BLACK OUT

BLACK OUT

John Lawton

GROVE PRESS
New York

First published in 1995 by Viking Penguin,
a division of Penguin Books USA Inc.

Printed in the United States of America

ISBN: 978-0-8021-4556-7

Grove Press
an imprint of Grove/Atlantic, Inc.
841 Broadway
New York, NY 10003

Distributed by Publishers Group West

www.groveatlantic.com

11 12 13 14 15   10 9 8 7 6 5 4 3 2 1

For

WPC Patricia Angadi
Women's Auxiliary Police Corps
Oxfordshire
1941–1943

Painter, Novelist and Copper

February 1944

§ 1

In the London borough of Stepney very little remained of Cardigan Street. Nor for that matter of Balaclava Street, Alma Terrace or of the untimely named Waterloo Place.

The Blitz had levelled them late in 1940. Four whole streets blasted into a sprawling mass of jagged, undulating rubble. In the spring of 1941 nature reclaimed them – blackberry and elder took hold, nettles thrust their yellow roots between the bricks, buddleia and bindweed appeared as islands in the ruins. By 1943 a wild garden covered the wilderness of war.

Winter. The first months of 1944. Children played a game of hopscotch chalked on the blue and red tiles that had been a kitchen floor.

The fat boy with the Elastoplast across his glasses was too clumsy to be allowed to play – an enforced bystander, he stood on the sidelines, bored by the game, occasionally staring into the eastern sky. The bombers were getting more frequent again. He'd missed them. Like any boy of his age he could tell a Dornier from a Heinkel, a Hurricane from a Spitfire. If they weren't up there, then there was simply one less game to follow. He glanced down to the low wall of black brick that separated what was once Alma Terrace from what was once Cardigan Street. A mongrel dog had leapt the wall with something long and floppy clenched between its teeth. The fat boy watched as the dog began a vigorous trot around the bombsite, cutting its own crazy course, across floors, over walls, through the fragmentary remains of windows, in and out of the open rooms, occasionally brandishing its trophy aloft and shaking its matted brown coat in an ecstasy of delight.

'Can you see that dog?' the fat boy asked his friends. They ignored him, their shouts drowning out his words. The dog didn't pause, not even to piss. The circular course seemed to be growing smaller, towards an unknown centre. There was method in his madness.

'It's got something in its mouth!'

Again he was ignored. The dog flounced, a shake of the mane, and as the fat boy turned to follow the dog's diminishing circle it rounded him in a swift move and dropped the precious gift at his feet. The fat boy stared, anxious to believe what he could see clearly for the first time. The shaggy hound had handed him the ragged stump of a human arm.

§2

Troy stopped the car beneath the railway lines on Ludgate Hill. It was pitch black and cold as hell. The fresh scar on his arm ached, his fingers were numb, and his nose felt ready to stream. He began to wish he'd made the journey in daylight, but something in blacked-out London held an indefinable appeal for him. He'd tried once to explain to his colleagues why he liked night work.

'It's like walking on water,' he had said to no reaction. 'It's Jungian I suppose – I feel I'm being allowed abroad in the collective unconscious of the city.'

Laughter. The blasphemy of Troy's first remark was beyond comprehension, this latter was merely risible, with its polysyllabics. If he were not careful Troy's fondness of night would lead him to become a dirty old man. Worse still, they said, a complete bloody tosser.

Abroad in that vast, smothering breadth of night, but not alone. The pinprick of light he had seen became clear as a torchbeam. An Air-Raid Precautions warden was waving the torch at him as he approached the car. Troy slid down the window and waited for the usual catechism of cliché.

'You can't go on – the Cathedral's had a near miss – you should have turned off at Ludgate Circus.'

Troy answered softly, 'Is the road blocked? I have to get through.'

'That's what they all say.' The warden paused. Any second now, thought Troy, the inevitable would gain utterance.

'Is your journey really necessary?'

Troy knew – one day such aphorism would drive him to violence.

'I'm a policeman. Scotland Yard. I'm on my way to Stepney Police Station.'

'Can I see your identity card?'

Troy had sat clutching his warrant card. He raised his left hand off his lap and held the card under the torchbeam. The warden looked from Troy's face to the card and back again.

'When I was your age I was in the trenches.'

Troy looked into the man's face. He was almost entirely in shadow, but his age seemed clear enough; the clipped moustache, the received pronunciation, the creaking joints all bespoke a man in his fifties – a generation Troy had come to loathe, with their constant justification of what they had done in the war, their jingoistic fervour that their sons should also risk their lives in another German war – a generation of drawing-room drones, League of Nations naïves, chicken-farming chunterers. Troy had long ago ceased to regard the ARP and the Home Guard as anything but a patriotic nuisance.

'I'm a copper. I think that says it all.' Inside Troy kicked himself. Why pick up the white feather?

'The war's out there, sonny!'

No, thought Troy, as he pressed the self-starter and jerked the old Bullnose Morris into reverse, it's here. War, like charity, begins at home. He turned south at Ludgate Circus and drove slowly down New Bridge Street. Eight years a policeman, five almost entirely spent on murder cases had led him to define all human relations in terms of conflict. The craters of Blackfriars and Puddledock yawned on his right. There had been a woman in '38 who had put a knitting needle through the eye of a faithless husband. Upper Thames Street and the blitzed arches of Cannon Street station passed overhead. In '41 a returning Buffs Major had dismembered a seemingly errant wife with a bayonet. Seemingly but not actually – he had gone to the gallows a contrite murderer of a blameless woman. Such cases required no solution – the murderers did not leave the scene of the crime, or if they did they walked into a police station a few days later and confessed. Looking south across Tower Pier the night over Bermondsey split open with the deep whumpf of a bomb, and a towering lick of flame rose brightly satanic into the starless sky. Here, or near enough, Londoners had bathed and paddled in the salt water of the Thameside in hot summers between the wars, on the artificial beach carved out of the Thames reach, just by Tower Bridge. A boy of eight had drowned in '39 in the last hours of peace – held under by his sister of eleven. Troy had patiently extracted her confession in front of disbelieving parents and withstood a cross-examination of fury in the witness-box. The litany could be endless. Only three weeks ago a man in Uxbridge had taken his wife's lover apart with an axe and had swung at Troy as he arrested him, nicking a piece out of his arm. Into a grating third gear as the car rounded the top of Tower Hill, and a cluster of bombs ripped up the night over Bermondsey once more.

Drawn to the noise and light, Troy drove out on to the deserted bridge and stopped the car. London seemed to have shut down. He left the car and stood on the pavement. Looking downriver, the Luftwaffe were swarming out of the south to rain bombs on Rotherhithe and the Surrey Docks. It looked to be one of the heaviest raids of the year. Another massive bang, another pillar of light rising into the sky, and a rapid surge of flame shot out across the water. They were aiming for fuel tanks on the south side and had clearly found them. Petrol flooded out into the salty tidal surge to set the Thames on fire. Blue and orange flames danced like motley demons towards the bridge, where Troy stood watching the absurdly attractive pyrotechnics of war, the witching way the fireball transformed the blackest of nights into a flickering chiaroscuro parody of day. The sky crackled with the pop-gun fire of ack-ack shells, exploding softly and uselessly like bursting paper bags in the hands of children. Tracer bullets soared heaven-ward on trails of shining carmine. An age ago, in the Blitz, Troy had watched it come down – Hitler's metal rain – preferring his chances in the open to the black holes underground. The gemstone sky of a night raid had never lost its fascination. On days when imagination and intuition held less sway than reason and analysis, Troy was inclined to see that this fascination might indeed be grotesque, part, perhaps, of some not so fine madness. A madness he had lately come to realise was far from unique. Tales had begun to circulate that Churchill drove his police bodyguard to distraction by standing atop Storey's Gate, at the far end of Horse Guard's Parade, to watch the show exactly as Troy himself was now doing. Of course, that was only rumour, but Troy had seen for himself the hordes of American soldiers clustered at the top of the Haymarket or on the steps of the National Gallery, staring wide-eyed into the south-east like winter natives stunned by the first burst of spring light. He had stood with a group of NCOs in Trafalgar Square, sharing their madness. One of them had turned to Troy.

'Nothin' like it,' he had said. 'Ain't never seen nothin' like it in the state of Kansas.'

§ 3

Even the desk copper at Stepney looked as though he had been brought out of mothballs to replace a younger man now square-bashing in Aldershot or Catterick.

'Yes?' he said.

Why, thought Troy, does no one call me 'Sir'? Just once would someone ignore age and pay deference to rank.

'Sergeant Troy. I'm here to see George Bonham.'

He held out the warrant card again. The constable peered with straining eyes. Troy could be holding a dead fish for all he knew. He turned to the open doorway behind him and yelled, 'Sarge! Someone for you!'

A bear of a man emerged from the back room. Size fourteen boots. The best part of seven foot when helmeted.

'Good of you to turn out, Freddie,' said Bonham, smiling broadly. He raised the counter-flap and stepped through. Troy's extended hand was gripped momentarily before he received an avuncular pat on the shoulder that seemed as though it would shatter his spine.

7

'Let's have a cuppa. You must be frozen. It seems ages since you were last here. Bloody ages.'

Leman Street had been Troy's first station. The alma mater of nicks. He had served under George Bonham at the age of twenty-one – glad to be accepted at an inch under minimum height – and had been nurtured and protected by Bonham for reasons he couldn't even begin to guess at. It had been Bonham who had urged him into plain-clothes. In 1939 the Yard had claimed Troy for its own. A rapid solution to a tricky case, together with the shortage of men in the phoney war, had made him into a sergeant a few months after the outbreak of war. Now, at almost twenty-nine, a brush with Bonham could still make him feel like a child.

In the back room Bonham set the kettle on its ring, and took a tea-caddy down from the shelf. Troy knew that Bonham's love of old-fashioned English ritual could string out tea-making into infinity. He glanced around the room. It had changed not one whit in the time he'd been at the Yard, the same eggshell colour, deepened into every hue of cream and ochre by generations of cigarettes.

'You must be near frozen,' Bonham said again.

'George,' Troy said, hoping his impatience with the ritual wasn't obvious. 'Could I see it straightaway?'

'It's not going anywhere.'

'All the same I'd like to see it.'

Bonham ambled over to the window, flicked the catch and brought a long brown paper parcel in from the window-ledge.

'Not having any ice I thought that was about the best place for it. It's not likely to go off on a night like this, is it now?'

He set the frost-glistened package on the centre table and tugged at one edge of the paper. The contents rolled stiffly out on to the table-top. It was a human arm, male, hacked off crudely just above the elbow. It was a left arm, complete down to the fingers, the third of which still wore a gold ring. The forearm was covered by a coatsleeve in some woollen dog-tooth pattern. Beneath that a greying shirt cuff stuck out still held by a silver cufflink. Troy stared. Then he circled the table twice. He stopped, turned the arm over so that it was palm up and studied the hand. Several minutes passed in silence. As he leant back against the cupboard and took his eyes

8

from the arm for the first time, the kettle whistled into the calm. Bonham slooshed out the teapot and pared off a portion of his diminishing tea ration.

'Who found it?' Troy asked.

'Kid. Late this afternoon.'

'Where did he get it?'

'Bombsite. Off east, towards the Green. Just came in, plonked it and ran. But that don't matter none. I've known him since he was in nappies. We'll have no trouble finding him again. His parents have a flat in the same block as me.'

'I'll have to talk to him.'

Bonham set down the pot and two cups next to the arm and looked down at Troy.

'Not tonight, surely, Freddie? It can't be that urgent.'

'How urgent can murder be?'

'Who said anything about murder?'

'Who sent for Scotland Yard?'

'That's just a precaution. I was worried when it didn't turn out to be one of ours.'

'No bodies without arms?' Troy said.

'I've accounted for everyone. I mean everyone. It's not local. I'd swear to it.'

'There've been heavy raids all month. London is littered with bodies. We could build up a wall with our English dead.'

'Not one of ours. That I can tell you.'

'People dying all over London, George.'

'Not this one. We've lost a few this week. Poor sods too slow or too stupid to get into the shelters. But they're accounted for. On my patch there's no one missing. We've dug out and identified every body. And nobody with their arm blown off.'

'This wasn't blown off or torn off, it was cut off.'

'I thought better o' lookin' that close meself.'

'Four strokes of the blade at least.' Troy leaned closer to the cut end of the stump, his elbows propped on the table. 'Something heavy, single-edged and broad. Tapered at the front.'

'Meat cleaver?'

'More like a machete or a bowie knife.'

Bonham handed a cup to Troy. The numbness in his hands shot

9

into painful life against the heat of the cup. He winced and turned back to the arm. The fingernails were neat and trimmed, neither broken nor bitten. The tips of the fingers were heavy with nicotine – Troy could almost swear he'd found a Capstan smoker – but the curious thing was the number of tiny marks, darkened patches of stained and roughened skin. Burns or scald marks of some sort. Well-healed for the most part, but one or two somewhat fresher – perhaps a month or so old at the most. Troy felt the prick of pain in the split tip of his thumb. He sipped at the distasteful brew – only faintly reminiscent of a good pre-war cuppa. He circled the old elm table once more and stopped next to Bonham – shoulder to shoulder, but for the fact that Bonham's shoulder was way above his.

'Oh,' Troy added, 'and he was dead when whoever it was did this to him.'

Bonham slurped loudly at his tea.

'Bugger,' he said softly.

'Where's the bombsite?' Troy asked.

'The kids call it the garden. It's over towards Stepney Green. Most of it used to be Cardigan Street, before Mr Hitler.'

'I used to walk that as a beat bobby.'

'Well, you can walk it again tomorrow.'

'The boy lives in your block?'

'Ground floor back. Terence Flanagan. Otherwise known as Tub. No trouble that I know of. His old man's a bit of a one for the bottle, but he's more inclined to spoil the boy than take his belt off to him when he's the worse for it. You know the sort. Showers the kids with everything that's in his pocket from a farthing to a silver joey when the mood's on him. But the mother's a good sort. Keeps him on the straight and narrow.'

'I can talk to him in the morning?'

'If you're up early enough. Stayin' the night are you?'

'If that's all right with you, George.'

'No trouble, bags o' room. The place is half-empty after all.'

Troy knew better. Bonham and his wife Ethel had raised three sons in as many rooms. Two walk-through bedrooms and a living room less than ten by ten, with a galley kitchen that also held a bath. The only reason it seemed less than cramped to Bonham was because he'd never lived anywhere else, and the only reason he termed it half-empty was that his three sons were in the navy and his wife had been killed in the Blitz of 1940. Troy had eaten many times with George and Ethel Bonham in the late thirties – arriving in their lives just as the youngest boy had signed his papers for Portsmouth. The Bonhams had fostered, fed, and, as Troy saw it, educated him throughout his first year as a constable.

Bonham tucked his helmet under his arm like a ghost's head and prepared to leave. Troy picked up the arm.

'You're jokin'?' said Bonham.

'No, let's take it.'

'Suit yourself.'

Troy rolled the arm back in its brown paper and tucked it under his own arm like a stick of French bread.

Bonham opened his locker and scooped a small, bloody, newspaper-wrapped parcel into his upturned helmet.

'A bit o' somethin' special.' He smiled at Troy. The smile became a knowing grin. 'The butcher's a pal o' mine. He's seen me right this week. Should stretch to two.'

He tapped the side of his helmet, much as he might have tapped the side of his nose, as though sharing some vital secret with Troy.

'I'm OK,' said Troy, tapping the frozen arm.

'Now you are jokin',' said Bonham.

§ 4

Bonham lived in Cressy Houses, a few yards from Stepney Green. A splendid, if blackened, redbrick and red-tile exterior, rising four floors and bearing the proud plaque of the East London Dwellings company. Where the building met the pavement in Union Place it was still shored up with beams and scaffolding – relics of the raid that had claimed the life of Ethel Bonham.

'Shan't be a tick,' said Bonham, shoving a set of keys at Troy, twisting his giant's frame out of the car. 'You let yourself in and get the kettle on. I'll just have a word with young Flanagan's parents.'

Troy climbed the steps to Bonham's front door on the second floor. The flat seemed more than half-empty. It smelt faintly of boiled vegetables, and while spotlessly clean and tidy seemed lifeless – occupied rather than lived in. He stepped into the tiny kitchen and lit the gas. He was struck by the first thing in which he recognised the hand of Ethel Bonham – a knitted bag for clothes pegs hanging on the back of the door. It pointed up just how little remained, as though Bonham had deliberately removed all trace of his late wife. The glass display cabinet that had once held an assortment of china, from a plaster dog to a couple of hideous red and gold crown Derby plates, stood empty against the living-room wall. In the spring of 1936 Troy had been the rawest of raw recruits, so fresh from the country that the tram and the taxi looked more likely as threats to his life and limbs than any criminal. Ethel had taught him city life, where and when, if not how to shop; how to darn socks, how to crack an egg with one hand and how to flip it without breaking the yolk. In the October of the same year Bonham had carried him home from the battle of Cable Street, when the police commissioner had been rash enough to try and clear a path for Mosley's fascists by sending the entire Metropolitan mounted corps against the overwhelming odds of a hundred thousand Londoners. Out of control and terrified, a horse had caught Troy above the left eye with its iron hoof. Ethel bathed and bandaged the wound. Troy still bore the scar, almost invisibly following the course of his eyebrow. Ethel had taught him self-sufficiency, had unwittingly encouraged him in the life of the city solitary which he now knew to be, irrevocably, his nature.

'All in order,' Bonham shouted from the kitchen. 'Tub gets a morning off school to show us where he found the arm.'

Bonham filled the doorway between the hall and the living room, ducking his head under the lintel. He unbuttoned his tunic and hung it on the back of a dining chair. He stood in his shirt and braces, unknotting his tie, the high-waisted regulation trousers, tight against his ribs, emphasising the belly-rise of a muscular man relaxing softly into his fifties. Troy hated being in uniform. Loved the anonymity of his plain black overcoat.

'A nice bit o' beef,' Bonham said simply, and flipped the back stud on his collar. 'I'll slip it in the pan. A few spuds. A few greens. And we'll open a bottle while they do. Come on, Freddie, get your coat off.'

He knelt by the gas fire and set it hissing and roaring into life with a Swan Vesta, as Troy pulled carelessly at the buttons of his overcoat.

Bonham sat before the fire, knees almost up to his chin, huge hands delicately cradling a glass of stout.

'You ain't lost anyone yet. Hope you never do. But because you ain't, you won't know. It takes some people different ways. With me ... well, I found it easier to accept being on my own, after twenty-three years a married man, without all the knick-knacks and the paraphernalia. Like I say, you won't know.'

'Sooner or later we'll all know,' said Troy.

Bonham took the loose abstraction for something specific.

'You mean the war'll go on and on and on?' he asked.

'No,' said Troy. 'The opposite. The war's nearly over. London's filling up with soldiers. You can't get on a train at a main-line station without seeing queues of soldiers. More and more often they're Americans. I think you can take Eisenhower's presence in England as a sure sign – there'll be a second front soon.'

Bonham spoke for Europe. ' 'Bout time,' he muttered into his glass.

'And maybe then old men will stop giving me the white feather.'

'What? Literally?'

'No, but any face under forty looks to any face over forty as though it should be in uniform. I get it all the time.'

'Copper's a copper,' said Bonham with a sense of finality.

Not once had Troy been tempted to enlist. Not that anyone else had started a rush. The second war did not slavishly follow the first. It nurtured its own brand of confusion. Part of which was a wave of xenophobia leading to the round-up of thousands of aliens after Dunkirk and the fall of Norway. Amongst these had been Troy's eldest brother – eight years older than Troy and unfortunate enough to have been born in Vienna (part of the Reich since the Anschluss of 1938) to Russian parents, inching their way across Europe in the wake of another great confusion known to history as the revolution of 1905. Released in the autumn of the same year, rearrested two months later, and released again in the following winter, Troy's brother now served King and Country as Wing Commander on the newly developed Tempest fighter. The grudge he did not bear his adopted country had, by some unknown mechanism, descended to Troy, who knew no other country, but which, for a number of reasons he would not dream of articulating outside the family, he would serve in no other way than as a policeman.

'I cannot understand why you're not angry,' he had said to brother Rod.

'No point,' came the reply. 'No point in rejecting Britain for its treatment of me. Count it merely as an accident.'

'An accident!' Troy had protested.

'Exactly, an honest mistake. Whatever I may subjectively feel about my adopted country,' he paused emphatically. 'My home – objectively it is on the side of the angels.'

'Fight the good fight?' Troy had sneered at his brother.

'If you like.' The characteristic family trait of *laissez-penser*.

'It all leaves rather a bad taste in the mouth, don't you think?'

To this the elder Troy had made no answer.

'Homeless,' said Troy.

Rod had waited, wondering exactly what his brother was driving at.

'Doesn't mean much. None of it means much,' Troy had said. 'Home, patriotism. It none of it means much to the homeless.'

'I know,' said Rod, thinking that Troy had at last reached coherence.

'Homeless in the heart,' Troy had added, blowing all coherence.

'What the hell is that supposed to mean?'

It had been Troy's turn to have no answer.

§ 5

Boiled beef, no carrots, spuds and greens of indeterminate species left Troy grateful for Bonham's generosity and wondering why the late Mrs Bonham had not passed on her skills to her husband in quite the same measure she had passed them on to Troy. Bonham had picked up a second bottle of stout and was rooting around for the opener when someone banged on the door.

'Evening, Mr Bonham.' Troy heard a man's voice at the threshold, hidden from his view by Bonham's back. In a block of dockers, costermongers, rag-trade workers and chars, Bonham stood for law and order, for the decency in which all believed but occasionally could not practise – one of us but not one of us. The voice was respectful without deference. The 'mister' was Bonham's undisputed right.

'I hear you found something.'

Troy stood up as quickly as if he'd been stung. Bonham was telling the man he'd better come inside, just so long as he wasn't wasting anyone's time. A short man in a ragged jacket and heavy, canvas trousers stepped slowly into the room. He was almost as wide as he was tall – almost a yard across at the shoulder – five and a half feet of stacked muscle.

Bonham introduced Detective Sergeant Troy of the Yard and Mr Michael McGee, and pointed the man at a chair.

'I hear you found something,' McGee said again.

'Mick, you know damn well that's not the way we play things.'

McGee set his cap on his knees and wiped a cowlick of hair from his face.

'Wolinski's gone,' he said flatly.

'Gone,' said Bonham. 'What d'ye mean, gone?'

'I mean no one's seen him for three days.'

Bonham inclined his head slightly, looking down at Troy as they stood side by side, backs to the fire.

'First I've heard of it,' he said. 'No one's reported him missing.'

'Who's Wolinski?'

'Lives above.' Bonham aimed a giant forefinger at the ceiling.

Troy spoke directly to McGee. 'Why didn't you report this?'

McGee simply shrugged.

'Wolinski's one of the comrades,' Bonham put in. 'Works down the George V docks, with Mr McGee here, when he's a mind to. And when he's a mind to he'll take off. True, I've not heard a peep from upstairs, but I paid it no mind. He lives alone, doesn't make a lot of noise.'

'So he just vanished three days ago and no one's said a word until now?' Troy's tone was a touch incredulous.

'He's like that,' said Bonham. 'They're all like that. Suspicious of the police. We're enemies of the people. And all that malarkey.'

McGee shrugged this off.

'Word is you've found a body down by Cardigan Street.'

'Not strictly true,' said Troy.

'But you found something all the same.'

'You think it might be Wolinski?'

'How can I know till I see it?'

Troy paused to change tack. 'How long have you been a docker, Mr McGee?'

'On and off since the bottom fell out of brickeying in twenty-nine.'

'And Mr Wolinski?'

'Almost as long I reckon. He came here from Poland in thirty-four or thirty-five I think.'

'Hold out your hands.'

McGee gave Troy a puzzled look but did as he was asked, palms upturned on the oilskin tablecloth. From the corner of his eye Troy could see that Bonham too was taking his questions with a quizzical pinching of the eyebrows. McGee's hands were a mess of old scars, fresh blisters and thick yellow callouses, as large as the corns on a beat policeman's feet.

'The body is not Wolinski,' said Troy. 'The hand I examined has no callouses. The dead man never worked in a dock or at any form of manual labour – ever. Mr Wolinski may be alive or he may be dead – but we haven't found him or any part of him. Now – do you want formally to report him missing?'

The legal-sounding precision of Troy's phrasing seemed to unnerve McGee for the first time. He looked to Bonham for help.

'Why don't you give it a day or two, Mick. Peter's been gone and come back a dozen times. This is no different like as not, and he'll not thank you for involving me.'

McGee seemed unwilling to accept reassurance, as though it was less than dutiful, less than justice.

'You might at least look,' he said obscurely.

'Look,' said Bonham. 'At what?'

'The flat. You're supposed to look for clues or something, ain't you?'

McGee dangled a set of shiny keys in front of him. Bonham finally flipped the top off his stout and said it was all a waste of time, but for Troy this was an invitation to simple nosiness that he could scarcely refuse, beautifully blurred as it was by the line of duty.

Refugees, almost regardless of origin, played forcefully on childhood's memory, of family legends, of nursery stories and a wealth of nonsense about the old country. That part of Troy's mind that was ready to dismiss such nonsense was perpetually in thrall to the power of such myth-making.

McGee sat purposefully out of the way on an upright chair, just inside the living room – as if trying neatly to avoid disturbing anything Troy might eventually term evidence. Room for room an identical flat to Bonham's, the contrast in content and décor could not have been more startling. At a glance Troy would have said the room held five or six thousand books, on all four walls, window-sills included, floor to ceiling. Where space had run out Wolinski had neatly tied books into bundles and stacked them under chairs. Under the table were hundreds of *Daily Workers*, *Picture Posts*, *Manchester Guardians* and the odd copy of *Pravda* – all tied up neatly with string and stacked clear of the knees.

Troy glanced over the shelves. The entire *Comédie Humaine* of Balzac – in French. Most of Dostoevsky – also in French. The twenty-four-volume Tolstoy of 1913 – in the original Russian. *Das Kapital* in German. Odd volumes of Kropotkin in English (almost heretical for a Marxist thought Troy) and on and on and on. There scarcely seemed a major work of literature in any European language that had not been read, or at least owned, by Peter Wolinski. The second room held a desk – a pen, ink and a blotter arranged with military precision – and yet more shelves of books.

Physics, chemistry – all double-Dutch to Troy, but a pattern emerged as Troy's eyes followed the shelves round to the desk, and dusty long-unopened volumes in German gave way to newer works in English, mostly dealing with stress in metals or the dynamics of chemical propulsion. On one wall Wolinski had found room for photographs. Two or three dozen or more, some no bigger than postcards, some as large as dinner plates. Young men outside pavement cafés, a young man in black gown and mortar board clutching a symbolic scroll, a mixture of old men and young men arranged as though to commemorate some academic gathering – a familiar mixture of the social hours and formal occasions in the life of a pre-war student, a Pole abroad in the Weimar Republic.

Troy stared at a striking photograph of the Führer in full flight and fury – gesturing with rigid index finger to the heavens in one of his stage-managed pieces. It bore the caption 'Hey you up there in the gallery!' It seemed so remote to think back to the days when Hitler had been a figure of fun. Next to it Wolinski had caught the transition in a shot of startling emptiness and chilling beauty. Early summer morning in the street of some unnamed Bavarian town, not a human figure to be seen, just the houses with their decking of flags stretching down to infinity – a long silent tunnel of swastikas.

Troy called out to McGee, 'What did Wolinski do before he came here?'

'He taught in one of them German colleges.'

'University?'

'Same difference. Munich I think it was. Till 'Itler drove 'im out.'

Only the bedroom remained. Had not the previous two rooms shown him a man of meticulous habits, Troy would have said this room had been ransacked. The twisted and grubby sheets, the dust on every surface, the clothes in higgledy-piggledy heaps. Nowhere to sit, scarce enough room to stand and just enough to lie. It seemed Wolinski ignored everything for the life of the mind. Troy could not have slept a wink in dust and dirt such as this. On the bedside table, spine upwards, was Wolinski's bedtime reading. Troy smiled – *The Code of the Woosters* by P. G. Wodehouse, in which whilst in hot pursuit of his Aunt Dahlia's cow-creamer, Bertie Wooster manages to defeat British fascism.

'Mr McGee, come here please.'

McGee called back from the first room, 'Won't I mess things up?'

'You can hardly make more of a mess than I've done. Just try not to touch anything.'

McGee ambled into the bedroom.

'Is it always like this?' asked Troy.

'Yeah. He always did live a bit like a pig.'

'Would you know if any of his clothes were missing or if he'd packed a suitcase?'

McGee pointed to the top of a cracked and blistered mahogany veneer wardrobe.

'His case would be up there. If it was here, that is.'

Troy led McGee back to the kitchen.

'And his razor would be here?' Troy pointed to the tiled strip next to the sink. 'Mr Wolinski is still clean-shaven I take it?'

'Oh yeah,' said McGee. 'Sometimes he treats himself to a proper barber-shave down the Mile End Road, but he's got a safety. I'm sure of that.'

'Do you see it?' asked Troy.

McGee shrugged again.

'Then I think we can assume that Mr Wolinski has gone wherever he's gone of his own accord. Kidnappers and murderers don't usually ask you to pack for the occasion. And the Luftwaffe doesn't much care whether it bombs the unshaven or not.'

'So Peter'll be back?'

'He didn't abandon a houseful of books in Munich. I hardly think he'll do the same in Stepney.'

Rather than reassured McGee seemed deflated by Troy's words.

'What do I do then?'

'Give the keys to Sergeant Bonham and if Wolinski isn't back by the end of the week report it properly at Leman Street. He can hardly swan around England for long these days.'

'Of course,' McGee said thoughtfully. 'There's a war on.'

'I had heard,' said Troy.

§ 6

Troy stood and shivered outside the ground floor back and watched his breath form clouds in the air.

'And don't give Uncle George no cheek,' Mrs Flanagan instructed her son Terence, alias Tub.

Troy and Bonham exchanged glances over the Uncle George. Mrs Flanagan did up the boy's coat buttons and straightened his socks in the wrinkle zone between knee and ankle.

'Doesn't pay to scare off the kiddies,' muttered Bonham.

'If you say so, Uncle George,' Troy muttered back at him.

'It got us the arm didn't it?'

Mrs Flanagan was speaking directly to Bonham.

'If he's any trouble just give 'im a back 'ander, George.'

'Will do, Patsy,' Bonham replied.

The child squinted up at Bonham – almost seven feet tall in his helmet – like a squirrel surveying the prospect of an oak. His one visible eye roved actively, the other hid behind a fresh slab of Elastoplast. He moved off towards the street without a backward glance at his mother. On the step, out in Union Place, a grim prospect greeted Troy and Bonham. Seven small boys ranged across the pavement, all looking expectantly towards Bonham.

'Oh no,' he said. 'What do you lot think you're up to?'

No one spoke. The expectant looks seemed fixed somewhere between joy and tears. Sergeant Bonham held power over the greatest, the most mysterious event in their short lives. Troy looked down at a motley of gabardine mackintoshes, outsize jackets tied up with string, brown boots, pudding-basin haircuts, bruised and scabrous kneecaps. Such an amazing array of ill-fitting hand-me-downs that only the peach-fresh faces challenged the image of them as seven assorted dwarves. Out on the end of the line, a grubby redhead, doubtless called Carrots, juggled a smouldering cocoa tin from hand to hand, an improvised portable furnace. Troy wished he had one of his own.

'You're supposed to be in school, you know that,' Bonham persisted. 'Now come on. Clear off!'

The boys stood their ground. A classic Mexican stand-off.

A lifetime spent on the sidelines, excluded but observant, had left Tub in no doubt about how leadership should behave when occasion arose. He knew the occasion and he knew how to rise to it. He stepped out from between Bonham and Troy and the mass of boys parted before him as surely as if they'd been struck by Moses' staff. He led off in the direction of Cardigan Street. The boys followed in their own pecking order – none of them overtook or even tried to draw level with Tub in his magisterial progression. He didn't speak and he didn't look back. Bonham and Troy followed on the end of the line, feeling faintly foolish and Brobdingnagian. Troy thrust his hands deep into his pockets to keep the stabbing nip of frost from his fingertips and wondered if the carrot-headed child could be persuaded to part with his invention for a shilling.

Tub stood on a level patch of fresh snow, and waited as Bonham and Troy struggled across the rubble and into the 'garden'. The boys lined up, respectfully not setting foot on their hopscotch patch, forming a hellish gauntlet that Troy would have to run to get to Tub. Troy stumbled to a halt at the end of the column.

'Here?' he asked. 'Do you mean you found it here?'

Tub nodded. Troy looked around. In all its ups and downs the bombsite seemed indistinct and uniform under its coat of snow. Bonham lumbered up, wheezing.

'If he's leading us on a wild-goose chase—'

Troy cut him short. 'How can you be sure?' he asked Tub.

Tub scraped at the snow with the toe of his boot, revealing a blue quarry tile. As if to some invisible cue everybody suddenly began to kick at the snow, scattering it clear of the old floor. Troy offered to hold the tin while the carrot-top worked, but he clutched it tightly to his mackintosh and scowled at Troy, hacking away all the time with the metalled heel of his boot.

Troy looked down at the kitchen floor and its fading hopscotch squares.

'Here?' he repeated.

'This is where we was,' said Tub.

'Yes, but is this where you found it?' Troy was reluctant to name the object, but eight pairs of eyes seemed to be daring him to do it. 'The arm,' he conceded. 'You found the arm here?'

'Nah,' said Tub. 'This is where we was when the dog give it to me.'

Troy heard Bonham mutter a faint 'Jesus Christ'.

'What dog?' he asked.

'Dog,' said Tub, as though this in itself were sufficient explanation.

Troy looked at Bonham, Bonham looked at Troy – both feeling more and more like Mutt and Jeff.

'First I've heard of it,' said Bonham. Troy was beginning to find the phrase all too familiar.

'Another fine mess, Stanley,' he whispered back. 'Are you telling me a dog came up to you and gave you the hand while you were playing here?'

'He wasn't playing,' chipped in the biggest boy. 'We don't let 'im 'cos he trips up.'

'So you didn't find the hand at all?'

'Yes I did,' Tub protested. 'It was me. Just me. Wasn't none of this lot. Dog came up and give it me. He didn't give it no one else. He give it me!'

'Do you have any idea where the dog came from?'

Tub seemed not to understand.

'Where did you first see him?'

Tub pointed to the wall between Cardigan Street and Alma Terrace, to where odd bits of houses still stood, to where a few dozen bricks remained in the order the brickie had lain them.

'Show me,' said Troy. The same ritually structured procession moved off towards Alma Terrace. Troy looked over the stump of wall. The morning's fall of snow had covered any tracks the dog might have left.

'George,' he said, 'we're looking for a needle in a bloody haystack.' He felt Bonham's size fourteen tap sharply against his shoe, telling him to watch his language. 'We're going to have to search it all.'

'Freddie, you've got to be joking. I don't have the men for that.'

'How else are we going to find anything?'

'What do you expect to find?'

'The rest of the body. Well, to be precise, bits of the rest of the body.'

Troy glanced at the boys, wondering how much they heard and how much they understood. Eight cherubic faces, and sixteen hard, ruthless eyes looked back at him. Preserving innocence seemed a fruitless ideal.

'How would you like to make some money?' he said.

'How much?' said the biggest.

'A shilling,' said Troy.

'Half a crown,' said the boy.

'You don't know what it's for yet!'

'It'll still cost you half a dollar,' the boy replied.

'OK, OK,' said Troy, 'half a crown to the boy who finds the rest.'

'Freddie, for God's sake,' Bonham cut in. 'You can't!'

He gripped Troy by the shoulder and swung him round into a huddled attempt at privacy.

'Are you off yer chump?'

'George, can you think of any other way?'

'For Christ's sake, they're kids. They should be in school!'

'Well, they clearly have no intention of going. And they don't exactly look like Freddie Bartholomew do they?'

'Jesus Christ,' Bonham said again.

'Don't worry,' said Troy.

'On your own head be it.'

Troy turned back to the boys, ranged in front of him in a wide semi-circle. 'I want you to look for ... ' he hesitated, uncertain what to call a corpse. 'For anything to do with what Tub found. OK?'

They nodded as one.

'And if you find it don't touch it. You come straight back and tell Mr Bonham, and nobody, I mean nobody, goes near it till he's seen what you've found. Understood?'

They nodded again.

'Or the half-crown's forfeit,' Troy concluded.

Tub spoke up. 'An' a bob for me for findin' and sixpence each for all of us for lookin' or you can just bugger off,' he said.

'Done,' said Troy, glad that things were now on a clearly established business footing.

'I must get out to Hendon,' he said to Bonham. 'The sooner we get a forensics report the better.'

'You're leaving me in charge of this lot?'

'Sorry, George.'

'It's a scandal, Freddie. If the mums kick up . . .'

'You know them, George. Is it likely?'

'You know, Freddie,' Bonham said softly, 'there are times when I think there's nothing like a long spell at the Yard for putting iron in the soul.'

'Just doing my job. Call me at the Yard this afternoon if anything turns up.'

Troy picked his way across the bombsite back to his Bullnose Morris and the gruesome parcel in the boot. The boys scattered to the points of the compass, dreaming of riches beyond belief. Behind him Troy could hear Bonham offering the carrot-top sixpence for his hand-warmer.

§ 7

Ladislaw Kolankiewicz had been a senior pathologist at the Police Laboratory in Hendon since it opened in 1934. One of the first recruits to the science of the gruesome, and bearing the recommendation of no less a figure than Sir Bernard Spilsbury, there were many who considered Kolankiewicz to be appropriately gruesome himself. Troy had come across him in 1937 and since then had watched his hairline recede to nothing only to re-emerge sprouting vigorously from his ears and nostrils and coursing along the backs of his fingers. He had grown stouter and more bent from his daily stooping over the dead and his English had not improved at all. Precise and flawless on technical matters, his colloquial use of the language was obscenely fractured. Policemen all over London and the Home Counties would relish visits to Hendon, simply because it replenished their fund of Kolankiewicz anecdotes, as he rolled words into each other in pointless, foul combinations along the lines of 'Fuck bloody off bastardpimpcopper', or as he now uttered to Troy, 'What the bollox you want, smartyarse?'

Troy was glad to see the room was empty. Too often Kolankiewicz had forced him to conduct conversations while he sawed away at a human skull or barked rapid summaries of a stomach's contents to Anna, his assistant and stenographer, perched on her stool in the corner. But today he was sitting quietly on the same stool, clean of apron, bloodless of hand, eating a spam sandwich and reading the *News Chronicle*. It was almost pleasant, despite the ever-present chemical reek that spelt out death to the senses.

Troy slapped his brown paper parcel down on the slab and pulled at the loose end. The arm jerked free and rolled halfway across the slab. Kolankiewicz shot out from his corner like a spider scuttling across its web. He seemed to stare greedily at the prize for a few seconds. Then he shrugged and looked up at Troy.

'What this shit?'

'It's an arm.'

'Mr bloody wiseguy,' Kolankiewicz muttered. 'I mean, smartyarse,' he yelled, 'where's the rest of it?'

'It's all I've got.'

Kolankiewicz raised his hands to heaven. 'Ach! Ach! Ach! What do you expect me to do with this?'

'Anything you can. We're looking for the rest now. There's plenty of fabric. A cufflink, even.'

'Ah! Cufflinks I like. Hallmarks. Craftsman's initials. Distinctive proportions of fine metals to base – all very informative. What do you know about where it was found? What's it been on or in?'

'Not a damn thing.' Troy stretched out a hand to hold down the arm as Kolankiewicz took a large pair of scissors to the woollen sleeve. A sharp stab of pain caught him in the upper left arm. He rubbed gently at the spot with his fingers. Bent double over the arm, Kolankiewicz looked up from beneath wild, bushy eyebrows.

'Nice workmanship,' he said. 'High-grade silver. What's the matter with your arm?'

A sentence in perfect English almost startled Troy. The absence of the ham element in Kolankiewicz's voice made him momentarily unrecognisable as the demented dwarf he had known. Kolankiewicz straightened up. 'Is that the one? Is that where you took the blow with an axe? Very stupid of you.' He came around the table, right up to Troy.

'Let me see,' he said.

'It's OK. I've seen a doctor.'

'I'm a doctor.'

'I know, but unlike most of your patients I happen to be alive.'

'Fucking snobbery. If you're in pain, show me. Don't play the fucking hero.'

Troy plucked at his overcoat buttons and began to ease his shoulder out of the garment.

'Would you mind washing your hands first.'

'Eh?'

'I don't know what you've been doing with them, do I?'

'I been eating spam sandwich and drinking tea.'

'And before that?'

'Jesus Christ. OK! OK!'

Kolankiewicz stood at the sink, rolled up his sleeves and made an ostentatious display of scrubbing up. Troy winced as the stubby, hairy, cold fingers poked at his arm.

'You know you're very lucky you didn't lose the arm. That was a very deep wound. You had a good surgeon. Lovely job.'

'Why does it hurt?'

'You have your arm almost chopped in two and you ask why it hurts?'

'Now. Why does it hurt now? What's wrong?'

'Swelling where the stitches came out – perhaps some minor infection of the needle holes, not the real wound. I'll give you some surgical spirit and you wash it down for a couple of days. You'll be fine. When did the stitches come out?'

'Three days ago.'

'Then you shouldn't worry. What you should worry about is why you let yourself get locked up alone in a room with a lunatic axeman.'

Kolankiewicz took a small brown bottle off the shelf above the sink, splashed a little of its contents over a swab and bathed the four-inch scar.

'This guy,' he went on. 'The one in the papers. Killed his good lady's paramour. Chopped off two of the postman's fingers. Broke

26

the wrist of a constable. And you walk into his house and tell him to give himself up. You're crazy! This Oxbridge—'

'Uxbridge,' said Troy.

'This Uxbridge axeman could have killed you.'

Kolankiewicz rolled down Troy's shirtsleeve and fastened the button at the cuff in a gesture that was curiously paternal.

'No – I don't think so.'

'Always the fucking hero.'

'Heroics has nothing to do with it. It was all down to knowing the man.'

'Psychology?'

'If you like.'

'Fucking guesswork I'd call it.'

'Have it your own way. But once he'd nicked me—'

'Nicked. Troy, you're full of crap.'

'Nicked me! – it was all over. He got what he wanted. He'd seen blood. The sight of blood was the culmination for him – it satisfied and defused him. After that it was a matter of simply sitting there and talking him out. He wasn't going to chop me into pieces. The only person he was ever going to chop into pieces was his wife's lover.'

'And while you – Mr Smartyarse – were talking him out, where was the axe?'

'On the floor between us.'

'And what did you do? Sit there with a home-made tourniquet on, hoping he'd surrender before you bled to death?'

'The old school tie. First use I've ever found for it.'

Kolankiewicz thrust the bottle at him. 'Twice a day till the soreness goes. Now scram. I give you my report as soon as I can.'

§ 8

The gas fire in Troy's office sputtered at him and refused the match. All over London, gas-holders sat squat on the skyline like gigantic gibuses. One of them must have been hit in last night's raid, Troy thought. He twisted the tap on and off in the hope of jerking the fire into life. He heard the soft click of the door opening and looked up to see the Squad Commander, Superintendent Onions. Onions leaned on the edge of Troy's desk and folded his arms.

'Been asking for you,' he said softly in his Rochdale baritone.

Troy stood up and flicked the dust off his trousers and wondered if this was a reprimand. Onions was a bull of a man – five foot nine of packed muscle – with a bull's unpredictability, stubbornness and unprepossessing appearance. Troy had never been certain of his age, but guessed at fifty – the hair, long since grey, was ruthlessly clipped at the back and sides, leaving the stubble of a crewcut along the top of his head – the bright blue eyes still burned brightly in the lined face. Onions looked sharp and bullet-headed, the intensity of his gaze at odds with his sheer bulk and with his almost thought-less appearance. He dressed habitually in the manner of the older generation; a heavy double-breasted suit in a dull shade of oxblood enlivened only by a thin scarlet stripe and wonderfully counter-pointed by regulation-issue black Metropolitan Police boots. It was, Troy reflected, the kind of suit Hitler favoured, but for the fact that the Führer seemed to have frequent difficulty finding the matching trousers first thing in the morning. Troy knew for a fact that in the complexity of Onions's nature there lay an element of insecurity – he wore both belt and braces. Onions it had been who'd rescued Troy from Leman Street and made him a sergeant. His advocacy of Troy had brought Troy to the brink of an early inspectorship. It was expected any day. But the relationship could be fractious. Outguessing Onions was pointless. Most of the time, in the privacy of his office or Troy's, they were on Christian name terms. But there were days when they weren't. And if they weren't they weren't.

'I've been to Hendon, Stan,' Troy told Onions, sounding his mood. 'I had to see Kolankiewicz.'

'Does he improve?'

'Foul as ever. You could never say he wears his heart on his sleeve.'

Onions unfolded his arms and laid his palms on the ripped and cracked leatherette of Troy's desk. Certain now of his footing with his chief, Troy took another shot at the gas fire and brought it hissing and spitting to feeble life.

'He'll have his hands full soon enough,' said Onions.

'A murder?' said Troy.

'That's why I wanted you. During last night's air raid an American soldier got his throat cut not two hundred yards from here.'

Onions's words shot through Troy like electricity.

'Where?'

'Trafalgar Square. Of all places. An infantry corporal walked out of a pub in the Strand about tennish and was found half an hour later by the bobby on the beat with his throat cut to ribbons.'

'Bottle?'

'Fragments of green glass still embedded in the victim's flesh.'

The gas fire popped and roared suddenly as the pressure returned. Troy put the matchbox back on the mantelpiece and moved round to the far side of his desk by the window, skirting the temporary beam that had been temporarily holding up the ceiling since the direct hit of 1941. He knew what was coming and he was wondering how best to avoid it. How best to state his case. In a game of stakes and odds, Onions held a full corpse to his one arm – he didn't even have a pair.

'This is murder too, Stan,' he said.

'What's murder?'

'The Stepney case. That's why I was in Hendon. I took Kolankiewicz the arm.'

'A bomb victim, surely?' said Onions, turning to keep track of Troy as he paced across the window.

'No. Murder. Sophisticated, brutal murder.'

Onions joined Troy at the window and looked out. People with views of the Thames seemed always to be looking out, expecting more from the promise than the view would ever deliver.

'Sophisticated?' Onions queried.

'The victim was killed and then dismembered – fairly systematically I should say – in an attempt to dispose of the body. It wasn't the heat of the moment, it wasn't blind panic, it was coldblooded and calculated. Somehow, something went wrong. The arm got missed, or the dog stole it – or whatever – fortunately the dog didn't eat it, and that's a small miracle, and it came into our hands. If it hadn't some poor sod out there would simply have disappeared without trace.'

'What've you got?'

'Just the arm. Bonham's searching the site now. Today or tomorrow I'll get a forensic report and of course a full set of left-hand prints.'

'It's not much.'

'It's murder. Not the work of some angry, despairing man who lashes out and kills. The work of a planner, someone who means to get away with it, someone with ice in his veins and steel in his spine, enough to patiently dismember his victim. Enough to overcome the horror of his actions. Someone who does not flee from death. I've usually profited from the fact that most killers want to be caught. They are, in a sense, the perpetrators of some awful accident rather than killers. They run and then turn themselves in, or leave a trail I could follow with my eyes closed. They want me. I'm the redemption. I'm a necessary part of coping with what they've done. Even if I'm just one stage on the way to the gallows. I've known men who've sat there hugging the corpse, willing the life back into it, I've known men confess one day and deny the next – anything to undo the deed, anything to repeat the act of confession. This one's not like that. Anyone who can do this once can do it again.'

'All that from an arm?'

Troy shrugged.

'Are you saying we've got a maniac on the loose?'

Even on Onions's lips the words had the unmistakable ring of the popular press.

'Far from it, Stan. We've a calculating killer on the loose. That's not mania in my book.'

Onions paced the floor between the window and the desk and paced it back again – practising as he did so one of his habitual gestures, slicking his palms along the sides of his head as though a rich mane of hair were there rather than the grey bristles of his short back and sides. Usually it implied thinking.

'What about Trafalgar Square?' he asked at last.

'Was the American robbed?'

'No. More than fifty quid in his wallet.'

'Was he black or white?'

'White.'

'Age?'

'Twenty-two.'

'I think you're looking at two possibilities. Americans have two vices – they sell from their own stores on to our black market and they have affairs with English women. Either one could lead to this.'

'Black market?' Onions weighed up the idea. 'If Corporal Duvitski had crossed a spiv they'd have got him in an alley somewhere. Even in the blackout no racketeer would risk murder in a place as public as Trafalgar Square.'

'Then I think it's best to talk to the men in his platoon. They'll hang together for a while, but soon enough they'll tell us who Duvitski's girlfriend was. Somewhere around there'll be a husband or a lover. He'd have had to have followed the victim from the pub, perhaps even trailing him for a day or two, so there'll be witnesses who can identify him.'

'Open and shut, eh, Freddie?' Onions raised a pepper-and-salt eyebrow quizzically at Troy's rapid breakdown of the case.

'No,' Troy answered, leaning back on the window-sill and sinking his hands into his pockets. 'Not open and shut. Just routine.'

'It doesn't need a detective?'

'Well – no – it just doesn't need me.'

'In the meantime you'll want to be getting on with your puzzle, putting the Stepney corpse back together, I suppose.'

'With your permission, sir.'

'Do you ever think that one day you'll overreach yourself, Freddie?'

Troy shrugged again and said nothing. Onions clapped him on the shoulder, called him a cheeky bugger and headed for the door. Halfway out he paused, looking back at Troy.

'And if this isn't a *crime passionnel*? If it's spivs and wide boys?'

'Then I'll call in my narks.'

Onions left. Troy warmed his hands in front of the fire, now glowing freely, and wondered how much of what he'd told Onions was really true, how much of it he might eventually prove. Every

31

fibre of his instinct, every shred of intellect told him it was true, but it was still guesswork.

§ 9

Sooner than Troy had anticipated Kolankiewicz telephoned.

'I done all I can with your arm,' he said. 'I'll give you the details now, the report you can pick up tomorrow.'

Troy reached for a notepad and switched on the desk lamp. 'OK,' he said. 'Fire away.'

'He was dead when they did this to him. Too much blood still in the vessels for any other interpretation. Though, obviously, there was some loss of blood. I'd say he was cut up within an hour or so of death – but I make no promises about that. And don't ask me how he died. Apart from being able to say he didn't die of having his arm chopped off I got fuck nothing. I'd put his age at forty-five, though I could be out ten years either way. An arm is not the best organ from which to make such judgements. If you find his liver, then we're talking. Height and weight, I can do better. He was a skinny little guy. About five foot four, less than nine stone. Not very muscular, never used his muscles to earn his living.'

Kolankiewicz paused. Troy could hear the rustle of papers as he looked among his notes.

'Ah – yes – the burns. The burns on the jacket are consistent with those on the hand. The hand was burnt repeatedly. Some scars are months, even years old. One or two only a matter of weeks. And they were caused by acid not flame. The edges are too neat. You getting all this?'

'Of course,' said Troy.

'Now – the clothing. The jacket is woollen, good condition, no darns or patches, no shine to the elbow. The way people wear things out these days, I'm forced to conclude it was fairly new. Who can afford to keep a jacket and not wear it? Only the guy who prints the coupons. The weave is very distinctive. A herringbone pattern favoured by the Bavarians. The cufflink backs

32

us up there. There's a Munich hallmark on the back, which dates it to 1907 and the initials W.W.L. If there weren't a war on it would be a simple matter to write to the silversmith's guild and find out who made it and for whom. As it is . . . ' Kolankiewicz let the sentence trail off.

'The last inch of the sleeve, at the wrist, is peppered with microscopic fragments of metal. All I can say is it looks like some sort of alloy. To be certain would require tests I don't have the facility to do. The entire sleeve is dusty with coal dust and coal ash. His blood group was O. And I got a clear set of prints for you. Lots of very distinctive scars. That's about all I can tell you. You want I should keep the arm on ice till you find the rest?'

'If you could. Thank you.' It seemed appropriate to say 'thank you, Ladislaw' but Troy had never heard anyone address Kolankiewicz by his Christian name.

'How's your arm? Still sore?'

'No . . . it's fine,' Troy lied.

'OK, I keep the meat. The report and the prints I trust to God and dispatch riders.'

He rang off. Troy sat and stared at his notes. Dumbfounded by what they told him. A German in Stepney? There were hundreds, thousands of Germans in Stepney, but not one of them could have a new German jacket.

§ 10

As darkness fell Troy began to feel that he had at last got his office in order – made some headway with the pile of paperwork that had accumulated while he followed Onions's orders and recuperated from the attack of the Uxbridge axeman. Itchy of foot, he was thinking he might drive over to Stepney again when Bonham rang.

'Dig into your pocket, Freddie,' he said, 'you owe one of the little perishers half a dollar.'

'George! You found it!'

'Well, it isn't an it and it wasn't me. It was young Robertson. The one they call Shrimp.'

'What do you mean it isn't an it? Is it in pieces?'

'Worse,' said Bonham, 'it's a bloody jigsaw. Come and see for yourself.'

§ 11

The same picket of urban cowboys met Troy at the lost junction of Cardigan Street and Waterloo Place. The same child's stare, suspicious of any adult, met his greeting to the boys. They were eight hours older, aeons wiser and waiting to be richer. Clearly it was *de rigueur* not to hold out the hand – demeaning almost, the posture of the beggar – seven pairs of hands stayed firmly in the pockets of jackets, while the eighth still juggled the smoking cocoa tin.

Bonham and Troy went into a huddle, backs to the boys, as they sorted out the change in their pockets. Then Bonham walked down the line with a stack of sixpences and passed them out like a priest of mammon at unholy communion. Hands flashed like the tongues of lizards, deftly trousering the loot. Troy approached the boy Bonham had pointed out to him, thanked him for his efforts and handed him a worn Edward VII half-crown. Shrimp Robertson produced a gleaming Ever Ready bullseye torch from under his jacket and flashed at the silver that had crossed his palm. He looked back at Troy – a bold, challenging eye-to-eye stare that Troy had often wished he possessed himself. If he could look like that he'd be the hard man of the Yard in no time.

'It's the real thing,' Troy said. 'Just a bit worn.'

The cowboys galloped off on imaginary horses, slapping thighs and whooping. Shrimp wandered slowly after, occasionally looking back at Troy as though he thought he'd been gypped. Troy could see the beam of his torch darting over the ground. It wouldn't be long before some old fool in an ARP helmet told him to put it out.

Bonham was pointing at a hole in the ground. A couple of battered doors had been pushed aside to reveal a stone staircase descending into the guts of the earth.

'I doubt I'd've found this,' he said. 'Young Robertson went home for his dinner at half-twelve and came back with his prize possession – that torch of his – kicked this lot aside and went down. He's got some nerve, that boy. That stack over there –' Bonham waved casually to where a forty-foot stump of blackened factory chimney jutted out of the rubble like Ozymandias's leg, 'connects up with the cellar. Not that I'd've thought of it. I wouldn't.'

He switched on the beam of a huge chrome torch and led the way down. A strong smell of carbide wafted up to Troy's nostrils, deepening the impression that he was approaching the first circle of hell. Hell surely stank as well as roasted? A uniformed constable was kneeling by a lamp, adjusting the flow of water – half a dozen carbide lamps were arranged in a rough semi-circle across the floor of the cellar, casting a hazy bluish light that flickered constantly in the draughts. The remains of the ceiling littering the floor threw giant, jagged, jumping shadows across the walls.

The constable stood almost to attention – hands pressed to the seams of his trousers. He could not be more than nineteen or twenty – a tall thin streak of a youth, his Adam's apple prominent and bobbing above the top button of his tunic. For a moment Troy looked at the constable the way he knew the older generation of blimps looked at him – any minute now this man, this child in police blue, would get his call-up for the big push, for Calais or Normandy or whatever strip of sand and slaughter Eisenhower had decided on. In that respect, thought Troy, death had already set its mark upon him.

'Bloody hell, Corker,' Bonham delivered his reprimand. 'Is this the best you could do? This lot must've come out of the ark.'

'Sorry, Sergeant,' the constable shrilled back. 'ARP took all our good stuff last month. It's all I could find.'

The smell was becoming familiar, nostalgic rather than demonic, reminding Troy of his first bicycle in 1926, and his brother's first home-made bomb in 1927.

'See,' Bonham was saying, 'they even dug a bullet out of the wall.'

Halfway up the far wall the dirt and mould had been scraped clear in a wide circle around a hole the size of a fist. Troy pushed his hand into the hole and crumbled brick dust between his thumb and finger.

'Neat,' he said. 'Almost scrupulous.'

He could see an old brass tap on a twisted lead pipe snaking up out of the floor in the corner where a stone gulley led to a small iron grating.

'God,' he said to Bonham, 'this place is tailor-made for murder. I don't suppose there's any sign of a cartridge case?'

Bonham waved dismissively at the pile of rubble that had once been the ceiling, now rotten with rat shit and decay. 'You must be joking,' he said. 'Even supposing it was an automatic . . . ' He let the sentence trail away to nothing.

As best he could, Corker adjusted the angle of each lamp in turn, aiming their beams at the large Victorian cast-iron furnace which took up one whole wall of the cellar. This industrial dinosaur had once powered a small factory and bore across its front the proud, cusped inscription Wrigley and Butterworth, Runcorn 1888. At about hip height was the firebox door. Bonham wrenched it open and handed Troy the ash rake, a long rod of steel ending with a welded half-moon plate.

'See for yourself,' he said.

Even with Bonham aiming his torch it was almost impossible to see into the brick cavern of the interior. Troy raked blindly and a few handfuls of flaky, grey ash spilled out on to the sacking at their feet, speckling Troy's shoes and Bonham's boots. Corker came closer, looking expectantly from the pile of ash to Bonham to Troy, faintly smiling in his nervousness. Troy locked on to what appeared to be something solid in the belly of the furnace. He hooked it and pulled sharply. A bone flew out of the firebox and broke in two on the sacking.

Corker's mouth opened silently.

'It's a femur,' Troy told him.

Corker looked blankly back at him.

'A thigh bone,' Troy added.

He delved into the furnace, once more stirring up a cloud of fine ash as light as talcum powder and with the fresh, tantalising smell of cooked meat. Tibia, fibula, clavicle, patella, humerus and a myriad of vertebra and tiny bones from ankle and wrist poured down in a stream of dust and death, swathed in the deceptive scent of Sunday lunch. All that remained of a human life cascading into a small heap at Bonham's feet.

Silently Troy and Bonham exchanged glances. As the minutes passed Corker had turned white. It seemed to Troy that whatever briefing Bonham had given him Corker was only slowly making the connection between this brittle carnage and a corpse.

'Let's get it over with,' said Bonham.

In less than ten minutes they had almost a full skeleton in disarray on the cellar floor. Many of the bones were broken or burnt through, others indistinguishable one from another save to the trained eye of an anatomist. Yet, Troy felt certain, they were all pieces of a single body and he'd seen nothing to dissuade him from the theory that there was only one arm in the pile. The amateur surgeon had done his job well. Nothing but dust remained of the victim's clothing, and more solid evidence, such as a gold tooth or the silver right-hand cufflink, would have melted into shapeless blobs – unidentifiable even if they persisted day and night with the mountain of ash.

Something solid, very solid, was jammed up against the back of the firebox. Troy jiggled the rod and pulled hard. A white ball shot out into the cellar. Instinctively Corker caught it like a rugby ball. He looked quickly at his catch and the smirk of achievement faded from his face. He screamed, threw the skull to Troy and ran to the iron grating in the far corner.

'Not there!' Troy yelled. 'For Christ's sake. Where do you think they got rid of the blood!?!'

Corker changed his aim in the last split second and puked into a green mass of rotting lath and plaster.

Troy held up the skull to the light of Bonham's torch. It was still warm to the touch. The lower jaw and part of the left cheekbone were gone. There was a large hole in the back of the skull and a smaller one at the front. Slivers of baked brain still clung to the inside of the cranium and a glossy gel of melted eye coated the sockets.

'Straight between the eyes,' said Troy. 'Took the back of his head off on the way out.'

'Nasty,' said Bonham without feeling.

The sound of Corker's retching cut through the reverie of discovery. Bonham weighed up the young man – he had turned from white to green – and sent him outside to wait and breathe in fresher air.

'It's his first time,' he said to Troy. 'I tried to tell him . . . but it's no use me telling him he'll get over it. I never have.'

Troy still held the skull cupped in one hand, playing Hamlet at Yorick's graveside. Jigsaw, Bonham had called it. It seemed a classic understatement and put him in mind of his own statement to his squad commander.

'You know, George, I've just told Onions we haven't got a maniac on our hands.'

'You think this ain't the work of a nutter?'

'It's the most meticulous nutter I've ever seen.'

'Doesn't mean to say they're not nutters. Not half a mile from here, not ten years before I was born, Jack the Ripper carved up brasses and got clean away. That took planning – being meticulous as you call it. And there's a lot round here still remember it.'

Troy tried the brass tap. It wouldn't turn. A sliver of icicle clung to the spout. He prised up the grating and reached down into it. His hand came up brown and sticky from a foul-smelling mess.

'Jesus Christ!' said Bonham.

Troy turned his hand slowly before his eyes as Bonham turned the torch on him. A coagulant slime clung to his hand from the fingertips to the heel of his palm, and began its viscous slither towards his wrist.

'Tap frozen. Drain frozen. Not enough heat from a burning corpse to thaw the place out, so they couldn't flush the blood away,' Troy said, smiling at the small success and holding out his hand to Bonham.

'Leave it out, Freddie.'

'Which means he was killed some time during this recent freeze up, some time during the last week.'

'Less than that,' said Bonham. 'Didn't freeze up till five days back.'

Carefully Troy drew a clean linen handkerchief from his coat pocket, wiped his hand on it and dropped it into the bag of bones. At the top of the steps they found Corker, helmet off, cigarette between his lips, the colour slowly returning to his face. He dropped the cigarette and attempted to stand straight up in the presence of the two sergeants, but his stance weakened as his eyes were drawn almost magically to the sack in Troy's hand.

'Finish your ciggy, lad, and then gather up your lamps,' Bonham told him sympathetically. 'We've done all we can for now.'

Troy placed the sack in the boot of the Bullnose Morris. As he turned round he found the Shrimp not a dozen feet off – still staring intensely at Troy, hands thrust deep in the pockets of his shorts.

Troy knew, had always known, that he had no gift, no way with children.

'Should you be out at this time of night?' he asked lamely.

Shrimp turned over a piece of broken brick with the toe of a brown boot and looked at the ground.

'I can look after meself,' he said.

Troy didn't doubt it.

'Was there something?' he persisted gently.

'You sound like that berk on the wireless,' the boy said.

'What berk?'

'Sam Costa.'

'Look, do you want something or not?'

'Depends.'

'On what? You've had your half-crown. You can eye it all you like – it's coin of the realm. You can blow it on all the bullseyes your ration book'll run to.'

''S'awright,' the boy mused. ''S'awright. Money's no problem.'

'Well, it's all you're getting.'

Troy turned the key in the car door, yanked it open and made a move to get in.

'Like I said,' the boy continued. 'It all depends.'

'Depends on what?' said Troy with a foot already in the door.

'On how much you want what I got.'

Troy slammed the door and squared off to the little extortionist.

39

'You've got something? Something you found down there? I told you not to touch anything.'

The boy shrugged – beyond intimidation.

'Withholding evidence is not only stupid it's illegal.'

'I couldn't give a toss. What I got'll cost you another half-dollar or you can whistle. And don't try any rough stuff . . . my dad has coppers for breakfast.'

How often, Troy thought, had he heard such phrases?

'This had better be worth it.'

The boy shrugged again.

'Let's see the colour of your money.'

Troy held out half a crown at arm's length. The boy moved up to striking distance. Troy snatched his arm away. Slowly the boy's hands came out of his pockets. Two clenched fists, knuckles upward. He held out his hands, tapped his fists together lightly and opened the right. It was empty. He tapped again. Opened the left. It too was empty. At the third tap he opened the right fist again and grinned. There was a balled-up child's handkerchief crushed into the grubby little palm. Troy picked up the bundle, spreading its snot-encrusted folds across his palm. There in the middle was a gleaming copper cartridge case – a huge bore – .45 or .44 at least from the look of it.

Troy placed the half-crown in the boy's open hand. It was trousered with the speed of a salamander.

'See,' he said, 'I never touched it.'

Troy dropped the shell into an envelope and gave the handkerchief back.

'Where?' he said.

'Next to top step,' the Shrimp replied. 'It was what made me go down. Be seein' ya.'

And he walked off into the night. From somewhere the bullseye torch appeared once more and bobbed like Corker's Adam's apple. It seemed to Troy that it waved in mockery all the way up Stepney Green.

§ 12

A cold coming out. Hendon was dark and deserted. Troy had to bang loudly on the door before the night-watch roused himself from his jobsworth's sleep of the just and gruffly consented to sign for the sack of bones. A cold getting back. Troy left his car at the Yard and cut a night-walk; a convoluted, nosy policeman's route home that defied the flight of the crow and took him where his feet led rather than his mind decided. Coming up Lower Regent Street into Piccadilly Circus he was reminded that it was Friday night. There were queues for the Eros Newsreel Theatre and for the London Pavilion. A warm hum of inviting human noise came off the Criterion Restaurant, and the same sense of life and release oozed from the other end of the social scale through the blacked-out windows of the Lyon's Corner House. The doors of The Monico, next to Saqui and Lawrence, and home of the 1/6d afternoon tea, banged ceaselessly with the flow of people in and out. The Luftwaffe scarcely needed to see the lights of London, surely they could hear it? He refused the invitation and headed towards Coventry Street.

He had been back at work only two days and it seemed to him that the weekend ought to be logically still further off. It also occurred to him that if this was Friday then he was due in court the next Monday. Just when he should be getting his teeth into the Stepney case. At the top of Haymarket, passing the Gaumont cinema, next to the long-defunct, boarded-up offices of Air France, he thought he heard someone call his name and turned to look back, but could see nothing in the blackness, as people blundered about trying to avoid each other, or not trying to avoid each other – depending on the urgency and promise of a Friday night in wartime. War, along with the inevitable increase in crime, had brought a new darkness and a new sexual licence – a freedom from one care flung out in defiance of all the others. At its crudest, do it now for we may be dead tomorrow. Troy crossed Leicester Square to Wyndham's Theatre, over into St Martin's Lane via the alley at the back, and turned into the entrance of Goodwins Court – a gate so strait Sidney Greenstreet could not have passed – to the small house in which he had lived since leaving Stepney. A sign of the times – the prostitute who usually stood guard at the corner of the Court and St Martin's Lane was walking off in the direction of Trafalgar Square, her arm hooked through the arm of a man in uniform, so indistinct that Troy could not tell if it was a Pole or a Canadian, an airman or a soldier. Her sashay, the swaggering buttock roll, was unmistakable, even in the blackout. Before the war any whore would have had ten times the discretion and ten times the need. Ruby felt and acted as though she was safe from reproach and restraint – she knew damn well Troy was a policeman, and when she wasn't trying to flirt with him was offering to fix him up with a friend, as she liked 'all her friends to be friends', which, it seemed, was how she regarded Troy.

The evening meal was a vague prospect. Troy could cook and clean better than most men of his age. Bachelorhood was not a waiting time to wallow in the pleasurable filth of one's own incompetence. The youngest of a family of four he had been accustomed from an early age to rely on his own resources and his own company – a much older brother being beyond his reach and twin sisters virtually a world unto themselves – and all Ethel Bonham had had to do was play upon the tendency to self-sufficiency that was all but natural in Troy. The trouble was, self-sufficiency could not make a meal of snoek or whalemeat. By comparison, five loaves and thirteen fishes were more malleable. Troy, like the nation, was bored and irritated by the wartime shortages. The longer the war went on, the worse, it seemed, the diet became. The national loaf, his uncle assured him, was nutritionally almost perfect, but it tasted like wet newspaper. Occasionally and bizarrely the diet was enlivened by the sudden short-lived availability of various fruits. Once, years ago, it had been cherries, then it was oranges and for days afterwards the streets of London were littered with peel as a reminder of the orgy. Troy turned to the kitchen cupboard and sought his salvation in a box of eggs given to him by his mother. Out on the heights of Hertfordshire, Maria Mikhailovna had turned her east-facing lawn into a chicken run and had quadrupled the size of the kitchen garden the day war was declared. In the spring of 1941 she had forsaken fripperies for the duration and given the orchid hothouse over to tomatoes. In the depths of 1942 she had surrendered her much-prized south lawn from the windows to the ha-ha and turned it over entirely to potatoes. By 1943 she felt there was little else one woman could give. Her regular treat for her children was a half-dozen eggs at any time, bolstered by fresh leeks all through autumn and a long summer of changing varieties of fresh, earthy smelling potatoes. At odd, unexpected moments one sister or the other would arrive on his doorstep tooled up with what appeared to be half a barrowload of Covent Garden's finest, from common spud to uncommon capiscum straight out of one of the greenhouses, thrust them at Troy and tell him he neither called nor visited often enough. Masha in particular would go through his kitchen cupboard and berate him for not meeting her standards. Troy felt that was entirely his business and none of hers and asserted that he looked after himself quite well.

The cupboard yielded an onion, greening a little on the outside, a couple of King Edwards and three speckled, large brown eggs. It called, Troy told himself, for a Spanish omelette – oh, for a capiscum out of season! – a meal that would be a treat in any restaurant, but for the fact that few restaurants in town would now run to a three-egg omelette. Such was the desperation to fill a menu nowadays that he knew of more than one restaurant that had served roast rook. Under the sink he had several bottles of wine from a cellar laid down by his father before the war. On his death late in 1943 Troy's mother had offered the cellar half each to her sons. Troy had paid no attention on those frequent occasions when his father had tried to teach him about wine, or when he had merely drunk enough to become lyrical on the subject. What discrimination brother Rod showed Troy didn't know, all he tried for himself was to remember whether such and such a year had been a good summer, and to follow the vaguest rule about fish and meat – not that this said anything about eggs. He reached for a Pauillac '27 with no recollection whatsoever of the weather, only that it was most certainly the summer his brother had blown up the old potting shed with the device he had cobbled together out of carbide gas and cocoa tins.

He had drunk his first glass – so fine a wine that he felt sure he was violating a long-held cache of his father's, knocking back some special reserve – and had softened the vegetables in a pan, when there was a knock on the door. A blast of cold air rushed in. Constable Wildeve stood on the doorstep sniffing the scents that wafted out from the kitchen and smiling expectantly.

'I thought it was you. I'd just stepped out of Joe Lyon's and I thought it was you. I called out but you probably didn't hear me.'

Troy swung the door back.

'Come in before all the warm air goes out.'

Wildeve followed Troy back to the kitchen still sniffing, smiling and hinting. 'Good Lord. Eggs. Real eggs. Do I see real eggs?'

'Yes. And if you hadn't just eaten your fill at the Corner House I might say it would stretch to two.'

'Ah ... I haven't you see. She stood me up, so I paid for my solitary cup of scummy tea and left. That's when I saw you.'

Troy reached for a second plate, set another glass down before Wildeve and pushed the bottle towards him.

'I thought you weren't due back until Monday,' Wildeve said.

'I felt fine, and I got a call from Stepney. My old station sergeant with a body on his hands. Onions didn't object. Although he did try to stick me with another case. I had expected to see you. I presume you had your head down?'

'In court. Two days cooling my heels at the Bailey.'

Troy tipped the eggs into the sizzling pan. Wildeve picked up one of the half-shells and fondled it.

'Real shells!'

Wildeve could be infuriating and inspired by turns. He could gossip at a moment that demanded high concentration, and drop acute insight into conversation as though it were scarcely relevant and he thought it worth a quick mention in passing. He picked at the gossamer lining of the shell in fascination.

'Just look at the speckles on this eggshell. I've seen nothing like it in, well ... months. I say, and that's real onion!'

Troy decided not to take the bull by the horns. He set the meal in front of Wildeve, let him eat, drink and prattle about the beautiful Wren who had left him with a cold cup of tea on a Friday evening, interspersed with the business of the day that had taken him into the witness-box at the Old Bailey. He rolled the omelette around his palette as though it were either scalding him or was as scintillating as the finest claret, and swigged finest claret like it was ginger beer.

As he held out his glass for a refill Troy buttonholed him and launched into a quick synopsis of the case so far. Wildeve's second glass sat untouched as he listened.

'Bizarre,' he said. 'Bloody weird. That bobby has my sympathy. I'm not sure I wouldn't have puked either.'

'The problem is,' Troy continued, 'I'm due in court myself on Monday. Bernard Leahy's up for the Portsmouth strangling at Winchester. I think there's a good chance he'll go for Not Guilty and deny the confession.'

'Ah,' said Wildeve, 'so you need me to ride to the rescue?'

He knocked back the second glass with a speed that would have appalled the late Alexei Troy.

'Not quite, Jack. I need you to go through the aliens' registration list at B3 over in Scotland House. Also the CRO. You might try the refugee organisations – though the first thing they'll want from us is what we want from them – a name. I've a full set of prints from the hand. They're in the top left drawer of my desk. Kolankiewicz biked them over while I was in Stepney.'

'Bugger.'

'Just do it, Jack. It's the only way to begin.'

'God, all that paperwork. You wouldn't think a German would be so hard to find. There's never one around when you want one.'

'If he was here in 1940, then he would almost certainly have been rounded up in that wave of detentions after the fall of Norway. He may even have been interned. That means fingerprints.'

'Well, he's hardly likely to have arrived since, is he?'

'It's that possibility that worries me,' said Troy.

§ 13

As Troy stepped down from the witness-box the defending barrister rose and addressed the judge. He might want to recall Sergeant Troy, would Mr Troy therefore not leave the court in the course of the day, or Winchester overnight. This caught the prosecution unawares. Sir Willoughby Wright got to his feet and indulged in a fabricated fit of coughing, whilst looking at Troy across the top of a white handkerchief the size of a government-surplus marquee. Troy made a circling motion with the index finger of his right hand as he had seen the ASMs do to the comedians at the Windmill when they overshot their allotted time.

'My Lord,' Sir Willoughby began, 'I believe Sergeant Troy has other, pressing cases at Scotland Yard. The court can hardly expect—'

'But the court does expect, Sir Willoughby,' said the judge sharply. He looked at Troy and added, 'You will remain, Mr Troy, and I need hardly remind you that you will still be under oath, and that you will not discuss this case with anyone.'

Out in the waiting room Troy cursed aloud, and a small man in a grubby mackintosh and a Homburg looked up from behind a copy of the *News Chronicle*. It was Kolankiewicz. Troy looked around for the duty officer, who was peeking into the court through the gap in the doors and sat down on the bench, next but one to Kolankiewicz. It would not do to be caught talking to another witness if the duty officer turned out to be a stickler for protocol.

'What are you doing here? I thought the forensic report was done by the local chap?' he whispered.

'Wrong side,' said Kolankiewicz cryptically, not even looking in the direction of Troy.

'What do you mean wrong side?'

'Here for defence.'

'What? You're the Police Pathologist!'

'I can take private cases just like Harley Street. Leahy didn't do it. That hand of his been useless for years. He caught it in a machine of some sort ten years ago. He couldn't have strangled anybody. And we should not be having this conversation as damn well you know.'

Kolankiewicz made a show of putting up his newspaper and pretended to be reading as a duty officer passed by them. The doors to the main court opened and there was a rush of trilbied, spotty-faced young court reporters looking for telephones that still worked.

'They've broken for lunch,' Troy said. 'Let's find a place for a cup of tea and a chat.'

Troy chose the third café they passed, far enough away from the court. Like everywhere else it was full of off-duty GIs, chain-smoking and flirting with the waitresses. Ahead of him in the queue, a blond, handsome infantryman was complaining pleasantly about the cold, learning the English habit of talking about the weather as a preface to anything – he had never seen his breath freeze in the air indoors before. His accent rolled along melodically, not quite a drawl.

'Where you from, dearie?' Troy heard the waitress ask, as he stood at the counter.

'Guess,' the soldier said.

The girl fired blindly at a map, 'Dodge City?'

'Fort Smith, Arkansas, ma'am.' And she was none the wiser.

Troy found his way back to the table with two half-pint cups of weak tea.

'I need to ask you something,' Troy said, as Kolankiewicz tipped the spillage from the saucer back into his teacup and slurped loudly.

'Most improper.'

'Sod Leahy. It's not him I'm talking about, and if you don't believe he's capable of strangling anyone you should have seen the bruises on my arms where the bugger grabbed hold of me when I was nicking him. I had the imprint of his hands on me like stigmata for days. He fought well enough for a man with a useless hand.'

'You have the foresight to photograph these bruises?'

'No – and Leahy's not the point.'

'So you keep saying, but we keep talking about him. A pervert's conspiracy, isn't it?'

'What you mean is conspiracy to pervert the course of justice. And it's that German I'm on about.'

'Ah, the late Herr Cufflink.'

'Precisely,' said Troy. 'How did you know the cufflink was German?'

'I told you. It had a Munich Guild mark on it,' replied Kolankiewicz. 'Miss,' he waved at a passing waitress, 'there would not be such a thing as a buttered scone?'

The girl looked at him for a fraction of a second as she squeezed

47

by, clutching a plate of buttered scones. 'Quite right,' she said, 'there wouldn't.' And she plonked the whole plateful in front of half a dozen laughing, leering young Americans. Kolankiewicz gazed forlornly after his lost scone, and watched as the waitress lined up a multiple date for the evening. Troy tapped the table to seize his attention.

'As a rule that kind of information would have taken you days to come up with. How did you happen to have it at your fingertips?'

'Easy peasy. I still had all the reference books and records out that I used last year.'

'Last year?'

'That other German. The one they found on Tower beach with bullet-hole in his cheek. I got out all the stuff on fabrics, hallmarks and you know what then. I identified him as German from the clothes. Labels cut out, but the fabric was a giveaway. It just happens that I never bothered to send the stuff back. You know me. I work best in a little chaos.'

'When last year?'

'April. May. I don't know.'

'How is it that I haven't heard of it? Where was I?'

'How the fuck should I know? It wasn't in the Met area. City Police you know. I believe their man handled the case. Idiot name of Malnick.'

'Oh God. Not Malnick.'

Malnick had been a uniformed Inspector with the City of London Police in 1939 when Troy was in his first few days at the Yard. The City Superintendent had requested help from the Yard when the case of the drowned eight-year-old boy seemed to have ground to a halt. Inspector Malnick had had his nose put thoroughly out of joint when Onions sent a twenty-four-year-old Troy, still only a constable, as the specialist help he thought they needed. He had earned Malnick's everlasting enmity by solving the case in forty-eight hours.

'I was in Liverpool in April. Could it have been then?'

'Possibly. But they didn't send for the Yard. Their man insisted on tackling it personally. But, like I said, he was an idiot.'

'Did they catch anyone?'

'Not to my knowledge. If the case ever came to trial they never

48

sent for anything from Hendon. My file is still open.'

'Why didn't you tell me this on Friday?'

Kolankiewicz swigged his tea and played for time.

'I forgot,' he said with a shrug, 'It was my assistant, Anna, who remembered.'

'Was there any other similarity besides the clothing?'

'That I'd have to look up. As you're asking me to compare a whole body to an arm and a bag of bones, I should say not much.'

'Shot in the face, you said?'

'Oh, that I do remember. It seemed, as you English would say, caddish. Certainly less than sporting.'

'A shot to the forehead badly aimed?'

'Don't ask me to guess. It's like pissing into the wind.'

'Any attempt at dismemberment?'

'No. I had a whole cadaver. Troy, why don't you talk to Anna? She can get out the file and tell you anything you want to know.'

At the back of the café Troy got through to Hendon on the phone. But Anna could not find the file. She told him she'd ring back. Troy hogged the phone and stood by it to prevent anyone else making a call. He watched Kolankiewicz slyly swap his empty cup for Troy's full one, and as the phone rang saw him snatch his coveted scone from a tray as the waitress had her head and her common sense turned by a provocative remark from one of the soldiers. He would hate to have to get between the cocksurety of any young soldier and the righteousness of Kolankiewicz.

'It's not there,' said Anna. 'I don't know what he's done with it. Even the cards are missing. I think that's why he didn't want to tell you, but I told him you'd ask.'

'What cards?'

'One of Spilsbury's methods, that we copied – everything that would go into a file also goes on quick reference cards. I fill in Kolankiewicz's. But they've walked or he's had them out and not put them back.'

'Do you remember anything about the case?'

'Yes. Mainly what a buffoon Malnick was. Kolankiewicz got right up his nose as you can imagine. Apart from that, the body was a man of about forty I'd say. I usually go through clothing and articles myself. Nothing of any help in the pockets, labels snipped out of his clothes with nail-scissors. The shot to the face killed him instantly. Bone fragment straight up into the brain, but that wasn't all. There was an aggravated wound to the leg. Can't recall which.'

'Aggravated? In what way?'

'As though he'd run, hobbled more like, for quite a way after he'd been shot. Bullet passed right through, so I've no idea whether he was shot twice with the same gun or what. But he'd increased tissue trauma consistent with using the leg muscles after the initial wound. Must've hurt like hell. Why isn't Kolankiewicz telling you this? The bastard hasn't sloped off has he?'

'Far from it. He's pretending he doesn't know me.'

Kolankiewicz had retreated behind his newspaper so as not to be seen eating the stolen scone. Troy saw the waitress turn round from the pleasures of the Americans and place a hand on her hip in a forthright manner. He knew what was coming. These days you could die for an onion, kill for a scone.

'Must dash. I'll call you when I can.'

' 'Ere,' the waitress was saying, 'you light-fingered so-and-so! Where is it?'

She pulled down the newspaper. Kolankiewicz's cheeks were stuffed like a hamster's. Even in the teeth of the evidence, he munched on stolidly, returned her gaze with knobs on and shook the paper free of her hand. As Troy struggled past the rows of tables to get to Kolankiewicz, the young Arkansian had risen from his seat and was offering to assist.

'He nicked it. So 'elp me the little bugger nicked it!'

'Who you calling bugger?' said Kolankiewicz, having swallowed the evidence, his accent thickening as he resorted to his Polish identity to feed his defiance. 'Is it for scrubbers to insult customers in this way?'

'Hey, now you hold on a minute there, buddy,' said the American, 'I don't know what you said but it sure sounds like no way to talk to a lady!'

'Scrubber,' said Kolankiewicz, 'by definition a female who courts the company of an organised body of men in the hope of procuring and offering sexual favour. I think you will find it has become a national pastime among the British.'

The American paused, somewhere between curiosity and anger.

'What d'he say?'

Before the waitress could answer, Troy slipped between them and took Kolankiewicz by the elbow, forcing him to stand up.

'He means,' he said, 'that he's very sorry to have troubled you both, and hopes that this will cover our bill.'

Troy slapped a florin on the table and steered Kolankiewicz to the door. Behind him he heard the waitress declaiming in predictable terms of 'damn cheek' and 'don't come back'.

Kolankiewicz shook free of Troy's grip and went through a showy display of realigning his hat. Troy knew that he might look more like a policeman if he too wore a hat. He might also look as silly as Kolankiewicz did now, standing on his injured pride and rearranging the visible symbol of dignity.

'The bullet that killed your German. What was the bore?'

'Bullets, schmullets. Don't ask me, Troy. I'm a flesh-and-blood man. The details of calibres and twists stay in my head long enough to dictate to Anna. Ask me about the state of a man's liver two years after I cut it out, chances are I will remember.'

'Did you have a chance to look at the cartridge case I left you before you came down?'

'Forty-five for sure.'

'Forty-five automatic? There's a Colt forty-five automatic that's a standard issue American-forces weapon.'

'Yes – but the black market these days. I know a pub in Mill Hill where you could buy a Howitzer over the counter.' Kolankiewicz gestured at the café window. 'Most of your colonial cousins would sell you anything from a pair of nylons to a half-track. You need a second-hand Flying Fortress? Try the Railwayman's Arms in Mill Hill. And the money they get they spend monopolising the buttered scones of Olde England!' The Arkansian smiled through the glass, easy grace letting good manners get the better of his temper. It was wasted on Kolankiewicz, who promptly turned his hand around and gave the man two fingers. Taking it for a Churchillian gesture, the American waved back with a Victory V. Kolankiewicz stomped off down the pavement. Troy felt he had witnessed some major national confrontation in miniature.

§ 14

It was Thursday morning before Troy got back to the Yard. Kolankiewicz had not spoken to him for nearly three days. Wildeve was out, but there was a message on his desk – 'Anna Pakenham called. Still can't find files. We have more German refugees than sheep in these islands. J W.'

Troy called Anna.

'What was the verdict?' she asked.

'I didn't wait to find out. Kolankiewicz's evidence made me look like a fool.'

'No, Troy, he's the fool. He's going to have to explain how a full dossier can just vanish. All I've got are my shorthand notes and I'm afraid they don't make too much sense. I use a pencil, which can look rather grubby twelve months on, and I only learnt when we lost the regular girl to the ATS.'

'The calibre of the bullet would help.'

'Forty-five. Numbers always go down in plain English.'

'Automatic?'

'Can't be sure. And before you ask the bullet was with the clothes and personal effects, such as they were, and they've gone too.'

'Kolankiewicz didn't mislay anything,' said Troy. 'Doesn't this sound more like they've been stolen?'

'I don't know. We've been burgled once and I put that down to a moonshiner. All we lost were fifteen quarts of pure alcohol. There's no value in the dossier on an unidentified man.'

'Unless of course you want to be certain he stays that way.'

§ 15

The weather broke. January had been unseasonably mild, February the aberrant frost, and now March seemed to offer the promise of an early spring and a wet one. At City HQ Troy sat in a damp basement while the desk sergeant burrowed into the stacks for 1943's file on an unknown man found dead on Tower beach, and watched the winds of March blow the rain in sheets down the dirty glass, thick as milk-bottles, set high up the wall at pavement level, while the snows of winter dissolved and ran in clanging streams down iron pipes en route to the Thames.

He heard the heavy uneven step echoing down the stacks long before Sergeant Flint limped into sight.

The man stopped by the table where Troy sat and set down a bundle of foolscap folders nearly a foot thick. He was breathing heavily and slumped into his chair sighing with relief.

'You weren't limping the last time we met,' said Troy.

'Bit o'shrapnel,' the sergeant replied. '1941. Doctors said I'll never walk right again. Afore the war o'course that would've been the end of bein' a copper. But ... things bein' what they are.'

He cut the stack in two like giant playing cards.

'If you wouldn't mind ... I've narrowed it down, but I just couldn't lay me hands right on it. Odd that, seein' as 'ow it's recent. Good job Mr Malnick is gone. Stickler for order he was. I let something slip he'd give me a rocket.'

Troy was already tearing halfway through April, setting files aside at three times the speed the sergeant could muster.

'Where did Mr Malnick transfer to?' he asked.

'It wasn't a transfer. He got accepted for the RAF.'

'What? At his age? He must be fifty. He was turned down by the RAF when I was here during the invasion of Poland.'

'That wasn't the first time neither. His wish was granted.'

'What do you mean?'

'I think someone pulled a string for him. He was out of the force with a speed that took everyone by surprise. I remember the Super commenting on it. He was a copper on Friday and a flight lieutenant on Monday.'

'When was this?'

'Straight after the case we're looking for. I suppose it must have been May last year.'

Troy had finished his pile and watched as Flint picked over May. He was painfully slow, as though to look and talk at the same time were beyond him.

'It surprised all of us, I can tell you. Mind, I wasn't sorry to see him go. I worked with him for eight years. Well, you saw what he was like yourself that time they sent you over when you was still wet behind the ears.'

'Thanks,' said Troy.

'Aunt Fanny we called him. A fusspot. Not even a good fusspot. Couldn't find a truncheon in his trousers without a torch – well, you know how they talk in a locker room.'

'But meticulous?'

'Oh yes. That all right.'

Flint had resorted to licking finger and thumb to get a better grip, and was slowly working his way down towards the end of May.

'Anything Mr Malnick left would be in good order?'

'Oh yes.'

Troy waited, trying to show patience with a man clearly not in the best of health, trying not to rush the obvious. After all, it was not so far away.

'Odd,' said Flint, 'it's not in your bit . . .'

'And it's not in yours.'

'Stripe me.'

'I'm not surprised, but I am curious. What kind of power, what kind of access does it take to make all trace of a man disappear?'

Flint sucked in his breath, pretending appraisal of a situation that was beyond his experience.

'You don't,' Troy ventured, 'by any chance know what airfield Mr Malnick is serving on?'

As it happens I do. He sent us a card this Christmas just gone. Said he couldn't tell us where he was, but to let us know he was engaged on work of national importance.'

'Aren't we all.'

'But it had a postmark. Bradwell in Essex. An' I know there's an RAF outfit there, 'cos my sister's boy 'Enry is on it. Mostly Poles and Canadians he reckons. A few English to . . . liaise . . . I think he calls it.'

§ 16

It took Troy most of the following morning to persuade the motor pool to fill up his Bullnose Morris with enough petrol to get him out to Bradwell-on-Sea and back. In the garage at the Yard, a man in greasy overalls had looked over his chit as though he thought Troy had printed it himself.

Troy was in his office stuffing a briefcase for the trip when the phone rang

'Ah. Found you,' said Anna. 'I have a definite match on blood group. That disgusting handkerchief you left is clotted with type O. Kolankiewicz is still being unspeakable, but says to tell you the bones in the bag could be part of the same body as the arm – that is there are no left arm bones in the bag, and the right arm is the same size, although many other smaller bones are also missing. Should stand up in court.'

'What news on the Tower beach corpse?'

'Worse. Everything. Every single damn thing is missing. The only option left was the body itself, so I enquired about the possibility of exhumation. Forget it. The cemetery took a direct hit six weeks ago.'

'So much for a fine and private place.'

'Sod Marvell,' she said, 'more like Hieronymus Bosch. A charnel house in the mud. Sorry.'

'Where is Kolankiewicz, by the way?'

'Scrubbing up for a dissection. Cambridgeshire constabulary have a tricky one for him. He spent part of the morning with that arm of yours and kept muttering about trousers.'

'Trousers?'

'That's what it sounded like to me.'

Troy rang off, hoping that when Kolankiewicz finally surfaced from his Polish misery it would all yield something constructive. Troy rooted around in his desk drawer to see if he still had toothpaste and a razor for a possible overnight. He looked up. Silently Onions had entered the room. He was clutching the chit. He sat in the upright chair on the far side of Troy's desk and scratched at his cheek with the hand that held the chit.

'I take it you can't handle this by phone?' he said.

'You've met Malnick. Any answers I can get out of him will mean nothing if I can't see his face when he speaks.'

'Do we call our fellow officers liars?'

'No. But I do call this one stupid and devious. And that's a bad combination.'

Onions took a fountain pen from his breast pocket and scribbled his signature across the chit. Troy closed his briefcase, and hoped he could make a getaway. The fringes of London could jam solid with troop convoys these days and a journey could take twice as long as it used to before the war.

'Hendon?' Onions asked simply, and Troy knew he had no quick escape.

'Everything's gone. Not a paper-clip left in place.'

'Ah ... so you smell conspiracy?'

'Smell it? Stan, I can touch it, it's tangible, solid, inescapable. If Malnick is part of it, which I very much doubt by the way, he'll be as slippery as an eel. As it is he'll play up his injured innocence and think I'm directly accusing him.'

'Which you're not?'

The door burst open. A breathless Wildeve rushed in and began to gabble before he had even noticed the presence of Onions.

'Do you know how many Germans and Austrians and other assorted enemies there are in this country?'

'About seventy-five thousand,' Troy replied.

'Oh. You do know.'

Onions stood up. 'Don't mind me,' he said.

Troy could have sworn that Wildeve blushed as Onions looked directly at him. He recalled that in his early days Onions's gorgon gaze had been utterly mysterious, as likely to be mere curiosity as silent reprimand.

'My brother was interned,' Troy continued. 'I looked into it. What have you found?'

'Well, they only fingerprinted those they interned in 1940, that is largely people in categories A and B, and that's less than a third of the total. Even then they reckon there were well over five hundred they never even caught up with. They said they couldn't mount a search themselves, but I've got a uniform on it, so it's being done.'

'How long?'

'Days. Perhaps a week. At least. Nothing in CRO. Whoever he was he had no form.'

Onions thrust the chit at Troy and left without another word.

'Have I upset him?' said Wildeve.

'No – I've just confronted him with a situation he hates. I think we can count Hitler and the Luftwaffe out of the conspiracy,' Troy said, 'but everybody else in.'

'What do you mean?'

'I mean,' Troy said, 'that the plot thickens. Unfortunately a lot now depends on Malnick, which is why I'm not giving him any warning. If I phone him he can get off the line and cook up a story. I'm playing it down for Stan, but I wouldn't trust Malnick to see old ladies across the road.'

'You don't surely think a policeman would destroy files?' Wildeve almost whispered the sentence, as though it were a heresy best unuttered.

'Somebody did.'

§ 17

Troy took the Bullnose Morris through the battered fringes of East London once more, a snaking crawl around pot-holes and debris out via the boroughs on either side of the Lea Valley where entire streets stood roofless and windowless, houses quilted in cardboard and tarpaulin, shops that had gone from being more open than usual – one of the war's more short-lived jokes – to being simply, perhaps permanently shut. He found it hard to believe a second time in the political daydream of homes fit for heroes – the heroes, as he saw it, had by and large been the civilian population, sixty-odd thousand of whom had died, and, heroism being a finite resource, many had fled from the Blitz never to return. He wondered what inducement other than the familiarity and illusory safety in one's own origins would lure people back, found it impossible to imagine East London recovering. Beyond this where London met Essex were places like Hornchurch, swamped by the RAF and the USAF, whose aerodromes were scattered up the east coast, shattering the nights of the sleepy dormitory towns of the thirties and the rural outposts of Langham and Bentwaters and Bradwell. The countryside purred with the sound of engines.

It was almost dusk. The sign of the Green Man swung in the wind blowing off the North Sea. Troy pushed on the door marked Snug and glanced around the bar. It thronged with young airmen, mostly Canadians and New Zealanders, and mostly looking as fresh-faced as schoolboys. There were only two faces over thirty, and they were making the least noise, the barman and a morose-looking figure who sat alone at a table in the bay with a glass of sherry in front of him. His hair rose up in ridges like corrugated cardboard and although only fortyish he was assuming the jowlly look of a lugubrious bloodhound. He stared directly at Troy and seemed not to recognise him. Troy knew him at once although he had not seen him since the days of his father's pre-war dinner parties when the old man had tried to woo him from his job at Lord Beaverbrook's *Daily Express* to his own *Evening Herald*. It was Tom Driberg, now MP for somewhere or other, better known as William Hickey. He had turned Alexei Troy down, but had gone on allowing himself to be wooed and dined on many occasions. Troy had no idea that Driberg had any connection with Bradwell. He approached cautiously, knowing his reputation, but telling himself he was too old and most certainly the wrong class to appeal to Driberg's cultivated taste.

'Do I know you?' he said bluntly.

'Yes,' said Troy. 'Frederick Troy. I'm Alex Troy's son.'

'Yes ... yes ...' he mused. 'Didn't you join the RAF?'

He motioned to the empty chair opposite, and his face began to shed its demeanour of thinly concealed misery.

'No. The police.'

Troy thought Driberg flinched, and was certain he saw the blood drain from his face. By way of reassurance he added quickly, 'I'm here to see an old colleague who's joined up. I thought he might be here.'

'Can I get you a drink?' Driberg said, composure regained. 'The dry sherry's passable and they keep a red wine just for me, not that I'd recommend it – but the thought counts. God knows where they get it.'

Troy asked for a glass of Indian tonic water and took the seat opposite Driberg. Over his shoulder he could see the bar, and that what he had taken for a large mirror behind it was in fact the view across the pumps and optics into the saloon bar. There was another crowd of RAF servicemen, almost a mirror image of the present crowd but for the presence in their midst of an older man who appeared to be holding forth on some subject that swung his young audience between laughter and derision. Tall, angular and at least twenty years older than anyone else around him, Inspector Malnick had traded one shade of blue for another and had teased out a clipped moustache into something approaching a parody of a handlebar. Troy watched in fascination, so pointedly that Driberg squirmed around in his seat to see the object of Troy's bad manners – Malnick's bony hands flattened out into the wings of an imagined aircraft swooping and rising as he told some tale that Troy thought was bound to be improbable. He thought he caught the word 'prang' filtered through the hubbub and urged on him by wishful lip-reading. On the chests of most young men around Malnick were the wings of pilots or the winged Os of the observers, and the ribbons of colour splashed against the pale blue of battledress where medals had been awarded. No such adorned Malnick's blouse. He was clearly ground crew and just as clearly hated it. As his hand brought his plane up into a sharp ascent his eyes met Troy's and they locked in a long, intent gaze shot through with fear, regret, suspicion and plain embarrassment. The hand froze. He snatched it back and shook it as though he had just been burnt. He blushed and the crowd of youngsters roared with laughter. One or two of them slapped him on the back, someone called out for 'another pint for the old bluffer'. Malnick continued to stare silently back at Troy through the row of optics, almost oblivious to the noise and the centrality of his own place in it, and Troy knew at once how he should handle Mr Malnick.

'You will excuse me, won't you,' he said to Driberg. 'But I think I've found what I was looking for.'

'Don't let the fool buttonhole you all night. The Raf turfed me out of the Lodge, but I've a cottage down on the quay these days. Come and have a nightcap. Bed for the night if you need one.'

Malnick turned his back on his audience and headed for the door. Troy met him in the hallway between the two bars.

'I'm so sorry, Mr Malnick. I really didn't mean to drag you away.'

'You have all the same. I take it this is of some importance?'

Troy stopped himself from reacting to the pomposity of the man. A little flattery in circumstances where Malnick was accustomed to none might yet yield a dividend.

'Truth to tell I rather need your advice about a matter. Can I get you a drink?'

'No,' said Malnick. 'It's time I was heading back to the Lodge. If it's as important as you say you'd better come up.'

Troy could hear Bradwell Lodge before he could see it through the evening gloom. It was as raucous as the Green Man. A child of nineteen or twenty came haring down the drive, trouserless and pursued by half a dozen others waving pillows and cushions. It was, Troy recalled, known in his schooldays – a time he looked back on with loathing – as a scragging. Malnick stepped swiftly aside, not even pausing in his polemic on the strategic importance of a ground crew and traffic controller to the national war effort – but England had long since overflowed with such people. Troy met on a daily basis men for whom the war had inevitably come down to a personal conflict between themselves and Hitler.

They had scarcely made it to the front door of the Lodge when the same pursuit swung full circle and the trouserless officer nipped smartly between the portals only to collide with another buffoon who had thought it a good wheeze to slide down the Adam staircase on a tin tray.

'And what's worse,' Malnick appeared to have changed the subject, 'I've known the bastards to spend an evening chucking a chamber-pot full of beer from one end of the hall to the other!'

It occurred to Troy that perhaps the source of Malnick's indignation was that no one had asked him to join in. It must be a soul-searing experience, he thought, to want so much to serve your country, in one guise or another, and to do so only in the capacity of a misplaced and unrespected housemaster.

Malnick flung open the door to what appeared to have been a breakfast room and now served him as an office. A wooden label on the outside said 'Mess Officer' but the word Officer had been crudely crossed out.

Malnick stretched himself out behind the huge expanse of a partner's desk that took up half the room, swinging gently on the revolving chair, revelling softly in the attention and deference Troy was fighting to remember to pay him. He flipped the button on one of the hip pockets of his battledress. He drew out a cigarette-rolling machine and a flat, round, worn tin of rolling tobacco. Another affectation of youth. When he and Troy had last met he smoked Black Cat cork-tipped from a packet. Malnick sprinkled the tobacco down the groove of the machine and rolled in a white paper, using every gesture to emphasise that Troy was waiting on his words. Troy wasn't. He was wondering how to get around to the subject of the man's identity.

'You were a constable, weren't you?' Malnick asked.

'Yes. I'm a Sergeant now. Perhaps I'll be an Inspector one day.'

'One day,' Malnick retorted. 'Now, what's on your mind?'

'Well . . . Yes, couldn't think who else to turn to. A rather tricky case.'

Malnick bristled with unrestrained pride. A flick of a minute lever on the side of his machine and a thin, bent specimen of tobacconist's droop popped pathetically to the surface. He lit it all the same.

'It's one you know already. A man was found shot in the face on Tower beach. About a year ago.'

'I knew it,' he exclaimed. 'I knew it. They couldn't crack it! They had to call in the Yard.'

Malnick chortled almost into open laughter. Troy could not be sure how much of it was fakery, but the pleasure in other people's failure seemed real enough.

'And here you are!' Malnick revelled.

'And here I am. They told me at your old nick that you might be here, so I . . . ' Troy let the sentence trail off, hoping that Malnick was at least reassured as to his motives.

'Quite, quite,' muttered Malnick, blowing smoke towards the ceiling.

'What I was wondering . . . ' Troy struggled for the right measure of helplessness and flattery, 'was about your notes.'

Malnick stared back, the smile of smugness fading fast. Troy knew at once he had wrong-footed himself and quickly threw in a qualifier.

'We all know things we don't put in notes. Certain feelings and suspicions that don't quite work on paper. Copper's intuitions, that sort of thing.'

'Of course.' Malnick paused. 'There was an element of the macabre.'

'Macabre?'

'A touch of sadism, I'd say.'

'Sadism?'

'They shot him twice, you see. Got him out on the beach and put one through his leg. Just for the fun of it if you ask me.'

Troy wondered. Was this just lurid fantasy? It so sharply deviated from the cool, scientific analysis that Anna Pakenham had offered.

'As though one of them wanted to hurt him. Deliberately wanted to hurt him.'

'What makes you think there were two of them?'

'Nothing. Just a feeling. As you say, not the sort of thing you'd put down in notes.'

'No footprints?'

'Tide had been in and out before we found him. I'm not surprised you're baffled. It was one of the trickiest I'd come across. Scarce a thing to go on.'

'It would help enormously to hear your reactions to the one concrete fact we do have. The body.'

'You've seen the picture.'

'There's a world of difference between a photograph and the flesh. It's how you saw it, how you first reacted to it that would help me now.' In for a penny, thought Troy, and ventured as offhandedly as he knew, the one question that mattered, 'Perhaps you could describe the corpse?'

Malnick seemed convinced by this preposterous bluff. He set down the damp stub of his misshapen cigarette and reached behind him to where a mountain of cardboard folders were neatly stacked on the shelves. He pulled down a volume that looked to Troy like a child's stamp album, or at least very like the one he had had himself, thick and tattered, bound in green leatherette with faded gold leaf lines on the spine and cover. Malnick laid the book on the desk, with the word Album facing Troy.

'I've kept this over a number of years. Never quite sure of its value, but pretty certain that one day the record of an honest job done by a serving police officer might be of some contribution to the science of detection.'

He flipped open the cover. Troy could not believe his eyes. The man kept a scrapbook of his cases! The arrogance of it! Furthermore the arrogance of a scrapbook not merely of his successes but of his failures, which he scarcely seemed to see as failures. Malnick flipped the pages, and the book lay open at the Tower beach murder of 1939 – the case of the drowned child. There was a clipping from a local paper of a proud Inspector Malnick outside the court. In the background, Troy was certain, the small man with his back to the camera was himself. Page after page of testimony to Malnick's egotism rolled by. Troy hoped the look on his face managed to pass off incredulity as awe. Malnick flipped on to a brown, fading chunk of newsprint depicting himself and the haul from a bullion robbery in 1941.

'Now,' Malnick was saying, turning a fat wadge of pages, 'you take a look at chummy here.'

An eight-by-eight police photographer's black and white filled a whole page. A close-up of a man's face, a man who had been shot in the left cheek. Troy heard the whistling intake of his own breath and masked his surprise. He could not believe that Malnick had kept a copy of this photograph. Nor would anyone else, particularly anyone who thought they'd successfully eradicated all trace of the victim from police and forensic records. He was in awe, not of Malnick's meticulousness or efficiency but of his own blinding good fortune. Malnick prattled again, taking Troy quite literally and offering a fanciful appraisal of the victim's character, where all Troy had been hoping for was a description, but Troy had ceased to listen. He turned a page. There was a full-length shot of the body as it had first been found, lying on its left cheek, with one arm flung out behind it and one leg twisted under the other. The grotesque puppet that was death.

'That chap in Hendon tried to tell me he was German,' Malnick was saying. Troy glanced up at him. 'Stuff and nonsense, of course. Since I've lived on the coast I can tell you there are rumours of Jerries landing almost on a daily basis. Not one of them has ever proved to be true.'

Troy noted that the eight-by-eight print was held in place by black gummed corners. It would be but the work of a moment to tease it from its page and stuff it up his coat.

'Quite,' he said, echoing Malnick's vocabulary. 'I thought as much myself, but it does leave us with a problem. Who?'

He prised the print from its corners and paused, looking up at Malnick with the open invitation to speculation, knowing full well that the picture itself was worth a thousand theories or fanciful descriptions.

'Crime isn't what it was.'

'I don't follow,' said Troy.

'It organises differently.'

As far as Troy was concerned this was hardly a revelation. The fact that crime organised at all was a back-handed tribute to wartime efficiency.

'Gangs,' said Malnick with a melodramatic emphasis. 'I'm talking about gangs. I felt quite certain that this was a gang killing.'

Troy closed the book and let the photograph slide silently on to his lap.

'I'll need a name.'

'The Spider.'

Troy was startled. Was the man an avid reader of Edgar Wallace? The Ringer, The Fixer, The Twister – The Spider?

'The Spider?' he said, hoping that it didn't sound like mimicry.

'The *nom de plume* or what have you of Alfred Maxwell Golding. I talked to him only the day before my posting came through.'

Did Malnick really see no connection between the case he was on and the suddenness of his acceptance into the RAF? Had he so deceived himself that he could pass it off as mere coincidence?

'Denied it, of course, but smirked like the cat that got the cream. Kept saying "go on, copper, prove it. Just you try." '

It was easy to see just how much Inspector Malnick intensely disliked being called copper. Troy had long ago accepted it as by far the least offensive, most convenient term – but then he had got out of uniform in record time. Malnick had worn his, with undoubted pride, from his first day on the force to his last. He had taken the jeering of children and the contempt of clever, briefed criminals and the blue had written itself into his soul like Blackpool through a stick of rock. It had rendered him as upright as a truncheon and about as flexible – and therein lay his problem. Who or what was Alfred Spider Golding? Was Troy witness to another of Malnick's fantasies – or had twenty years a-coppering given the man some insight into the villains on his own patch?

'A Mr Big I take it?'

'The Mr Big. Holds court most evenings in the Cockle and Trumpet in Cary Street. King of the skivers, fence and receiver, Mr Five-bob-on-the-quid, dodged conscription from day one and recruited every other Tom, Dick and Harry that thought flogging nylons and forging coupons was more patriotic than doing a bit for one's country. They're more organised than they were before the war. So much of the competition's out of the way, and the force is depleted.'

So far he was talking sense. Troy slid the photograph under his coat, a short step away from safe concealment in the armpit.

'I've no firm evidence that he kills people who get in his way, but I know in my bones he's responsible for two killings in the City district – he's the sort of man that likes to make examples of people. Kill and let it be known. This has all the hallmarks of such a disciplinary killing.'

Troy risked the obvious.

'Then why do you say it's a difficult case? Why doesn't the Yard's failure surprise you?'

'Because to anyone that doesn't know the manor it's like looking for a needle in a haystack. You were lucky in thirty-nine. Ninety-nine per cent of the time you can't just breeze in from the Yard and put your finger on a quick solution. Can you buggery! Most of the time it's down to local knowledge. To the kind of savvy you can only learn by the soles of your feet. This man was a minor member of some team, a firm as they call them, who got his comeuppance. The only reason I didn't get a chance to put a name to a face is that London, as well you know, is awash with new faces. There's a sign up on the Great North Road – "Send us your bent, send us your crooked." '

'You really don't believe he was German?'

'Twaddle,' said Malnick with the emphasis of finality.

Troy feigned an itch to scratch and the photograph found home. He had what he came for, more than he came for. And if Malnick chose to fly in the face of the best forensic science in the world then he was a bigger fool than even Troy had thought. Malnick prattled, returned to his theme.

'When they got that poor sod on the beach they punished him before they killed him. Someone on that firm really likes hurting people.'

It was the only part of Malnick's argument that struck Troy as being worth a moment's attention.

§ 18

Driberg had burnt the toast. Twice. For the third attempt he handed the toasting fork to Troy and decided he was far better suited to uncorking the wine.

'You're the youngest, you say?'

'Yes,' Troy replied. 'Rod is eight years older than me, the twins five. I'm the afterthought. Their only English-born child.'

'Would you say you knew your father well?'

Troy could not see what Driberg was driving at. The man had a penchant for gossip, but this, surely, was not simply his idea of chewing the fat? Not only did Driberg have a journalist's nose – whereby there was no such thing as an idle question – he came from that same inter-war school of chequered, idealistic politics that characterised his own family. Troy knew for a fact that Driberg had been a card-carrying Communist – although why all Communists had to carry their cards instead of leaving them at home as most people did their gas-masks Troy could never work out.

'I saw more of him. They sent me away to school later than any of the others. I was one of those sickly children. Always being told to wrap up well even in summer. But I doubt I knew him better than my brother. Rod at least knew him as an adult for fifteen years. I didn't.'

'Y'know it's always puzzled me. Why did he accept that wretched title?'

Wretched? Did Driberg put the same question to the Sitwells? To Beaverbrook? Why wretched? Driberg adored title and ritual, from the imperial pomp of a coronation to the order of knives and forks on the table, so wickedly designed to intimidate the lower-middle classes. Troy recalled as a teenager watching the housemaid slap down the silver in no particular order, knowing full well that his father would eat a six-course meal with a wooden spoon and pass no comment, and later seeing Driberg surreptitiously arrange the implements at his own place into their proper lineage.

'He didn't accept it. He bought it from Lloyd George when I was four or five. I have absolutely no recollection of any of it. By the time I was old enough to ask I didn't much care. After all, inheriting it was Rod's problem not mine. I do remember Rod asking the old man a few times, and the answer was always the same. For a foreigner to be accepted in London society a little recognition was essential. Although to be honest I think he called it window-dressing. At the same time one couldn't cross any of those very English invisible lines. A peerage slapped on to an unshakeable foreign accent would have been a mockery – he'd have joined the rich Jews of Westminster, ennobled for their wealth and despised for it too – or so he said – at the same time the only title worth having had to be hereditary. So a baronetcy it was. Result – as he would have it – no one thinks he's muscling in on anything as privileged as the Lords, nor is he quite as parvenu as a knighted brewer. He is – or was – Sir Alexei Troy Bt., publisher, newspaper proprietor, Englishman and wog – and no one much minds. The power has a respectable coat to its back. Why? Why do you ask?'

'I was curious about its part in the game. Whichever one your father happened to be playing at the time.'

Troy knew better than to be offended. He had seen the game first hand on so many occasions. Driberg had more acuteness in so phrasing it – and, Troy felt, if the truth be known it summed up his father better than any of the so oft applied words such as 'mercurial' or 'unfathomable'. The elder Troy played not the game *of* English society but the game *with* English society. He had seen his father entertain the insufferably brilliant Sir Oswald Mosley – brilliant by the acclaim of his peers, insufferable because he knew it and abused it – the pompous, loud, but scarcely charmless Bob Boothby, fresh from his meeting with Hitler, and the shy, determined Harold Macmillan, son-in-law to the Duke of Devonshire, whom he had endeavoured to steer away from the Conservative Party at the depth of the Depression, when it became obvious that Macmillan was not prepared to toe the National Government line and accept poverty as an incurable fact of life that was beyond intervention. Alex Troy was nothing if not an interventionist. Most intervention came to little. Boothby and Macmillan never came again and, to the best of Troy's knowledge, Mosley was never asked. Driberg was. The Troy household was one of those in which he could bank on meeting a vast cross-section of British political life, even if it lacked the Boothbys and the Mosleys. Where else could he find himself seated between the earnestness of A. J. Cook, the miners' leader, and the banality of Chips Channon, Conservative MP and social butterfly? Where else could he appreciate the seeming inconsistency of a newspaper proprietor who had condemned Stalin right up to the Nazi–Soviet pact and then swung around to suggest in an editorial he wrote himself that all good men should bide their time, at precisely the time when the good men were burning their Communist Party membership cards, and the fellow-travellers were doing whatever fellow-travellers did to resign from an organisation to which they had never belonged? But, then, neither had Alexei Troy belonged – he had been some sort of Plekhanovite back in the old country, perhaps the only one, and had cut a course of his own choosing. He had seen circulation of the *Evening Herald* drop by twenty per cent after his editorial – yet had gone on arguing his case, and printing the letters of dissent, until the week before the invasion of Russia when he had written another leader saying it was time to 'stand by our new ally the Soviet Union'. History had proved him right. Rather too quickly. The game continued. For the last year of his life he was once again a mercurial oddity. A titled wog no easier to pin down than a sprite. People came just to hear what he would say next. For a fellow-traveller, he travelled exceedingly well, and exceedingly well heeled. Bt., he was wont to joke, stood for better times.

'I wondered, you see,' Driberg was saying, 'what he thought of you becoming a policeman. All his life – picking and pricking at order like a gnat on a dinosaur's backside, and then you choose the law and with it the order he so despised. I think it must have hurt him deeply.'

'What makes you say that?'

'Because,' Driberg said, turning for the *coup de grâce*, 'he never talked about it.'

Perhaps the man was right. Words flowed from the elder Troy. Anyone who spent the currency of language like an Irish sailor on a drunken roll surely had a damning reason for silence? He had, for example, never answered any questions about the origins of his fortune. What use would the truth have been – that he had looted more than a million pounds' worth of jewellery back in 1905? Some gnat's prick.

'And I was wondering,' Driberg continued, 'whether this too wasn't part of the game?'

Troy said nothing. He watched the slice of toast on the end of the fork burst into flames and topple off into the fire, heard Driberg mutter 'bugger it' and listened to the generous gush of red wine filling up a glass.

§ 19

Alone in his office the following day Troy propped the photograph he had taken from Malnick – mentally avoiding the word stolen – against the telephone and contemplated it as the last light of afternoon slanted from the west to pick out the dead man's face and wink wickedly off the brass on the inkwell. A day to think, half of it spent driving Driberg back to London in pleasing, unstony silence, had left him with the beginnings of a pattern forming in his mind. He came into the Yard to find it peaceful and Saturdayish. No sign of Wildeve, and Onions was most certainly out on his allotment in a disused railway siding in Acton. Who these Germans were he had no idea, but he felt confident that the two crimes were related and that what they were was nestling just beneath the surface of the few facts he had. For a while it made sense to regard the two bodies as one – a two-headed creation from the castle of Baron Frankenstein. The phone rang.

'I been thinking,' said Kolankiewicz lazily.

'So I heard.'

' 'Bout trousers.'

'Heard that too.'

'And the beauty of trousers.'

'Form and function in perfect harmony. Two holes exactly where your legs are.'

'The beauty, the real beauty is in the turn-ups. Their capacity for capturing, storing and then yielding up to scrutiny the most surprising, the most overlooked items.'

'What have you found?'

'What would you want me to find?'

Troy looked at the scribbles he had made on the back of an envelope. The disparate parts of a whole that only existed in his guesswork.

'I was wondering about the relationship between the bits we have. In particular what little forensics has revealed so far. Fragments of an alloy trapped by the fabric of the sleeve, you said. Acid burns, you said. And I was asking myself what's missing that should be obvious in this time of death and glory?'

'And?'

Troy paused, fearful of improvident word magic, as though utterance would invite divine denial. 'Cordite,' he said. 'You found cordite in the late Herr Trousers' turn-ups.'

'I am sorry to have taken so long about it. When you see as many dead as I do they begin to blur into one colossal corpse. The world-carcass. It came back to me about an hour ago. Some smell, something that came wafting to me across the next-door neighbours' compost heap – and there it was, the memory of cordite, delicately overlaid by the black stench of Thames mud in which the poor sod was found. Twelve months old, as vivid to the nose as *petit madeleine* to the tongue. You know what I think we have? A munitions worker. Acid, metal, cordite. Put them together and they go bang.'

'A German munitions worker? Two German munitions workers?'

'OK. OK. That takes some figuring. I leave that to you.'

'How far up Herr Cufflink's sleeve did you look for these fragments of metal?'

'Up as far as the arm went.'

'Did you find anything after the first couple of inches?'

'No. I told you that already.'

'And the same on Herr Trousers?'

'Ach – I'd be reading backwards from my present opinion. Settle for the cordite. That I am certain of. My nose tells the truth. I am the Proust of filth. The smell of a man's rotten liver will find its way back to me years later. Makes it almost impossible to eat in a British restaurant, I can tell you.'

'Very well. Look at it this way. A munitions worker wears an overall. He does not wear his best tweed jacket to the factory. What do you wear, most of the time?'

'You know fuck well.' Irritation was bringing out the Pole in Kolankiewicz once more. 'You seen me hundreds of times. A white lab coat, for Chrissake.'

'Which stops leaving two inches of cuff sticking out. Sod's law. Toast always lands butter-side down on the carpet. Lab coats never fit. What we have here is a member of your own fraternity. Cufflink, probably Trousers too, was a boffin. Someone working above factory level in the bombs and bangs business. The sooner you put those fragments out for analysis the better.'

'I've done it, but, take it from me, that alloy is nothing I've ever seen.'

'You mean it's...' Troy failed to find the word he wanted. '...New...?'

'New? Troy, it's from another planet! For all I know it fell off Flash Gordon's rocketship.'

And suddenly Troy realised exactly what they had unearthed between them and how complex and how dangerous the ramifications of that knowledge might be.

§ 20

Troy's Uncle Nikolai always reminded him of a character from Edward Lear – a fitting subject for a limerick. But since none had fitted precisely he had made up his own at about the age of ten and had got as far as 'There was an old man from Nepal, Whose face was incredibly small . . . ' but no further. Of course Nikolai's face was not incredibly small, it appeared so because it was buried by a mass of hair and a full beard, and, often, spectacles. Overall, small was somewhat appropriate. At five feet two he needed not one soapbox but two from which to harangue the crowd at Speakers' Corner of a Sunday morning. Troy knew that he stood on tiptoe just for the extra couple of inches that allowed him to lean across the makeshift lectern and gesture at the crowd.

Troy had caught him mid-speech and mid-harangue, in a Leninish pose, left arm flush along the top of the lectern, the right sweeping across the crowd in a broad intaking motion that could imply open-handed inclusiveness, a commonality from which none could escape, or, as the palm closed to leave a pointing index finger, single people out as though his words were aimed solely at them.

' . . . And it is to the Britain of the post-war years that we must now turn. It is time to talk of many things—'

'Of cabbages and kings,' yelled a literate wag from the crowd.

'Sod cabbages,' replied a wittier wag, 'I seen enough of the bleedin' fings the last five years to do me a lifetime!'

Beneath the grey curls that wrapped around his face it was impossible to see whether Nikolai Rodyonovich was smiling or not.

'After the last war we were promised—'

'Whaddya mean "we"?' came another voice from the crowd. 'You're about as English as frogs' legs and sauerkraut!'

'I am, as you know full well, Mr Robinson, a Russian. You yourself goaded me with this fact, as I recall, in the summer of 1938, in such abusive terms that a member of the London constabulary felt obliged to step in and restrain you!'

Troy had been the constable in question. Off duty but uniformed. Speakers' Corner had seen too many incidents that summer of general Jew-baiting and wog-bashing. A small surge of xenophobia that was untypical of the British, and untypical of this war — Mosleyites excepted. Without telling the old man he had privately undertaken to afford him some measure of protection. It seemed curious to think that Nikolai drew a regular crowd, as though he had a personal following, year after year, but, as Troy recalled, Robinson, a Bill-Sykes lookalike with a fair, even hatred of all foreigners, had had his cake and eaten it by dubbing Nikolai a 'Russky, Commie, thick-lipped, Jew-boy arsehole who had better bugger off back where he came from'. Nikolai had no such plans. In 1919 when Troy's father, some ten years older than Nikolai, had raised the issue of naturalisation for the family, he had made the decision for his wife, his daughters and himself – his youngest son, after all, was British-born – but had merely urged it on his younger brother and his eldest son, both of whom he felt should decide for themselves. Neither had bothered. Hence Rod, thanks to his birth in Vienna as the Troys crossed Imperial Europe at a snail's pace, had found himself an Austrian and a categorisable alien at the outbreak of war, and Nikolai had found it impossible to clarify his allegiance by becoming British – no one had been allowed naturalisation for nearly five years. Yet British was how he saw himself. Britain was his home. He loved it dearly. Troy doubted if this could ever be conveyed to the crowd, but why else did the old man get up on the stump week after week on the endless subject of Britain if not from love of country?

'*We*,' he said with an italicised emphasis, 'were promised homes fit for heroes. A promise we all knew to be hollow within a few short years. Now we are told it is different. This war has been total war, it has required such a degree of motivation on the part of the British that government has been obliged to inform and to educate us almost as much as it has deceived us. And as the culmination of this new-found awareness of the basic fact of life on earth that if we do not pull together we shall most certainly sink together, they have come up with a notion that startles them, and they expect us to be startled by it too. Sir William Beveridge has spoken of a system, an organisation of our human resources that could offer us care, protection and education – from the cradle to the grave. And it goes by the name of the Welfare State. Who are we to believe? Are we to believe that Churchill will allow what he clearly believes to be a thief's charter to become the way of the land, even the law of the land. Are we to trust the victor of Tonypandy?'

Troy heard a murmur buzz through the crowd. Churchill had survived a spectacularly ill-organised vote of no confidence in the House a couple of years ago, and since then had been virtually unassailable. He had survived cock-ups such as Dieppe, and withstood the constant pressure at home and amongst the Allies for a second front. But, as far as the public were concerned he was royalty – and behaved like it. An attack on Churchill could hardly be well received. Where was Nikolai's argument heading?

'Are we to trust a man who opposed the British worker in 1926, at a time when the miners were fighting for a living wage against the pay cuts imposed by profiteering mine-owners?'

The buzz had become louder. Heads began to turn. Muttered exchanges. The man next to Troy said flatly, without tone or movement, 'He must be barmy to knock Winnie at a time like this.' Troy glanced quickly around to see if there was a uniform in sight. If he had to step in in civvies he would likely as not get his block knocked off.

Up at the front a heckler took up the invitation that Nikolai had proffered with a pause. 'What are you tellin' us? Vote Labour? I don't need no one to tell me that. What I need is a chance. I ain't had a vote since 1935. We none of us 'ave! We've had the same soddin' government for ten years!'

'My friend,' Nikolai resumed, 'I have been addressing you from this stump since 1928. In all that time have I ever once urged you to vote for any given political party? Time after time Mr Robinson has called me a Commie. Have I ever once urged you to vote Communist or told you to join the Communist Party? We have witnessed these last five years the most radical transformation British society has ever undergone. We have pulled together, of course we have, or Hitler would be goose-stepping up Whitehall today. We have learnt a new measure of co-operation, and with it a new definition of democracy. Even the King has a ration book!'

Troy thought this was fatuous. When the palace had been hit during the Blitz Queen Elizabeth had remarked famously that at last she could look the East End in the eye again – such equality was illusory. Only when Buckingham Palace had been flattened and the family broken up and the young princesses stuck on a train for darkest Derbyshire with brown paper parcels and labels around their necks would Troy have seen a recognisable equality. He had no faith in this new definition of democracy. But then, unlike his uncle, he could not say with any confidence that he loved his country.

'What will the end of this war bring?'

Another voice from the crowd rang out, ' 'Ere 'alf the time. It ain't over yet!'

'Will it bring a furtherance of our new-found co-operation or will we waste it all in a return to the deadlock simplicity of a two-party system that leaves the fundamental inequalities of society untouched? What, in the hands of Labour, let alone the Conservative Party, can the Beveridge idea achieve but a crude tinkering with the economics of injustice? How quickly will we be made to forget that we pulled together and survived together? That we recognised for the first time as a people the necessity of mutual aid?'

At last Troy knew Nikolai was on course, knew where this deviation had all been leading – to the argument that underlay any public speech he had made in the last thirty years, his habitual endorsement of the old Russian anarchist ideas, of the devolution to the most basic level of everything that could be made to work at that level, of the factory as a village, of the field as a workshop, of the community as the basis of a social non-order, of the end of hierarchical society, by Kropotkin out of Tolstoy and not so much as whiff of Bolshevism. He had heard it all before. Certain that he had caught the old man's eye he sloped off to a park bench at the back and pulled out a copy of yesterday's *Manchester Guardian*,

75

wondering whether there would be any news that had slipped by the censor or whether all the British needed to know on a fine spring morning was that careless talk still cost lives and that Mars Bars somehow contributed to the war effort, particularly if sliced like Battenberg.

Quarter of an hour later Nikolai had wound up and the crowd that had dwindled from forty or fifty to the last dozen or so of the faithful – hardly an accurate word as half of them had stayed to argue the toss – was breaking up. Troy looked up from the paper. The old man was not far off. Running his fingers through his beard as though disentangling it. In his full-length coat with its astrakhan collar, Homburg shoved back on his head, it was easy to see why the roughs so often mistook him for a Jew. All this produced in Nikolai was Jewishness, and if they had called him an Assyrian – surely the most minor of minorities – he would have found an Assyrian turn of phrase and embarked on identification and defence. Perhaps the core of anarchism was its refusal to be pinned down, its willingness to assume any identity?

'Boy, haff I got a treat for you!' Nikolai said as he approached.

The contrast between the Americanism and the forgetful relapse into his native accent with the 'haff' startled Troy.

'Why don't you try "what brings you here, nephew?"'

'Ach – am I to be surprised to see you? You're a policeman. They pop up everywhere. Now, drop the twaddle and come see what I haff for you.'

More than seldom Nikolai reminded him of Kolankiewicz. If Poland was not so much a country, more a state of mind, then Russia was less a country, less a state of mind than an hysterical heart. Nikolai led him at a brisk trot to the edge of Park Lane. There, just off the road, was a large tarpaulin concealing God Wot Not.

'Voilà!' Nikolai yanked at one corner of the tarpaulin sheet and threw it clear. 'Ecce bicycle!'

Whatever it was it was huge. A motorcycle and sidecar combination on a colossal scale. 'What is it?' Troy asked.

'It is poetry, it is glory, it is heaven cast in shining silver, the wheels of man and the wings of angels. In short, a Matchless Model X 1000cc V Twin, 1936.'

'Really?'

'I was out at your mother's last week – she says, by the way, that you could visit more often – and from somewhere she had got hold of five gallons of petrol. It was a pleasant afternoon, so we got that old Crossley 6, you know the two-litre 1930 model, down off its blocks and went for what your mother insists on calling a "spin in the country". Hertfordshire can be very pretty at this time of year. We passed a row of tied cottages, and out in front of one of them was a young woman in ATS uniform with a stall of items for sale. Brown boots, a set of fishing tackle, a shotgun or two, a gramophone and, as it happens, a Matchless Model X motorbicycle combination. I asked her the purpose of the sale. She said that while she was away doing her bit for Britain her husband had sought consolation in the arms of a Land Army girl, and this was her vengeance – ah, the poetry of vengeance! I had to admire the woman's imagination. While he was out rolling his master's winter wheat she was selling off every last thing he owned to the first passing customer and to hell with her husband. I bought this and one of the shotguns. The boots, alas, were far too big. And I gave up fishing years ago.'

'Can you actually start it? You must need a kick like an angry jackass.'

'A properly tuned motorbicycle will start with a tickle, and as I, having no access to cheap petrol, spent yesterday converting her to run on alcohol – which, after all, I can make for myself – this particular baby starts if an angel breathes on her!'

Nikolai grabbed the handlebars and raised a leg high off the ground. Troy tapped him on the arm.

'Half a mo' – what's that?'

'What's what?'

'That other tarpaulin, wrapped around the sidecar.'

'That's my treat.'

'I thought the bike was your treat?'

'This too!'

Troy seized the initiative and peeled back the covering from the sidecar. Wedged into it nose-down was a bomb. Its tail fins stuck up at a rakish angle, pointing back at the sky from which it fell.

'It's a dud.' Nikolai smiled his reassurance at Troy.

'What do you mean it's a dud? What's the difference between a dud and an unexploded bomb? Have you taken complete leave of your senses trying to drive a thing like this through the middle of London? You could kill yourself and a couple of hundred others along with you!'

'Calm down. Believe me, it is a dud. It's one of the new German one-hundred-and-fifty pounders. Very small bomb. Devastating effect. We've been trying to get hold of one intact for weeks. Thing is, they go off like they're five hundred pounds. We rather suspect that Jerry is on to something completely new.'

'We' meant Nikolai's team at Imperial College, where he, Professor Troitsky, led a university Applied Physics department into the application of anything that flew or blew.

'I picked it up off the RAOC at first light. It fell in Islington churchyard last night. Believe me, it's safe as houses.'

That particular metaphor did nothing to reassure Troy. So many houses in Islington these days were nothing more than rubble and dust.

'See,' the old man said. He drew a curly stem pipe from his waistcoat pocket and tapped the casing with the bowl.

'You're not getting me on that thing with an unexploded bomb sitting in the sidecar. They'll have to bury us in a sieve if it goes up!'

Halfway down Park Lane, Troy had cause to admire Nikolai's fine-tuning of the engine. Clinging on for dear life as the old man put the bike through its paces he felt certain he could hear the bomb start to tick above the gentle sound of the engine's purr. They rounded Apsley House at over fifty and shot off along Knightsbridge in the direction of Kensington Gore and Imperial College, nestling out of sight behind the Albert Hall. Over his shoulder, the Homburg now rammed down firmly to his eyebrows, Nikolai told Troy he felt sure they could top ninety on the straight.

§21

Nikolai cleared an upright chair of a sheaf of papers, a stack of magazines and a pile of oily rags with which he had recently cleaned his motorbike and told Troy to sit down. He threw his hat neatly on to the prong of the hatstand by the door and peered into the mirror behind his desk, ruffling his beard as he had done in the park, muttering about the shortage of good barbers in wartime, all too busy with short back and sides in Aldershot, and finally, still playing with his reflection in the mirror, asked Troy what had brought him out on a Sunday morning. Troy had thought long and hard about how to broach the subject. He reached into the inside pocket of his overcoat and took out the black and white eight-by-eight of Herr Trousers.

'This,' he said simply. If it broke the issue with a huge short circuit and finally seized his uncle's attention, so be it.

Nikolai shrugged off his overcoat and let it fall behind him. He took the photograph from Troy's hands, sat himself on the edge of his desk chair and flicked on the green-shaded reading lamp. From where Troy sat it picked out his face like a limelight. He watched as Nikolai rummaged around on the complete mess that passed for a desk-top and slipped on his half-moon reading glasses, peering intently, adjusting the angle of the nosepiece and screwing up his eyes. Troy watched as a tear formed in each eye and rolled gently down his cheeks. This was not what he had anticipated. Nikolai stared at the image in the photograph, still and silent for longer than Troy could tolerate. He was about to speak for the sake of speech when the old man looked up at him.

'When did this happen?' he asked.

'Almost a year ago. I . . . I didn't realise you knew him . . .'

'Isn't that why you're here?'

Nikolai at last put the photograph down. Without self-consciousness he wiped each eye, and looked back at Troy expectantly.

'I'm here because I'd worked out that he was some sort of boffin. Quite likely a boffin in your own field. I've no idea who he is, let alone that you knew him. If I'd known I'd . . .'

'No, no. Don't apologise. It's perfectly reasonable to presume that I would haff some knowledge of most people in my field. It's a very small world. Or at least it was before the war.'

He took off his glasses and leaned back in his chair. He wiped his right eye once more with the back of his hand.

'Do you remember when you were about eighteen – the summer of 1933 – the year your father wanted you to go up to Oxford and you steadfastly refused – I was still with Handley Page, on fighters. I went to the last Munich University conference, the last because Hitler would never again let a German scientist swap notes with a British, although truth to tell the British made me sign the Official Secrets Act before I went. There were whizzbangers, as you used to call them, from all over Europe, one or two of my own age, many, many more bright young men almost fresh from their first degrees. I was very concerned in those days with the development of light alloys. I gave a paper on that subject – although after Handley Page had vetted it there was little left in it that a twelve-year-old couldn't haff found in a school textbook. I haff often found it ... how shall I say ... a source of encouragement ... refreshment, in its pre-cafeteria meaning ... to find enthusiasms in the young for ideas and practices I haff advocated all my life ... after all I haff no children. I found myself rethinking my own work at the age of fifty-odd. Some of those young men were brilliant. None more so than this young man.'

He nodded in the direction of the photograph.

'You haven't told me who he is,' said Troy gently and persistently.

'Oh ... he was Gregor von Ranke. A Hessian. Quite, quite brilliant. So unGerman. Or at least unGerman in the way we haff come to think of the Prussian as the characteristic German. Forever quoting poetry, he brought Goethe alive for me. We spent evenings with him reading the German out loud to me and then translating it as he went. In return I would read him Blake, the story of Orc ... fiery the angel fell ... We wrote to each other for years afterwards. I wasted yards of paper trying to get him to leave Germany before it was too late. He was a gentle man. Nazism was anathema to him. I never understood why he would not leave.'

'Do you know what became of him?'

'I'd be guessing, but if Speer did not recruit him for his Todt machine I'd be very surprised and the Germans would be far stupider than I know them to be?'

'Todt machine?'

'Organisation. Todt organisation. Franz Todt was Hitler's resources manager. He ran the business of the war. He was killed in a plane crash in forty-two. Since then Albert Speer has run it. It covers everything from raw materials to boffins, as you call them. In most respects Germany is very disorganised. It's one reason we will win this war. For us it's total. Our whole economy is geared to it. Germany's is not. Speer is a rare example of Hitler's much vaunted fascist efficiency. He does more than make the trains run on time.'

Nikolai took up his spectacles and lost an emotional moment in the polishing of them.

'He was the gentlest of men – the gentlest of men. Tell me, Frederick, why did they do this to him? How did you get the picture out of Germany?'

'I didn't. He was found on Tower beach.'

Nikolai raised a bushy eyebrow. 'So he came after all.' He paused. 'But if he was killed here ... who would ... ?'

'That's my problem. What was he doing here? Who killed him? Why? I take it there's no possibility that von Ranke spent the war here?'

'It's possible. I like to think he would haff got in touch with me. I'd even say I'm certain he would haff. More than that he would haff been interned in 1940 and somewhere in the corridors of Whitehall someone would haff realised who he was and I'd haff found out that way. I went to see a dozen or more men of near-genius that we had locked up on the Isle of Man. There was one poor man, worked on submarines for us – killed himself as soon as he was told he'd be interned. I think we'd haff jailed Einstein if he'd been here. Gregor could haff been very valuable to the war effort. Even on his own, without the rest of the team.'

'What team?'

Nikolai pulled the centre drawer of his desk out and began to ferret around.

'I haff somewhere here,' he was saying, 'a picture we had taken in Munich that summer. Ah ... I haff it.'

Troy came round the desk and looked over his uncle's shoulder at the sepia print that he held under the reading lamp. He watched the old man's finger rove over the ranks of figures, twenty or more, trying to put names to faces.

'That is Gregor, you see. And of course that is me on the end there. Now he worked with two fellows. Another German, a Munich man I believe ... Bertoldt ... dammit ... he always used Christian names in his letters ... talked endlessly about them but always in Christian names or initials ... Bertoldt was BB ... ah, yes ... Brand, Bertoldt Brand. And the other I knew less well. A Pole. That's him on the other end. His name is on the tip of my tongue ... the tip of my tongue ...'

But it was on Troy's lips.

'Wolinski,' he said softly. 'Peter Wolinski.'

§ 22

Troy rode the District line out to Stepney Green. Kicking himself that he had walked over to the park rather than taking the Morris. Kicking himself that he had seen that photograph on Wolinski's wall only ten days ago and utterly failed to recognise his own uncle. He was fatter, less grey, but unarguably recognisable. In his mind's eye he could see the very same print sandwiched between Wolinski's picture of himself in full academic garb and that chilling early morning shot of sunlight on the swastikas. By Mark Lane self-recrimination had given way to a deepening concern, the near certainty that he had now upped the body count from two to three. Except of course that no one had yet reported the body of Peter Wolinski. Perhaps there was a gradient of efficiency for the killer. Corpse no.1 – found intact, corpse no.2 – disposed of but for the chance finding of one arm, corpse no.3 – gone for good? Burned, sunk in the Thames or some newly devised grisly method of total concealment? Tomorrow morning he would face the unpleasant task of informing Onions that since they last met an unsolved murder on their patch had, to put it simply, tripled in the course of a quiet weekend.

Bonham's front door was an inch ajar. As Troy pushed against it he heard the slam of a door closing directly above him. He slipped quickly into the hall, listened to the rapid pick-pock of a woman in heels descending the top staircase, and watched a tall, slim woman pass the front door and disappear at the end of the corridor. As her shoes rang out on the next staircase Troy grabbed Bonham's old brown mackintosh off the back of the door and burst into the living room. Bonham was in his shirt and braces, poring over a government freesheet on how to make steak and kidney pie out of cardboard and tea leaves. He looked up, startled, but caught the coat that Troy threw at him.

'George! A woman just came out of Wolinski's flat. Get after her. Follow her, find out who she is, where she lives. You can't miss her. Must be six foot in her high heels, black two-piece cut like it cost a packet and she's a looker.'

Bonham managed a rightie-ho, fumbled with his coat and made a quick grab at his helmet as he passed the door.

'George, you can't trail someone wearing your helmet!'

Bonham glanced down at his size-fourteen regulation police boots.

'Be as quiet as you can.'

Bonham nodded – puzzled but obedient – and was gone, crunching down the concrete steps. Troy took the shiny set of keys that McGee had left off the mantelpiece and climbed to the top floor. Wolinski's door was deadlocked. So he was right, he had heard the rattle of keys a split second after the door slammed. He let himself in. The first room smelt of scent, a burnt cinnamon scent that was familiar. It was not, he thought, that favoured by either of his sisters – but they complained bitterly that supplies of any scent were short since the fall of Paris and few women could adhere to their taste. The room looked untouched, exactly as he had seen it the last time. He followed the trail of scent into the middle room. That too was intact – but then she had hardly looked the type to ransack a room. If his eyes told him true she'd be more at home leafing gently through the pages of *Vogue* than upending drawers and waste-baskets.

Directly ahead of him was the wall that served as Wolinski's gallery. A rectangular patch of light, clean wallpaper had appeared among the fading red and green nondescript flowers of the paper pattern. Between sunny morning with swastikas and young man with scroll was a gap where his uncle's photograph should be. Nothing else had gone, only the team shot of the bombs and bangs boffins of 1933. He stepped into the bedroom, the trail of scent died. She had not been in there. Troy stood in front of the wall of photographs and it seemed to him she had made a beeline for the picture, that she had come expressly to take it. But how could he be sure? Unless he searched the place. He looked around. Taken literally, a daunting task. But, the bedroom apart, Wolinski was an ordered, meticulous man. Start with the desk and the contents of the drawers?

An hour later, Troy was none the wiser. Wolinski saved nothing. The hoard instinct that caused him to store old *Manchester Guardian*s in neat bundles applied only to the life of the mind. The drawer yielded not so much as a gas bill, a cheque stub – surely the assumption of a working-man's life had not meant Wolinski adopted it wholesale? Troy's own desk was chocka with the written paraphernalia of his life, of the life of a man of his class, bills from his tailor or his shoemaker, the accounts held with local tradesmen. Bonham, he knew, had no bank account, he had never met a working man who did. Onions only had one because of rank, and even then was often clueless as to what they really did for him. How could Wolinski function in the cash-to-pocket, hand-to-mouth fashion? Not only that, the sentiment, the power of memory and relationship seemed to stop with his exile. None of the photographs on the wall had been taken in Britain. He had no letters or postcards from anyone. A section of the bookshelves held diaries for the late twenties and early thirties, but the last volume was for 1933. No volume referred to Britain. Wolinski had dropped to England like a nut fresh from the tree. Troy struggled with school-boy German and read a terse account of his meeting with Nikolai – who was held to be 'unspeakably eccentric if well-meaning'. Wolinski's working life might as well have been in code – meetings and discussions were simply summed up as 'lab all morning with B'. Or 'argued with G. Cannot agree on details.' Even if Troy knew the vocabulary of physics, all that mattered had stayed between Wolinski's ears, as though, even then, he had been covering his tracks. He had lived a life in secret and it now seemed to Troy that he had died his death in one too. Herr Trousers – Troy had difficulty thinking of him with a real name like Gregor von Ranke – had snipped the labels out of his clothes. Peter Wolinski had snipped them out of his life.

§ 23

At seven o'clock the next morning Troy's front door shook to the pounding of a fist.

'Let me in, Freddie, I'm freezin' to death,' came Bonham's voice from outside.

Bonham lurched in as Troy held back the door. His mackintosh glistened with frosted dew, his skin was grey, his lips near blue and the bags under his eyes deeper than ever.

'God,' said Troy. 'You look dreadful.'

'So would you, you been up all night.'

Troy was on his second cup of ersatz barleycorn coffee of the morning. Bonham grabbed it from his hand and took a deep warm swig.

'Aaagh!'

'I know it's awful. But it's all there is.'

'No,' Bonham muttered. 'No bloody sugar!'

Where Bonham came from the spine-chilling politeness of 'one lump or two?' had not yet arrived. In the cafés of Leman Street the only way to get tea without sugar was to put your hand across the cup before they could spoon it in. Such habits were almost solely responsible for British teeth.

Bonham perched on the edge of the sofa and stretched out his hands towards the orange glow of the gas fire. Troy stirred a tablespoon of granulated white into the cup and poured a second cup for himself.

'She didn't go home till nearly midnight. The woman's got no blood in her veins. She sat most of the afternoon in Kensington Gardens, no topcoat nor nothin', and read the papers – not a paper, Freddie, but half a dozen of 'em. Then she schlepped over to South Kensington and had tea in a caff with a friend . . .'

Troy stopped him. 'A friend? Man or woman?'

'Hold yer 'orses. I say a friend. It looked to me to be nanny. Some old woman in the get-up those women wear for pushin' prams in the park. God knows I saw enough of them in Kensington Gardens. It was her old nanny. She was doin' the toffs' number of afternoon tea with the old retainer. I s'pect you do the same.'

Indeed, Troy did.

'After that she went to a lecture at Wigmore Hall. The Future of Mankind or some such. Lots of Brains Trust types. Cost me a bob to get in. I'll have that back off you if you don't mind. Come nine o'clock and it looks to be all over and blow me if they don't start natterin' among themselves and by the time the caretaker comes along to tell 'em he's got a home to go to even if they haven't it's half past ten. She grabs a taxi, I have to leap in one to follow her. You try convincing a London cabbie you're a copper when you haven't got yer 'elmet! Anyway that cost me another one and fourpence. She gets out in Chelsea. Tite Street. Just off the Embankment, number fifty-five. I seen the lights go out about a quarter to midnight. But I don't know who she is. So I settled myself on the area steps of the house opposite and waited for the milkman. He come along at a quarter past six. I showed 'im me boots and me blue shirt and me braces and he says maybe I'm not a fifth columnist after all, perhaps I am a real honest-to-goodness London bobby and he tells me she's Diana Brack. B-R-A-C-K. Single. Lives at number fifty-five with a maid, and a cook. Man-servant got called up.'

'Sterling work, George.'

'The only sterling I want is me two and fourpence.'

A little warmth had begun to seep through to Bonham's tortured flesh. He shrugged off his mackintosh and slurped at his flavoured cup of syrup.

'Tell me,' Troy began, 'did she pass anything to anyone? She had a black handbag under her arm. Did you see her open it?'

'Quite a few times. She paid the bill at the caff, she paid the cabbie.'

'But she took out nothing that might be a photograph.'

'Not as I saw. But then I didn't have her in sight all the time or she'd have seen me.'

'Did anyone strike you? Did you find out who else she talked to at the Wigmore.'

'One geezer told her he was somebody or other from the BBC. But it wasn't a name that meant anything so I didn't clock it. The feller who gave the speech was name of Strachey. John Strachey. But she didn't talk to him. I really couldn't get close enough. I looked a berk as it was. People tried to chat to me. I said I was with the caretaker, just waitin' to lock up. Truth is I look like a copper. Even in me civvies I look a copper.'

Bonham paused. Set his cup down on the floor. Looked straight at Troy fastening his tie.

'Freddie, you wouldn't mind telling me what's going on? Why was I following that woman? McGee came into the nick on Friday afternoon and said you'd told him he could formally report Wolinski as missing. Is he missing?'

'No, George. He's dead.'

Bonham said 'Jesus Christ' softly. He picked up his cup, crouched over it, cradling it gently and sipped at it. Slowly he straightened up, sipped at his cup again and let his head loll back across the chair, staring up at the ceiling, two hands wrapped around the cup as though he might crush it to dust. 'Jesus Christ,' he said again. 'Jesus Christ.'

§ 24

Troy arrived late at the Yard to find he had exchanged one large policeman warming nicely in front of the gas fire for another. Onions was sprawled in front of the fireplace, puffing on a Woodbine and reading the morning's post. Wildeve was at his desk and shot to his feet as Troy walked in.

'The Superintendent's been waiting to see you, Sergeant,' he squeaked in breathless formality.

Troy put down his leather case on Wildeve's desk. Wildeve was making for the door, anxious to escape the stifling silence that was Onions. Troy put a hand on his shoulder and pressed him back into his seat.

'No. Don't go, Jack. The Superintendent and I would both like to hear from you. Good morning, Stan.'

Onions stuffed his correspondence into a jacket pocket and turned to matters in hand.

'Up with the lark I see, Freddie.'

'I was actually.'

Troy turned around the visitor's chair by Wildeve's desk so that he could sit facing Onions.

'I've had ex-Inspector Malnick on the blower,' said Onions. 'He was, how shall I put it . . . ?'

'Shirty?' said Troy.

'Shirty will do very nicely. He seems to think you have something of his.'

Troy reached into his briefcase and handed Onions the photograph.

'Ah . . . the Tower beach case.'

'Codename Trousers. But I know who he is.'

'You have a positive identification?'

'I know who he is. Gregor von Ranke.'

Onions just nodded and kept on nodding as Troy brought him up to date on his meeting with Nikolai and Bonham's pursuit of Diana Brack. Then he asked precisely the question Troy had asked of Nikolai.

'Team? What team?'

'It appears from what my uncle knew of them that they were little short of being geniuses. They were developing lightweight alloys, tough, non-corrodable, thin. And then they were also on to a thing called a ram jet – I don't know what that is – on to chemical propulsion. Well, I've lit a few of those myself on November the fifth – it means rockets. I asked Nikolai what use all this could be to anyone and he said the military potential was enormous. He saw it in terms of pilotless flying bombs.'

Onions raised an eyebrow. A silent 'what is the world coming to?'

'And rockets of enormous speed, with nuclear fission warheads. But what they talked about was their dreams, not the use they might be to the Reich. They said that if they were left alone with all the right resources they would put a man on the moon by 1960.'

Onions stared back at him silently for a moment. Troy realised how odd this must be to a man of Onions's age. He had been born into another world. He was of an age with the novels of H. G. Wells and Jules Verne. He had been seven when two bicycle manufacturers took their dream down to Kittyhawk, South Carolina, and made it fly. Up till then the bicycle itself had seemed like science's front line of achievement, and the car was a noisy nuisance that no one really cared for. To Troy, 1960 was a long way off. To a man in his fifties it was the day after tomorrow, and the motor car was something he'd only recently come to terms with.

'Jesus Christ,' he said softly. Then, 'So you're pretty certain that the arm, which is where we came in, belonged to this Brand chap?'

'It does seem logical.'

'What was he doing here? What were any of them doing here? They seem unlikely choices for spies.'

'I don't think they were spies. Wolinski, at least, had genuine refugee status. How's that coming along, Jack?'

This startled Wildeve. His mind had been elsewhere.

'Er ... I ... er ... I don't think I'm getting anywhere. There's just too much of it. Too much bumf on everything. Without names to go by it was damn impossible. Checking out von Ranke and Brand should be easy now. But if I draw a blank then, well that's it really.'

'Even if they were legitimate refugees I'm not sure what that tells us,' said Onions. 'They came here, they registered, they died. We have no motive and no suspect. After all, your Brack woman's a lead, but she's hardly your suspect.'

'The motive surely lies in what they knew and what their work was? But, of course they didn't come here as refugees. Nikolai was involved in sifting out interned enemies who could serve the war effort. If they were here as refugees, barring a cock-up, they would have been arrested in 1940. Sooner or later Nikolai would have heard.'

'What about Wolinski?'

'Friendly alien. He would have been allowed to go about his business. And as he buried himself in the docks and his books, no one would have noticed him.'

'So, what next?'

'I'd like a meeting with MI5. Who's their liaison with the Met?'

Onions took a tiny pocket diary from his inside pocket, licked his finger and turned the pages.

'Pym. Squadron Leader Pym.'

'Neville Pym?'

'It says N. A. G. Pym? D'ye know him?'

'I was at school with him.'

'My, my, my. That old school tie'll be the death of you.'

'I'll talk to Pym.'

'Are you going to tell me why?'

'Just a hunch. I have a feeling that this might be their turf rather than ours.'

'Bodies on the streets of London is always our turf,' said Onions.

From the corner of his eye Troy could see imminent flapping in Wildeve. He was on edge, trying and failing to interrupt.

'Spit it out, Jack. Whatever it is.'

'Well ... it's just ... well, you did say the woman you had followed was called Brack. Diana Brack you said. Diana Ormond-Brack?'

'Could be.'

'Well ... I rather think I know her. Or at least I used to. She's old Fermanagh's daughter.'

'Am I supposed to guess what that means?' said Onions, turning Wildeve to beetroot. 'Old MacDonald would mean more.'

'Jack means the Marquess of Fermanagh,' said Troy. 'He's one of the powers behind the throne. One of those Conservative Party king-makers. It's said he helped keep Churchill in the wilderness for ten years.'

'She was a friend of my brother's at one time,' said Wildeve, blushing a little more at the euphemism for lover.

'Well, well,' said Onions, getting up from his chair, stubbing his last Woodbine out at the mantelpiece. 'It's a small world. And as this appears to be the only lead you two have got, I suppose I'd better leave you to it. I wouldn't want to be treading too close behind you with the Pyms and the Fermanaghs in this Lobster Quadrille. You never know, I might wear me brown boots with me blue suit, and that would never do.'

As the door closed behind Onions, and Wildeve resumed an approximately normal colour, he asked quietly of Troy, 'Do you suppose that was sarcasm?'

'Probably,' Troy replied.

Wildeve got up. 'I suppose I'd better get back to B3.'

'No, Jack. Just tell your uniform what he needs to know. Let him draw the blank.'

'You seem very confident.'

Troy shrugged. 'Is it likely that Diana Brack will remember you?'

'Only by name. I was fourteen or fifteen the last time we met.'

'Get over to Tite Street as soon as you can. Watch, follow, and then come back and tell me. Who she meets, where she goes. It's too early to steam in and ask her anything.'

Wildeve reached across his desk and gathered up a loose collection of papers and dumped the lot in Troy's in-tray. As he looked out at the Thames Troy heard the door close softly behind him.

There was more than sarcasm, more than counter-snobbery to Onions's remark. The conspiracy that Troy had told Onions was all but tangible required a conspirator or two of enormous power. But peers of the realm didn't have people bumped off just to cover up the indiscretions of a wayward daughter, did they? Surely Stan wasn't thinking in that direction?

Troy called MI5 in St James's Street and asked for Squadron Leader Pym. It took a while for the switchboard to put him through. He heard the line crackle repeatedly and was beginning to think they were cranking up some sort of security apparatus when a loud click heralded the connection.

'Squadron Leader Pym,' a voice said loudly and brusquely.

'Good morning. It's Frederick Troy here.'

There was a pause.

'Troy?'

'Frederick Troy.'

There was a deafening silence, then Pym spoke again almost *sotto voce.* 'What do you want?'

'I think I need to talk to you . . . '

The usual waffle about wanting information, the usual flattery about only 'you' can help, the usual lie about it being 'just routine police business' was cut short. Even more softly than he had spoken before, Pym said, 'Not here, not now.'

'Sorry,' Troy said. 'Have I called at a particularly bad time for you?'

'How innocent,' Pym replied. 'Of course you have. Any time would be a bad time.' He paused again. 'Come to my flat this evening at seven. I'm at Albany. E6.'

And the line went dead. E6 was not a postal address in the East End. It was the apartment number. Albany was, as Onions would have said, the 'swankiest' address a single man about town could have. A beautiful, exclusive apartment building on the north side of Piccadilly. It was an address that would have suited such as Lord Peter Wimsey or Albert Campion, although, if Troy's teenage reading served him right, it was Raffles who had lived there – and Raffles wasn't on the same side as Troy. As a bachelor apartment, with its uniformed porters and its famous ropewalk, Albany was without equal in the whole of London. Pym had done well for himself. From an office at MI5 HQ Pym could walk home in a matter of minutes. If Pym had grown into a man about town then he could be about town minutes after leaving work at the flip of a collar stud.

§ 25

A day on paperwork wore away much of Troy's patience. When the top-hatted porter at Albany stopped him, he produced his warrant card and declined to give his name, state his business or be announced. Pym had seemed so reluctant that he didn't want to give him any opportunity to put him off any further.

When Pym answered the door on the second floor he was

wearing a deep burgundy smoking jacket, and he was smoking. .
He was smoking a Passing Cloud. A ridiculous cigarette that was
oval rather than round, and looked as though it had been recently
sat on. Troy thought it was smoked only by fools who wanted to
attract attention to themselves.

'You're early,' he said, and looked somewhere over Troy's head,
so pointedly that Troy himself thought there might be someone
behind him and turned to look.

'You've come alone?' asked Pym.

'Of course,' said Troy.

As Troy stepped past him into the hallway Pym looked both
ways outside the door before he closed it. He led Troy into a huge
mock-Palladian drawing room, the height of the ceilings alone
would have been intimidating but Pym had added to the effect
with an expensive array of Regency furniture. Troy found too
much red and gold oppressive, the trappings of a circus – he found
the furniture uncomfortable. Pym stopped at a sideboard and
poured a small glass of sherry for Troy. Troy perched himself on
the edge of a glittering circus chair, Pym leaned against the marble
fireplace and plucked his glass off the mantelpiece. He had gone
grey above the ears since Troy had last seen him, and had acquired
the soft, loose look of face that characterised a man who took little
exercise and took most of his pleasures in restaurants. Pym was
running rapidly to seed and looked as though he meant to enjoy
every moment and ounce of it. Somewhere in his attic was a
portrait that was forever young.

'I see no reason why we can't be civilised about this,' he said.

He looked down at Troy, softly arrogant, the merest quaver in
the rich ruby port of his voice, resuming its natural lush, suggestive
tone that reminded Troy of his schooldays, rather than the false
RAF bark with which he had greeted him earlier or the equally
false stage whisper with which he had ended. Troy had no idea
what he was talking about.

'You're not the first to phone up out of the blue and come
crawling round here.'

Troy still had no idea what Pym meant, but thought 'crawling'
a bit beyond the pale.

'I'm only doing my job,' he said.

'And what precisely do you consider your job to be? I suppose you're going to say pestering me is a public service?'

'Well, I hadn't really thought of it in that way. I can't tell you it's routine because it isn't. It's a pretty serious police matter as these things go.'

Troy watched the blood drain from Pym's face exactly as it had done from Driberg's at the mention of the same word.

'You've told the *police*? You fool, you complete and utter bloody fool.'

Pym set down his glass again. Troy saw that he was now almost white and thought he might faint.

'Pym, I don't know what stupid game you're playing with me, or what misapprehension you're labouring under, but you are, are you not, the MI5 liaison officer with the Yard? If you're not say so now and I'll bugger off and you can stuff your damned sherry. Just tell me who I have to call.'

'You're a policeman?'

Troy wondered. Had he really not told that girl on MI5's switchboard that he was calling from Scotland Yard? If he hadn't what on earth had Pym thought he was after? And then it dawned on him. The Driberg reaction was for precisely the same reason. The homosexual's habitual fear of the Vice Squad. At school, Pym, some four years older than Troy, had been a bully. But then that was the job of every older boy – to bully the younger. As bullies went Pym was hardly the worst. He had no taste for the brutality, the beatings that prefects had the power to inflict on small boys. His tongue was feared – he had a remarkable capacity to inflict abuse and humiliation but that was about it. Troy's closest friend Charlie had been Pym's boy, not his fag – for a while Troy himself had held that unenviable post – but his lover. Troy had thought nothing of it, and being Pym's lover had afforded Charlie some measure of the protection that a thirteen-year-old boy who looked like a blond, Nordic princess needed in a system that was, at least for the duration of school life, predominantly queer. Charlie had long since grown out of it. The availability of women in the outside world had given him a choice and he'd made it. Pym too had made his choice, and as Troy looked at him puffing furiously at his Passing Cloud, struggling to regain his composure, propped against the fireplace like a character in a play by Noël Coward, he realised that the choice had been to stay as he was.

'Neville,' said Troy, venturing the Christian name tentatively, 'I'm with the Murder Squad. I hold no brief for the Vice Squad.'

Pym glugged back his sherry, poured himself a large brandy and sat back in the chair opposite Troy.

'You wouldn't believe how many of them still come around. People you thought you'd never see again after they opened the gates on that fucking school and turned us loose. You know I rather think our parents sent us to the wrong school. It seems to have turned out a lot of chaps who appear to be habitually down on their luck, and most of them seem eager to describe themselves to me as "old friends" – I'd no idea I'd so many friends. I've been touched for a loan – usually accepted with an ungracious "just to tide me over" – half a dozen times in the last couple of years.'

'If you've been blackmailed you should report it.'

'In my position?'

Troy shrugged.

'I think you'd better tell me why you've come.'

'I have a murder on my hands. I believe the victim to be German. I'm ninety-nine per cent certain he's not a refugee. In fact I'm pretty damn certain he arrived on these shores rather recently.'

'So?'

'If he was a spy, if you have lost a spy, I will need to know.'

'A body you say. Dumped on your doorstep or what?'

'Shot, dismembered, burnt.'

'Troy, we don't shoot spies, we turn them. And if we can't turn them or we have no use for them we put them on trial and then we hang them. I can tell you now the answer is no. And before you ask, the chances of the Germans having spies in London, at least spies even the Yard can spot as German, without us knowing about it are virtually nil.'

That was the answer Troy had anticipated. He watched Pym inhale the aroma hovering in the brim of his balloon glass and thought of the wording of his next question. The issue he had so far declined to discuss with Onions or Wildeve.

'There is another possibility,' he began. 'I need to know if your

95

people have brought anyone out of Germany or the occupied countries who has subsequently gone missing.'

Pym sipped at his brandy and thought for a moment.

'That's a very tall order.'

'No taller than the last.'

'Spies come over. They get caught. Everyone knows that. The Germans have been known to send poor Dutch bastards across in rowing boats armed with nothing more than a dictionary full of pinpricks for their codes. And the poor sods do it because their families are hostage. Those men are dead the minute they set off. The Germans would be better off putting a bullet through their heads. What you're asking is very different. You're asking what our people are up to over there. I've no authorisation to answer that. Even for Scotland Yard.'

'But,' said Troy, 'you'll ask.'

Pym got up, a huffy dignity, a piqued sense of self-importance showing in his expression, and went into the other room. The phone jangled as phones do when someone is dialling on a badly wired extension. Troy tried the sherry. He had always thought the stuff tasted awful. This specimen did nothing to change his mind. He looked around for a plant pot in which to dispose of it. In most homes in England he would have found a handy aspidistra perched on its high table, but Pym had no plants. Every table and niche was occupied with some sort of statuary, an arresting array of nude males. Over by the door where Pym had just gone was a largish plaster copy of the Michelangelo David. It was rumoured that when Queen Mary had visited the British Museum the staff had had a fig leaf made to cover the offending cock on their own cast of the statue. Pym did not care for such modesty. The cock bloomed for all to see. Any 'old friend' who did turn up to touch Pym for a fiver would know at a glance he was on to a good thing. Did the man invite blackmail? After all, there were plenty of other places he and Troy could have met if the prospect of turning up at MI5 was more than Pym could contemplate. It crossed Troy's mind that Pym might just enjoy the risk.

Pym returned in less than five minutes, and took up his old pose by the fireplace.

'I've had a word in the appropriate quarter,' he said. 'The

answer's no. We've brought out no one we can't account for. And that constitutes no admission on our part that we have brought anyone out, you will understand.'

'Quite,' said Troy. After all, even in the height of his momentary panic, Pym had had enough sense not to admit he was still queer. It had been understood unspoken. 'I'm almost sorry to have troubled you.'

He rose to go and began to button his overcoat. Pym took a huge stone table lighter off the mantelpiece and lit another of his awful cigarettes. The 'almost' in 'almost sorry' had bounced off Pym, now safely esconced in his own conceit once more.

'There is one last thing,' said Troy just before he reached the door, aiming for the suggestion that what was high in his list of priorities was perhaps a mere afterthought – a cheap ploy of detective stories that he had learnt from the daddy of all cheap detectives, Porfiry Porfirovich in *Crime and Punishment*. Pym blew smoke down his nostrils. Troy had often thought that however impressive the trick it must feel deeply unpleasant.

'We're not the only army in these islands, are we?'

'What do you mean?' Pym looked surprised.

'I mean, it's just as likely that the Americans would have brought out a useful foreign national.'

Pym said nothing, waiting for Troy to ask and offering no invitation.

'I'll also need an answer to the same question from them.'

'I'll see what I can do.'

'I'll need to know pretty quickly.'

'As I said. I'll see what I can do. I can't speak for the Americans. All I can do is ask. I'll call you tomorrow.'

§ 26

Better than his word, Pym called Troy at half past nine the following morning. The rain ran down the window in sheets; Troy was sitting with his back to the torrent, listening to a bleary, yawning Wildeve

97

give his account of Diana Brack's movements the night before, when the telephone rang.

'Troy, listen,' said Pym imperiously. 'The Americans will see you. God knows why, but they will.'

'You have a way of making it sound as though they're above the law,' said Troy.

'What you don't grasp, Troy, is that they run things now. And it's not a point I'm about to argue with you. Do you want this meeting or not?'

'Of course. When?'

'I'm afraid it's eleven o'clock this morning or not at all. They have an office in St James's Square, at Norfolk House. You see a chap called Zelig – Colonel Zelig.'

'Who is he? Your opposite number?'

'I've no idea. Quite simply he's the man who'll answer your questions. Isn't that enough?'

'Of course. I appreciate your help, Neville.'

The use of his Christian name seemed to be an affront that stung Pym.

'You've used up any favours I owed you, Troy. Remember that.'

He rang off before Troy could say a word. The precise point of the outburst was lost on Troy. He looked up at Wildeve, trying to dry his hair on a pullover, while his coat steamed on a radiator and his shoes made puddles in the waste-paper bin.

'I'm seeing some American this morning.'

'Where does that connect with my end of things?' asked Wildeve.

'I've no idea.'

'Ah ... where was I?'

'You and Lady Diana had just sat through *Major Barbara*.'

'Right.' Wildeve sat down opposite Troy and pushed a lock of damp brown hair from his eyes. 'She walked home. Could've strangled her. All that money and she doesn't take a cab, she decides to walk all the way from Shaftesbury Avenue to Chelsea. Do you know how long it takes to walk from—'

'Skip it, Jack. Doesn't it strike you as odd that a woman of her class does all this alone?'

'Eh?'

'She has a drink at the Cri, she goes to the theatre, she meets no one. You've no sense that someone she expected stood her up?'

'Freddie, you've seen Lady Di. You'd have to be blind to stand up Diana Brack!'

'Yet she tackles the social round of her class without an escort.'

'A lack of eligibles perhaps. They're all in the Toff's Rifles or the Mummersetshire Yeomanry. I tell you, in her time most of the eligible chinless in the country have paid court to Diana – my brothers to name but two – and a fair smattering of lounge lizards and silver screeners. There was a lot of talk about her and Jack Buchanan for a while. Al Bowlly was reportedly mad with frustration because he couldn't get within a mile of her.'

'Get to the point,' said Troy, checking his watch against the clock high on the wall above Wildeve's head.

'Sorry – what I mean is she isn't that sort. She's . . . well . . . she's a bluestocking I suppose. Furiously intellectual – and I do mean both of those words. I saw some fine set-tos between her and Old Fermanagh when I was a boy. She despises the rituals and mores of her class. Johnny Lissadel once told me she'd rather spend an evening with Sidney Webb than a day with the Aga Khan.'

Troy smiled at the contrast. At the familiarity – her class was their class, his and Wildeve's, and if they too did not in some measure despise the mores and rituals of their class they would scarcely have become policemen. Troy wondered if Wildeve recognised this.

'I can't say I'm surprised at anything so far,' Wildeve continued. 'A bit boring, a bit spartan. Just what you'd expect really.'

'So you followed her home?'

'I did indeed. She spoke to no one until we got into the square just north of Tite Street. It's all down to allotments now. She had a few words with an old feller who's raising a pig there.'

'Anything in it?'

'Good manners. That's about all. A kind word to the lower element.'

'Should we be looking at him?'

'I doubt it. He was in a Civil Defence outfit. LCC Heavy Rescue. Must be sixty I suppose. Big fellow. Completely bald. Whatever she may think now, it's still second nature to her to take a little deference from the deferential classes. I had a quick word with him. Lady Di keeps the allotment next his – last vestige of a short spell in the Land Army. As I recall they called her up and slung her out in less than six months.'

'And so to bed?'

'Quite. But I was there till one just to be sure she didn't go out again.'

Troy got up to look out of the window, skirting the beam that kept Scotland Yard from falling on his head. Outside it was what Troy called Noah's Ark weather. The street was empty of pedestrians, the buses rolled by full to the brim, and the Thames itself was high against the containing wall of the Bazalgette's embankment. Wildeve had his head on one side and was attempting to dry one ear on a large monogrammed handkerchief. He resembled a morris dancer *manqué* rather than a policeman.

'Jack,' said Troy 'You can have the night off. I'll watch her tonight.'

'Thanks. I do appreciate it. I'd hate to drown while we clutched at straws.'

Beneath the *ingénu*, beneath the upper-class frothiness, Wildeve had a mind that from time to time could startle Troy by its blunt appraisal.

'We have a definite connection,' he said. 'Brack was at Wolinski's. She did steal a photograph of our man.'

'Precisely put, Freddie, she probably stole a photograph of someone we think might be our man. But you surely don't think Diana Brack's got herself mixed up with a murderer?'

§ 27

The windscreen wipers on the Bullnose Morris scarcely kept pace with the rain. Troy inched the car carefully round St James's Square, with the side window down, looking for the familiar marks of an American base. Two caped, white-helmeted MPs stood in front of Norfolk House on the eastern side. As Troy eased his car in behind a large Packard in camouflage browns one of them came over and banged on the roof at him. Troy stepped out into a solid wall of rain to see the man pointing at the Packard and shouting over the noise of water drumming on steel.

'You can't park here!'

'Business,' said Troy, moving towards the shelter of the doorway.

'Oh yeah. With whom?'

Once under cover, Troy held up his warrant card. The second soldier had raised a hand to his hip under his cape as though holding the butt of a gun.

'It's OK, Lou,' said the first soldier. 'He's a cop!' He handed the card back to Troy and asked, 'Who you seeing?'

'Zelig. Colonel Zelig.'

He beckoned to Troy to follow and stepped into the house. He pulled a clipboard from the wall, took off a glove and ran a finger down a list of names.

'Eleven o'clock, right?'

Troy nodded.

'Basement. Two floors down.' He pointed towards the staircase curling around a brass lattice-work lift-shaft. 'Show your ID to the guy in the corridor when you get down.'

Two flights and one ritual later Troy found himself in a windowless, warm room forty feet under the streets of London. The room was empty. All that security just to guard a desk and a typewriter, thought Troy. The door swung open and a WAC backed into the room, keeping the door ajar with her hip and swivelling round to face Troy. She carried a cup of coffee in one hand and a greasy, steaming brown paper bag in the other. As she turned Troy found himself face to face with a small, good-looking blonde, with hair so short and and masculine it was almost a crewcut.

'You want Zelly?' she asked in a voice rich with deep, throaty vowel sounds.

Troy nodded, still taking in the startling appearance. Her uniform fitted her like a glove, tucked and pleated, outlandishly emphasising the hour-glass figure, with its tightly rounded bosom and pinch-bottle waist.

'Gimme your name and I'll tell him you're here. You caught him at elevenses.'

'Very English,' said Troy.

'Also very Zelly,' she said. 'Any excuse to eat.'

She went through the same motions again, flicking down the handle of the inner door with her elbow and shoving it aside with her hip. Troy caught the door and propped it open. She smiled momentarily at him as she ducked under his arm.

'Your name!' she whispered hoarsely.

'Troy,' he whispered back.

Looking past her Troy saw the Colonel get up from his desk. He yanked a blind down over a map of Italy.

'Dammit! Can't you knock?' he croaked.

He pulled down another blind over a map of France in a showy pantomime of secrecy. The WAC set Zelig's elevenses on his desk.

'It's OK. I think he's one of ours. Mr Troy. He's your eleven o'clock.'

Zelig ignored Troy and snatched at the paper bag. The door banged shut as the WAC left. Zelig had done and said nothing to indicate his acknowledgement of Troy's presence. He bit into the hamburger and yelled through a mouthful of bread and meat.

'Tosca!!!'

The WAC stuck her head round the door.

'Whaddya want?' It hardly seemed the way for a sergeant to address a colonel.

'Is this mayo? I asked for mayo. I always have mayo on my burger for Chrissake.'

'It's English,' she replied simply.

'English what?'

'They call it salad cream.'

Zelig pulled a face of disgust and stared down at the mess in his right hand.

'I guess,' she added, 'it's what they eat when they can't get mayo. You could call it ersatz mayo.'

She pulled back and closed the door. Zelig was still staring at his hamburger, with enough meat in it to use up the average British ration for a week. Troy sat down in the only chair on his side of the desk. For the first time Zelig seemed to notice him. He took his seat again and with it a huge bite at his burger. However distasteful he seemed hell bent on finishing it in three bites. Troy thought if he didn't speak soon he would try counting his chins, or perhaps the hairs on his head. He was fifteen stone and bald but for a halo of stubble that circled his skull just above the tops of his ears.

'Sho?' Zelig said, showering the top of his desk with breadcrumbs.

'I'm Sergeant Troy of the Murder Squad at Scotland Yard. Squadron Leader Pym at MI5 referred me to you. There's one or two things you might be able to help us with.'

'I doubt that.' Zelig gulped down enough food to choke himself to death and snatched another bite and a slurp of coffee. The hamburger was reduced to a moon-shaped sliver. For someone so obviously addicted to food he seemed to extract remarkably little pleasure from it.

'I need to know if your people have brought anyone out of France or Germany—'

'My people?' Zelig emphasised 'people' as though it were a meaningless word in a language he did not speak.

'Your...' Troy sought for the right word, 'agents ... You do have agents in Europe?'

'No comment.' '

Troy felt like hitting Zelig. Surely Pym had briefed him on the purpose of the visit. Why else was he seeing him? Why then was he forcing Troy to dot the i's and cross the t's?

'You don't seem to be in the picture, Colonel.'

'Rough me up a sketch. I'm all ears.'

All gut more like, thought Troy.

'We are investigating a death – murder we believe – we also believe that the victim was German.'

'One less Kraut to worry about.'

Troy ignored the remark. 'I've established that he was not a spy, and as far as I can that he was not a refugee. I was wondering therefore if he was...'

Troy couldn't think of the right word – there seemed to be no single word which simply and precisely described what Troy thought the late Herr Brand to be. But, spoken or not, Zelig seemed to know it.

'Nothin' doin',' he said.

The door opened again and the WAC hurried in and placed a note in front of Zelig.

'Hey. Just a minute, Sergeant.'

She held on to the door and coyly looked back at him over her right shoulder. Troy followed Zelig's gaze, from her backside down to her stiletto heels.

'Is that skirt army issue?'

'It's green, isn't it?' she replied.

'So're dollar bills 'n' apples. It's too damn tight – grips your ass like it's been stuck on. You walk like you been sewn together at the knees. And those shoes.'

'What about 'em?'

'They ain't regulation neither.'

'Up yours,' said Tosca, and banged out.

It occurred to Troy that there was a certain choreography to their banter – a vulgarian's Burns and Allen, and it all seemed to be so timed as to prevent Zelig ever getting to an answer. If Troy did not seize the initiative now he might as well forget it. He turned on his best copper-in-the-witness-box style in the hope of dragging Zelig back to the subject.

'Have you brought out any Germans who have subsequently gone missing?' he said clearly and succinctly.

'Like I said,' the fat man replied almost nonchalantly, 'nothin' doin'.'

'Do you mean that you have or you haven't?' Troy persisted.

'I mean,' said Zelig, 'that it's none of your damn business.'

For several seconds they sat in a silence emphasised and punctuated by the sound of Zelig finishing hamburger and coffee. Troy weighed up the odds. If the man really was the buffoon he appeared to be then he probably knew nothing – after all the British army was full of desk-bound majors, pushing paper around simply to prevent them repeating the charge of the Light Brigade, and what better use for the Colonel Chinstrap of the American army than to have him liaise with the British. Or was he so consummately playing the buffoon that he would never reveal a speck of what he knew? The mystery remained. Why had Zelig gone to the trouble of seeing him? Just for the pleasure of saying no?

Troy got up, thanked Zelig for his time in the briefest of polite terms and headed for the door.

'Any time,' he heard Zelig croak as the door closed and he found himself once more looking at Sergeant Tosca. Clearly, he had interrupted something. A tall, languid-looking American in the uniform of a major sat on the end of her desk, one leg swinging gently, his head bent over to her as though simultaneously signifying relaxation and flirtation – sharing a secret. He chuckled deeply. She smiled in return, and as Troy's presence became obvious the two pairs of eyes swivelled towards him.

'All through?' she said.

The Major was extracting a cigarette from a large silver case. He snapped it to and tapped the end of the cigarette on the desk-top.

'You have a light?' he said to Troy, and aimed the cigarette towards him.

Troy shook his head and blinked at the sudden flash as Tosca struck the wheel on a Zippo lighter and held it out to the Major. He bent closer, drew on the tobacco and muttered something Troy couldn't hear. She laughed in response, listening to the Major but looking at Troy.

'Yes thank you. All through,' said Troy.

He left feeling that a shared, exclusive joke just about summed up his dealings with Britain's closest ally. He sat in the car listening to the rain beat a tattoo on the roof, wondering how much of this was down to Pym, how much of it simply natural bloody-mindedness on the part of Zelig. Would Pym have gone to such trouble to make a fool of him? Was he too just passing the buck – making Troy chase Zelig with questions for which Pym already had the answers?

The Packard staff car was still in front of him. The driver's door opened. The WAC lieutenant-chauffeur walked around the boot between the Packard and the Morris, and stood erect by the near passenger door. Troy looked back at Norfolk House. One of the MPs was coming across the pavement opening a large umbrella, the other stood to attention by the door. Suddenly Troy knew exactly who they were expecting. He reached the step just as Eisenhower walked under the cover of the umbrella. He'd crossed some invisible frontier – a forearm, half-buried in leather gauntlet, swung gently across his chest, and the MP spoke softly to him.

'Far enough, buddy. Whatever it is, now is not your moment.'

For a second Troy and Ike were eye to eye, then Ike was in the staff car and moving out into St James's Square.

'Sorry. You weren't down to see the man were you?' said the MP.

'No,' said Troy, 'no, I wasn't.'

The rain was beginning to soak through his overcoat. He went quickly back to the car. Was it worth the try? One bald-headed American was probably much the same as any other bald-headed American. The only difference lay in the amount of scrambled egg on the cap. Though, being fair, Troy felt certain Ike had better table manners.

§ 28

The woman at the front desk at MI5 HQ in St James's Street looked at Troy's warrant card and phoned up.

'Squadron Leader Pym is in conference,' she told Troy. Throughout the day, at odd intervals, she told Troy the same thing over the phone to Scotland Yard. At six o'clock Troy was debating with himself whether to tell Onions, buttonhole Pym at Albany or relieve Wildeve at Tite Street as he had promised. He tried Pym's home number, which he had memorised the night before.

'I've been trying to reach you all day.'

'So I've heard. Troy, you just don't know when to give up do you?'

'I'd be a poor excuse for a copper if I gave up in the face of a crude stonewalling like the one Zelig gave me.'

'That's got nothing to do with me. I can't help you any more than I have.'

Troy could hear the tremor in Pym's voice, the tone hovering somewhere between exasperation and anger.

'If Zelig had no intention of telling me anything, then why did he agree to see me?'

'I don't know, and I wish to God you'd stop asking. I cannot, cannot, cannot talk to you!'

Troy was silent for a moment. He heard Pym sigh deeply and knew he had let slip something he now regretted. He wondered what kind of a dressing-down Pym had spent the day listening to. Who had been giving him the hell that betrayed itself now in his exhaustion and nervousness? Blurting out the one thing he should not.

'You know, Neville, if you wanted me to give up there was no more sure fire way of ensuring I didn't than by telling me what you just told me. Who's told you not to talk to me?'

Pym's tone was subdued now, spent of anger and shot through with weariness. 'Troy, I can't help you. Really I can't. If only you knew ... If you have any sense of ... if you ... for God's sake let this one drop.'

'I can't do that.'

'Then don't drag me down with you.'

Troy heard Pym put down the receiver. Whatever doubts he had had about the cover-up of von Ranke's murder and the motive for it – for Brand's and Wolinski's – blew away like will o' the wisp. Pym had lit a flame in his imagination and he could feel it tingle down into his fingertips – the sheer pleasure of pursuit. He caught the bus out to the Chelsea Embankment to meet Wildeve.

§ 29

At the corner of Tite Street and Royal Hospital Road Wildeve was nowhere to be seen. But that was just as well. If Troy could see him so could anyone else. He walked on towards the Chelsea Embankment.

'Psst.' He heard as he passed the house opposite number 55.

'Psst.' Again. With more urgency if a psst could have it.

Troy looked down to see Wildeve's hand groping towards his ankle from the area steps of the house.

'Down here!' he whispered.

Troy swung open the gate to find Wildeve sitting on the steps with his eyes at ground level. He slipped down next to him.

'These people seem to have closed up for the duration,' Wildeve whispered. 'Absolutely perfect. The better hole, eh?'

'Jack, if they've gone away why are we whispering?'

Wildeve opened his mouth, but Troy waved it shut. 'What's happening?'

'Absolutely nothing. I got here around noon. Took me that long to dry out. I know she's in. I've seen her at the first-floor window a couple of times.'

'Alone?'

'I think so. The girl's come and gone a few times. And there's been the usual handful of tradesmen up and down to the basement door. If there's anyone else up there with her they've been here since the morning. I've seen no one.'

'OK,' Troy said. 'Go home and get warm.'

'Good-oh. I was beginning to think you'd never get here.'

'Who is it tonight?' asked Troy.

'Another Wren. All the nice boys love a sailor.'

Wildeve looked both ways at the top of the steps, and then left again, like a child observing a thoroughly dinned kerb drill, and headed off in the direction of the river. An hour and a half later, Troy sat in the pitch darkness, feeling frozen stiff and utterly bored. How had Wildeve stuck it for the six or more hours? He stood up to ease the cramp in his right leg, rubbed at the scar on his arm, which seemed to ache in the damp, and dusted off his trousers. A flash of light came suddenly from the first-floor window, and he caught a quick glimpse of a woman's face, a hand at the blackout making some minor adjustment. It was unmistakably, even in the briefest glance, the same woman he had seen in Stepney. A face so striking one could hardly forget it.

Troy crossed the street, staring up at the window, but no further light or movement came from it. An impulse seized him. He walked up to the front door and rang the bell. He heard the clump of lazy, tired feet banging up the stairs from the basement, and the door inched open. A young housemaid, cap awry, stockings crumpled as though pulled up in a hurry, stood in the doorway.

'Yes?' she said.

'Sergeant Troy,' said Troy, showing the card.

'Tradesman's entrance downstairs,' said the girl, and swung the door to. Troy jammed his foot in the way and braced an arm against the door. Tradesman's entrance! Good grief, could the woman not hear the toff in his voice? Had a few years on the beat rendered him indistinguishable from the butcher's boy? He reached into his jacket pocket and handed her one of his private calling cards, the pre-war ones without rank and giving his parents' address.

'Take this and hand it to Lady Diana. Tell her Mr Troy would like a word. Now!'

The girl snatched the card and ran, leaving Troy standing in the hall. A minute passed in silence, then the girl returned.

'The mistress says as how I'm to show you up,' she said half-whispering. 'Coppers is always tradesman's door. That's what cook says,' she added impudently.

Diana Brack contrived a dramatic entrance. She strode the width of the room to meet Troy, her hand extended in a firm, masculine handshake.

'Mr Troy. I'm so sorry. The usual cliché applies. One cannot get the staff nowadays.'

She stood at least five foot ten and was dressed in Vesta Tilley garb. A tailored and pleated version of men's striped trousers flapped around her long legs and pinched in tightly at her waist — a black silk shirt, complete with silver cufflinks, rippled from broad shoulders across a small bosom. A single strand of pearls at the the throat. This was hardly a gesture to femininity, for the whole appearance contrived femininity in irony. Her skin was china white. Her black hair shone with a rich lustre, curling thickly a couple of inches above the shoulder, and flopped carelessly over her right eye. As she took back her hand she flicked the strand clear of her face and Troy looked into eyes that were a rich, deep green. It was, he thought, a snook cocked at fashion with more panache than he had seen in a long time. A devastating study in black and white. He appreciated the frustration of Wildeve's brothers and the late Al Bowlly. Here was a face to kill or die for. Diana Brack was beyond doubt one of the most beautiful women in London. Troy thought it must plague her father badly that she was still single at thirty-four. Not that her age showed. He would have put her somewhere in her mid-twenties, but that her manner showed more self-assurance.

'Do sit down. Can I get you anything? Daisy tells me you're a policeman. What a surprise!'

They sat opposite each other. Either side of a huge oak fireplace – she on a Knole sofa, legs crossed at the knee, one foot swinging gently and showing a glimpse of black stocking at the ankle, Troy on an armchair, resisting the languor she seemed to exude. The floor between them was a sprawling mess of newspapers, and face down on the pile, spread open at halfway, was a book – Troy raised an inner eyebrow at Engels's *The Condition of the Working Class in England*.

'Are you sure I can't get you something?' she asked again, and again seemed not to wait for an answer. 'It must be terribly cold out.'

'No, there's nothing. Just a few questions and then I'll be on my way.'

'Questions for me? Good Lord.'

The *faux-naïf* air of innocence was irritating. It called for drastic action.

'I'm investigating a murder,' said Troy.

It was the sort of remark that shook people, made them sit bolt upright. Brack's expression did not change. She was neither smiling nor looking worried. Whatever concern she felt registered only in her voice. Troy could read nothing in the green eyes.

'And you want to question me?' she asked with the merest hint of incredulity. 'Who exactly do you think has been murdered?'

'That I can't tell you.'

'Then I think you'll have a hard job asking me any questions.'

'Why were you at Peter Wolinski's flat on Sunday evening?'

It was a remark that shook. Just. There was the merest perceptible change in her posture; her head drooped slightly, the lock of hair fell into her eyes once more. She brushed it aside, looked up at Troy again. She gripped her knee tightly, and the blue veins stood up in the backs of her hands as the long fingers locked together.

'Good God. You're not saying Peter's been murdered?'

'I'm not saying anything of the sort. Why were you there?'

'I was just curious. I hadn't seen Peter for a while. I hadn't heard from him. I thought I'd drop in and see.'

'You just happened to be passing?'

'Of course not. One doesn't just pass Stepney Green. One goes out of one's way to get to Stepney Green! Anyway, how do you know I was there? I don't deny it for one second, but how do you come to know?'

'You were seen.'

'Ah. I was seen. Am I being spied on now Mr Troy?'

Was there a petulance added to the innocence? The hint of a pout? Was the woman playing with him? Her posture relaxed once more as she unlocked her hands and sat back. Troy felt that the slight lift in tone was an inadequate response to what he had inferred. Diana Brack seemed to have none of the outrage that was typical of anyone who thinks the police have invaded their privacy. This was as true of a cat burglar as it was of a lord. Her responses were too subtle for innocence. She was playing the game too well. But whether it was his game or hers he had yet to tell.

'Of course not,' he said. 'But Mr Wolinski has been reported missing. We are curious as to his movements.'

'Well, I haven't seen him in over a fortnight. If you were watching then you'll know he wasn't at home when I called.'

'The last time you saw Wolinski—'

She cut him short, anticipating the question. 'Was in the Brick-layers Arms. That's the pub on the corner of the street where he lives. And no, he didn't do anything that struck me as suspicious. He didn't seem worried about anything. And he certainly didn't mention a damn thing about doing a bunk.'

Troy changed tack. If she thought she could shake him off by a barrage of words, she would have to think again.

'How do you come to know Wolinski?'

'We share certain concerns.'

'Concerns?'

'Political concerns.'

'Wolinski is, I believe, a Communist.'

'Well, that's hardly illegal, is it? Yes – I know Peter through the Communist Party. I met him a year or so ago in Whitechapel.'

'But you're not a member are you?'

'No, Mr Troy. I'm not.'

'You're a fellow-traveller.'

She smiled widely. Beautiful, even white teeth that had never fallen foul of pre-war dentistry. 'Mr Troy, do I detect a note of snobbery? I do not think I can be called upon to explain or to apologise for my politics. After all, it is often better to fellow-travel hopefully than to arrive.'

Troy smiled. He'd asked for that. 'And you see him occasionally?'

'No. I see him frequently.'

'But not lately?'

'I think this is where we came in.'

'And you didn't go into Wolinski's apartment?'

'Apartment?' She drew the word out slowly, investing it with the power of several extra syllables. 'Peter was not at home. I knocked. No one answered. I left. I don't know where he is, or why he hasn't been in touch. I'm terribly sorry, but I really don't see how I can help you.'

It was the sort of line that if uttered in a play by J. B. Priestley would lead to the host getting up to heave on the bell-pull prior to the butler showing the detective his way out and his place in society. But Troy knew that his place in society showed through every syllable he uttered. Only the dimmest of parlourmaids could ever fail to miss it. Diana Brack did not. He also knew she was lying. The sound of that door closing rang clear and distinct in his memory. Besides, the scent, the burnt cinnamon smell that had drawn him through the first two rooms was at this very moment drifting across the short space that separated him from Diana Brack as she leaned forward rather earnestly.

'Look. You come here, you tell me you're investigating a murder. You won't tell me who. Yet you also won't tell me that it's Peter. You say I was seen, as though there were any secret in the fact of my friendship with him. You have, clearly, followed me here. Now, just what do you think has happened to Peter, and what do you think it has to do with me? I rather think I've a right to know.'

'I really don't know what has happened to him. Like you I'm concerned. I had hoped you'd be able to shed more light on his disappearance. It's really as simple as that. In fact,' Troy added, pulling his notebook from his overcoat pocket, 'if there's anything you can think of that might help us, I do hope you'll give me a call.'

He scribbled down Whitehall 1212, a number every sentient being in Britain knew, and as he did so watched her out of the corner of his eye. She glanced quickly off to her right to the half-open door into the next room. A look so fleeting as to be all but imperceptible. As Troy raised his eyes from the paper she was looking directly at him once more. She smiled and took the page from him, and he knew as certain as eggs were powdered that there was someone hiding in the next room.

§ 30

He gave it five minutes and then doubled back to the area steps of the house opposite. A quarter of an hour later the door of number 55 opened. Brack came out, stood on the pavement, looked up and down the street and turned back to the doorway. Troy heard a whispered 'all clear' and a tall, well-built man in a brown gabardine mackintosh, belted tightly at the waist, came down the steps and wrapped his arms around her. As they separated the man dipped his head forward to put on a trilby and in the light that poured from the open door Troy saw clearly who he was. It was the American Major he had seen in Zelig's outer office. He was in civvies, but he was quite unmistakable. He smiled at Brack in the same way he had smiled at Sergeant Tosca. The way the wolf smiled at Red Riding Hood.

Brack watched the American walk up the street. She stood too long in her affection for Troy's comfort. By the time she had closed the door and pulled the blackout to, Troy's quarry was out of sight. Certain he had heard the man's feet echo the length of the street Troy ran across Royal Hospital Road and stopped at the corner of Christchurch Street. There was no sign of him. He kept going north and came to the edge of Tedworth Gardens, a London square long since stripped of its railings and hedged in with a tangle of barbed wire and boards. Getting used to the darkness Troy could see that it was down to allotments and was dotted here and there with Nissen huts and Anderson shelters. He walked down between the strips of vegetable plots. Out of the darkness a voice spoke.

'Looking for the Major, old cock?'

Suddenly a face appeared in the glow of a cigar end as its owner dragged on the stub and brought it brightly to life. Troy went over. It was a huge, bald, fat man, in a Heavy Rescue blouse, just as Wildeve had described him. Sitting on the backless stump of an old chair. And there at his feet was a large white pig.

'Evenin',' said the man. And the pig added a grunt of its own by way of greeting. 'Turn right towards St Leonard's, then left into Smith Street, and you'll find yourself in the King's Road. Quickest way to Sloane Square Tube, old cock. If you run you should catch sight of the Major. Mind, you'd better not let him catch sight of you. You got copper written all over you.'

Troy didn't wait to ask how he knew. It was possible the old man was in cahoots and had been told to say just what he had said, but Troy had little time and no choice and hurried on to Smith Street. As he turned into the King's Road he wondered again. The man would have to be a magician to cook up a bluff like this. The street was full of people on foot and most of them seemed to be men in trilbies and mackintoshes. In weather like this most men might be seen in a mackintosh and trilby, but at least the American had the added distinction of height. There weren't many Englishmen over six feet two. He followed the old man's hint and set off in the direction of Sloane Square, walking briskly and hoping that he didn't run into the back of his man in the dark. By the time he crossed the second side street he felt pretty certain he had singled out the American from the small throng of men heading up the King's Road. They crossed the square only thirty feet apart and Troy saw him go into the Underground station. He waited in the street, long enough to let the American buy a ticket and and head down to the platforms. He followed halfway down the steps to the eastbound platform – the logical route into central London – and peered on to the open platform. There were half a dozen people right at the bottom of the steps. Enough for concealment. He joined the end of the crowd, turned up his collar and tried not to look in the obvious direction. When the train pulled in he would be first to step forward, but would not get in until he saw the American do so. One carriage apart would be best. He looked across the tracks at the other platform as he heard the rattle of an approaching westbound. The crowd on the other side instinctively edged forward. There, right at the front, was the American, looking up the line towards the train. Had he looked across the track he would have been looking directly at Troy. The train pulled in between them. Troy ran for the steps, across the bridge in the ticket hall and made it down the steps to the other side just in time to slip in as the doors hissed shut. The District line rose so near the surface that the train had been blacked out to meet ARP regulations – only small diamonds cut into the blackouts let out light. The darkness outside was infinitely preferable to the dim, muggy interior of the train. It was like stepping into a circle of hell. The carriage was full to capacity. Troy looked down the carriage. In the middle by the double doors the American was standing with his back to Troy. He was no more than twenty feet away. The train screeched into South Kensington, one of the open-air stations. The man was in the first half-dozen off and headed for the lift down to the Piccadilly line. The queue for the lift was long enough to make Troy gamble on a race down the spiral stairs to platform level. To follow in the same lift was impossible and to wait for the one behind ran too great a risk of losing him. Troy arrived at the bottom just as the lift doors opened – he waited at the edge of the stairwell and saw the American emerge and go down on to the northbound line, which would take him into the heart of London via Knightsbridge and Piccadilly.

At this level a walk along the platform meant competing with the nightly shelterers. Troy had almost forgotten the experience. He rarely used the Underground and had never taken shelter there. A hundred feet below the surface, thousands of Londoners were camping out with their bunk beds and their Primus stoves, safe from Hitler's bombs. This aspect of London life became part of folklore in the Blitz of 1940, and had made a sudden return with the heavy raids that had begun again in February. People no longer waited for the siren to announce the Luftwaffe's imminent arrival but took to the deep-level tubes as early as they could. Children bagged places for whole families from early morning, well in advance of the official permitted time in winter of 4 p.m. By the time of the last train the platforms, the corridors and even the stopped escalators would be littered with sleeping bodies. It was better organised second time around – metal rows of bunks, three tiers high, lined the platforms and chemical lavatories were stuck at either end. The overwhelming presence of two thousand-odd people in a small space, whatever the improvements in conditions, still made the open space preferable. A choice between the smell of humanity – heavily laden with disinfectant – and the smell of cordite, between the risk of death and the safety of what was a glorified dungeon by any other name. The spread of the sub-terraneans left little room for people still travelling. Once on the platform Troy could hardly move more than a few feet without protest from both shelterers and passengers. He got as close as he could, but the cries of 'who do you think you're shoving?' seemed too much like unwanted attention. He joined the narrow band of passengers closest to the track. He could only be at most a few feet away from the American. Behind him a young mother was trying to put a small girl to bed. Next to them a woman in her seventies was brewing tea. On a top bunk an old man already had his head down and was snoring loudly. Troy faced the adverts rather than look at a private life rendered embarrassingly public. It was probably, he often thought, why the English upper classes sent their children to public schools – and even why they were called public when they were so obviously exclusive – to teach them the value of privacy by forcing them to live out their formative years in public. Public baths, public bedtimes, public beatings. He could not resist the backward glance and looked over his shoulder at the mother and child. While the mother clearly had some self-consciousness about the matter, the little girl had none and chattered aimlessly as her mother folded her clothes and zipped her into a siren suit for sleeping.

Troy rode the train into London one coach away from the American. The sliding glass windows between the two coaches were down for ventilation and he could see across the gap into the next car. The man had the end seat by the door and had buried himself in a copy of the *Evening News*. The stations swept past – Hyde Park Corner, Green Park, Piccadilly Circus – and still the

American did not move. He looked up as the train pulled into Piccadilly Circus just to check the name, but returned at once to the contents of his newspaper. At Leicester Square and Covent Garden he did not even glance at the station names. Where was he going? Troy had fully expected him to alight at either Leicester Square or Piccadilly Circus – the obvious stations for the West End, for Rainbow Corner, the huge American Servicemen's Club in Piccadilly itself. As the train approached Holborn the American got up, shoved the newspaper into his pocket and stood by the doors. A second before they opened he gave a fastidious tug at the brim of his hat, then ducked and stepped out on to the platform as the door glided past. Holborn was worse than South Kensington. It was packed so tightly that passengers were all but fighting their way down to the exit, and the feeder tunnels were pouring yet more people on to the platform. Struggling to keep his man in sight Troy trod on a leg. It kicked back. Somebody yelled at him not to waste his time trying to get out – there was a raid on.

With his eyes on the disappearing back of the American Major Troy edged his way along. He passed what appeared to be a heated argument between a middle-aged cockney housewife and a uniformed American corporal. He kept going. The American had made better headway. Troy was within seconds of losing sight of him completely, when he heard the row just behind him explode with anger, and with it the unmistakable ring of danger.

'I'm telling you, lady, she's gotta have it.'

'Come orf it, she's only fifteen. Who yer tryin' ter kid?'

Troy instinctively turned. The corporal had seized a young woman by the upper arm and with his free hand was threatening the housewife. Troy looked back to see the American almost at the exit.

'Who am *I* trying to kid? She's had five quids out of me, and she's gotta have it!'

'You bastard. She's too young to be on the game, can't you see?'

'Frankly, lady, I don't give a damn. All I know is she came on to me like a real commando.'

The American disappeared into the exit tunnel. Troy turned just in time to see the corporal strike the woman in the face with a clenched fist. He ran, regardless of people underfoot and grabbed the corporal by his free arm. The man let go of the girl and pushed Troy backwards over a huddle of bodies. As Troy struggled to his feet the man was dragging the girl away. She screamed.

'Mum! I didn't! Honest I didn't!'

Troy dived for the man's legs but failed to bring him down. He didn't have the weight to rugby tackle a six-foot, fourteen-stone man. He felt himself dragged to his feet as the man seized him by the lapels. He smashed Troy backwards into the row of bunks. Troy got off one punch straight to the nose. It stopped the corporal momentarily as both hands left Troy and covered his face. All around them women were screaming. Before Troy could duck out, the man had him by the throat and pulled him into a side tunnel that led to the emergency spiral staircase. He banged Troy against the wall, pulled him off and swung him round full circle, banged him two or three times more, swung him full circle again and slammed him hard against the wall directly opposite the staircase. He let go and began to lash out wildly with his fists. Troy slumped, brought up a knee into the man's testicles and as the hands stopped flailing at him neatly slipped one end of his handcuffs over the man's wrist and closed it. He clipped the other over his own left wrist and with his free hand got off three or four hard blows to the face. The American collapsed on top of him, and suddenly all the world was dark and black and hot and smelt unbearably of cordite. And the screaming stopped.

§ 31

Troy was crawling. It was a large open, muddy field under a blood-red moon. Away on the hill stood a figure he could only see as a silhouette, and Troy knew that he should move towards it. He tried to stand but found the mud sucked too powerfully on his hands, so he crawled on as the figure beckoned. His nightshirt clung wet and sticky to his back. Overhead the sky lit up with the searing glare of rockets. A man stood over him. His face resolving from a blur to recognisable features as the moon rolled away into the light of day and the figure on the hill vanished into transparency.

'Freddie?'

It was Wildeve. It was Wildeve. What in hell was he doing here?

'Jack? What are you doing here?'

Had he spoken? It seemed the words had not come from him.

'Freddie. Do you know where you are? You're in the Middlesex Hospital in Mortimer Street. You've been in an air raid.'

'What?'

'You got hit by a bomb.'

The room behind Wildeve shaped itself into form. It was a small hospital ward. He could see the beds opposite. Wildeve sat on the edge of his bed.

'Sorry, Jack, I wasn't quite in the world.'

'You were almost out of it permanently.'

'Tell me what happened.'

'You were found in the corridor at the foot of the emergency stairs at Holborn station. Do you remember that?'

Troy nodded.

'A bomb hit the air shaft. Went straight down the spiral stairs like a hot knife through butter. Must have exploded about fifty feet above you. Turned the stairs into instant shrapnel. We found you handcuffed to an American soldier. He saved your life. Completely cushioned the blast. There was almost nothing left of his back. One piece of the stairs went right through him and stopped just short of your chest. He died outright. So did the others.'

Troy was aware that Wildeve was almost whispering to avoid spreading alarm with his grisly tale, but felt he had to ask. It all seemed so vague.

'Others? What others?'

Wildeve looked around him to be certain he wasn't being overheard and leaned closer to Troy.

'The shelterers.'

'What . . . ?'

'Freddie, everyone in that corridor died except you. Most of the people on the platforms were killed. The Rescue boys reckon the total will be around six hundred and fifty. You've had a very lucky escape. They found you handcuffed to a corpse!'

Wildeve paused. Troy sighed deeply, from tiredness not shock.

The chance in six hundred hardly registered. There was a deep, numb throbbing in the back of his head. He saw in his mind's eye the young American slamming him against the tunnel wall over and over again and felt the pain in his head and shoulders – a pain that had hit him so quickly he had not known he'd felt it until now.

'What were you doing there?'

'I was following the American. He came out of Brack's house. I followed him to Holborn.'

'Damn. I suppose that lead dies with him,' said Wildeve.

'No. Not the same man.'

'What?'

'Not the same man. Another American. The man I was with wasn't the man I was following. He got away from me. Down the exit tunnel.'

'Lucky blighter.'

Troy tapped Wildeve with his leg. He got up, and Troy threw back the covers and tried to swing his legs off the bed. His head swam and the room turned the same shade of bloody red he had seen in his dreams. Wildeve placed his hands gently on Troy's shoulders and pushed him back.

'Don't be stupid, Freddie. You've had an almighty blow to the head. They want to keep you in for another day or so.'

'Another? Jack, how long have I been here?'

'Three days.'

'Oh God.' Troy sighed. 'Jack, you'd better get over to Tite Street and watch for him.'

'I've been at Tite Street most of the time. The only reason I'm not there now is that Diana is not an early riser. It's only seven in the morning. Not that I'd expect you to know that. In fact you probably don't know it's Saturday morning. Now who is this chap?'

Troy told him.

'You didn't mention any American but Zelig,' said Wildeve.

'I didn't think it was important. But now it's very important. We must find out who he is.'

'Well, it's got to be me. You're going to be out of it for a while.' Wildeve paused, trying to take in the pieces Troy had dropped into his lap. 'Do you think he saw you?'

Troy remembered seeing the American gliding slowly and silently away from him, saw himself in pursuit, then leaping over the prone bodies, racing to meet the look of terror on that young girl's face. Had she survived? Had she been blasted to pieces or burnt alive? Wildeve touched his shoulder, dragging him back to the present.

'What?'

'I said, do you think he saw you?'

'No. I'm almost certain he didn't. He took a devious route into London, but I think that was just instinctive caution. He wasn't looking for a tail.'

'Do you think he's our man?'

'I don't know, but he's there, isn't he? It would be an odd coincidence for him to be in Zelig's office and at Brack's house. And he hid from me at Brack's. He didn't want to be seen. Zelig wouldn't say anything about any possibility of a connection between the Germans and American operations, but somebody tore a strip off Neville Pym for letting me get that close. We now have that connection. The American, Diana Brack, Wolinski, to Brand and von Ranke.'

'You know, Freddie, I haven't a clue where all this is leading. I really couldn't follow what you told Stan on Monday. I doubt that he could.'

Troy tried to speak, feeling all the time the pain in his head get worse, begin to form above his left eye into a red, tumbling cloud, blown across his vision by the propellent power of his words.

'I . . . I can't tell you at this stage. It's not clear in my own mind. Not clear at all. Do you see what I mean? It's pieces, only pieces.'

He had no idea whether Wildeve believed him. He prayed he would not press the point now.

Wildeve stood up.

'I ought to be going,' he said. 'I'll look in tomorrow with your clothes.'

'My clothes?'

'They had to be cleaned. Your overcoat's come up OK, but your shirt's had it. It was impossible to get the blood out. I've ordered a new one from your man in Jermyn Street. Onions stumped up the coupons. He says you owe him, but I doubt he gets through a month's clothing coupons in a year. He'll be in to see you later, by the way.'

Troy sighed again. He didn't relish seeing Onions, who would ask a dozen questions for each one Wildeve asked, and was unlikely in the extreme to be as easily put off. The red cloud hovered in the corner of his eye. He put a hand up to his forehead to see if it would brush away. He rubbed at his temple and felt the gritty residue of the blast. His hair was full of flakes of concrete. For days afterwards he seemed to find it everywhere.

§ 32

He had stood so long in the cold and the dark he had come to wish he could stamp his feet and flap his arms like a cabbie, just to keep his circulation going – but it would, almost by definition, be a poor attempt at shadowing anyone. Instead he leaned and yawned in the porch of number 23 St James's Square, saw readers at the London Library go up the square, saw the staff come down as they left for the evening, and showed his warrant card to a constable.

As the man stopped on the pavement to look up at him, Troy was struck by just how ridiculous a bobby looked in a cape and helmet and how glad he himself had been to get out of uniform. Glistening with rain and spattered with mud, this constable clearly felt nothing of the sort. He looked directly into Troy's face and spoke firmly. 'Waiting for someone, are we?'

Why, oh why, thought Troy, does no one call me sir? He quickly held up his card. The constable angled his shaded lantern towards it. 'I'm on duty,' said Troy, and pocketed the card. 'Keep out of the way.'

'As you wish,' replied the constable. 'If you need me I'll be round again in forty minutes.' He plodded slowly on, his boots ringing squarely on the pavement, glancing quickly into each doorway as he passed.

Troy let his gaze linger on the man's back a fraction too long. In the blackout even a quarter moon was difficult to see by, and as he looked up again a woman in uniform was passing out of sight on the far side of the Square. If it was her he'd have to run to catch her. As he reached Norfolk House she was turning right into Charles II Street. He couldn't even be sure it was her, and in the effort to catch up he lost all the feelings that had plagued him as he waited. Why was he hiding? He'd have to speak to her sooner or later. What was he going to say to her? Still he had no idea, but finding her in the first place now seemed all important. For no reason Troy could see, she crossed the street, glanced at the traffic and crossed back again. High heels seemed to be no obstacle to a fast walk – she moved rapidly in and out of the shadows, setting a pace Troy found hard to match. She had almost reached Lower Regent Street before Troy arrived at the thirty- to forty-feet gap at which he felt comfortable when tailing. She walked into Lower Regent Street and he lost sight of her. Seconds later she reappeared walking quickly back towards him, looking straight at him. There was no turning he could take and it was obvious she'd seen him. She came right up to him and stopped only four or five feet away. But for her stilettos she could not have been more than four foot eleven, and in the tight precise uniform she was puffing herself up like a young pigeon, ready for the confrontation. Troy seemed to tower over her in a way that did nothing to intimidate her.

'You following me?'

Troy fumbled for his warrant card. 'Troy,' he said feebly, 'Sergeant Troy.'

She glanced only momentarily at the card and looked back at his face, hard and inquisitive.

'So how come you're not in uniform?'

'We don't all wear uniforms.'

'Aha.' She paused. 'I'm a sergeant too.'

'I noticed.'

With three conspicuous stripes on each olive-green arm he could hardly not notice. She half-turned as if to walk on and then turned back. She looked him down and then up, fixing her eyes on him again. They were a clear chestnut brown with not the slightest speck of green or hazel. She seemed to be trying to read his intentions in his face. Troy wished he knew what they were. The rosebud mouth flickered into something he took for a smile.

'Ah well – no point in following on like some cheap gumshoe. We might as well go together. Your place or mine?'

Troy said nothing. He'd no idea what she was talking about. She stared, she smiled. Still Troy said nothing – she walked on. Troy watched almost to the street corner. Zelig was right. The skirt was far too tight. Her backside moved like two ostrich eggs in a bag. She came back.

'Are we gonna fuck or what?' she said.

'I ... er ...' Troy almost choked, never having heard that word spoken by a woman outside of drunken scenes in police stations.

'Now this is stupid. Or maybe you're stupid. For Chrissake we can't do it on the sidewalk. Come on, shake a leg as you guys say. I don't live too far away – you'd only of had to follow me to Orrnnjj Street.'

Troy wrestled with Orrnnjj Street and realised she meant Orange Street – a narrow, gently serpentine lane that ran between the Haymarket and the Charing Cross Road – two pubs, a chapel and a short row of Georgian houses. They crossed Lower Regent Street and the Haymarket almost in step. Once or twice she looked at Troy as though she thought he was a complete fool – very much what he felt. Into Orange Street the light disappeared suddenly and completely and the air seemed cold and quiet. He could hear the pick-pock of her high-heeled shoes on the pavement, but he couldn't see her. She stopped. He bumped into her and heard her curse softly. Then she was rattling keys at a door and a piece of the night seemed to open up and swallow them.

'Stay close behind me, right? Top floor, five flights, and there's no light 'cos there's no blackout. OK?'

He followed blindly up two flights of stairs, groping his way hand over hand on the banister rail. Rain and moonlight slanted in through a broken pane on the second floor and he caught sight of her standing in the fraction of light, invisible from the wasp waist upwards. He tripped and banged a kneecap loudly on the stairs.

'I told you. Stay close behind or you'll break your goddam neck before we're halfway up.'

She bent down into the light so that he could see her face, and seized his right hand with her left.

'You must be the clumsiest, dumbest bastard ever tried to pick me up.'

With a gentle strength she guided and pulled him to a small doorway on the top landing. She rattled the keys once more.

'Why did you wait in the rain all that time? You know where I work. OK. We're in.'

She flicked on the light and slammed the door shut. Troy found himself in a large bed-sitting-room that spanned the whole top floor of the house. At the front and back the roof came down almost to meet the floor, but in its vast centre the room held a large double bed, a dining table, a battered horsehair sofa, a wind-up gramophone and a wide, untidy scattering of woman's clothing.

'No apologies for the mess. I work most of the time. Come to think of it, if you'd told me last week you were coming I could have told you I don't get off till past nine.'

She kicked off her shoes and crossed to a large Kelvinator refrigerator. She'd stopped looking at Troy and he followed her with his eyes. She peeled off her battledress, aimed it at the sofa, gave Troy a grin and yanked open the fridge door.

'How do you feel about bourbon?'

She almost disappeared into the fridge.

'I don't know. I've never tried it.'

It was physically impossible for her to look over the fridge door. She darted him a quick glance round the side and rummaged in the ice-box.

'I got ice here. And I got a good Tennessee sour mash somewhere around.' The door hissed and sucked shut. She put two glasses and an aluminium ice-tray down on the table. 'The PX is pretty good. It's not always Tennessee, but . . . goddam it there's a war on.'

She paused, looked him up and down once more, fixing him where he stood, lamely silent with his hands in his pockets like a recalcitrant schoolboy.

'You gonna take your coat off or what?'

For reasons he refused even to guess at, simply unbuttoning his sodden black overcoat in front of her reminded Troy of undressing before his mother aged ten or eleven, past the stage where he needed her help or supervision but too young to convince her of his need for privacy. He pressed his palm against a large cast-iron radiator and draped the coat over its feeble heat to dry. When he turned she'd found the bourbon and was drowning two lots of ice-cubes in a generous four fingers of sour mash. She pushed a glass across the table to him. Without coat or shoes she seemed even smaller. Troy felt his slight five foot eight to be lumbering and ox-like. He picked up the glass of whiskey for the sake of something to do with his hands. She took a large gulp of whiskey and sighed with the pleasure of it – eyes and lips still smiling at him.

'First of the day. Always the best.'

For a minute or more they faced each other across the table. She seemed animated, even when stood stock-still and quiet. Troy felt grotesquely that he must be blushing or trembling. Only the width of the table separated them, but he felt it would take an earthquake, or – much more likely – a bomb, to move him. Only a single sixty-watt bulb lit the room, half-muted by its shade and several years of dust, yet Troy felt as though a searchlight had picked him out. Her gaze seemed warm, open, honest and searing. She belted back the rest of her drink and clunked the glass down. Troy sipped slowly at his. In a swift movement she peeled off her non-regulation blouse and it floated down on top of her battledress. Her bra was non-regulation black silk, and as her skirt pooled around her ankles Troy could see that the pants matched in an expensive, black-market, strictly non-issue set. Even the stockings were real not painted.

'Wassamatterbaby? Cat gotcha tongue? Would you like me to put the light out? Is that it?'

'Yes.'

'Yes what?'

'Yes I'd like you to put the light out.'

In the darkness, groping towards the bed, he heard the sudden swish as she tore back the covers.

'There's just one thing – what's your name?'

'Troy.'

'I know that, dummy – what's your Christian name?'

'Frederick.'

'OK. So I'll call you Troy. You can call me Lara.'

Troy heard the rapid double snap of elastic and the springs creaked as she lay back on the bed.

'Lara?' he said.

'Yeah. Like short for Larissa.'

'Sounds Russian.'

'Yeah. But only on my mother's side.'

He pulled off a shoe. He was wet to the skin. Suddenly, freed from her gaze, buried in his elemental darkness, it seemed a relief to be getting out of his clothes.

§ 33

Nearer the dawn a bomb moved Troy. A dull repeated whumpf somewhere off to the south woke him and drew him to the window. He groped for his shirt at the foot of the bed, slipped it on and peeled back a corner of one of the blackouts – he could see part of Nelson's column and the square as it swept over towards Charing Cross. Somewhere beyond Lambeth an orange-red glow flickered on the skyline.

'Hey. You OK?'

Her voice startled him.

'Yes, I'm fine. There's a raid on. I was just looking.'

'Is it close?'

'No. New Cross or Lewisham, I should think. Somewhere out that way.'

'Thank God for that. I hate going down the subway in the middle of the night. It stinks. You know that? It really stinks.'

'Half of London sleeps down there permanently.'

The dull whumpf again – then the burst of flame from the same direction. A single heavy blockbuster followed by smaller incendiaries. He turned back to look at her. The light from the open blind cut a cheese wedge into the room. She was looking at him, again.

'Why d'you put your shirt on?'

'I don't know,' he lied.

'Come over here.'

Troy moved slowly towards her, stepping into the point of the wedge of light.

'Take it off. No buts. Take it off!'

He sat on the bed and tossed the shirt behind him.

'Ain't gonna bite. Least nowhere I haven't already.'

She traced his ribcage on the left side, bringing her fingers up to the shoulder and down his left arm.

'Baby – you're a mess of scars.'

'Occupational hazard,' he said simply.

'What are you? A flyer? Soldier?'

'I don't follow . . .'

'Sergeant you said. Sergeant of what?'

'I'm a police officer.'

'Whaaaat?' She sat bolt upright, almost screaming.

'I showed you my card.'

'So? Ace of Clubs. Jack of Diamonds – I didn't look.'

She flopped back on to the pillows, her fists pounding her temples in a mockery of amazement.

'My God. My God. I screwed a cop.'

'There's a first time for everything,' said Troy.

'So there is.'

She sat upright and kissed him on the lips. 'OK. So now tell me about the scars.' Her fingers stroked a weal on his ribs, an inch or two below the nipple.

'That's a knife wound.'

'Flick knife?'

'No . . . actually it was a potato peeler.'

He could see her grinning.

'I got between a wife-beating drunken Irishman and his beaten drunken wife. She stabbed me with a potato peeler.'

She bit her lower lip, restraining the laugh and silently moved her fingers over to his arm.

'Bullet from a Webley point thirty-eight. I went to arrest a member of Her Majesty's Household Cavalry, who tried to deter me with his service revolver.'

'But you got him?'

'I got him.'

'You're not such a chickenshit after all.'

'Whatever made you think I was?'

'Oh – you should have seen yourself a couple of hours ago!'

'Point taken.'

Her hand slid across his left thigh to the knee. 'And this little piggy?'

'Nothing to do with the job. My brother pushed me off a bicycle when I was eleven.'

'What's all the new stuff?'

'Eh?'

'All these scabby little nicks on your hands.'

Troy held his hands, backs up, in front of him. He could see nothing. Rubbing one with the other he could feel the cuts and weals the blast of brick and concrete had left there. He remembered how he got them – it brought him back to his subject, slightly amazed that for an hour or two at least he had allowed it to slip from his mind.

'That was a bomb blast on the Underground. Actually, I was following a friend of yours when it happened.'

'A friend of mine?'

'The Major. The one who sat on your desk. You lit his cigarette for him.'

Troy felt her squirm deep into the bed, avoiding his words, pulling the blankets higher.

'So ... you're not off duty. Tell me, do you always fuck on the company time?'

'I just thought you might know who he was.'

'Sure I know him. But you gotta wait till morning. I tell you now, you might arrest me before I get my beauty sleep.'

Troy walked around the foot of the bed and slipped in the other side. For a minute or two they lay like spoons in a cutlery drawer, then she wriggled and jammed her backside up against him, and with a half-audible mutter of 'lousy copper' she sighed her way into sleep. Before he too dropped off Troy felt almost certain she was faintly snoring.

§ 34

The whistle of a full kettle rattling on the iron hob woke Troy with a wrench. He looked down the room. Tosca sat on a stool in front of the ironing board, reading a battered copy of *Huckleberry Finn*. She was dressed even to the tie, but for the skirt that lay draped across the board awaiting the long rev-up of a primitive electric iron.

'Welcome to the world, sunbeam,' said Tosca.

She splashed a pint of water into the coffee-pot. 'Today we have real coffee.'

'Good Lord.'

'From the PX like everything else. Stick with me kid an' I could show you a good time.'

'Overpaid, oversexed and over here,' said Troy.

'Come again?'

'Gives new lie to an old cliché,' he muttered.

'Oversexed, eh?'

She picked up her book and looked at him over the top, a caricature of the seductive secretary – Katharine Hepburn or Barbara Stanwyck.

'I always read ten pages of Huck. Every day. Kinda like my Bible. Reminds me of home.'

'You're from Missouri?'

'Don't be stupid, I'm from New York.'

She slapped the book down and brought two cups and the coffee-pot to the bedside. Curiously elegant in olive green and high heels. Curiously naked without her skirt.

'I'm from Manhattan. Or did you think I talked like this for the fun of it?'

Troy eased himself up in the bed, once more ludicrously conscious of his nakedness; the whiteness of his skin in the morning light.

'I seen men's nipples before, you know.'

He let go of the sheet and made an effort to be less shy.

'Now – about Jimmy.'

'Who? Aagh!' The coffee cup burnt his fingers and he thrust it quickly back at the table.

'Jimmy. Jimmy Wayne. The guy you were so indelicate as to grill me about at an intimate moment.'

'The Major. Yes. Tell me. What's his regiment ... I mean unit?'

'OSS.'

Troy stared, not understanding.

'Office of Strategic Services. Dirty tricks. Nasty things overseas. You know. That sort of thing.'

'And here?'

'Here nothing. They're just based here.'

'Does he work for Zelig?'

'Sort of. But sort of not. Like they're ... equals.'

'And who does Zelig work for?'

'Directly? For David Bruce, the OSS station head here, and before you ask the whole shebang is run by Donovan. Known as Wild Bill. Don't ask me why.'

'And he works for ...?'

'For Ike, of course. Dammit we all work for Ike one way or another. Why, what's Jimmy done?'

She swilled back coffee so hot Troy still found it scalding and returned to her skirt. Three or four deft strokes of the iron and she had the pleats in line and was stepping into the skirt before Troy had worked out what to tell her. She turned her back to him and pointed.

'There's a hook and eye thing at the back I never can reach ... can you ...?'

Troy leaned towards her, fingers fumbling.

'I think it's all that makes a girl marry. Just to have someone around to do up the fasteners at the back. Still not gonna answer me, eh? Boy you expect a lot.'

Tosca slipped on her battledress, peered into the wardrobe mirror, running a slither of bright red lipstick across her pout. She blew him a kiss and headed for the door.

'Let yourself out, copper. Slam it good and hard. And when you finally decide to tell me Jimmy's been monkeying with food coupons, let me know. Maybe I could help. Same time tonight?'

Before he could answer she was gone. Troy heard her feet dance down the stairs, and felt the house shake as she banged the street door. He reached for the coffee, sipping cautiously at it, wondering what he was going to tell her and why Huck Finn should remind anyone of New York and feeling that familiar, troubling mixture of guilt and happiness wrap itself upon him.

§ 35

As a child Troy was much troubled by his sisters. He had no way of grasping the twists, the utter volte-faces of character that could inflict such vicissitudes upon him and upon the family as a whole. Only when his brother gave him an edition of Saki for his thirteenth birthday did he realise that Sasha and Masha were each both Aunt and Clovis within a single, shared character. They could be, beyond all prediction, first authoritarian, displaying a governessy lack of humour, and then mischievous, undermining all they might stand for as Aunt with a Clovis-like taste for trouble and an acid wit.

Now they turned up on his doorstep in the first calm of early evening. Solicitous of his welfare. They'd called the Yard only to be told he was off sick. Now Masha fussed about his kitchen, opened the doors of all the cupboards and made herself insufferable. Sasha tidied his bedroom, picking his clothes off the floor and lingering nosily over his shirt, clucking sternly over the lipstick on the collar, and warning him off women who wore cheap perfume. Then the twist – just what he was not expecting.

'We're going out.'

'What?'

'Out, my boy. Out, out, out! There's a new concert on at the Adelphi. The new work from this Tippett chap and you shall accompany us.'

The 'shall' was a defining archaism. It allowed of no possible disagreement. Every so often the social bug seized one sister or the other out in Hertfordshire where they had lived in self-imposed exile with Troy's mother since their husbands volunteered – Hugh for the navy, where he now captained a minesweeper, and Lawrence for the army, for whom he did some mysterious staff job at the War Office – and they would breeze manless into London feeling deprived and out of it, insistent on knowing what was what, and where anyone who was anyone was to be found. Not that Troy knew, so they would whisk him off to one of their traditional haunts, to the Four Hundred in Piccadilly, the Millroy in Berkeley Square or the Bon Viveur in Shepherd Market, to wave at minor royalty and to be hugged and smothered by the expansive bodies and personalities of European exiles. Troy hated every minute of it. Became easily bored with the Count of this or Prince that. Hated any restaurant or club they chose, almost on principle, and found nothing cheering in the latest craze to hit the sisters – contemporary music. He would often take calls at the Yard from them in the Wigmore Hall or the National Gallery, for which they expected him to drop everything, murder included, for the pleasure of lunchtime with Myra Hess. He usually declined and knew he could risk their displeasure by hanging up, as they had the combined memory span of the average dog. He had never heard of a composer called Tippett but he knew it meant a tuneless evening of scraping catgut.

'No,' he said. 'I've something else on.'

'Oh,' said Sasha. 'Miss Lipstick I presume?'

He had silently promised to see Tosca at nine. He realised this only as he tried to think of a lie to tell them. He had recalled only his silence not the assent which it had become for him. He had no idea what Tosca expected, but knew now that left to his own devices he would turn up at Orange Street at nine. He could not use the truth, however fresh from the mould of thought, as an excuse. The last thing he wanted was his sisters' involvement in any further aspect of his life.

They arrived at the Adelphi with ten minutes to spare, and he found they had taken a box from which to see and be seen by all their friends. He hated their eccentricity, for much the same reasons he relished Nikolai's and even Kolankiewicz's. It was so very unEnglish. They swung their moods with a Russian whimsicality, overbearing or overfriendly, and dressed in a manner that was a joke. They looked like little Anna Kareninas, identical to a T in their blacks and velvets, in their high-laced boots and their winter muffs. He would not play piggy in the middle and sat on Masha's left.

In the little time they had left she endeavoured to explain to him what the music was about.

'*A Child of Our Time* is about this Polish–Jewish refugee fleeing the Nazis.'

The notion that music was or could be 'about' something was not an idea Troy readily accepted, but he listened patiently to the music and much to his surprise he found he rather liked it. Then the choir came in with a chorus of Negro spiritual – singing 'Steal away'.

He leaned close to Masha. 'I thought it was about the Jews,' he said.

'It is. This is sort of about slavery and freedom. The Negroes sort of stand for the Jews in this bit.'

'Stand for?'

'They are the Jews, then. The composer sees them as symbolic of one race enslaving another. Taking away their status as human beings.'

'That's what I call a strained analogy,' said Troy.

He looked around from the near-global vantage point they had given him by taking a centre box in the dress circle.

Across to the extreme right a woman had leaned forward resting her hands on the balcony rail and her chin on her hands. Troy leaned across his sisters and took Sasha's opera glasses from her lap. He focused on the woman across the pit. Her eyes were closed, she was smiling serenely as though enraptured by the power of the music, the undeniably dramatic swell of voices – 'Steal away, now, Steal away' – and it was Diana Brack. And just behind her was a man, smoking a cigarette, halfway into the shadow of the box.

The house lights rose with the applause at the end of Tippett's piece. Troy picked up the opera glasses again. Brack sat back and the lights revealed the face of Major Wayne, chatting to her and doing up the buttons on his mackintosh. Troy dropped the glasses and ran. He estimated three doors from the end of the row to correspond to the box they sat in, and as he rounded the curve in the corridor he could see that the door was open. He took the steps three at a time and reached the ground floor just as the stalls released a flood of people into the foyer. He elbowed his way through the crowd and rushed out into the unlit street. He looked up the Strand and down it. He could see no sign of the American. A needle in a haystack would be understatement. He stood on the steps, reluctant to give up the pursuit as a bad job. The audience flowed out to either side of him, swamping the street in the sound of chatter. A hand pinched at his upper arm, Masha tugged him gently in the direction of the foyer,

'There you are. I wondered where you'd got to. Now you do remember Diana, don't you?'

She was looking off over his shoulder. He turned around and there was Brack, pleasantly nodding and smiling at Sasha's inane banter. She smiled him her wide smile – the perfect teeth again – and Masha simply bridged the gap by asking the same question.

'Diana. You do remember my little brother, don't you?'

Brack extended her hand. He had little choice but to take it.

'Of course I remember Freddie. Though it must be years and years. My how you've grown. I should think it must be twenty years. No, no. I have it. I have it. It was the year of the strike. 1926. I was sixteen, you must have been eleven or twelve and you'd been given a bicycle for your birthday. The girls brought me home from school to stay for a fortnight that summer, and you had such a tussle learning to ride that bike. You fell off and grazed your knee and you cried so and I bathed it and bandaged it for you. Surely you remember?'

He remembered the pain. What she called a graze had required eight stitches. He remembered a young woman with gentle hands and exotic scent who hand-cleaned the wound in warm water and disinfectant and embarrassed him with the fuss and had kissed him not on the cheek but on the lips when she had done and turned embarrassment to sexual confusion. He remembered the bicycle and the smell of the carbide lamp, and with it the added memory of that stinking charnel house in Stepney that had reeked of carbide gas. What he did not remember was Diana Brack.

He felt more than faintly foolish to realise that she had known all along who he was. It had, he was sure, no real bearing on the case, but it made him feel more and more that her calm and assurance when he had interviewed her was the sang-froid, the arrogance of someone who was playing a game for two people in the conceit that only one of them knew the rules. How far did her arrogance go? Above the law? Pursuit now was pointless. Brack would be looking over her shoulder and he could not let her see him following Wayne. Knowing about Wayne was the one thing he had that she didn't. It was not to be wasted fighting through the crowds of West End theatreland as discreetly as a bull in a china shop. For the while he had lost Wayne – again. He looked at his watch. It was just after ten. With any luck he could put his sisters in a cab to his father's town house in Hampstead and be in bed in half an hour. The idea that he was due, overdue, at Orange Street had slipped completely from his mind.

§ 36

Wildeve had a good mental image of Major Wayne. Although what use Troy's description of him as having 'bedroom eyes' was to be in the blackout was altogether another matter. But mostly he was sitting down the area steps in Tite Street on the assumption that any tall man emerging from number 55 was likely to be the American. He sat all evening on the rashness of such assumption, uncertain as to whether Diana Brack was in or out. The mist slid off the Thames curling up the street to put a chill in his bones, and he was nodding off at about ten thirty when the slam of the door opposite woke him. He peeked out above the pavement. A cab was moving off and the light behind the door was momentarily visible before the blackout was smoothed down. Dammit, he thought, someone had come in and he'd not so much as caught a glimpse. Half an hour later he heard the door open again. A tall man emerged and walked off towards the river, a wraith vanishing into mist. He stepped quietly into the street. Wayne was standing at the corner of Tite Street and the Chelsea Embankment. As long as he stood there Wildeve could hardly move. Wayne's hand shot up. Wildeve saw a cab pull over to him, and the American got in. Wildeve raced for the Embankment to see the taxi slowly pulling out into traffic. By sheer good luck there was another cab cruising slowly towards him only a dozen yards away. He flagged it down.

'Where to, guv?' said the cabman.

'Follow the cab in front,' said Wildeve.

The man looked back at him in silent, contemptuous disbelief.

'Honestly. I'm a policeman,' said Wildeve without the strength of conviction.

Wayne's cab turned into Chelsea Bridge Road. The traffic was light at this time of night but the mist that had wafted off the river now seemed to have the makings of a London pea-souper, and the two cabs in tandem moved slowly up Sloane Street to emerge in Knightsbridge. The smog took on the characteristic yellow hue of a killing cloud.

'This ain't easy you know,' the cabman said over his shoulder to Wildeve. 'You can't see your hand in front of your face, let alone another bleedin' cab!'

Wildeve said nothing. He rolled down the window to see out, but all he achieved was to let a dogtail of the smothering London smog slither in. For all his protestation the cabman seemed to have cat's eyes. Wildeve was no longer sure where they were in the tangled streets of the city. He felt that the level of traffic noise after a right turn was probably fair indication of Park Lane, but he soon lost all sense of geography as the cab cut a zig-zag course across the small streets of Marylebone to the north of Marble Arch. He felt tempted to ask.

'We haven't lost him have we?' he said, leaning over to the glass divide.

'You can thank your lucky stars if we haven't. I reckon that's your man just up ahead, but I'm not about to swear on a Bible.'

'Do you know where we are?'

'Manchester Square, guv'nor. That I will swear to.'

§ 37

The cab inched around the north-western corner of the square and ground to a halt in the stalled traffic. The smog was so thick that most sat it out in silence. Only the odd burst of pointless honking punctuated the enveloping stillness. Anxiously the young policeman slipped open the door and leaned out to see what he could see. Odd points of light bled into the darkness like running watercolours. He could tell nothing from it. The door was yanked from him and as he fumbled to keep his footing he was blasted back into the seat by a gunshot. He was dead before he hit the leather. A yellow tongue of creeping smog curled in through the open door to lick the corpse.

§ 38

Troy slept a rich, warm, painless sleep. A fierce hammering at the door fought through to him – more like the rattle of dried peas on a tin drum. He found himself in bed in his underpants and socks. He grabbed a blanket and all but fell downstairs. He pulled back the door a fraction and the night was a mustard cloud wrapping itself around the colossal bulk of a night sergeant from the Yard.

'Mr Troy. You'd better get dressed. There's been a murder in Manchester Square. I've a car at the end of the street waiting for you. I did try to phone but you've not been answering.'

'Sorry,' said Troy, and let the door swing back as he headed for the stairs. Pulling on his trousers he yelled down, 'Where in Manchester Square?'

'In the Square itself. I'm told it was right in the street. I can give you the details as we drive.'

Troy fumbled around for the rest of his clothes, pulled a grubby shirt over his head and caught a faint whiff of scent. Tosca's? He had picked up the shirt Sasha had dropped disdainfully on the bed. It was strange how the scent lingered and provoked. He had not noticed it at all on Tosca. Whereas Brack's was as vivid as an image. He had only to think the smell to feel it. Only to feel the smell to see the woman. But then he wasn't thinking of Tosca as a suspect for anything — he knew scent much the same way Kolankiewicz knew human offal. He snapped out of the reverie and looked at his watch. He had come in from the concert with his head splitting and fallen straight into bed. It was nearly midnight. He'd been asleep for less than an hour, but it had felt like five years on another planet.

They stepped into the street and instinctively Troy pulled his coat tighter around him, turned up the collar and sunk his hands deep in the pockets. He felt the grit of the bomb blast under his fingernails, and for a split second the blood-red cloud appeared over his eye and he winced at the pain of it, before mentally pushing it over the horizon.

'I know,' said the sergeant, reading Troy's expression wrong and leading the way out into St Martin's Lane. 'I've never seen anything like it. This bugger'll choke off more than the Luftwaffe tonight.'

§ 39

A Special in uniform stood by the open door of a taxi, wrapped in his cape. Troy begged a torch off the night sergeant and told the car to go. There'd be enough chaos with two pairs of police feet and a photographer to deal with. Troy looked at the bobby. He was smiling. It seemed absurd, but he was smiling. He was fat and fiftyish and he was smiling. It was just possible that if you volunteered as a Special there was nothing better than a good murder.

'Well?' Troy said.

'I've touched nothing. I've stood guard since I heard the cry go up.'

The phrase seemed a quaint leftover from the peelers. It irritated Troy. He thrust the torch at him and climbed into the back of the cab.

The Special peered over Troy's shoulder. 'Struth,' he said as the torch hit the mess of blood and brain in the back of the cab. 'Struth!'

There was little left of the face. One bullet had caught him in the cheek, another in the mouth and a third had entered at the forehead and taken off the back of the head. Most of his brains were spread across the rear window, and his clothes were drenched in blood. The body lolled against the seat, the head tilted back, lifeless eyes gazing upward.

'Hold that damn torch steady,' said Troy. 'I want to go through his pockets.'

Troy closed the eyes, fished into the inside jacket pocket and pulled out a wallet and a piece of blood-soaked cardboard. He wiped it clean with the fleshy side of his hand.

'He was a policeman,' he said softly. 'It's a Met warrant card.'

'Struth!' said the Special again.

Troy peered at the name on the card, and ducked back out of the cab. The Special was still smiling. Troy realised it was his natural expression, as fixed as rictus.

'Where's my constable?' he asked.

'Behind the hedge,' replied the Special. 'Tossing his supper. It's hit him bad.'

'Get him.'

Troy climbed back into the cab. He patted down the man's pockets and tried to breathe shallowly to avoid the stench of death. He was searching for the policeman's notebook. It wasn't there.

'Freddie?' came a bleating voice from outside.

Troy faced an ashen Wildeve on the pavement.

'Who was he, Freddie?'

'Miller. Melvyn Miller. Detective Sergeant. Special Branch. Are you OK to talk?'

'I think so.'

'You'd better tell me what happened.'

Troy set the Special to guard the cab and took Wildeve over to the edge of the park.

'I'm sorry, Freddie. I didn't see a damn thing. The traffic had stopped completely. I gave it a couple of minutes and the urge to get out and walk hit me and of course it dawned on me then that Wayne was probably feeling the same, so I got out just to see if he'd quit the cab and set off. I was two cars behind this one. I thought this was Wayne's cab. So did my cabbie. He swears this is the cab he followed from Tite Street. When I got to it the door was open, the chap inside was dead and the cabbie was slumped over the driving-wheel with a lump the size of a hen's egg on the back of his head. I damn near fainted I can tell you. For a couple of minutes I didn't know what to do, then I ran for the nearest police box, got them to call you. The Special showed up pretty sharpish, but the traffic started to move again, and I lost Wayne. If I ever had him in the first place that is.'

'You didn't hear shots.'

'No. He used a silencer I should think.'

'Even that makes some noise, but then fog does tend to swallow sound.'

'Freddie, you don't suppose Wayne thought that chap was me?'

'I wouldn't think about it if I were you.'

'It just seems like ... well ... like chance. The worst kind of rotten luck for this poor chap to slip in between me and Wayne in the fog like that.'

'Jack, he was a Special Branch officer, doesn't that tell you anything?'

'I don't know.'

'I'd like to say take the night off and go home, Jack. But you can't. I want you to get Onions out of bed and tell him. Then get your head down in the office until we send for you. It's gone midnight now. Onions will have a car sent to Acton to pick him up. It'll take about another hour and a half.'

Troy watched the police photographer do his work. Then the ambulance crew took away the body, and he climbed back into the cab to look for the bullets that killed Miller. The torchbeam was too feeble to go by. He judged the trajectory from the angle of the body and felt along the blood-sodden seat with his fingertips. There were tears in the black leather. It was probable the bullets had gone right through the cab. He turned out the contents of the boot and found one slug lodged in a horse-blanket the driver used to wrap the engine and had folded over at least sixfold to form a dense mass that had stopped the bullet as surely as a sandbag. The other two had come to rest in the tarmac of the road. He prised them out with his penknife, but they were splayed beyond any recognition. One out of three wasn't bad. He knew Kolankiewicz would be able to identify the slug. It was surely a .45? If only they had another to match. The Special Constable was down on his hands and knees on the pavement feeling around in the dark for the casings. Troy could hear him grunting and cursing as his hands found everything from cigarette ends to shards of glass.

'Buggeration,' he was saying. 'Buggeration.'

Then 'Gertcha!' The final grunt of triumph, and the man stood up with two spent shells in his fist and brought them over to Troy. The permanent rictus smile made his expression seem like a look of great satisfaction.

§ 40

Onions had shaved before coming out. Nothing in his appearance would have given away the fact that he'd been dragged from his bed at past one o'clock in the morning to be driven across London at a crawl. By the time he met Troy in his office it was nearer 4 a.m. He sat in his overcoat behind his desk, looking as though he was waiting for an early commuter train.

'You look dreadful,' he said.

Troy looked at himself. His coat was filthy again, he had no tie, his shirt was black at the cuffs and his shoes were sodden. Next to him Wildeve looked scarcely better and smelt of vomit. He was having difficulty staying awake and Troy could see him fighting the inevitable flutter of his eyelids.

'I called the Branch from home,' Onions said. 'I talked to Charlie Walsh, the CI in charge of Miller. He was grim about it all, but he'll let us get on with it.'

'That won't stop him carrying out his own investigation. I've never known them not to look after their own.'

'There's not many Special Branch officers killed in the line of duty. In fact I can't remember a case. That's our lot more often than not. I think you'd better give him a day or so on the paperwork.'

'What?' This struck Troy as an outrageous request. 'A murder. A copper shot to death on the street and he wants a day or two?'

'I get the impression this Miller was bit of a loner.'

'For god's sake, Stan. This is madness!'

'A bit of a loner,' the timbre of Onions's voice changed slightly but in a way that spoke volumes. 'You know the sort of bloke. Doesn't keep his Super up to date. Goes wandering off on his own.'

Troy knew he had gone too far in raising his voice to Onions. He was now coming around the desk heading for the hapless Wildeve, who had fallen asleep with his legs crossed and one foot sticking idly into air. Onions kicked the foot and it shot to the floor tilting Wildeve's posture so that he almost fell off the chair.

'Wake up, boy!' Onions yelled in his ear.

'Yah worra,' Wildeve said, his head pivoting madly in a desperate attempt to locate his bearings.

Troy steadied Wildeve with a hand and shot him a 'say nothing do nothing' look.

'You'll have plenty to do,' Onions went on.

'I'm doing it. The bullets have gone off to Hendon. I got Thomson and Gutteridge out of bed. One to watch at Tite Street, the other at Norfolk House. And I've two chaps in uniform doing the cab ranks to find the driver of Wayne's cab. The driver of Miller's is in the Paddington Hospital. They won't let me see him till tomorrow. I'll be ready for whatever Walsh has by seven o clock.'

'Chief Inspector Walsh to you. And, like I said, give it a day or two.'

Troy pushed luck. 'You have at least established that Miller was following Wayne?'

'It's hardly a coincidence, is it?'

'But Walsh did confirm he was following Wayne?'

'I'm satisfied that he was following Wayne.'

'Why?'

They were both standing now, squared off to each other across the desk. Onions opted to lower the stakes, resumed his seat, slicked back his hair in his habitual gesture and waited a few quiet seconds until Troy too had sat down again.

'I've known Charlie Walsh the best part of twenty years. If he has a slight problem...'

Troy bit his tongue at the word 'slight', but forced himself to say nothing.

'...And needs, say, twenty-four hours' grace, I'll let him have it. We know Miller was following Wayne. That's what matters. And at seven o'clock you'll be too damn busy with MI5. You're not the only one getting buggers out of their pits. I had that ponce Pym on the line and told him I wanted to see him and Zelig and whoever else is in charge of this mess a.s.a.p. He offered me noon, we compromised on 7 a.m.'

Troy would have hated to be in Neville's shoes when he took that call.

'Ah,' he said. 'I see. Walsh can't talk until he's gone through channels.'

'That's not what he said.'

'No, but it's what he means.'

Onions leaned forward, elbows on the desk.

'We're stabbing at shadows, Freddie. Give him till tomorrow evening, or this evening as it now is. If nowt comes through, call him. And if you talk to him the way you talk to me he'll knock your block off. Now if Sparky here can keep his eyes open we've a couple of hours for the pair of you to tell me everything before you and I have to set off to meet the spooks. And I mean everything.'

He reached into his pocket and took out a packet of Woodbines and a box of Swan Vestas. He lit up and sat back in patient, authoritative, listening mode.

§ 41

If looks could kill Pym would have assassinated Troy in the wink of an eye. He opened his office door to Troy and Onions looking white and drawn. Being up this early did not agree with him. Troy had not seen him in uniform before. The muted blue of the RAF contrasted sharply with the efflorescence of his off-duty image.

The office was barely big enough for the number of people it now held. In front of Pym's desk sat Zelig. On his left almost in the corner of the room was a woman in a charcoal-grey twin-set. Pym took the chair on Zelig's right, which left two facing for Troy and Onions. It formed a tight, antagonistic circle.

'There'll be no introductions,' Pym said. There was a weariness and a paper-thin tolerance in his voice.

Troy did not know the woman. Apart from Onions she was the only one who looked at all comfortable or presentable at this ungodly hour. She was small, the wrong side of fifty, but it was still evident that she had been good-looking. The signs of age showed most clearly in the lines around her eyes and lips – the eyes of someone who had spent years with small print and reading lamps, lips that had drawn on too many cigarettes. It was not a face to have been destroyed by laughter lines. It had an intimidating, humourless look. Her arms were folded across a small bundle of buff-coloured foolscap files, grasped to her bosom like a deterrent barrier. If Pym was anxious to avoid revealing an identity it could only be hers. Zelig coughed and stared at the floor between them. He looked jaundice yellow and distinctly unhappy about the situation in which he found himself.

'Colonel Zelig has a statement he wishes to read,' said Pym.

Zelig unfolded the single sheet he had sat clutching. He read in a hesitant, jerky voice, as though unfamiliar with the meaning of the words he used. He coughed frequently and had clearly skipped breakfast in his haste, as his stomach rumbled all the way through.

'We have been informed by MI5 liaison that Scotland Yard is investigating a shooting that took place in Manchester Square last night at approximately eleven fifteen in the evening. We understand that you wish to interview in connection with this incident Major James Wayne of the Office of Strategic Services. The High Command of the United States Forces in Britain, and the Commander of the Allied Forces are anxious to co-operate in any way that will further the interests of justice. Between the hours of ten thirty p.m. on the night of the nineteenth of March and three a.m. on the morning of the twentieth Major Wayne was in a planning meeting of Operational Command in General Eisenhower's Headquarters at Chenies Street, WC1 with General Eisenhower and General Patton.'

Zelig looked up, folded the statement away once more, and for the first time found himself looking straight at Onions, a pose he could not sustain more than a second. As his eyes darted across to Pym, Pym spoke.

'I think that concludes our business, gentlemen. I do hope that answers your questions.'

'That's it?' said Troy. 'That is it? You cook up an alibi, a complete tissue of lies and tell me that's it. Like hell it is. Where is Wayne? I want to talk to Wayne.'

'That won't be possible,' said Pym.

Troy leaned forward to Pym and said slowly and quietly, pegging back the anger he felt, 'I have a witness who saw Wayne in Chelsea at eleven p.m. I saw him myself in the Strand at ten past ten. He was not in a meeting with Ike as damn well you know. If you do not produce this man I'll swear out a warrant for his arrest on a charge of murder.'

'That won't be possible,' Zelig echoed with a croak in his voice. 'The Major isn't your man. Don't you see that? He's innocent. This proves it.' He waved the paper feebly.

'Will Eisenhower sign an affidavit to that effect?'

'Now you're being silly,' said Pym.

Troy turned on him. 'I didn't come here to listen to this buffoon. What the hell do you think you're playing at? This is murder. Not one murder but four. One man shot to death, another cut up into little pieces and burnt, a third simply vanished into thin air and now a London policeman shot in the face on the streets of London. You're not hiding this man behind anything. There's nothing big enough for him to hide behind.'

Onions sat in silence, looking in turn at each speaker, with not a flicker of expression on his face.

'You're forgetting, Troy,' said Pym, 'that well-worn phrase, a matter of national security. Major Wayne, I am assured, by our allies, is engaged on work of national security. It will not be possible to hear his statement except in the form you already have.'

Troy got to his feet.

'For Christ's sake this is murder! You can't hide murder behind national security.'

The twin-set woman spoke from the corner in a deep, assured voice, cutting through Troy's anger, with the power of emphasis on his own name, seizing his attention without raising her voice even to a normal speaking pitch. 'Mr Troy. While we're on the subject of national security . . .'

Pym looked at her in surprise. Zelig squirmed on his chair in an effort to see her face. Clearly neither of them had been led to expect any interjection from the chair in the corner. She took advantage of the unnatural hiatus and one by one tossed the foolscap files on to the carpet so that they lay facing Troy at Zelig's feet. In letters an inch high they were labelled Troy–Sir Alexei, Troitsky–Nikolai, Troy–Rodyon and Troy–Frederick. The last slapped down on to the pile leaving Troy's name for all to see.

Zelig flapped visibly, chins wobbling, his gaze flying between the files and the woman. Pym sighed faintly, the weary sigh of a man seeing the best efforts of mice and men go astray. Troy glanced at the file, and stared back at the woman expressionless. Of course he had long suspected such files existed, there was less in the surprise than she might have thought. But then he did not think the gesture was being made for him in the first place.

'What's in a name, Mr Troy?' she said simply.

For half a minute there was total silence. Then Onions got up and opened the door.

'Good day to you, madam, gentlemen,' he said, as if nothing had happened, as if he had not sat through the entire meeting in utter silence, and walked out without looking at any of them. The woman smiled a self-congratulatory smile. Troy followed Onions. Behind him, a second before someone closed the door on them, he heard Zelig say, 'Now what the fuck is going on here?'

§ 42

Onions leaned down to the window of the car and spoke to his driver. 'I'll walk a while. Pick me up at the bottom of Carlton House steps.'

They walked along King Street and around St James's Square anticlockwise. Within sight of Norfolk House, and a conspicuous Constable Gutteridge, Onions at last spoke.

'Who was she? Any idea?'

'Muriel Edge,' said Troy. 'MI5. F4 section head.'

'You know her?'

'No. I've never set eyes on her before. But there's only one woman in a position like that in the whole organisation, and if she's got all the files on my family then it's pretty obvious that she's F4, which monitors British left-wingers, and F4 is Edge. Ergo she is Edge.'

'How come I've never heard of her?'

Tricky one, thought Troy. 'I'd call it one of the few disadvantages of rank. At your level you don't hear quite as much as a sergeant.'

'Understood,' Onions replied. 'But why the bloody pantomime?'

They crossed Pall Mall in the direction of Waterloo Place. Onions walking at a steady pace, not looking at Troy. Troy let the silence run on a while wondering what reply he could possibly give.

'I don't know,' he said lamely.

'You wouldn't be holding out on me would you, Freddie?'

'There's nothing to hold out. I've told you everything. The only reason they have a file on me is because they have them on my father and my uncle whose politics are a matter of public record. Mine aren't. How I vote is nobody's business and it isn't important. And as there hasn't been an election since 1935 it's also irrelevant.'

They reached the foot of Waterloo Place, the top of Carlton House steps. The squad car was already at the bottom, waiting in The Mall. Onions paused by the Duke of York's statue.

'They're clutching at straws,' Troy concluded.

'They're not the only ones.'

Onions moved down one step and turned to face Troy, putting them almost eye to eye.

'Your evidence is thin, you know that don't you?'

'Yes.'

'You ask for a warrant you'll get it but he'll be on the streets again five minutes after his brief shows up.'

'Habeas corpus?'

'Open and shut. Charge him or let him go. I don't reckon much to putting Wildeve's identification of your Yank on a foggy night up against the word of the American General Staff. From what I gather, Wildeve had never seen the man before anyway. You saw him at ten past ten. Just leaves time for him to be in Ike's bunker by half past. They were lucky. It fits their story as well as it fits the truth. If that lunatic Pole out in Hendon matches the shell you found in Manchester Square to the one you found in Stepney, all it tells us is that the same gun killed Brand and Miller. Wayne will have ditched the gun by now. We'd never be able to tie him to it. If we find the cabbie who drove the bastard last night, that might be something. But as of now we've got bugger all.'

Troy did not know what to make of this. Onions was breathing deeply as he spoke, as though holding back feeling. Surely he was not turning over the prospect that the case was a dead duck? Surely he wasn't revving up to telling Troy to drop it?

'But I don't like being lied to. I don't like being fed a cock-and-bull story by a bunch of spooks who've appropriated the notion of what's in the national interest entirely to their own interest. I won't be told to ignore my job and my duty just because a brasshat with a Gabby Hayes accent waves a scrap of paper at me and tells me a murderer has a cast-iron alibi as long as I don't push my luck. I'll be buggered if the Metropolitan Police Force will be talked to in that way. I'll be buggered if a shite like Zelig and a jessie like Pym can lie to a superintendent of the Yard with a smirk on their faces.'

Onions was close to rage. His face was reddening by the second, his voice had risen almost to shouting. He waved a hand off in the direction of the Royal parks, and locked his eyes on to Troy's.

'Nobody shoots coppers on the streets of London and tells me to look the other way. Nobody shoots coppers on the streets of

London and tells me there's not a damn thing I can do about it. I want you out there. Bring me this bastard!'

'You want me to find the evidence?'

Instantly Troy regretted such a lame remark. Silence would have been smarter.

'Find it? Right now, Sergeant, I don't care if you have to invent it! Get out there and do your job!'

Troy watched Onions's back all the way down the steps and into the car, trailing shards of fury.

§ 43

Troy jammed the telephone between his neck and shoulder and doodled on the blotting-paper while he waited for someone to answer. On the eleventh or twelfth ring someone did.

'Special Branch.'

'Chief Inspector Walsh, please.'

'Who's calling?'

'Sergeant Troy.'

'Hang on.'

Troy heard muffled voices as the young man put his hand over the mouthpiece. He already had Zelig – Wayne . . . Brand on the blotter and added another dotted line and the name Edge, followed by a question mark. For good measure he underlined the name.

'Walsh here.'

A much deeper, older, more assured voice than the last. Troy felt he could read rank in it. If man diminishes himself to a mere surname he must be very confident of his status.

'Sergeant Troy. I'm on Stanley Onions's team.' He paused, hoping Walsh would not make him spell it out. Walsh said nothing. 'Look. I'm only two floors below, could I come up and talk to you?'

'I've already spoken to your Super.'

Yes, and you told him bugger all, thought Troy.

'I'd like to talk to you myself.'

'You can talk to me, son, but not in this building.'

'Where then?'

'D'you know the Princess Louise, Holborn?'

'No, but I can find it.'

'Six o'clock tonight. Get 'em in. Mine's a pint o' mild.'

'How will I know you?'

'I'll know you, Sergeant Troy.'

He rang off. The 'you' had been emphatic. Troy tore the sheet off his blotter and thought better of throwing it in the bin. If whole files could just vanish, doubtless waste-paper bins could be searched. Late in the afternoon as he walked north along the Victoria Embankment, he scattered its pieces and let the March wind carry them out across the Thames.

At six o'clock of a March evening the Princess Louise had not yet blacked out. It had been a clear if crisp spring day, and Troy felt pleased that he could see the last of it blowing westwards over the frosted glass and the inscription 'Saloon'. It seemed unlikely to be a pub that had a trade of regulars – too far west to be a local, too far east for the night-life of Soho. Almost anonymous in its Victorian greens and browns. Troy thought Walsh had chosen it for precisely this quality and its emptiness – the exact opposite of the concealment Troy himself would have sought, a private conversation buried in a noisy crowd. Less mysteriously perhaps Walsh had chosen the pub for its open fire. The place was three-quarters empty and the half-dozen American airmen standing around the fireplace scarcely kept the barman busy. He seemed curiously engaged in conversation with what Troy always thought of as a Bill Sykes dog, with its black-eye patch, perched on the bar. He addressed all his remarks to the dog, and the man propped against the bar answered – neither seemed to look at the other as though the dog were present as an essential mediator – the dog said nothing, simply staring meanly at Troy as he asked for service. No sooner had the barman set half a Guinness and a pint of mild in front of Troy than a large, heavy man – unmistakably a policeman – swung in the door and sat without a word in the empty chair opposite. He looked to be of the same old school as Onions; bowler hat, heavy, worn overcoat, boots and a greying moustache that all but concealed his upper lip.

'This one mine?' He gestured at the pint.

Troy asked himself if he could get what he wanted without Walsh resorting to whole sentences. Walsh even sounded like Onions, and Troy wondered if the same no-nonsense approach might lead to a brief statement of the facts in the same blunt, broad Lancashire tones.

'Mr Walsh,' said Troy by way of a greeting, with the right hint of deference. Walsh took an inch off the top of his pint and began to rummage around in his overcoat pockets. A frothy strand of beer clung to the ends of his moustache like candy floss. From one pocket came a straight-stemmed pipe, from the other a pouch of tobacco. Slowly he filled the pipe, glancing once or twice at Troy. Troy had always thought of pipes as a way of passing off vacuity as thought, the hollow man's way of seeming less than hollow.

'I'd like to compare notes with you, Mr Walsh.'

'D'ye have a light?'

'No.'

Walsh unbuttoned his overcoat and laid his bowler on the third chair. Beneath the coat was a double-breasted grey jacket, beneath that a cardigan with small leather buttons like macaroons and, Troy realised, as Walsh reached into it for a match, the man also wore a waistcoat. The swathed layers added much to his bulk, added to the sense of gravitas he so clearly wanted to create. Or perhaps he just felt the cold. He lit up and spoke to Troy through the first puffs of tobacco. A waft of Burton's worst shag floated across the table at Troy.

'You've nowt to compare – you've come up wi' nowt.'

'So you're still in touch with my Super?' Troy tried to make the obvious sound like a question.

'Of course. It's your investigation, d'you think I'd not know how you're doing when it's one of my own involved?'

'But you are conducting your own investigation?'

Walsh sucked deeply, paused and exhaled. 'No,' he said, 'I'm not.'

Troy almost started in surprise. 'What? A Special Branch officer's shot dead and you're not investigating?'

'Murder is your department. It is, is it not, the sole function of Superintendent Onions's office to investigate the act of murder within the Metropolitan area and as otherwise requested?'

He sipped another inch off his pint and sat back to look at Troy, making Troy feel that his patience was a limited indulgence.

'That's just nonsense. You always chase up your own.'

'Always? Mebbe. But not this time.'

Walsh leaned forward, injecting a touch of confidentiality into tone and gesture, the deeply nicotined third finger that had tamped his pipe prodding at the table-top. 'I've been told. From this end it's closed. Orders. You understand? Now, I say again, you've got nowt. You've not found the cabbie that drove this Yank – in the best part of twenty-four hours no one's come forward – you've no witness, you've not found your Yank – and I gather he's come up with an alibi. Even if I could investigate there's not a lead I could catch hold of. What's his alibi by the way?'

'His CO says that he and Wayne were in a meeting with American High Command. A meeting so secret that he won't tell me where or what, just conveniently when. Among the also-presents were Patton and Eisenhower, and nobody's asking Ike if he wants to alibi a murderer.'

'They've got you by the balls, son, can't you see that?'

'No. I bloody can't. What I can see is that a copper's been shot in the face on a London street.'

Walsh looked around the room, checking to see if heads had turned at Troy's outburst. He leaned closer. His voice dropped and the tone of shared confidence became one of rank and authority.

'Listen to me, Sergeant. I've been on the force thirty-two years. Nobody blows my men away like chaff if there's a single damn thing I can do to stop it. But I'm a police officer, just like you, and I learned the day I joined that taking orders is what keeps us on the straight and narrow. If we can't take orders, if we don't respect our superiors then we're just like that lot –' He gestured out towards the street with the wet end of his pipe. 'We're scum and we're rabble.'

He sat back red-faced and angry. His pipe had gone out and he laboriously went through the sucking and puffing of relighting it.

'I've had my orders. You've had yours. That's all there is to it.'

'My orders are to continue,' said Troy quietly and pointedly.

'Then I wish you well of it. From what I hear, following orders hasn't been your strong suit of late.'

'I want to see Miller's file on Wayne.'

'Sorry. I can't help you.'

Walsh sank most of his pint. Troy's Guinness sat untouched. He hadn't wanted the drink in the first place, had not in fact touched alcohol since his night with Tosca, but not to have a glass in front of him would have been so openly hostile.

'I don't understand,' he said. 'You told my Super that Miller was following Wayne.'

'I said no such thing.'

'I need to see that file. The only reason we didn't insist on it last night is because we thought you were investigating too.'

'I do not have the file.' Walsh paused for the effect. 'If such a file ever existed.'

'Miller was following Wayne. He kept notes. We all do – those notes will be a matter of record. There must be a file.'

Troy hammered out his logic to be faced with the same curt denial.

'As I said, I can't help you.'

'If you're not investigating and you do not hand over that file, it could be construed as withholding evidence. If you make me I'll request it through formal channels. I don't care what gentleman's arrangement you've reached over my head . . . if you make me I'll get it the formal way . . . I'll have Onions do it.'

Troy half-expected Walsh to explode – he could hardly be accustomed to being threatened by his juniors. Instead he made one last generous suck on his pipe and knocked it out in the ashtray. He took a silver smoker's penknife from his waistcoat pocket and went into the ritual of scraping and tapping – looking across at Troy every few seconds as he did so.

'Tell me, Sergeant. Do you know what vetting is?' he asked, raising a bushy eyebrow in feigned innocence.

'Roughly.'

'Well – more precisely than roughly – yours only just measured up to scratch the last time it was done. I know. I conducted it myself back in that fifth-column panic in 1940. Lot of nonsense, and we all know it, but if you go on digging around in this way, you may come up against that catch-all line "a matter of national importance" – could be anything from the price of eggs to secret weapons – and you may give our lords and masters cause to examine that vetting and consider . . . shall we say . . . its marginality?'

'You're talking about my family.'

'Amongst other things. That uncle of yours at Imperial is a bit of a barm cake – ranting at Speakers' Corner – I ask you – the man's a clown. And your brother – in and out of internment. All adds up y'see. And it all adds up to the sudden necessity of keeping your nose clean.'

'My brother's collecting his DFC from the King next month,' said Troy.

'Doesn't make you a hero. You know what I mean, lad.'

'So I mustn't ask for non-existent files?'

'I think we understand each other at last. Sorry not to have been more help, Sergeant.'

As quickly as he had appeared, Walsh had picked up his bowler and was gone. For ten or twenty seconds Troy sat in bitter disbelief, until the penny dropped. He ran out of the Princess Louise and looked down the street. Walsh was walking solidly, back bent, one hand to his hat in the stiff evening breeze, in the direction of Holborn viaduct. Troy ran after him and caught him by the sleeve and shouted, 'You can't give me the file because you don't have it. And you don't have it because Miller didn't report to you!'

Walsh shook free of Troy's hand and looked down at him. Six foot and heavy-set it seemed that he could crush Troy underfoot like a beetle.

'Split hairs, Mr Troy, split hairs.'

Troy walked hurriedly alongside Walsh until he stopped again.

'If Miller didn't report to you, who did he report to?'

Walsh sighed deeply, as though bothered by a persistently stupid child.

'You're a good copper, Troy. I've admired your work. We all have. There's not many have come so far so quick. But you've got to learn to take orders. If we can't take orders then the rule of law means bugger all, and if you can't grasp that then you're not one of us. I'll bid you goodnight, Troy. If you follow me again, I'll slap the cuffs on you and clip you to a railing.'

He walked off, still at his steady policeman's pace, clumping westward. The wind flapped and tugged at Troy's coat as he watched Walsh disappear into the evening's rush for the Underground. He stood immobile, thinking – until a man bumped into him, jabbing him in the back with his gas-mask case and told him to mind himself. In that mind a dotted line had become firm, solid, continuous – almost tangible. Edge.

§ 44

Troy and Wildeve met for lunch in St James's Park. Troy, having no appetite, brought nothing. Wildeve brought the sandwiches his landlady had made up for him. Nothing could be less appetising than national loaf, the merest smear of butter and a spread of four-year-old raspberry jam. Wildeve would have given an arm or a leg for a piece of veal and ham pie or a slice of lean roast beef on white bread. Instead he had given his food coupons to his landlady and bitterly regretted it.

'I can't eat this muck. I really can't,' he said to Troy. 'I don't suppose you . . . ?'

Troy got up from the bench, took the sandwiches and walked towards the pond. 'Let's see if the ducks will eat them,' he said.

Wildeve sat and shivered. 'And then perhaps we could eat the ducks. Though I don't suppose we could get an orange for love or money. Do you know there are kids nowadays who've never seen a banana or an egg you didn't have to shake out of a packet like cheap custard powder?'

'Stop whining, Jack. We're in a Royal park. Those ducks are the King's property. You're talking treason.'

Troy broke the stodgy bread into pieces and dropped it into the quacking mass of ducks that had gathered around him.

'It's cold as hell, Freddie. Why do we have to meet here?'

Troy hurled a piece of greyish bread towards the middle of the water and sent half a dozen ducks scurrying towards it. Wildeve sat with his back to The Mall and Troy turned to face him looking quickly down the path in each direction. From this position he could see anyone within a hundred or so feet in any direction.

'I don't want ears pressed to partitions or keyholes in the office. I don't want anyone to know what you're up to.'

'Me?' said Wildeve.

'Don't worry, Jack. It's orders.'

'Whose orders?'

'Mine, Constable.'

'And Onions?'

'No. In fact Onions doesn't know and I don't want him to know. If you end up in the shit you were just following orders, the buck stops with me.'

'Oh.'

'I want you to put Muriel Edge, head of MI5 section F4, under surveillance.'

Wildeve muttered 'shit', stuck his hands deep into his pockets, strolled to the path and sent a stone hurtling down it with the toe of his shoe.

'Shit,' he said again, more loudly than the first time, 'shit, shit, shit.'

The *ingénu* pretence was over. No longer the whining schoolboy, he turned his shining morning face to meet Troy's gaze, bright of eye and cynical.

'I want her followed from her office in St James's Street, I want her home watched, I want to know when and how I can talk to her without any of her people knowing. There'll be a Special Branch man somewhere around most of the time I should think.'

'Shit!' Wildeve said again.

'It's possible that as a section head she has a permanent shadow. All I need is a gap in her life when I can be certain she isn't being watched.' Wildeve looked across to Horse Guards Parade, towards Whitehall, as though imaginatively weighing up the magnitude of his task.

'Freddie, I don't suppose you could tell me why?'

'I don't see why not. I met with Walsh from Special Branch last night. He's been told to drop Miller's murder. His orders come direct from MI5. Now, he tells me . . . and I believe him . . . that he doesn't have Miller's papers on Wayne.'

'He must have. Miller was his man.'

'If he had been Walsh would be locked on to this case like an alligator. He's that sort of man, believe me. At first I thought I was getting the same runaround that I got from Zelig – but Walsh is the cleverest operator I've ever met. He pointed me in the right direction, he warned me to watch my back, and all anyone over-hearing him would have heard was a Chief Inspector dressing down a sergeant. His hands are tied, but he made damn sure we kept after Miller's killer. Miller was not his, Miller reported directly to Edge. If a file exists, Edge has it.'

'But surely it's Edge who's told Walsh to lay off?'

'I don't think so. I think that came from higher up.'

'Such as?'

Troy fell silent as a bowler-hatted civil servant approached the water and opened up his gas-mask case. He pulled out a few crusts, tossed them at the ducks and walked slowly on.

'Such as?' Wildeve repeated.

'I don't know – but someone who can tell both Walsh and Edge when to jump. Her immediate boss is the divisional director Roger Hollis. He'll answer directly to Sir David Petrie. Whoever made them jump they jumped – they backed off the case. You and I are the only people looking into Miller's death.'

'Then why haven't we been keelhauled too?'

'Simply because we don't take orders from MI5. Only Onions and the Met commissioner can tell me to stop an investigation. The route MI5 have to the commissioner is through the Home Secretary, and I really don't think they want to have to explain to Herbert Morrison why the streets of his city are getting littered with corpses. Pym and the Americans can stonewall us by not answering questions or invoking national security – but unless they go to the Home Secretary and convince him to tell the commissioner then there's bugger all they can do to make us quit.'

'Short of adding us to the pile of English dead, you mean?'

'Oh no. They won't do that. Not for a while anyway. Miller's death upset the applecart ... I don't know how ... but I doubt they'll risk another.'

'I thought Petrie was an ex-copper,' said Wildeve. 'I can't imagine how he could just sweep the death of another policeman under the carpet.'

'An awful lot of them are ex-coppers. I'm not sure past loyalties matter a damn. Besides Edge was never on the Force, neither was Hollis. This business may not even have reached Petrie. The chain of command could stop well short of him.'

'I see. Just as it does with Onions?'

'It's not that I don't want Stan to know – honestly, Jack, at the moment Stan doesn't want to know. He wants results. If I get them, he'll put his blind eye to the telescope. I can't follow her myself. She knows me. Any thick plod they've assigned to her will have been told to look out for me. You have to do it.'

Troy scattered the crumbs from Wildeve's sandwiches, and tossed the paper bag on to the water.

'Any idea where Mrs Edge lives?' asked Wildeve.

'Fifty-two Edwardes Square.'

'And I don't suppose I'm allowed to ask how you know this?'

'Quite right, you're not. And I need to know quickly.'

Three days later Troy knew.

§ 45

Edwardes Square is in west London, just south of Holland Park. A quiet, leafy expanse of late Georgian elegance. Quiet because it lies tucked away from the Cromwell Road and Kensington High Street, and has houses on only three sides. Leafy since the square itself is a large private park cordoned off for the benefit of residents only by high iron railings. Before the war the scene in front of Troy would have been lit by the dull glow of ancient gas-lamps, still perched awry on their fluted stems. It was a Hollywood idea of London. Capes, top-hats and hansoms – the detective furnished courtesy of Mr Chesterton and the Club of Queer Trades.

The plain-clothes copper on the door was getting restless. He kept glancing at his watch. Each time he waited less and was now looking in less than a minute. From the dark side of the square, where the high wall that ran along the backs of the houses in the High Street threw him into deep shadow, Troy could see the man and thought he knew the type well enough. Beery and fortyish – passed over for promotion and hobbling lazily towards a pension at the earliest date, war permitting, and his place next to the fire. If Wildeve was right, any second now he'd slope off to the pub at the south-east corner of the square and be gone a good half-hour. The copper pinched out the end of his cigarette, placed the stub carefully in a tin and slipped the tin back into his overcoat pocket. A gesture at once both neat and petty, but it was a common enough sight nowadays to see a man roll a fresh cigarette from the stubs of a dozen old ones. He turned up his collar, gave a desultory glance into the square and was gone.

The gate into the park stood open. The light would be good for another twenty minutes. Troy could just make out Mrs Edge, kneeling in front of a large well-kept flowerbed – shielded from the street by a thick hedge of variegated privet. Something cracked beneath his feet. He felt sure she must look up, but she carried on rooting out and pulling at something unwelcome in her flowerbed. A small Pekinese dog perked up at the sound, walked warily towards him and then turned and ran back with a single soprano yap as though announcing Troy's presence. Edge stood clutching something brown and shrivelled. Without turning she said, 'My fuchsias – they never seem to survive the English winter.'

She crumbled them to dust between her hands. Peeling off her gardening gloves she turned to Troy.

'What kept you?' she said simply.

Troy sat on the nearest bench and watched as she undid her headscarf and tucked it into the pocket of her fawn suit. She looked less the county lady without it.

'A little matter of certainty,' Troy replied. 'And the man on your door.'

Edge sat down next to Troy – delicately perched and ramrod straight. 'Yes. He is a nuisance, isn't he. So tiresome, but I tell myself it's all for my own good.'

She reached inside her jacket and brought out a thick wad of paper folded many times.

'Rather messy I'm afraid, but I think our friend would have noticed if I'd tried to walk the dog clutching a cardboard file.'

It was too late to read. Troy merely felt the weight of the paper and slipped it into his inside pocket.

'Of course Sergeant Miller only records facts. Facts and observations. He doesn't – didn't – speculate, but then I don't suppose he was trained to theorise. You people aren't, are you?'

Troy wondered if an insult phrased in the semblance of a question really required an answer. 'How much did you tell Miller?' he asked.

'Enough for him to know what to look for I hope.'

'Not enough to prevent him getting killed?'

The soft mockery vanished as she turned her hard, rich blue eyes on him. The lines around her mouth drew in sharply. She looked to Troy like a vicious bird of prey.

'You knew Wayne was a killer, didn't you?' Troy persisted.

'I suspected it. But then I suspect a lot of things. The whole point in having Sergeant Miller was to find out what was true and what was not.'

'He killed a man as long ago as April last year.'

'At which point I did not know of his existence. No, Mr Troy, I didn't know he was a murderer. I asked for a Special Branch officer only in November last year. You'll see. Sergeant Miller's notes go back no further than the last week of November. I'd received too many reports of this mysterious American involving himself with the London Communists. They may well be stupid enough to take him at face value – I'm not. I could see him as a plant at once. It was simply a matter of finding out exactly what he was up to and tracing him back to . . . ' she fumbled for the right word, ' . . . to . . . source.'

'Source?'

'To his masters. To the men who authorised American penetration.'

Troy could feel her anger rising. She could hardly shout at him without attracting the attention they both wanted to avoid, but her shoulders shook gently with the suppression of rage, and he felt her looks would turn him to stone if they only could.

'Mr Troy, I'm a section head. Do you know what that means?'

It too required no answer.

'I've worked all my adult life for my country. I love my country. I'd die rather than see it go Bolshevik. But that does not mean I will surrender any part of it to an alien power simply because that power assures me that we're fighting the same battle. I don't expect you to understand, you're only a policeman – but Wayne is OSS. That pernicious organisation has a foothold here. One granted to it by sheer necessity of the common cause – the special relationship.'

Roosevelt's words seemed spat out with a contempt he could surely never have meant them to convey.

'This war's nearly over. We're already fighting the next. So are the Americans. We all know who the next common enemy will be. But fight that war in England by usurpation of our sovereignty, of authority granted to me ... they shall not. It would merely be to invite in one plague in the hope of exterminating another. Yet ... if the OSS succeed in arrogating the pursuit of Communism to themselves now ... what is to stop them continuing to do so in two or in twenty years' time? Do you see what I mean?'

The tirade had stopped. She seemed calmer now, less rhetorical, for once genuinely concerned that Troy should have an answer for her.

'What –' Troy paused. 'What do you want from me, Mrs Edge?'

'Want? I want you to catch him of course!'

'You've just told me that that's your prerogative.'

'Not my prerogative, Mr Troy, my duty.'

'Then do your duty, Mrs Edge.'

Edge sighed. Her spine relaxed from its schoolmarm rigidity and she leaned back on the bench as though worn down by the effort of her own anger.

'No. I need you for that.'

'Go through channels. You could talk to Hollis, Hollis could talk to Petrie, Petrie could talk to the Home Secretary ...'

'No I couldn't. This matter isn't going anywhere near the Home Secretary. Isn't that obvious?'

'Yes – but I can't help wondering why. Petrie is a former police officer. He's hardly likely to want a murderer loose on the streets of London – particularly a murderer of policemen.'

'And your commissioner is a former soldier – stop this line of argument. It's leading nowhere. Take it from me. There are channels, and those channels are blocked by common consent at levels higher than either of us. Believe me, Troy, if I could I'd pick up a phone and call your superintendent myself, but I'd be cutting my own throat. There's procedure and there's protocol – if you can't see that you'll be a sergeant all your life.'

'If I'm being used I like to know what for. You know, Mrs Edge, I can't help the feeling that this is being kept clear of the Home Secretary because no one knows which way Mr Morrison will jump.'

Edge stood up, dusting flecks of earth and bark from her skirt. The dog took its head off its paws and stirred in the expectation that the ordeal of waiting was over.

'Do your duty, Mr Troy.'

The dog looked hopefully from Edge to Troy and back again.

'Without fear or favour?' Troy asked.

'Meaning?'

'My policeman's oath, Mrs Edge.'

Troy stood ready to leave. The dog hopped around in delight.

'Was it necessary,' Troy said, 'for you to invoke fear for my favour?'

'Ah. I see. You don't like to be reminded of your origins. Well, shall we say it was first necessary to gain your attention?'

'Was it necessary to draw the suspicion of everyone else?'

'I should think Pym and Onions know all about you by now. Your uncle's obvious, transparent. If I thought he was anything more than an academic hooligan I'd have a file on him a foot thick.'

'And Zelig?'

'Zelig's a fool. A rubber stamp for the Americans. He lets Wayne operate with a free hand and lets that secretary of his make most of the decisions. If he's suspicious of you, of your motives, of what you might turn up, it would be a minor miracle. It might just add a touch of healthy animosity. Keep you on your toes. If you follow Miller's notes, believe me you will find the evidence you need. Goodnight, Mr Troy. We shall not meet again.'

§ 46

Back in Goodwins Court, Troy spread out Miller's fifteen badly typed pages. Edge had a point. It did not seem to have been in the man's nature to speculate. He recorded times, dates and places with meticulous care but added up nothing in the approach to meaning. Troy could almost touch the reliable solidity of the man in the witness-box – proceeding in a westerly direction at precisely 11.37 a.m. The plod of boot on flagstone. Honesty without imagination. A man who did not know when his time was wasted. A man who did not know when his life was in danger.

November yielded nothing. Simply the fact that Wayne had other girlfriends besides Diana Brack and from time to time would pick up whores in Soho, doubtless equipped with a gross or two of Uncle Sam's government-issue condoms – not risking a dose of the clap in the service of his country.

Troy reckoned that Wayne had been on to Miller from roughly late December. For two weeks Miller had tailed him to meetings in the public houses of East London – including two in the Bricklayers Arms in Hannibal Road, only yards away from Wolinski's flat, and a short walk from the scene of Brand's murder. Wayne had disappeared into private meetings in Jubilee Street and Jamaica Road, and Miller had scrupulously turned to the electoral roll and recorded the names of the householders – Edelmann, Sidney Lewis and McGee, Michael Eamonn. Shortly after Christmas 1943 Miller had begun losing track of Wayne at Tube interchanges all over the City of London. Time after time it was recorded 'lost sight of suspect at Moorgate . . . Holborn . . . Liverpool Street . . . Monument' – and once or twice Wayne had clearly given Miller the runaround . . . 'lost sight of suspect at Earls Court . . . Hammersmith . . . Paddington . . .' And from then on Miller had wasted two months reporting nothing but the social high-life of an overpaid American officer. On the supposed night of Brand's death, 24 February – supposed because forensic insisted on a wide margin of error, what with the sub-zero temperatures and the fact that Kolankiewicz had but a single arm to work from – Miller had at least come close. He had kept up with Wayne through his attempt to lose him at Baker Street, but had been shaken off at Liverpool Street. It was, Troy thought, about as late as Wayne could leave it. He could walk to Stepney from there. So could Miller. With a single spark of intuition, the only such he had shown throughout, Miller had gone straight to Jubilee Street and waited outside Edelmann's house. Wayne, not surprisingly, had not appeared. Troy was certain that he had met Brand and Wolinski at Wolinski's or in a public house, and had killed one or both of them after luring them to the bombsite on the Green. Luring? Troy's own logic struck him as novelettish, but he remembered the sight of Miller's body. The back of his skull now in a dozen pieces at the bottom of a Cellophane bag – the black holes in his face and forehead, matching the holes in von Ranke's face, the holes in Brand's skull. Was this too how Wolinski had died? Miller's notes grew worse, sketchy.

In March, Wayne had been markedly inactive. For days on end Miller had nothing to report. Wayne had been more adept than usual. Miller had reported neither his visit to Zelig nor Troy's presence outside Brack's house. The last two weeks of March were unaccounted for. He had written up nothing from his notebook. Miller had grown casual and sloppy, typing up his notes only once a week before reporting to Edge. A sloppiness that had got him killed. Did the man not have enough sense to connect Wayne's presence in the East End on 24 February with the arm that had been found only three days later? Did he not know that he was dealing with a man who killed and took pleasure in killing? It was possible that he had not seen Wayne again. Until he slipped clumsily between him and Wildeve's tail, and Wayne saw him.

Troy asked himself why Wayne had killed Miller when he did. Why not sooner? Perhaps he had labelled Miller as incompetent and was not worried until . . . what? Until Troy's own appearance? But Wayne would not have risked killing Miller knowing that he or Wildeve was following. Only a madman would take such a risk. Wayne could not have known how close Troy was or that Wildeve was right behind him. It was likely, probable even, that he had not seen Troy that night at Holborn. No – Miller had died for the contents of his notebook. Wayne had decided to find out for certain how much Miller knew, and had provided himself with an impeccable alibi – and now, for reasons Troy couldn't even guess at, the powers-that-be had chosen to back him. In taking out Miller, Wayne had effectively got Special Branch off his back for good.

'All the evidence you need,' Muriel Edge had said. But, really, Miller offered only two things, the confirmation that Wayne had been somewhere in the vicinity of the murder on the day in question, and Messrs Edelmann and McGee.

'Zelig is a fool,' she had said. 'Lets that secretary of his make the decisions.'

Troy remembered he had silently promised to meet that secretary four nights ago, on the day that Miller had died. Miller's death had thoroughly eclipsed that urgency – now there were other reasons to keep the appointment.

§ 47

Tosca slammed the door on his foot.

'You're a week late, you bastard!'

Some of the weakest lines in a man's vocabulary sprang to mind.

'I can explain, honestly.'

Troy shoved against the door. She backed off. He could just make her out in the shadows, wrapped in a blanket from bosom to ankles, wearing her army shirt and an unforgiving expression. She turned and ran for the stairs. There was a flash of leg as she passed the window on the first floor and the thump of running feet. He closed the door quietly and groped for the banister.

Her door was an inch ajar, a shaft of light cutting into the spidery gloom of the landing. He pushed at it and stepped cautiously into the room. Tosca, he thought, had the mark of a thrower. Sure enough her arm came up and a pillow hurtled towards him, badly enough aimed to plump soundlessly against the wall four or five feet away from him. She was sitting up in bed, the remains of a consolatory feast scattered around her. Half-eaten doughnuts, the silver wrappers off Hershey bars and months old copies of American magazines – *Life*, the *Saturday Evening Post*. The radio was on, tuned low to the Light programme and a late evening concert of Big Band music. Elsie Carlisle crooned her seductive croon – 'You got me cryin' again'.

'You think you can just breeze in here when it suits you? Is that it?'

'I . . . er . . .'

'You couldn't phone?'

'No I couldn't. Things have happened since we last met.'

'Short of the second front opening – and I kind of think I'd hear about that before you did – it ain't good enough, whatever it is.'

'Major Wayne—' Troy got no further with the sentence. She screamed.

'Aaaaaaaaaaaaaaaaaaaagh!!!!! Don't mention that name to me, you bastard!!!!! If you think you can fuck on the company time—'

Troy kicked the door to and rushed to the bed, clapping a hand across her mouth before she could make enough noise to bring out the neighbours, the ARP and the fire brigade all at once. She bit into the side of his hand, and he snatched it back.

'If,' she hissed, as though she'd taken the hint, 'you think you can kill two birds with one stone as you aphoristically minded English would put it, take me for what I know, give me a quickie and then fuck the hell off, then think again, copper. Get your clothes off now or get out!'

Troy was astounded. He knew she could be direct, but it still surprised him.

'You don't mean that?' he said.

'Wanna bet? Show your grit, do your bit or pack your kit.'

'Good Lord,' he said almost involuntarily.

'Good Lord,' she mimicked, squirming out of the bed into a kneeling position in her shirt and stockings, beginning to pull at the knot in his tie. 'You guys kill me.'

She locked her lips on to his, gently forcing them apart with the tip of her darting tongue. She pulled back, grinning hugely, smiling in the depths of her brown eyes. She tossed the tie aside and tugged at the buttons of his overcoat.

'If you so much as mention work – yours or mine – before first light, you're dead. *Capiche?*'

Troy nodded.

'Now my tight-ass London baby, lie back and think of England.'

She pulled off his clothes, and had him naked before he became conscious that the light was still on. Once he had noticed it hardly seemed worth mentioning. He'd never made love with the light on before. Nor, for that matter, had he made love with the wireless on, to the sound of music – and that was so decadent it didn't bear thinking about. But then Tosca's motto seemed to be that there was a first time for everything.

§ 48

He lay awake. She stirred in the dark and reached out for him.

'What're you thinking about?'

'England.'

'You don't have to think about England afterwards only during. It's to take your mind off the wickedness of female flesh. What about England? What do you think of if you think of England? Churchill? The King? Hyde Park? Beefeaters?'

'No. None of that. I think of the yellow of primroses in spring. The furry folds of beech leaves unfurling in their bottle green.'

'Furry folds, huh?'

'The long white ribbon of hawthorn in its May blossom, quilting the fields in Hertfordshire.'

'Hertfordshire. That where you from?'

'Yes. And when it comes down to ·it I think of custard and overboiled cabbage.'

'What? What the fuck has that got to do with springtime?'

'Nothing. I was thinking of England, and sooner or later England makes me think of custard . . . '

'And boiled cabbage?'

'Yep.'

'You know what? I think you're hungry.'

'Not for boiled cabbage I'm not. I don't care whether I never see a plate of boiled cabbage again.'

'A week without it and a girl can forget how much spent seed can exhaust a man. They wiggle it about for thirty seconds and the next thing you know they're fast asleep and they always wake up hungry.'

She leapt naked from the bed and ran to the refrigerator. The fridge fought back for a second or two, then sighed deeply and with one last, begrudging suck yielded up its treasure.

'I got just the thing for you. Now it's cold, and I guess it should be eaten hot, but I've never found it too bad straight from the ice-box.'

She came back to the bed. Troy had to drag his eyes from her breasts to the plate she proffered.

'What is it?'

'Try some.'

It looked a mess. A rippling blood-and-custard mess, reminiscent of the company colours of the London Midland and Scottish Railway.

'Go on, be an American. Eat with your fingers.'

Troy tore off a piece of the mess.

'Not bad. What's the brown stuff?'

'Anchovy.'

'And the blobs?'

'Capers, I guess.'

'And the sausage?'

'Pepperoni.'

'Not bad at all. What's it called?'

'Pizza.'

'Pete Sir?'

'No. Peezah! I just got it from the PX. They set up a bakery somewhere out in the boonies for making New York's native dish. Keeps the troops happy, I guess.'

'You'd think they had better priorities.'

'That's nothing. We got a Coke-bottling plant in crates waiting for D-Day. First beachhead we get we start bottling Coke for the boys!'

Troy almost choked laughing.

'I'm serious. Anyway you're not supposed to know that. It's classified. You ready for more?'

Troy nodded thinking she meant the pizza.

'Boy, I thought you'd never ask. What you have to do to get laid in this town!'

With one hand she grabbed him by the cock and with the other flicked out the light. Darkness and Tosca enfolded.

§ 49

They woke to a common consequence of a raid.

'Goddammit! No gas again.'

Tosca padded softly around the room, muttering and complaining.

'No breakfast. No coffee. How does Hitler expect me to get through the day?'

Troy slipped from the bed. Judging by the angle of the sun slanting in across Trafalgar Square, filtered by the dirt of the back window, it was still early. He had a little time. He slipped on his shirt.

'What do you have for breakfast as a rule?'

'Eggs, toast, coffee. English muffins, when the PX has them. Funny thing is you can't get them in England. I mean is French toast French? Do Mexicans eat chilli? It kinda shakes your faith in the world order.'

It sounded like nonsense. He ignored it and pulled open the fridge. There were a dozen eggs and an unopened pound slab of white American butter. A bigger piece than he'd seen in one lump since before the war.

'OK. Sit yourself down.'

'Where?'

'Anywhere you're comfortable.'

She sat cross-legged on the floor between the fridge and the bed, still startlingly naked. Troy took command of the situation, gathered knives, plates and a fish-slice and plugged in the electric iron. Then he sat down opposite her. He upturned the iron, and handed it to her.

'Now. I haven't done this in a while. But at one point during the Blitz I cooked this way for a fortnight. It's terribly important you hold the iron steady. And it would have been a little better if you'd worn something.'

She wriggled and pouted. Her breasts shook, and she blew a mock kiss in his direction.

'Suit yourself,' he said, and tore a strip off the butter wrapper. He greased the flat of the iron and waited for it to bubble.

'You're kidding!'

'No I'm not. And please keep still.'

She gripped the iron firmly in both hands. The hot plate hovered inches above her thighs. Troy cracked an egg on the side of a plate and dropped it sizzling on to the flat.

'My God!' she said. 'It's cooking. It's really cooking.'

'It does take a while. Have a little patience.'

'That's OK. We got lots to talk about.'

Troy said nothing, waiting for her to lead.

'Like Jimmy's not been diddling coupons, has he?'

Troy shook his head and looked at the egg rather than at her.

'It's serious. You come in with that conscience-of-the-world look on your face, so it's serious.'

'He's murdered four people.'

'Whaaaaaa!!!!'

Her grip slackened, the iron tilted and the egg slid sideways. Troy caught it neatly on the fish-slice before it could land on her. The hot fat dripped stinging on to her thigh.

'Ow, ow, ow.'

'I think we'd better stop. It might be easier to get through breakfast on another subject.'

'No, I'll be OK. You can't quit now. I'm made of tough stuff. I just wasn't expecting it to be that serious. Who's he killed?'

Troy slid the egg back on to the iron, and cut a slice of bread ready for it.

'A couple of German refugees. A Pole who worked in the docks. And a policeman who was following him.'

'Holy shit. Why would he do a thing like that?'

'It's his job. Dirty tricks you said.'

'I also said not here.'

'What precisely is his job for the army?'

'I'm not supposed to know.'

'But you do.'

'Jimmy's a boaster. He can't resist telling. He pulls off something fancy, sooner or later, he'll start hinting at it. Over the last year or so it's become obvious what he does. He's one of those guys gets parachuted into occupied France. Does a few heroic stunts, gets pulled out again. He's got good French and German. It figures.'

'Does he bring out people? French, Germans, Resistance fighters, people who might be useful to our war effort?'

'Yes. We do that a lot, but don't ask me for cases. I know the general drift of what goes on. There's no way Zelly would ever let me see anything on an individual operation. He hates putting things on paper.'

Troy slid the egg off on to a slice of bread, took the iron from her and set it down end-up on the carpet. He handed the plate to her. She bit into the egg, yellow yolk cascading over her bottom lip, a puzzled look on her face as she stared at him over the top of her breakfast.

'Shame there's no coffee.'

'Can you find out if he brought out a German round about February this year?'

'You're asking me to spy on Zelly?'

'Yes.'

'I guess so. I'm not crazy about it, but if I didn't spy on him half the time anyway all I'd know about Allied Operations is what I learn from typing his letters to the Supply Officer complaining about the lack of peanut butter and mayonnaise in the PX.'

She finished the sandwich in silence. Something evidently on her mind.

'Who'd he kill last?'

Troy handed her the iron again, and began to cook breakfast for himself.

'The policeman. Last Tuesday night.'

'The night you didn't show.'

'I was in Manchester Square, putting bits of human brain into Cellophane bags.'

She winced and grimaced at the words, but pressed on. 'On Wednesday morning there was the most almighty panic going on in the office. Zelly was in before me, which is unheard of, and the scrambler on his phone was never off. I had to put my ear to the door. He talked to Jimmy and he talked to some of the top brass and he was in a stinker of a mood. He talked to a couple of guys at your MI5 too.'

'He'd just come from a meeting with me at MI5.'

'You were gunning for him, huh?'

'Yes, but the matter that worries me is who's gunning for me?'

'I don't follow.'

Troy talked as he ate. She put a finger to his lips, retrieved a precious smear of yolk and licked it.

'The first time I saw you, were you expecting Wayne?'

'No. He drops in occasionally. But he certainly wasn't due that day. In fact you were the only appointment Zelly had, and that put his blood pressure up. He sure as hell didn't want to see you.'

'I've been wondering why he did. He told me absolutely nothing.'

'Beats me.'

'Unless, of course, he wasn't seeing me. Wayne was.'

'Huh?'

'Wayne came just to get a look at me. He knew there was a policeman tailing him. Sergeant Miller of Special Branch. He was alarmed at the idea that the man was now in touch with Zelig. He came to see me and to be seen. If I was the man he'd spotted, if I turned out to be Miller, his fears would have been confirmed. He was too close to things and Wayne knew he'd have to kill him. I wasn't the policeman he'd seen. I was me. I'd no connection with Miller and what Miller was on to. I didn't recognise Wayne. If I had, if I'd shown the faintest flicker of recognition, I would be lying in the morgue with a bullet in my head too. Sergeant Miller gained a few days of life. Wayne killed him when it was most convenient. But he could just as easily have killed me. What he didn't know was that I spotted him later the same day coming out of his mistress's house. That I'd made a connection he couldn't even guess at. If he'd known I was on to him I doubt he'd have killed Miller.'

'Well. He came in. He chatted about nothing. Then he left. But close to what? You're investigating the murders. What else was he doing for your man to be close to?'

'I'm guessing, but I think he's infiltrated a Communist cell in the East End.'

'No way! That's not his brief. In London he just cools his heels. Gets in some R and R. He's not supposed to do a thing in England.'

'But he does. He kills people.'

'Commies? He kills Commies? I thought you said he killed a couple of Germans. I don't get it.'

'Nor do I.'

For a minute or two Troy ate in silence. Then Tosca leapt up and began to rummage around in the top drawer of the dressing-table. She tossed a key on to the carpet, and sat clutching a piece of stiff, white paper.

'Take it,' she said. 'It's my spare. By tonight I should have something for you.'

'There's something I need now. His address?'

'You don't know his address?'

'I haven't a clue where he is. I've staked out Tite Street and . . . '

'And you've staked out my office. That guy in St James's Square is a lemon. No – I doubt Jimmy will show his face. His official address is at that apartment block in Curzon Street we took over for officers. Marriot House. He has a couple of rooms, but I've never found him there. I figure he uses it as a letter drop and that's about it. I had to go in once. It smelt stale. He keeps a change of clothes there, but I figure he spends a night there once in a blue moon. He lives with his women. Wherever they are. This is what you really need right now.'

She laid the paper face up on the carpet. A mass of tiny photo-graphs, six or seven to a row, perhaps thirty in all. Miniatures of Major Wayne, each marginally different, as though frozen from a moving picture.

'It's called polyphoto. Camera with a motor drive. They were all the rage in Washington, summer before the war. I had one done to send to my mom. I guess it brings out the cutes in people. I guess even Jimmy thinks he's cute, though God knows you'd never think it yourself.'

It was signed 'Jimmy XXX'. The full, moist upper lip, so much bigger than the lower, the liquid, smiling eyes. In a myriad of self-conscious poses.

'I didn't ask for it. He just gave it to me one day. I don't even know why I kept it.'

On his way back to Goodwins Court to bathe and change, Troy wondered about Tosca's response. She had accepted everything he had said. Shocked, but accepting. There had been no questions along the lines of 'How do you know?' or 'Are you sure?' But then Wayne's role was to kill. That, surely, was the ultimate dirty trick and commonplace enough for a soldier in wartime. Of course, he had lied to her about the connection. He knew why Wayne had gone to the trouble of cracking an East End cell, even though he was surprised to learn that the task was above and beyond orders. But, as ever, he wanted to put evidence before utterance. He couldn't help wondering about the modest assessment she made of her own role at Norfolk House and the contrast it made with Edge's version. He couldn't help wondering about the game of slapstick that she played with him. Perhaps this was simply the way she was with men. But where in the Manhattan slapstick was there room for words like 'aphoristically'?

§ 50

Kolankiewicz was perched in front of the gas fire in Troy's office. Hidden behind his *News Chronicle*. Wildeve laboured on an immense pile of papers, yawning all the time. Troy walked past them and pinned the polyphoto to the notice-board on the office wall and tapped it.

'That's our man,' he said.

Kolankiewicz dropped the paper and scuttled across the room, looked up at Wayne, fixing his spectacles to his nose with one hand.

'Nasty piece of work,' he said.

'How can you tell?'

'A mean expression.'

'Which one?'

'All of them.'

'That's great. You should be a detective.'

'Don't be so fucking cocky. When you seen what I got you'll be bloody impressed.'

He pulled open his briefcase, and set three Cellophane bags on Troy's desk.

'I have good news. I have bad news. First shell, second and third shells, bullets from Manchester Square. You keep them. What can vanish once can vanish twice. The bullets are forty-five. The shells as you so rightly said were fired from an automatic. There are spring-loading clip marks on the sides, the like of which you do not get with a revolver. Now the good news.'

He took out two large photographs and pinned them to the board next to the myriad faces of Wayne.

'Now, in the absence of any other bullet with which to make any comparison I did all I could with the shells. These enlargements will show you what I mean. If you take the clip marks as indicating nine o'clock, then the firing pin in each case would appear to have hit at ten past two – in archery terms an inner. So far, so thin. I don't rate such evidence. There is too much room for coincidence. But...'

He took two more photographs from his briefcase and tacked them over the first set.

'Look at these. Blown up to the power fifty. Look at the pattern of the pin upon the cartridge case.'

Troy looked as closely as he could.

'They're identical.'

'Quite so. Presuming the same place on the clock, the two shells, from Stepney, from Manchester Square, bear the marks of being detonated by the same firing pin – or at worst two firing pins that have worn in precisely the same way.'

'That's ... that's brilliant!'

'Effectively the two shells were fired by the same gun. Not as conclusive as having the bullet that killed Herr Cufflink, but ... scientifically far from inexact. Now the bad news...'

'Bad news?'

'It won't stand up in court. At least, it's never had to, because no one's ever tried it.'

'Shit,' said Troy.

'Think how many points of similarity you need with fingerprints. Think how likely it is that your man has ditched the gun.'

'Think how often we catch them with it. Almost a sentimental attachment – killers for their weapons. They go on clutching it long after they've fired their last bullet at you, even though it's as damning as Bill Sykes's dog.'

Kolankiewicz shrugged. 'I offer this for what it's worth. My feeling is that to date we have only circumstantial evidence, piss in wind. This, this I will go into court with. But we'd be the first.'

Troy bent to look more closely at the photographs. He felt Kolankiewicz's hands on the back of his head, probing in his hair.

'What are you playing at?'

'I heard you been in the wars. That's quite a lump you still got. When was it?'

'It was . . . it was . . . '

Troy realised he could not remember when he had been in Holborn station when the bomb had hit. He remembered the pain in his head and the blood-red cloud and the thought of them now seemed to bring both back. But he could not in honesty say whether the bomb had been last week or last month, and for a second or two could see Kolankiewicz only through a red mist, hear him only through the drumming of a blood-vessel somewhere over the left eye.

'It was the week before last,' said Wildeve.

As little as that? Kolankiewicz looked all around Troy's head, umming and aahing a little, and then took his head in both hands, twisted his face to the window and looked deep into his eyes.

'You got eyes like a Polish peat bog,' he said. 'But the bad news is they let you out too soon.'

'They didn't let him out. He discharged himself,' Wildeve said.

'You're a smartyarse.'

'So you keep telling me.'

'Bangs to the head can be trouble. You get any headaches?'

Troy did not answer.

'I see,' said Kolankiewicz. 'Troy, see your doctor. As a favour to me. Don't fuck with the head. It's too near the brain.'

'Don't worry,' Troy lied, 'I will.'

§ 51

The silver moonlight picked out Cable Street in every crack and pot-hole. What there was of intact road surface shone as though the tarmacadam had been Brylcreemed, throwing the piercing silver gleam back to the roving moon in its cloudless sky.

Troy and Wildeve left the Bullnose Morris by Leman Street Post Office and walked along Cable Street parallel to the arches of the London to Tilbury line out of Fenchurch Street. Two drunks swayed towards them from the Shadwell end. One silent and giddy, the other raucous and leaping from pot-hole to pot-hole.

'By the light of the silvery moon, we'll sit an' spoon, honeymoon, honeymoon, hunny wossaname . . .'

He stopped mid-puddle.

'George, I've forgotten the bloody words.'

George seemed hardly to care. He broke wind loudly and contemplated the dilemma.

'Gizzanother then. Gizz bluebirds over the white fuckin' cliffs of fuckin' Dover. I ain't 'eard that since this mornin' at least. Wossa fuckin' war comin' to. I arst yer. Just when you want Vera fuckin' Lynn an' 'er white fuckin' cliffs of white fuckin' Dover there's never one around. Just like fuckin' coppers.'

'Right you are, George. There are bad times just around the corner, just you wait an' see. There'll be Messershmitts over the white fuckin' cliffs of wossname, just you wait an' see . . .'

Troy and Wildeve parted around the songbird who teetered at the end of a nine-foot crater of a puddle. He took one step and sat down hard on his backside in a foot or more of water.

'Aagh! I'm wet. My arse is all wet!'

For the first time he seemed to notice his onlookers.

'Gizzahand mate,' he said to Troy.

Troy looked down into the drunken, pleading eyes. 'Sorry, mate,' he said. 'There's never a copper about when you want one is there?'

A wail of self-pity went up. As loud as any siren. They walked on, deftly side-stepping George, and followed the line of arches.

'Freddie, what exactly are we looking for?'

'Signs of life.'

'You don't mean that people actually live in these?'

'Not exactly, but Bonham reckons Edelmann has a shelter here.'

When the Blitz first hit, the provision of shelters was appalling. Sydney Edelmann, Communist and local councillor, had kicked up a fuss about the conditions, persuaded MPs and the press down to the East End to look at the way the East-Enders had to live. Striking into the heartland of privilege he had even led a march on the Savoy to protest about the private shelter constructed deep underneath the famous hotel for the exclusive use of patrons. Dozens of Stepney's disaffected crowded into the hotel at the sound of the alert; demanded shelter only to be met with the police. Reading an account in the papers the following day Troy had laughed out loud at the news of Edelmann rightly meeting and defeating the challenge by invoking the Innkeeper's Act. In his way he was the subtlest of barrack-room lawyers. Without his agitation Troy doubted that proper provision would ever have been made by way of mass shelters. The poor would have gone on spending their nights in stinking cellars with no lavatories and no water. But, victory achieved, on the return of the bombers for the 'little' Blitz Edelmann would not use the new shelters himself, preferring, it was said, the privacy of his fortified railway arch.

They had passed and looked over more than a dozen arches. Most had been covered in with sheets of corrugated steel and served as scrap-metal yards – 'Help Build a Spitfire' was daubed in peeling paint across the doors of one arch, a relic from the summer of the Battle of Britain – or garage workshops, but from one high arch a narrow chimney emerged in a serpentine twist, puffing plumes of white smoke into the brilliant night air. Troy stopped and tugged gently on Wildeve's coatsleeve.

'I think we've found it.'

Wildeve looked blankly at the steel doors. The smoke abated between puffs, and he saw no sign of life.

'Couldn't we just catch him at home?'

'I've never known Edelmann to knowingly admit a copper without a warrant – look there it goes again.'

The chimney breathed, exhaling its wisp of smoke towards the sky.

'And you reckon they spend all night in there?'

Troy thumped on the door. They heard the slow unslipping of bolts and chains and the door opened a fraction of an inch.

'Who's there?'

'It's old Bill,' said Troy.

'I don't know anyone called Bill,' came the reply.

So much for the value of our native argot, thought Troy.

'Tell Sydney it's Sergeant Troy of the Yard.'

The door closed on him. A minute or more passed. A train roared overhead drowning out any sound from the interior of the arch. The door opened once more, wide in its dark welcome. From the depths a disembodied voice called to Troy.

'As I live and breathe, Mr Troy!'

A small dark man shuffled into the moonlight, his back bent under the perpetual burden of a hunch, spine twisted so badly that he looked up at Troy and Wildeve with his head at a painful angle, one eye popping, one eye almost closed.

'Lads, lads. It's my old friend Constable Troy!'

Edelmann gestured expansively with his hand, flinging the door open, knuckles of the hand only inches from the ground. Troy walked in. Wildeve followed, wide-eyed in a foreign land. They entered through an inner door into a colossal metal box spanning out its square within the circle of the brick railway arch. Half a dozen men sat around a central fire, some playing cards on the top of a packing case, others reading until disturbed by this palaver. The walls were lined with bunks. Eyes like foxes stared out at them from the depth of their burrows. It was clean, carpeted, well-ordered and, but for the present intrusion, friendly and homely. Sound vanished easily into the vastness of space giving it the soft whisper of worship, a steel cathedral.

'It's Sergeant Troy now, Sydney,' said Troy.

'My my, but you've come up in the world, my boy. I always said you'd do well.'

Could we knock off the Dickens impersonations? You're not a patch on Bransby Williams, and I've come on business.'

'O' course. O' course. 'Orace, you get Mr Troy and his friend a cuppa char. I shall be with the Sergeant in my office.'

He shuffled ahead of Troy, leading the way into a cubicle made by the arrangement of a small group of packing cases.

'Business you said.'

Troy laid out the photograph of von Ranke on a packing case.

'Looks very dead, poor sod,' was all Edelmann said.

'You didn't know him?'

'No.'

Troy put down the photograph of the young Brand blown up from Nikolai's group shot.

' 'Im neither.'

'You're certain?'

'If I knew I'd tell yer. There'd be no 'arm in that. On account of whatever your next question was I like as not would tell you to get stuffed.'

Troy laid down the third photograph. One he had had enlarged from the dozens Tosca had given him. Edelmann said nothing. He looked down, he looked up and he looked back at Troy.

'And what would your next question be, Mr Troy? Afore I tells yer to get stuffed that is.'

'My next question would be did you know you'd been infiltrated by the opposition?'

Edelmann drew in his breath with a faint whistle. He uncocked his head, the squint vanished from the half-closed eye, and he leaned back as though appraising Troy.

'Just supposin'. Just supposin' I should go along with this. What proof can you offer?'

Troy jabbed at the photo of von Ranke with his forefinger.

'He did that. Shot him in the face.'

'Nasty.'

'He did for him too.' Troy pointed to Brand. 'Chopped him into little pieces.'

Edelmann shook his head slowly from side to side. Troy had no idea whether it meant disbelief or despair.

'And I think he also killed this man.'

Troy slapped down a blow-up of the young Peter Wolinski, like a card-sharp playing a trump. Edelmann got up and walked out. Troy sat still and waited, heard his voice boom across the partition.

' 'Orace, where's that bloody tea?'

Troy heard Edelmann shuffling around the room. As near as possible for a man so misshapen he seemed to be pacing the floor. After several minutes he returned carrying two half-pint mugs of tea. He sat down opposite Troy.

'I'm listening,' he said. 'You have my attention.'

'I think Wayne – you do know him as Wayne, don't you?'

Edelmann nodded.

'I think he's a hit man, a military assassin for the American army. I know he killed these two. They're old colleagues of Wolinski's from before the war. I think he killed the first man a year ago when he tried to reach Wolinski. I think he killed the second man as he got to Wolinski. And that's when he killed Wolinski.'

'Nobody's seen 'im,' said Edelmann simply. 'Not for weeks. He was always a risk. I kinda guessed. Knew, if you like. What I never knew was why.'

'Nor do I. When did you last see them?'

'February. The twenty-fourth.'

'How can you be sure?'

'Study group meeting. Same time every month. I saw Peter in the afternoon. He said he'd be there. Wayne was there. He'd been coming on and off for about nine months.'

'Why did you let him in?'

'Bona fides. 'E 'ad 'em, didn't 'e. Letters from my sister's brother-in-law in Pennsylvania. Saying as 'ow 'e'd been a member of the United Workers of the World back in the thirties. Truth to tell I was quite pleased. It was another arm for the movement. Not one you expect. Russians and Poles we got by the dozen. It was heartening to be getting news from America. Made us feel we were getting somewhere. He'd give us all the news, all the gen on the unions over there. What a con the new Deal was. All that kinda stuff.'

Edelmann seemed for a moment to have wound down to silence.

'And Diana Brack?' Troy prompted.

'She come along with 'im. That helped. Added to his bonas. I knew 'er. She'd been at conferences and meetings I'd been at. You expect the odd toff or two. Some are slummin', some are serious. Believe it or not it was H. G. Wells introduced me to 'er. I think it was 'is way of testin' out both of us. A quick 'allo and a handshake. Wells calls me the Stepney Quasimodo. She smiles. So I 'ave to. Bastard.'

'Didn't you check out Wayne through your contacts?'

'What do you think I got? The Kremlin's home number? I ain't even got Harry Pollit's home number. It don't work that way. It don't.'

'Was Wayne close to anyone?' Troy asked.

'Close? It ain't a social club.'

Troy knew better, but refrained from saying so.

'Did he have particular friends? Did Diana?'

'No to the first. He chipped in whenever we got round to something he knew about. But he tended to stick with 'er. I knew 'im better than most, but that ain't sayin' much. Diana's different. She'll pick out someone and home in on him. Did that to me second time I met 'er. Sees me across a room and just cuts through the crowd like she'd just one thing on her mind. Oblivious to anyone else. People buttonhole her she just smiles 'er toff's smile, polite as Miss Manners, and they sod off like they just 'ad a tooth filled. She likes to have a special friend. So 'appens in this lot it was Wolinski. I reckon she worked out after one meeting that 'e was the only one she 'ad anything to learn from.'

'Were they lovers?'

'I wouldn't know. We in't the mind police, whatever the papers say. Certainly in't the fuck police.'

'This special relationship – it didn't extend to Wayne?'

'No – I hardly saw 'im and Peter exchange a word. Wayne's no egghead. He'd've bored Peter stiff as socks on a frosty morning.'

Edelmann paused.

'The twenty-fourth,' Troy prompted.

'The twenty-fourth. Wayne was there. We have a pint in the Merchant in Matlock Street and move upstairs for the talk. We'd been going about ten minutes or so when Alf – that's the landlord of the Merchant – comes up and tells me Peter's phoned to say he can't make it. He was like that. Peter. Always considerate. Now, Lady Di – I was expectin' 'er too. She used to be pretty regular. Bought a lot of the books for my boys. And if the buggers couldn't be arsed to read 'em she'd like as not be able to tell you all about 'em anyway. But she don't show, and I 'ear not a word from 'er. Nor 'ave I since. A couple of minutes after I gets Peter's message Wayne gets up and makes his excuses to leave. Can't remember what 'e said. But it was the last time I saw 'im. The last time I saw either of 'em. I'd not put two and two together. Not in my conscious mind that is. Till you walked in. I suppose at the back of my mind I was expecting you or someone like you. I'd have shown you the door and the back of my hand otherwise, wouldn't I? And now you're tellin' me Wayne walked out and killed Peter, aintcha?'

'I think I am,' said Troy.

'Dear oh dear oh dear,' said Edelmann, and slurped deeply on his tea. 'And now I have to rely on you for justice. Dear oh dear oh dear.'

'It's the business I'm in,' said Troy.

Edelmann said nothing. Just pushed the mug of tea across the packing case at Troy. A train rumbled overhead, trundling in from Tilbury. They sat in silence.

'I 'ate coppers,' Edelmann said eventually, quietly. 'More than that I 'ate bein' dependent on coppers.'

Another train crossed above them, from the opposite direction. Troy counted the clicks on the plates, the mathematical music of trains rattling their metronome beat into the vast peace of night, and listened to Edelmann sipping loudly at his tea and silently hating Troy. Troy felt it was time to leave. He rose and said, 'I'll be in touch.'

'Bloody right you will.'

In the main room of the shelter Troy looked around for Wildeve, not immediately recognising that the back nearest to him in the group sat talking around the fire was his. It struck him as odd. He would not have expected Wildeve to strike up any easy conversation with these people. He was hunched over in a half-whispered, earnest discussion – letting the sepulchral tone of the shelter induce a churchy respect into his voice. Only when the eyes of the men shifted up to Troy did he turn and see him waiting. Two of the eyes now looking at Troy belonged to Michael McGee, the innocent who had first showed Troy Wolinski's flat. Outside, Troy buttoned up his overcoat and waited for·Wildeve. McGee came out first.

'What you going to do?' he asked quietly. An air of resignation to he knew not what.

'I'm going to make an arrest,' Troy said simply.

Wildeve emerged in time to hear Troy's reply. There was a silence of awkwardness. McGee waited for more. They waited for McGee to accept that Troy would say no more and return to the shelter. Troy set off down Cable Street. Wildeve caught up with him.

'Freddie`– just who are we going to arrest?'

§ 52

Two hours later, the clock was crawling towards ten and Troy sat on the edge of his desk looking out at the river. Onions had gone home by the time they had got back from Stepney. Troy was pleased. A day's or even just a night's grace for what he was about to do would be priceless. He heard the door open, and turned a little to see Wildeve enter.

'They're back,' said Wildeve.

Troy had thought better of going himself. Better of sending Wildeve. The job had fallen to Thomson and Gutteridge.

'I've put her in the interview room.'

Troy slipped off the desk and began to button up his overcoat.

'No. Put her in the cells.'

'What?'

'She's not here to help with enquiries. She's under arrest.'

'What about the warrant?'

Troy fished around in his pockets for his gloves. The knowledge that Troy was about to leave seemed to baffle and exasperate Wildeve.

'Isn't one,' said Troy. 'I told Thomson to pull her in under the Emergency Powers Act. I don't need a warrant. Just see that you caution her before you lock her up for the night. If she asks for her lawyer you've gone deaf. If she asks for food, make it bread and marge. If she asks for a cup of tea, make sure it's lukewarm. I'll be in at seven. We'll see how she responds to an early start.'

Troy set off down the corridor. Wildeve hared after him.

'Have you gone completely bloody mad? Emergency Powers. Fermanagh will have our balls for chestnuts!'

'Fermanagh's in Ireland. Retreated to his country seat after Dunkirk. It'll take days for him to stick in his two penn'orth. Emergency Powers is perfectly legal. We have two dead enemy aliens. A missing Pole and a fugitive American. Her connection with the matter is now evident. Emergency Powers will do nicely.'

Wildeve managed to slip ahead of Troy on the staircase and brought him to a halt with the flat of his hand placed squarely in his chest.

'What, what on earth do you hope to gain by putting Diana Brack in the cells for a night?'

'Think back. Back to how you would have reacted to it in the days before you knew it all as a policeman. You and I would both have found it very tough to get banged up in a cell with scratchy blankets and awful food. Look at it from her point of view. It's hardly a matter of routine. Think of it as the princess and the pea. She won't sleep a wink. Perhaps in the morning she'll feel like answering a few questions. She was the last person to see Wayne. It's time she talked.'

'And if she doesn't?'

'I reckon we'll have about three days before we have to let her go or make something out of the Act. If I can't get the truth or some portion of it out of her in that time you can take my warrant card and never call me copper again.'

Wildeve sighed and reluctantly accepted Troy's logic. They walked out of the Whitehall entrance of Scotland Yard side by side.

'What now?' asked Wildeve.

'I have other engagements.'

'At this time of night?'

'What's that supposed to mean?'

'Oh . . . just . . . well, Kolankiewicz seemed to think you needed rest.'

'Goodnight, Jack.'

Troy walked off along Whitehall in the direction of Trafalgar Square. In the direction of Orange Street.

He let himself in with the key Tosca had given him. The gesture gave him cause to halt. He weighed the key lightly in the palm of his hand. It seemed that he had accepted an awful lot in accepting the key. He went on up the stairs. Her door was open. No light came from it. She was at the back, standing in the south-facing window, looking out over Pall Mall and the Square. She was dressed in her army blouse, but was shoeless and skirtless, standing in the glare of moonlight in just her stockings. It was, he realised, her habitual way of ending the day. She cast off her uniform and with it the job. Like the habitual first drink of the day, which she grasped in her right hand, as her left came around the back of his neck to draw his face nearer to hers. A stockinged foot coiled around his leg and locked itself behind the knee. She tilted her head back, grinned and began to sing in a breathy imitation of Dietrich.

'Once upon a time, before I took up smiling, I hated the moonlight. Shadows of the night that something something seemed flat as the something. Once I awoke at seven, hating the morning light. Now I awake in heaven and all the world's alright.'

She stopped. Eyes alight, head nodding, encouraging him to pick up the refrain. He could not for the life of him think what the bloody song was.

'My God, does nobody know the verse to anything any more? "Blue Moon", dummy. Y'know, Rodgers and Hart?'

'Sorry. I only know the bits you can whistle.'

'It's true. I hate the moonlight. Leaves you no place to hide.'

'You have to hide?'

'I was being poetic. I guess I was wasting my time.'

'It makes a silver ribbon out of the river.'

'Sheeyit. Is that the best you can do? That's your idea of poetry?'

'Shit has only one syllable.'

'Shuttup.'

She kissed him lightly on the lips and began to sing again. Soft, breathy, and, her usual speaking rasp considered, surprisingly in tune. 'And then suddenly there appeared before me, the only one my arms will ever hold, I heard somebody whisper "please adore me" . . . ' She put her lips to his ear for the last line. He felt her breath hot upon him. 'That's like a hint, y'know.'

He remained steadfast in his silence.

'Sing dammit!'

'Sing what?'

'Please adore me.'

'I'm not ready for that.'

'God, you're no fun, copper.'

She uncoiled and went off for her customary struggle with the fridge door.

'Pull the blackout and let's have some light in here.'

In the blast of electric light she set down a large bourbon for him. Next to it on the table was a large green cardboard file. She tapped it with her finger.

'Make the most of it. It goes back in the morning or my ass is dogmeat.'

Troy flipped it open and sipped at the bourbon. She put the wireless on low. A faint murmur of Ambrose's Orchestra wafted across the airwaves.

'Where d'you get it?'

'Same place I got this one.'

A second file – buff-coloured and foolscap landed on the table from behind him. He looked at the familiar name upon it, and turned to look at her.

'Who is he?'

'My father.'

'Well . . . looks like you gonna be a rich man one day. Even if you inherit only a piece of your old man's action.'

'I already have. He died in November.'

'Sorry. The file ain't up to date. It was in Zelly's safe. There was one with your name on it too. But there was nothing inside it.'

'Nothing?'

'Nothing. Just a brand new empty file.'

So, Edge had been bluffing. He opened the green file without picking it up.

'What's OHQ 5 stand for?'

'Cockfosters. We have a base out there. Some old country mansion the Brits commandeered on our behalf.'

'OK,' he said. 'I'll read it in the morning.' He flipped the file shut and picked up the glass of bourbon.

'Am I hearing things? You don't want it all now? You can wait? You have, God forbid, other priorities?'

Troy said nothing. She put down her glass of whiskey and approached on tiptoes, still well short of being eye to eye. She took his glass from him, locked her hands behind his neck and looked up.

'Well – you're beginning to learn the house rules.'

'It might help if you printed them and stuck them on the wall. Like a seaside boarding house. You know. No spitting. No women after ten p.m.'

'No women after ten p.m! What an uptight asshole country this is.'

She kissed him lightly on an ear-lobe.

'Birds do it, bees do it, even something something . . . '

'Educated fleas,' Troy prompted.

'Even educated fleas do it!' Her voice soared to a loud mock growl. 'LET'S DO IT!!!'

They tumbled sideways on to the bed. He ended up on top. She kissed his eyes, his ears, his throat and then paused dramatically, one index finger across his lips.

'Y'know,' she said, 'this is the first time I haven't had to drag you between the sheets. However, before this gets to seem like unseemly haste – great phrase that, huh? unseemly haste. Have I been reading Jane Austen or what? – I have a treat in store for you. Look in the ice-box.'

'What?'

'Go look in the ice-box.'

Troy slid off the bed, dropped his jacket to the floor, wondering what she could be up to. The fridge was almost empty, but there on the middle shelf stood a cream-coloured screwtop jar. Troy picked it up and looked at it in the light. J. P. Davidson's Own Mayonnaise, made and packed in Baton Rouge, Louisiana. Fresh Olive Oil. Real Eggs. Accept no substitute. Not genuine without Ole JP's signature.

'I thought you couldn't get this stuff.'

'I can't. Zelly can. It was in his safe too.'

'Won't he miss it?'

'Nah ... he had like two dozen jars. And if he does, fuck 'im. As Marie Antoinette probably said, let 'em eat salad cream.'

Troy sat on the edge of the bed with his back to Tosca and unscrewed the top.

'Gorgeous,' he said, inhaling from the jar. 'Pity we've nothing to eat with it.'

'We have,' she said out of sight.

'Such as?'

'Such as ... me!'

He turned. She had taken off her blouse and was unhooking her brassière, unleashing a bosom of such magnificence as to stagger the beholder. She grasped the jar and upended it over her torso.

'OK, baby. I'm yours. Sauce me!'

§ 53

She slept through the first light of morning. Troy sat up in bed. The file told him what he had guessed and one or two things he hadn't. It detailed Wayne's missions. Mostly into occupied France, but an odd excursion to neutral Sweden, and several to Switzerland. Three trips to the area around Lille. Meetings with the Underground. Wayne's assurances to OSS that the men he met would arrange a meeting with Brand – the man who had finally surfaced as an arm in the grip of a dog's jaw, whom Kolankiewicz had dubbed Herr Cufflink – and, on the final trip, the meeting with Brand and the pair's escape to England by a daring night landing in French fields by a small USAF plane. What the report didn't say was why they wanted Brand. But Troy guessed that the file's function was to record actions and not reasons, thereby preserving some sort of secrecy if by chance people like Tosca indulged in a little safe-cracking. The report recorded Wayne's comments that Brand had proved very unco-operative during his debriefing at

Cockfosters. This was followed by a note initialled simply B McK expressing incredulity, 'Have we got the right man? Twice in a row. He's got to be a plant. What the hell do the French think they're playing at?' But Troy knew that Brand wasn't a plant. He'd just taken everything the Americans offered and then on the morning of 24 February had disappeared from Cockfosters never to be seen again. The file did not record any mention of pursuit or capture. But then, Troy thought, it wouldn't would it? On 27 February a rubber stamp had been applied and a thick black smudge marked the case as closed. It was initialled J W.

Tosca stirred in the tangled heap of sheets and blankets and pushed herself up on her arms like a stretching cat. She yawned and began to pull faces at him.

'Um. Yah Worra. Yuch. Boy – icky is not the word. I feel like someone glued my legs together. Worse,' she glanced down into the pit of sheets, 'I think my tits have fused.'

'When I was a boy I used to make models of Great War aeroplanes in balsa wood. Mayonnaise made a first-rate glue as I recall.'

'You better be kidding!'

She staggered from the bed, grabbed a towel and opened the door. Across the landing was a bathroom. Troy put the kettle on, pulled on his shirt and trousers, allowed enough time to let her settle and then followed, clutching the green file. Tosca was almost up to her neck in bubbles, and the skylight steamed up, cutting off the rays of spring sunshine.

'Bliss,' she said. 'I hate those days when there's no hot water. Y'know a true romantic wouldn't sit perched on the john. He'd drop his duds and get in the suds. You put the coffee on?'

Troy nodded. She closed her eyes and sighed with pleasure.

'There was nothing on a man called von Ranke last April?' Troy asked.

'No. Just a lot of mayonnaise, a lot of chocolate and a black book with telephone numbers and girls' names. I stole some of the chocolate. We ate it around midnight if you recall. I figured you meet enough hookers in your line of work not to need Zelly's black book so I didn't bother.'

Her eyes flickered open momentarily. 'Do you still think Jimmy killed this guy?'

'Yes.'

'Does the file prove it?'

'No. It adds to the weight of circumstantial evidence, but that's never enough. I need a witness.'

'Sorry, can't help you.'

'Why would the OSS send Jimmy to neutral countries?'

'A whole bunch of reasons. What did you have in mind?'

'He was in Sweden earlier this year. Just the once. He's been to Switzerland half a dozen times since 1942.'

'We have our man in Switzerland. It's a handy place to watch the Krauts from. It's also a handy place to do business with the Krauts.'

'Business? With the enemy?'

'Happens all the time. If you don't have any way of talking to them how do you expect to know when they're ready to call it quits? Sweden's another matter. Low-key from our point of view. As a rule it's nothing more than escaping refugees. For Jimmy to go in person they'd have to be someone special. He's not into helping the victims of Nazism for the sake of his health. They'd have to have something he wanted. There was a major flap on about Sweden not so long ago. I don't know what, but our people over there had gotten hold of something important.'

'Some*thing* not someone?'

'I'm certain of that. It was all coded stuff, but there's ways of telling. There was a lot of ranting and raving from Zelly – "Where the hell is Jimmy? Just when we get a piece of the action he's nowhere to be found!'

'A piece of the action?'

'His exact words.'

'What does it mean?'

'That's kind of ambiguous. It doesn't translate too good.'

She sank down into the foam, squeezed her breasts together to create a small mountain of white soapy bubbles and blew hard in Troy's direction. Froth flecked his face and shirt. She started to giggle and he knew his audience was at an end. He made coffee and left. She did not ask when he would be back, but then Troy read the lack of a question as indicating her knowledge of the answer. Wild horses, or more appropriately, wild murderers would not keep him away this evening.

§ 54

Troy let Diana Brack wait – on the assumption that waiting itself was something to which she could scarcely be accustomed. He had one of Scotland Yard's larger meeting rooms cleared and sat her in it, dwarfed by the emptiness, with only a WPC sitting by the door for company, which company had been minimised by Troy's instruction that the WPC was not to converse with the prisoner.

'I suppose you'll tell me this is all psychology?' Wildeve asked.

'If you like,' Troy replied without looking up from his desk.

By noon Brack had been cooling her heels for more than four hours, Troy was up to date on his paperwork and ready for her.

'Come and get me in an hour,' he told Wildeve.

'Eh?'

'Come and get me. Interrupt. Invent something. A telephone call. Anything.'

Brack was pacing the floor when Troy came in. Her anger was tempered by discretion. She had little intention of letting the cheap tricks of police work get to her. She did not use the opportunity to complain about the cell or the tea or the dreadful food.

'I suppose,' she began, 'that you'll tell me you have good reasons for this.'

Troy sat down at the trestle-table and gestured with an open hand to the vacant chair on the other side. She stood behind it but did not sit. A night in the cells had scarcely dented her. She still looked fresh. Troy hid his disappointment beneath his practised policeman's blank expression, and carefully arranged a series of files in front of him on the table. They were all empty. Edge's trick was worth the try.

'And I suppose you'll tell me chapter and verse of the law which lets you keep me here?'

'Emergency Powers Act (Defence) 1939 and subsequent extensions thereto,' said Troy. 'The word "defence" is in parentheses, by the way. Lady Diana, why don't you sit down? The sooner you answer my questions the sooner you'll be out of here.'

She hesitated. The look on her face told Troy she did not believe him. Then she sat, hitched her long black skirt up an inch or two, crossed her legs and slipped her cloak on to the chairback.

Troy went into the numbing routine of times and dates and places and bodies, and listened to her explanations and alibis. He found no reason to disbelieve her. If she said she went to bed early with a migraine on the night of 24 February, he was inclined to accept it. After all he could check with the housemaid and no amount of loyalty would enable the girl to withstand a few minutes of police badgering. The night Miller died he had walked with her and his sisters from the Strand to Trafalgar Square, stood awhile in the fog as they gossiped and then had seen her flag a cab, some twenty minutes after losing sight of Wayne, as she pointedly reminded him. But he had no interest in these answers any more than he had in the questions. Wayne was unlikely to have had any eyewitnesses to his killings – and certainly not such as Diana Brack – who would by now have torn themselves apart in reliving the nightmare. He pushed no further. After an hour Wildeve duly interrupted. Troy hesitated in the doorway and flung out over his shoulder the only question that mattered.

'Where is Major Wayne?'

'You tell me,' she replied.

Troy left her to wait in silence once more.

In the afternoon Troy asked the same questions again, and again and again. He pushed her towards the point of exasperation. It was a long journey. She answered Troy's questions with a firm air of being bored. Troy waited for her to say 'tiresome', but she withheld even that small satisfaction. The slight variations in her answers served to convince Troy that she was telling the truth. Exactitude would smack of rehearsal, of a planned, contrived story. At 6 p.m. he returned her to the cells, having asked only one meaningful question and having received no answer.

'Why?' asked Wildeve.

'She knows.'

'Knows what?'

'Knows that Wayne kills. She knows it and conceals it and lives with it. That makes her tough. One of the toughest people I've ever had to deal with. I would prefer it if she were at her wits' end when she tells me all about Wayne.'

'What does she have to tell? You said she wasn't a witness.'

'She is a witness to the man not the acts.'

Troy went home – to Tosca.

§ 55

Late in the morning of the second day Brack met the same inane questions with the first show of resentment.

'I went to bed with a migraine! How many times do I have to tell you?' she snapped.

This was fine with Troy. The first crack in the ice. He tapped on the table-top with his pencil. Stood, stretched and ran his fingers through his hair. The display of a man at a loss for words.

'All right,' he said in a tone of weariness. 'Tell me about the Major.'

'Tell you what?'

Troy resumed his seat, still stretching and yawning, and listening for every variation in the tone of her voice and the rhythm of her breathing.

'Anything . . . how did you meet?' he mused. 'Yes. That's it. Tell me how you met.'

For a moment Troy thought she might not take the bait, but she sighed and looked at the ceiling and began with a breathy air of indulgence, the hint of relief that the subject had changed.

'I don't see how this can possibly be of interest to you – we met at a Left Book Club discussion in a hall in Bloomsbury.'

'I see. I wouldn't have put the Major down as an intellectual.'

'You wouldn't put him down as anything because you don't know him. And if you did you'd realise your suspicions are absurd. Instead I think you've been talking to Edelmann and you're repeating his opinion verbatim. Jimmy is no intellectual. What of it?

He has an intelligence Edelmann would never perceive. A native intelligence. He's curious about so many things. An . . . an animal intelligence, do you see?'

Troy saw exactly. Animal intelligence fitted his idea of Major Wayne very well.

'Everyone I know describes you as a bluestocking. I'm at a loss to know what a woman like you would see in a man like Wayne. An ordinary soldier.'

'He is far from being an ordinary soldier. As much as you are from being an ordinary policeman.'

'What's an ordinary . . . ?'

A voice in Troy's head told him not to ask. Too late. She was going to tell him come what may.

'What's an ordinary policeman? A man who wears size-ten boots, a bowler hat, suits from a fifty-shilling tailor and has celluloid · collars to his shirts. Your shoes are from Jermyn Street, a single pair would pay a bobby's wages for a month. Your suit is tailor-made by a man in Savile Row with whom I expect your father opened an account as soon as you went into long trousers. Your shirts are handmade in St James's Street or thereabouts and your hat if you were ever so conventional as to wear one would be from Cork Street. That's pretty damn far from being a run-of-the-mill copper as you well know.'

Troy was surprised to learn she had observed him so closely. He assumed a face of prolonged boredom.

'In his way Jimmy is as different from the run-of-the-mill as you are.'

She paused, as though unsure how far to go.

'Imagine what it is like to be me. I spent a large part of my life surrounded by people who don't think and being told not to think myself. I come from a class that substitutes acceptance for thought. Imagine my childhood. I was brought up by one of Britain's unsung tyrants. A man who by the time I was twelve had turned his life into one long moan of resentment that he hadn't been allowed to fulfil his promise. That fate or worse, his own party, had conspired to cheat him of leadership. As his first-born I deeply offended him by not being male, and by adolescence I compounded the sin by turning out to be the tiresome kind of child that asks questions. His response was to bully. Not just me, but my brothers too. We did his bidding or we were thrashed. We thought as he thought or we were thrashed. Is it any wonder George and Johnny are drunks and lounge lizards? I have been a constant irritant to my father. The boys have been a constant embarrassment. Of the two he found embarrassment easier to handle. Pay their fines, pay off the mothers of their bastards and pay to have them dried out occasionally. What he could not handle were questions. My father didn't want me to go to university. Women simply didn't. If he'd known what Oxford was like between the wars he would not have found cause to worry. It was like belonging to a rather fashionable, inane club. If he'd read Evelyn Waugh he'd know that, but then reading isn't his forte. When I came down in 1931 I think he had one last fantasy that I might make a good marriage and be off his hands, but I soon disabused him of that.'

Troy knew how she had disabused the old man. Wildeve had regaled him with gossip – her unpublicised but notorious affair with H. G. Wells, a man old enough to be her grandfather, must have driven Fermanagh to distraction. Compared to Wells, Al Bowlly would have been a welcome relief.

'I was looking for challenges,' she added simply.

'You're not going to tell me that in rejecting family and class you also rejected the high life?'

'No. And I'm not going to answer gossip either. I wasn't interested much in the social round. But it's there. Let's just say that it amuses me sometimes to play the game. After all there's such pressure to do it that to give in from time to time eases the strain. I've never had much difficulty combining the dinner party with the political party. I'm surprised anyone should think them incompatible. If you want your politics crudely cooked, then you may turn to phrases like "it pays to know your enemy" or "to see how the other half lives" – I know how the other half lives. I am the other half. I can and do return to their world. But that's not the point. The point is this world. Trying to describe that without making you sneer isn't easy. I don't think you and I have ever moved in quite the same circles. You would surely understand if we had. The Left Book Club, the Fabians, the Communists are simply ways of meeting people who think. London is so full of people who don't.'

She paused. Searching for a clincher.

'Tell me. Have you ever met Sidney Webb?'

Troy had met so many people at his father's table. The Webbs included.

'He has a fine mind. The energy of a man half his age. But talking to Sidney is like discussing the state of the municipal drains with the borough engineer. And there are so many like him. Social planners for whom there is adventure in ideas but no idea of adventure. The sheer solidity of it weighs me down. I'd given Socialism ten years of my life. I was tempted. I was on the verge of giving up – not the belief – but the organisation. And then I met Jimmy. Jimmy is everything the Fabians aren't. When he walked into that hall in Bloomsbury it was . . . electric. He moved unlike anyone I'd ever met. He had conviction with calm. He talked and he listened with a composure that was new. The dreadful thing about the Left is that they long ago mistook outrage and urgency for efficiency and conviction. The number of pointless rows I've witnessed. I was fed up with them beyond measure . . . when suddenly a man appears with . . . dammit, with life in him! Edelmann is right in only the most limited sense. Jimmy is intelligent, he has a way of going to the heart of a matter in a few simple strokes, a few questions. He brought a new way of looking at things, a new way of . . . I . . . I . . .'

She stopped, looking at Troy, exasperated.

'Oh God. You haven't a clue what I'm talking about have you?'

Troy felt he knew quite well what she was talking about, although it might pay to be less than understanding. In Wayne she had met a man who blew the cobwebs out of the old British plodding Socialists. About time. They'd bored him silly throughout childhood. He not only understood, he agreed – except that she had fallen for the front put up by a man Troy perceived as a first-rate charlatan.

'What does a man have to do to get you to lie for him?'

'What do you mean?'

'You did take the photograph. You did conceal Jimmy when I called on you in March. What did he tell you?'

'Nothing. He wanted the photograph. He didn't want to see you. It's as simple as that.'

'And you didn't ask why?'

'No. I saw no reason to.'

'You've spent your life asking questions and you didn't ask Jimmy why he wants to avoid the police?'

She mustered defiance in not answering. Trying to stare back at him, but no longer calm, her determination dented.

'He's killed three men, and quite possibly a fourth too. Lady Diana, only a fool would attempt the degree of self-deception you're practising.'

She was redder in the face now. Troy thought she might be on the verge of tears.

'Where is he?'

'I don't know,' she said for the umpteenth time, but this time the sad mechanics of repetition and deceit told. Her voice was weak and the words carried no conviction. Troy knew she was lying.

The following morning he got her out of bed at six thirty, and she seemed pleased to see him. Whatever she had passed a sleepless night pondering was worse than any conversation she could have with him. Troy suspected that simply bringing her father into the matter had unlocked a floodgate. She talked and she talked and she talked. The same old song – understand me, imagine me. If only Troy would do this he would be able to see Wayne through her eyes and stop his pointless pursuit.

Troy sat through this potted biography, this dilettante's history of British radicalism, and let her unravel. He spread his folders out on the desk in front of him – but today they were not empty.

She changed her mind about gossip and proceeded to compare the absent Major to Wells – a quality of mind, a quality of presence. Troy interjected that murder was unlikely to be one of the many ways in which Wells had offended society. But Wells's shortcomings were nothing compared to her father's – she moved from one man to the other with a speed and complexity that was hard to follow. For a while it seemed to Troy that Wayne and Fermanagh and Wells all represented aspects of a single man – a Promethean creature of her own making.

Troy opened one of the files while she was in mid-flight on the subject of her father. He slipped a picture of Brand's broken skull in front of her. She stopped.

'What is this?'

Troy said nothing and took out the photograph of von Ranke.

'Why are you showing me these?'

Troy looked at her. She looked at the photographs.

'These are the men you think Jimmy killed?'

Troy nodded. 'Would it surprise you to learn,' he said, 'that these are the men in the photograph you took?'

'No, no – that was Wolinski.'

'And Brand and von Ranke – I expect Wolinski's body to turn up one day. Or perhaps you can tell me how the Major disposed of it?'

The blood had drained from her face. She stared at the pictures in disbelief, looking between them and Troy, searching out some shred of reassurance.

'Jimmy couldn't do that. Jimmy couldn't do that to anyone.'

Troy reached for the photograph of Detective Sergeant Miller – taken only minutes after his death – bloodier by far. She gasped out loud. For a moment or two she could find neither voice nor words. Her face was down, her eyes fixed on the photograph. As she looked up at him, brushing the forelock from her face, he thought he caught the beginnings of tears in the corners of her eyes.

'He didn't,' she whispered. 'He didn't do this!'

'He shot each of these men in the face. I think that's a peculiarly American technique, don't you? The ritual of gangland. Sergeant Miller was shot three times at point-blank range. Once to the mouth, once to the cheek and the bullet that killed him took the back of his head off. I scraped his brains off the cab seat myself.' Troy stabbed at the photograph with his index finger, pinpointing each bullet-hole with a thump of the table. Her mouth opened in a silent scream. She cupped a hand to it and fought for words.

'He didn't do it! He couldn't do it!'

Troy stood up and began to gather up his files, leaving the shot of Miller on the table in front of her.

'I think you know damn well that he did. I think the man you've

200

spent two days describing to me as admirably, attractively different is different to you precisely because he can do this.'

She breathed deeply for several seconds, regaining some composure, some voice.

'What does that mean? I don't understand.'

'I'll leave you and the late Sergeant Miller to ponder that.'

As he reached the door she found voice enough to shout, 'I know he didn't do this, I know! Please believe me, Troy, I know! Troy, please!'

After lunch Brack was shown once more into the meeting room. Troy had left the lights off and stood over the far side of the room against the shuttered windows on the southern side. The door closed behind Brack. She stood a moment or two in stillness, and then, as Troy did not move or turn to face her, she instinctively crossed the room towards him. Counting her footsteps Troy swung off the iron bar that held the shutters and let it swing free, clanging like a pendulum against the wooden frame. He prised back one leaf of the shutters and sunlight shafted into the room. He opened a second and before he could even turn to look at her Brack was shrieking. And nothing on earth would still her cries.

The shaft of light became a flood picking out in every detail the blood-caked holes in the face and skull of the corpse that lay on the trolley between Brack and the window. She put her hands to her cheeks and screamed through her fingers, but her gaze was fixed on Miller's face and until her legs gave way and she sank into a pitiful, bowed heap upon the floor she made no attempt to shield her eyes.

Minutes passed. The screams became whimpers. She said 'No' over and over again through stifling sobs. Troy stood still, framed in the open window, the shadow of his head cast across her face by the southern sun. The door opened and Onions stood in the doorway. A constable just behind him. Scarcely even raising his voice to normal speaking pitch, he said over his shoulder, 'Get that thing out of here, then fetch a WPC.'

He stood aside as the trolley was wheeled past him, his hands in his pockets. He looked at Brack without a flicker of expression on his face. Slowly he crossed the floor and stood next to Troy, looking out of the window, as calmly as a man surveying his rose garden from the french windows of suburbia.

'This had better be worth it,' he said quietly, watching the sunlight play upon the Thames. 'Are you gettin' much?'

Brack sobbed, louder than either of them speaking.

'Lies,' said Troy. 'I'm getting lies.'

'You've not got much longer. Her father's outside. Brought his brief too. Flown in from Ireland special,' Onions said in the most matter-of-fact way possible.

'I've been expecting this. Can you stall him?'

'I've stalled him the best part of an hour already.'

'Is he asking for her?'

'No. He's asking for you.'

'Then I'd better see him.'

They turned and crossed the room. Neither looked at the shrunken heap of clothing that was Diana Brack, but they parted around her automatically, like men avoiding an importunate beggar in the street. As they left a WPC came in. She looked at Brack and turned on her heel to speak to Troy.

'What do I do?' she asked.

'You do nothing,' Troy replied. 'And you *say* nothing.'

Onions strode off ahead. Troy quickened his step to catch him. It had always been part of the plan to let Brack sweat it out alone. Onions's intrusion was not yet regrettable – it might even be timely.

The Marquess of Fermanagh waited in an interview room. He stood by the window, stooping slightly, with his back to them as Onions and Troy came in. Slowly he swung around, drawing himself up to a towering six feet six. As tall as Bonham and half his weight, he was skeletal thin, with a sharply pointed nose and a gleaming mass of white hair combed back away from the forehead. Troy put him at seventy-four or five. He had his daughter's dark green eyes, but his lips were thin, drawn on to that cadaverous face by a pencil. He bore a striking resemblance to the actor Ernest Thesiger, in particular, thought Troy, to the role of the demented genius Thesiger had played in *The Bride of Frankenstein*. Troy found him instantly repulsive, exuding an evil born of political power rather than mere cinematic association. He found it impossible not to view the man through his daughter's eyes. It seemed as though over the last three days Fermanagh had joined Wayne as a ghost that lurked in the space between Troy and Diana Brack.

Fermanagh's solicitor attempted introductions only to be cut short by his client rapping on the table with the silver knob of his cane.

'Enough! Enough! Shuttup Pumphret! The Sergeant knows very well who I am! What matters is what he has to say for himself.'

Onions assumed a position of judicious abdication. He sat on a radiator and feigned indifference. Fermanagh seated himself at the table. Troy sat opposite him, leaving the solicitor nervously grasping the back of a chair, unsure whether to pull it back and sit or whether to keep well clear. A nod from Fermanagh told him to sit and Troy knew that this would not be a three-way conversation but a dialogue. Mr Pumphret had been brought along to show the briefcase and the bowler hat and give a gloss of legitimacy to the proceedings. Fermanagh would do his own bargaining, if indeed that was why he had come. Men like Fermanagh could not be accustomed to bargaining.

Troy recited, 'I am holding your daughter under Emergency Powers legislation. I am investigating a case involving the activities of certain enemy aliens. I have reason to believe she has information affecting the case. Unless you have been able to procure a writ of habeas corpus, I intend to go on holding her.'

He paused long enough for the solicitor to begin, long enough for Fermanagh to launch into his bluster, but neither man spoke.

'I take it then that you don't have a writ?'

'Writs be damned!' said Fermanagh. 'Let's hear the evidence! If you dragged my daughter in here you must have some evidence.'

Troy felt Onions looking straight at him over the head of the Marquess. He found Fermanagh's tone hard to read – for a moment it almost seemed that he wanted Troy to have a case. Why was he not simply barking his insistence, crying outrage, scorching opposition? Since when did men like Fermanagh care for facts? They rattled the crockery and frightened the horses.

'Lady Diana was seen leaving the house of a man closely connected to the case, who has disappeared – quite possibly the man has been murdered. Your daughter entered his flat after he was reported missing and took a photograph representing two enemy aliens and the third man.'

'And you have a witness to this?'

'Yes.'

'And he has identified my daughter?'

'Yes.'

'Who is he?'

Troy was not about to admit that it was himself.

'I can't tell you that.'

'And this man saw my daughter in this missing man's flat?'

Troy had smelt Diana Brack, he didn't need to see her, but that was a subtlety not to be wasted on Fermanagh.

'Yes,' he lied.

'But this missing man, your third man, is not an enemy alien?'

So far Fermanagh was doing well. He had in a few easy moves succeeded in bringing Troy to the weakness in his argument. Onions, he knew, would uphold his refusal to admit and define his own role as a witness, but he was unlikely to defend a lie on this issue.

'No,' Troy conceded. 'He is not.'

'A foreigner?'

'Yes.'

'Be precise, Sergeant. If that's at all possible.'

'A Pole.'

'Ah . . . an ally in fact?'

Troy said nothing. Fermanagh nodded and aahed as though weighing it all up. Pumphret stared at the crown of his bowler.

'It's thin, I say. Pretty damned thin. Wouldn't you say, Pumphret?'

Pumphret didn't say.

'Enemy aliens. Dirty business. Dirty business. Fifth column. Nazis in our midst.'

Fermanagh seemed to be musing out loud. Troy recalled reading in his father's newspaper in the thirties that Fermanagh had been one of a group of senior Tories who had called for talks with Hitler, who had endorsed Chamberlain's 'peace for our time' as 'a just agreement with our natural ally' rather than the delaying device it so obviously was. Not that this would colour his thinking now.

Patriotism was a last but ready refuge for scoundrels like Fermanagh. Troy knew exactly where this line was leading.

'But you don't have any direct link between my daughter and these people, do you?'

Troy stared at him, determined to offer no answer unless forced to.

'And without that link . . . you cannot charge her . . . you cannot detain her under 18b . . .'

Regulation 18b permitted detention without trial – it had been used to intern hundreds of aliens and several dozen suspect Britons, the Mosleys among them. Troy had no intention of invoking this and Fermanagh knew it. Pumphret might look like a fool but he had briefed his client well.

'You will . . .' the Marquess reached his point, '. . . have to let her go.'

Troy waited as long as he could. Hoping that Fermanagh would fill the silence. He did. Out of sheer cockiness rather than discomfort at Troy's unblinking gaze and utter silence, almost casually, smiling through stained, wicked wolf's teeth, he threw in an unnecessary 'Sooner or later'.

'Quite,' said Troy with the speed of a striking snake. 'Later. When *you* have got your writ.' And the house of cards Fermanagh had so carefully built came crashing down even as he smiled.

It was obvious to Troy that Fermanagh had no wish to apply for the writ. Now he could read the man and the game he played. He wasn't here to save his daughter, he was here to save the family name. He didn't, Troy concluded, give a damn about her. Any halfway decent father would have asked about her well-being before playing police politics with him, and as the 'sooner or later' showed the old bastard probably thought a day or two in the cells was good for a wayward daughter he had all but disowned ten years ago. Troy knew that he had no case on which to hold Brack, that Fermanagh could walk out of Scotland Yard with his daughter, that he could obtain a writ of habeas corpus almost at the snap of his fingers, but he also knew that he wasn't prepared to push the matter to a court appearance. He had gambled on Troy not recognising a bluff, gambled on the intimidating power of class and title. And he had lost. Troy got up – 'If you'll excuse me, sir,' he said to Onions –

and left. He could hear Fermanagh barking his name all the way down the corridor.

Troy relieved the WPC, pulled over an upright chair and sat six or seven feet away from Brack. She acknowledged his presence by looking up once. Her make-up ran in black rivers down her cheeks. Her sobs, though subdued, were still audible, and as he sat waiting for the time to begin again they seemed to swell to fill the room with the bottomless depths of her grief.

Twenty minutes or more passed to this single sound. Then she looked up again.

'He didn't do *that*,' she whispered. 'He couldn't do . . . *that*.'

Troy returned her look without blinking. 'Oh yes he did,' he said at the same whisper pitch. 'And you and I are the only people alive who know that. The only people who know him for what he is.'

Her green eyes flashed. She bowed her head and resumed the slow rhythmic sobbing. The door opened. Onions jerked his head at Troy to summon him outside.

Troy pulled the door to quietly behind him. 'What's Fermanagh saying?'

'Lot of tosh about how he has respect for the due process of the law, greased with knowing the Prime Minister . . . '

'Winston won't lift a finger for Fermanagh.'

' . . . Half the cabinet, not to mention the Met commissioner – "but all the same, the law is the law". He's full of "on the one hand, on the other" kind of malarkey. I think he'd dearly love to strangle you, but he'd prefer it if I did. He's implying a lot and saying nowt.'

'Will he call the commissioner?'

'No, I don't think he will. But –' Onions paused. 'I'm going to have to let her go.'

'I'm not prepared to do that.'

'You misheard me, Sergeant. *I'm* going to let her go!'

'Stan, there's no need. Fermanagh's bluffing. He won't chase a writ. He doesn't even have to do that. All he has to do is stand on his dignity and raise hell and he'll walk out of here with her, writ or no writ, because I haven't a leg to stand on and he knows it. But that's not all there is to it. He doesn't want to walk out of here with her. In fact, he doesn't even want to see her. He's enjoying tossing points of law around with me and pissing all over his own solicitor. He won't go for that writ.'

'Why not?'

'Because he knows bloody well that I have only to pick up the phone to the editor of any one of my father's papers to have it splashed across the lot, with every other daily to follow, that Old Fermanagh's daughter's been held under Emergency Powers with all that implies, and there's not a thing he or his team of libel lawyers can do about it. He came here hoping that we'd just give in at the first whiff of grapeshot, a title and a reputation. God knows it's probably worked for him all his life. I'd imagine rural chief constables jump when he barks. But I don't and nor do you. So he opted to mix the bluff and bluster with a little fact and negotiation – and there's the rub. That mixture doesn't work. It's so thin it's transparent. He hasn't the guts or, more importantly, the will to fight for his own daughter. He knows her well enough to know she's been up to something, and whatever he thinks it is he doesn't want it made public. He came here to learn what I knew, not to set his daughter free. The truth is he cares more for his own reputation than he does for her. After all, what's a few nights in a cell when your idea of punishing a child was to beat her senseless with a leather strap and lock her in the coal cellar overnight.'

'How the hell do you know that?'

Troy was startled. He had no idea how he knew. A distant, fogged memory of conversations overheard between his sisters and the young Diana Brack? Conversations that until now he could not have said he remembered in the slightest detail.

'That's not the point. The point is we've still got her until he makes us give her up. And he hasn't done that yet.'

'What more do you expect to get out of her?'

Troy knew the truth would be pointless. That he had no idea what she might say next and that therein lay the point. Onions would not deal in such intangible stuff as Troy's certainty that Brack knew Wayne was guilty and if she could be made to admit this 'who knows what might follow?' He offered a mundane matter of fact. 'Her movements and Wayne's the night Brand died.'

'She knows where Wayne was?'

'I'm damn certain she does.'

Onions pushed the door open. Brack had not moved. She lay curled in her dying-swan position, puddled in black. Soft sobs came from her. She had wept a full hour or more.

'Well. There's more than one way to beat them senseless and I don't think you'll get another bloody thing,' he said softly and firmly. 'That's my opinion, and I'm acting upon it. She walks.'

Onions recalled the WPC. She helped Brack to her feet. Onions and Troy stood looking on. Next to the WPC, even hunched in her despair, Brack seemed lithe and powerful. The WPC did her best to steady the larger woman, to steer her into the corridor, back to the front desk where she could collect her belongings.

She passed Troy with her head down, stepped two paces past him, turned and caught him on the cheek just below the left ear with a well-aimed right hook that wrenched her free from the WPC's guiding hand and sent Troy crashing to the floor. She stood at last at her full height, breathing deeply, staring down at the floored Troy through her tears. The blow had been aimed with all the skill of a man but not with the force. Troy lay amazed but unhurt and watched her disappear into the corridor. Onions said nothing, but left without extending a hand to help him up. It seemed to Troy that the gesture had overtones of 'I told you so'. He lay on the floor and stretched out in tiredness, cursing Onions for his unpredictability and his decency and that the two should ever so meet.

§ 56

Later than he liked Troy set off for home. At the entrance to Goodwins Court, Ruby the Whore stood sentry duty. Back from one commando raid and awaiting fresh orders. She propped a ladderless nylon-stockinged leg against the wall and blocked the narrow alley.

'You won't be needing me tonight then, Fred?'

Troy never did. There was a silent pause as Troy waited for her to drop the leg and let him pass. Nothing on earth would have induced him to grab hold and simply lift it out of the way. The joke milked, Ruby straightened up and brought her heels together with a click, and her lips together with a mocking pout. She blew a kiss. Six feet on he stopped. Something in the music-hall routine of her regular mickey-take was out of joint. The question. The fact that she was telling not asking.

'What do you mean?' he asked, turning back to look at her.

'She's a looker, my boy, an' no mistake.'

'Who is?'

'Dunno. But she's been hanging round your door a good hour and a half.'

There was no light to see by. He walked as quietly as leather soles would allow up to his front door. No sound or movement rippled the air. The alley was pitch black, breathless and deserted. He stuck his key in the door and a hand closed over his.

'I have to talk to you,' she said only inches from his ear.

'You've had three days of talking to me. Isn't that enough?'

Her hand tightened on his, forcing him to turn the key in the lock or physically shake her off. The door swung open.

'I have to talk to you,' she said again.

Troy said nothing. Stood on the doorstep, turning towards her to see her shape and features resolve out of the blackness. A voice became an outline, an outline a shadow, and when the shadow spoke, he saw the merest flash of white teeth. He could not see the eyes, but knew they were locked on his.

'He has gone.'

'Of course he's bloody gone. I've had half the coppers in London looking for him for days.'

'No. I mean gone gone, really gone. He was in our apartment at the Savoy. But now he's not. This time he's really vanished.'

Troy muttered 'Jesus Christ' and stepped inside. He crouched over the gas fire in the living room and put a match to it. He heard her follow softly behind him, and reached for the light switch. It was dead.

'The power's off all over the West End,' she said.

She materialised out of blackness by the pink roar of the gas fire. She knelt and held out her hands to it.

'I'm frozen to the marrow. I was an age out there.'

'I couldn't give a damn. Why didn't you tell me about the Savoy this afternoon.'

'Do you think I have no loyalty?'

'To a killer?'

'I don't accept that.'

'Then why are you telling me now?'

'I have nowhere to go.'

She slipped her cloak from her shoulders and curled her feet under her. Troy stood with his hands in his pockets. Coat on. To sit or to take off the coat would be tacit acknowledgement that she was there on his say so rather than against his will.

'You've a bloody expensive house in Tite Street, a lodge on the old man's Irish estate and a cottage in Suffolk.'

'I mean no one to go to.'

There was a long silence as Troy avoided her meaning and gave rapid thought to picking her up and throwing her into the street. She sighed deeply several times. If she was on the brink of tears Troy was no more likely to be moved at home than he was at the Yard.

'My father,' she began, 'my father took the Savoy apartment in 1938. He was terribly afraid of the Blitz. We all were. He foresaw London in ruins. And of course the Savoy has one of the strongest shelters in town. When he went back to Ireland in 1940 he passed on the lease to me. Not out of generosity – he'd simply been unable to sell it. Truth to tell I never used the shelters. Once a raid started I was rooted to the spot. I used to turn off the lights and stand in the window and watch the bombers across the river. Then I stopped using it at all. Until I met Jimmy and we needed somewhere to be together. Somewhere away from people, from time to time. When you came along with your silly allegations it seemed the perfect place. No one else knew I had the apartment. Not even the servants.'

'Not the Americans.'

'Certainly not the Americans. He stayed there while you looked for him. I could only visit when your men slipped up. Which they did often enough.'

She paused and breathed deeply.

'Naturally I went straight there from Scotland Yard. I walked along the river. No one followed me and I was there in minutes. And he was gone.'

Troy was angry and exasperated. He flung himself down in the chair by the fire. She was almost sitting at his feet.

'I suppose you think I'm a bitch. It's the only lie I told you. If I had told you where he was . . . '

Troy leaned forward as though about to throttle her, hands outstretched, his voice strained almost to shouting. 'If you'd told me where he was I would have arrested the murdering bastard!!! Can't you see the danger you're in?'

She seized both hands in hers. He had transgressed, crossed the narrow line that separated them. He should never have allowed the creature so close. She leaned her forehead against the backs of his hands. He heard the swift intake of breath that presaged tears and as she roved across his knuckles and fingers with her face he felt the hot wet tears fall upon his hands. He told his arms to withdraw and they did not move. He told his fingers to disentangle from the web and and they were paralysed. He told his legs to stand and they cheated, pitching him forward on to the floor. Almost nose to nose with his adversary, like two enquiring dogs. She let go of one hand and pushed her fingers into his hair at the temple. He had transgressed.

'When I was a girl I was fascinated by the darkness of this boy. Your hair so black and thick, so low on the brow. It still is. And the blacker black of your eyes. The darkness, the nothingness, the strength of silence. Was this child real, did he exist? Eyes let you see into the person. Yours just reflect back at the beholder and give nothing. I look into your eyes and I see myself as in a looking-glass. In a child that was disturbing. It seemed as though I must find a way to force a response out of you, out of silent eyes.'

That smothering kiss. Troy thought of the clear, fleckless brown of Tosca's eyes which smiled at him regardless of her expression. Of Wildeve's innocent, wide-eyed washed-out blue – the blue of jackdaws' eggs. And Brack's own bottle-green. He never, he realised, looked into a mirror except when he shaved. The nothing-ness she spoke of scarcely surprised him but he passed most of his life unconscious of its effect.

'That smothering kiss,' he said out loud, and in the utterance offered an invitation that could not escape her. She pressed her lips upon his. A momentary glance as their eyes met before she closed hers and time past overflowed into time present and the smell of her scent threatened death by drowning and with it the awful, inescapable stench of carbide gas and the brief glimpse of the swirling dust of carnage before his overloaded senses forced it from his mind and the touch of Brack drenched him.

He put out a hand to her breast. Cupped it. Enveloped it, small as it was. Her tongue ran hard across his lips, searching out his mouth. He reached down to her calves, bunching up the fabric of her dress, riding it up across her thighs, under the loose silk of her knickers to rest his hand warm and wet upon her cunt. He gripped her pants and began to drag them down towards her ankles. Her mouth withdrew. Her eyes opened once more, staring into his. She raised her knees and curled her legs and pulled at her pants and with her free hand tossed them behind him.

'I cannot see you,' was all she said.

In a position that threatened imminent cramp Troy squatted awkwardly and peeled back his overcoat, tore at his trouser buttons, freed his cock and collapsed into her as she locked her hands into the hair at the back of his neck and pulled him down upon her.

'I shall come,' she cried softly. It sounded to Troy like a promise she was making to herself. But it was he who came. Instantly. Almost without movement. Emptying into her in wave after wave.

He relaxed on to an elbow, his face towards the dull glow of the fire. Brack lay on her back, uncurled one leg. In profile she was silhouetted against the gaslight. Was she smiling? He had not seen her smile since the night she had trounced him at the Adelphi with her tale of the boy and his bicycle. She had not had cause to smile. She slept. Her breathing came so regularly it must be sleep. It seemed an age. Her eyes opened. Closed. Opened again. She turned fractionally towards him. Ran a finger up his cheekbone and wrapped the hand into his hair.

'There is a bed, I take it?'

'Of course. Upstairs.'

'Help me up.'

Troy stood. The most foolish position ever devised for a man he thought. Trousers around ankles. And held out a hand to pull her to her feet. She walked past him and up the staircase. He heard her feet in the room above, the clump on clump as she kicked off her shoes. He prised his off, toe to heel, and stepped out of his trousers. It came to him that he had no idea how to undress, how much to undress, how to get up the stairs dressed, half-dressed or naked. But knew he could not walk upstairs bare-arse naked. He slipped off his jacket, socks and tie and stood a while in his shirt and pants. He could delay no longer, bought himself a fraction of time by dutifully turning off the gas fire and followed her up.

She had lit a candle by the bedside and was undressing with her back to him. The flame danced in the draughts of an ancient house. She stepped out of her skirt and pulled her blouse over her head in that cross-armed action that only women ever seemed to master. She reached her arms behind her to unclip her brassière and suddenly was naked. Her shape outlined against the candlelight, the long, curving waistline, the broad shoulders, the willowy legs and boyish hips, was at once irresistible to Troy. She stood stock-still. He did not know if she was waiting. Her shoulders heaved gently with the weight of breathing, and her sigh, scarcely audible though it was, seemed to fill the room. He approached and kissed the back of her neck at the hairline. She squirmed her head, turned her whole body to him, kissed him on the mouth, and wrapped her arms around his neck. Without shoes she was still a good three inches taller than he, a shadow looming above him, cutting off the dancing light, and she tilted her head on one side to nip gently at his bottom lip. His hands were level with her upper thighs, he slid them between her legs and felt the crisp, puckered skin where his semen had dried upon her. He drew his fingers to her seam and felt the nip as her teeth tightened on his lip. He stroked slowly at her. She shifted softly on her feet, parting her legs. She let go of his lip. It stabbed with pain. She lay back on the bed legs spread looking back at him. Foolish. Man alone in shirt and underpants. The child too bashful to share communal showers until forced. Who needed a candle at the bedside every night but made his

213

mother turn her back as he undressed. He unbuttoned his shirt. Dropped it to the floor. Foolish and foolisher. Man in underpants. He felt her eyes settle on the final item of clothing. Watching the erection that thrust up his pants like a tentpole. She would not be the one to speak, she would not be the one to release his foolishness with a provocative, jokey 'get 'em off'. He let them go and climbed on to the foot of the bed. Foolish no more. She crooked an arm and scratched lazily at the pectoral of her left breast. He heard the rasp of nails on skin. He advanced an inch or two over her on hands and knees. She rose up and sank her teeth into the muscle above one of his nipples and worked his cock with both hands. He grew and burned and his chest needled and stung. He pushed her back against the pillows, tangled his fists in the dense black hair and took her. Rising and falling, thrusting hard as she arched her back against him, twisting vainly to bite at his hands. The wind shook the windows, caught the candle. The flame blew cleanly out and in the dark she screamed.

§ 57

He awoke to the sound of clapping. The irony of applause did not escape him. It was almost dawn. He was alone. The bedroom window was open and the blackout clapped in the rising breeze of morning. He went quietly downstairs. The front door was open, shifting gently back and forth in the same breeze. He found his trousers and pulled them on. Barefoot and shirtless he stepped into the street half-expecting to see her simply standing waiting. From what he knew it seemed in character. No light had yet penetrated the court. He peered to the left, out towards the obvious exit into St Martin's Lane. It felt like a clenched fist. High and fast, catching him on the side of the head right between the eyebrow and the ear and pole-axing him with a single blow. His vision was green and sightless but for a moment or two he remained conscious. Almost enough to know that someone was giving him a damn good kicking. The head, the kidneys, the ribs. Then green turned to

red. Blood mist, blood moon. It was familiar. Almost welcoming.
He had transgressed.

§ 58

Again he woke. Stretched out on the sofa in the living room. A
blanket across him. Ruby the Whore sat in the armchair, drinking
tea. Troy found he could speak. The blow to the head had missed
his jaw.

'How long...?'

'About ten minutes. I heard the rumpus from the other end of
the alley. But he'd gone by the time I got to you.'

Troy groaned. Tasted blood. As he drew in breath his ribcage
expanded into cutting pain. He leaned over the side of the sofa and
vomited.

'Go on, Freddie, you puke it all up. Make you feel a lot better
that will. I seen some kickings in my time. You been worked over
by a pro.'

Troy wrenched himself back on to the sofa, feeling his whole
body come back to life in one searing jolt of pain.

'Wasstime?'

'About six thirty.'

'Call Bayswater 6242. Ask for Jack.'

Troy leaned over the sofa and puked again. Just before he passed
out he heard Ruby dialling Wildeve's number. When he woke
again Wildeve was standing over him. He raised himself up on one
elbow. Wildeve furrowed his brow.

'How do you feel?'

'Bloody.'

'You need a doctor.'

'No. Just get me on my feet.'

'Freddie, for God's sake. Someone's kicked the shit out of you!'

'Someone? Someone? I know damn well who it was!'

'You must see a doctor.'

'No.'

'Why not?'

'Onions will put me on sick leave if he gets so much as a whisper of this. We're close, we're that close . . .'

'Close? Close to what?'

'He's here. She thinks he's flown the coop, but he's here.'

'Who does?'

'Brack.'

'Freddie, what on earth are you on about?'

Troy fell back on the sofa.

'Wayne is back,' he said.

'Wayne did this?'

'Why do you doubt it?'

'It . . . it . . . doesn't seem credible. Why would he take the risk? Look, I've got to call a doctor. For one thing that cut on your head is bleeding rather badly.'

'No,' said Troy. 'Get Kolankiewicz. I can't afford to be laid up by some stickler of a quack now. We have to get back out there. He's here, he's here!!!'

The expression on Wildeve's face, the silent exchange of looks between Wildeve and Ruby told Troy that he was yelling, that to them he was a bleeding, battered, hysterical fool. He breathed deeply in an effort to slow the pace of heart and mind. Ruby came over to him and fussed silently. Pulling the blanket up to his chin, propping a cushion under his head so that he could see Wildeve without straining, wiping a rivulet of blood from his eyes. Wildeve leaned over once, pulled a face of mild disgust and turned his back on him. Moments passed to the tune of a thumping blood-vessel. The room swam a little, then steadied itself like a ship righting itself from listing. Troy heard Wildeve on the phone telling Kolankiewicz he knew what time it was but and but again.

'He's on his way. Are you settled now?'

Troy nodded.

'Then tell me about it. Slowly.'

'Onions gets to hear nothing of this. Agreed?'

'Agreed. I'll cover for you until you're on your feet.'

'OK. OK. Wayne was hiding out in the Savoy. He's probably back there now.'

'Well I'll be blowed,' said Wildeve. 'Spitting distance the whole bloody time!' He paused, then added with the merest hint of incredulity, 'How do you know?'

And Troy realised for the first time that he could not tell Wildeve how he had come by this information. Worse, he could not think of a fitting lie.

§ 59

Ruby slept stretched full length in front of the fire. Wildeve sipped tea and kept out of the way. Kolankiewicz raged.

'What did I tell you? What did I tell you!'

He shone his Ever Ready penlight into Troy's eyes, and plucked at his eyelids. Troy winced at the pain and at the breath of the man. Who in their right mind ate garlic liver-sausage for breakfast? Where on earth did he get the stuff off the ration? It could hardly be on it.

'How many finger I hold up?'

Dozens danced like Mickey Mouse's demonic broomsticks dashing to the well and back. Troy hesitated.

'Tell the truth for once,' said Kolankiewicz.

'Two,' guessed Troy.

'Jesus Christ. All five, you lying bastard! How do you expect me to help you. Trust me I'm a doctor. Trust me or I kick you in the balls right now!'

'Too many to count.'

'Ach ... ach ... smartyarse. Listen, Troy. You got pressure on the optic nerve from the blood-vessels at the back of the eye. Not serious. All you need is rest and darkness. The swelling in your head goes down and the pressure on the nerve with it. But if you arse about you play with trouble. You got me?'

'What sort of trouble?'

'Trouble trouble. You are at risk.'

'What do you mean?'

'I mean you could go blind.'

Kolankiewicz rummaged around in his bag and came up with a curved stainless-steel needle.

'You need stitches in your head and on your chest. Two or three in each case. I got no anaesthetic and I hope it hurts. It might convince you to stop getting bashed about. Otherwise I predict a good chance you will join my regular client list.'

It hurt. Troy yelled. Wildeve excused himself to the kitchen. Ruby awoke with a start and followed him. Kolankiewicz tied the last knot and dived into his Gladstone bag once more. Troy watched the needle spurt as Kolankiewicz held the hypodermic up to the light.

'You sod,' he said, 'you had anaesthetic all along.'

'Not anaesthetic,' Kolankiewicz said, 'sedative.'

He whacked the needle into Troy's arm before he could protest.

'You got about five minutes to get yourself upstairs to bed. I give you enough to put down a brewer's dray horse. If you show your face at the Yard within a week Onions hears everything. You understand me? Good. Now, if you excuse me the dead are waiting.'

He slammed out. Troy felt the first giddy, sub-orgasmic rush of the drug and called for Wildeve. Wildeve hooked an arm around his shoulders and lugged him up the stairs. The staircase spun, Troy's legs abandoned him and a delicious narcotic elation flooded swiftly through his veins. The world was a painless, pleasant place. From outside the crystal bowl of his euphoria Wildeve's pleading reached him.

'Freddie, what the hell do I tell Onions? Where are you for the next week?'

Troy thought fast with what little power of thought remained.

'Norfolk,' he muttered. 'Suffolk. Lots ... lots of air bases. Gone to ... catch ... catch ...'

He resisted the pool of warm, pink light that invited him in and struggled with a final thought. There was something terribly important he had to tell to Jack. Terribly important. If only ...

'Savoy,' he slurred out. 'Check apartment. Wayne. Brack. Check apartment.'

He sank back on to the pillows. Ruby elbowed Wildeve aside and from nowhere produced a pair of striped winceyette pyjamas.

The last thing Troy saw was her pulling off his trousers and trying to thread his legs into the pyjamas.

§ 60

He woke from dreams of flight. He had been a kite high over Hampstead Heath tethered to Wildeve, who pulled on the wire and swirled him above the clouds. The view of London was tremendous. Night fell with exaggerated speed, the rolling night of trick photography. London lit up like Regent Street at Christmas. And not a bomber to be seen. He sat up in bed wondering how he could have such a vision of the city, somewhat in awe of the power of imagination until he remembered watching a night of the Blitz from atop Primrose Hill years ago. Incendiaries roaring up like gas jets off a stove. Suddenly it all looked remarkably like the view from Primrose Hill. Hardly quotidian but less the feat of untramelled imagination. He swung his legs off the bed. He ached dully but felt nothing he could honestly call pain. He pulled up his pyjama jacket. Two inches below the right nipple blood had caked around three black stitches. Connecting him but unconnected to him it seemed. He ran his fingers through his hair and felt the ridge of blood above his right ear. He stood. Less giddy than lightweight. His feet floated where his brain half-heartedly said they should go.

From the top of the stairs he saw Ruby with her back to him. She was ushering a man gently out into the street with a hand in the small of his back. The door closed, she leaned against it and tucked a ten-shilling note into the top of her stocking. Then she felt Troy's eyes upon her.

'Don't get moral. I've a living to earn. And if I did it in all the old familiar places there'd have been no one here to look after you.'

Troy said nothing. He sat on a step about halfway down. She smiled.

'I could cut you in of course. But that would be living off immoral earnings.'

She held out a hand to Troy. He stood and padded softly down the stairs, dishevelled in his pyjamas.

'What time is it?'

'Just after eight. It's Sunday morning. You've had a nice sleep since Friday. That nice Mr Klankiwitch phoned last night to see how you were. I told him you were sleeping like a baby.'

Troy made a mental note to ask Kolankiewicz what he had put in the Mickey Finn he called a sedative. Ruby pulled the curtains open. Troy could not remember when he had last seen the light of day; it seemed like another lifetime. Morning sun slanted into the yard from the east. For once it looked like spring. Temptingly like spring.

He bathed, he dressed, he went out. As he pulled the door behind him he caught sight of Ruby looking at him across the top of a magazine. He had no idea how long she intended to stay, but could not wrap his mind around the problem of letting a prostitute ply her trade out of his parlour. He smiled, imagining Onions's reaction. He realised that he was still under the Mickey, or he would never have seen the funny side of it. He set off westward. If he could make it as far as Green Park then he might make up his mind where, if anywhere, he was going.

At Piccadilly he stood and looked back in the direction he had come. Across Leicester Square the sun shone gloriously in a sky that was bluer than blue and virtually cloudless, the like of which he could not remember having seen before. He was wrapped in his black overcoat, readily accepting that his mass of bruises was in some way to be equated with childhood illness and a voice in his head had told him maternally that he should not go out without his coat. At the foot of Eros's pedestal two young women sat in shirtsleeves, daring all for spring sun, and shared a single cigarette.

He walked on into Piccadilly, watching his shadow dance before him. In the brightness of such light the city contrasted sharply with the weather. London thawed. London budded. London ached. Like muscle stretched and strained for too long it yearned to relax. The sense of action, the sense of an ending being almost tangible, Troy found himself wondering if the city would not expire with the first breath of spring like some old man who had spent his energy enduring the depth of winter and had none left for the simple pleasure of living. What the sun revealed was a city of peeling, blistered paint, of broken, boarded-up windows, of shattered walls and open roofs, of four long years of make do and mend. It was a city scorched and scarred, patched and tattered in the light of spring.

At Half Moon Street he crossed the road into Green Park. A squad of United States military police, white-helmeted, white-gaitered, stood to attention. From somewhere in the park he had heard the sound of 'The Star-Spangled Banner'. As he came closer to the band, as yet unseen, they took up the tune of 'Little Brown Jug' and the soldiers swung into action, drilling to the upbeat of Glenn Miller's arrangement, swinging their rifles from shoulder to ground and through cartwheels on to the other shoulder. The precise ballet of military training.

Troy sat on a bench, marvelling at the beauty of it, cynically curious as to what use it would all be on a French beach in a few weeks' time. More cynically he had bet Onions ten shillings that the second front would open in Normandy. Onions had taken him up, a firm believer in the *Pas de Calais*. No one, not even the few Belgians Troy knew, was betting on the coast of Belgium. Dunkirk was all very well in such use as 'the spirit of', but who in their right mind would risk it all a second time?

The soldiers switched to formation-marching to the tune of 'Chattanooga Choo Choo'. A crowd of more than a hundred had gathered, and a huge cheer went up as the Americans mapped out their military squares and sang a massed chorus of 'Pardon me boy'.

All around him the park eased into leaf – hawthorn in its deepest green, the paler green of oaks and chestnuts. And, lagging behind, with hardly a bud to show for themselves, the elm and the ash – ash, always the last to burst into leaf in May and the last to grudgingly give them up, often hanging on until early December. Across the park the mingled scents of spring floated towards Troy. Mayflower, of that he was certain. Lilac? Wasn't it too early, too optimistic to be thinking of lilac? They separated out like streams of water. Yes, it was lilac, it was lilac. And mingled again, the softness of the lilac overlaid by the sharpness of mayflower, never far from cat's piss at the best of times.

A couple strolled by arm in arm. A young chattering woman on the arm of an American first lieutenant. Her scent, caught on the breeze, added itself to the trail of blossom and suddenly Troy knew where he was going. He ran out into Piccadilly, stopped sharply on the pavement, feeling his head spin and his feet tread air, and hailed a cab.

'Tite Street,' he said.

At Tite Street he told the driver to drive on. They passed Detective Constable Gutteridge at the corner, slyly smoking on duty. In Tedworth Gardens Troy stopped the cabbie and paid him off. He had surrendered to an irrational hunch, as was so often necessary, and had been right. There, in the middle of the allotment, stooping over a hoe and gently shoving at the weeds was Diana Brack – tattily in mufti; jodhpurs, wellingtons and a moth-eaten Fair-Isle pullover, her hair pulled back into a single pony-tail by a rubber band.

Troy entered the square through a break in the fencing, tucked his hands in his pockets and approached. A few feet away from her the big man in Heavy Rescue uniform was on his knees in front of a large tin bath washing the pig. The pig looked up at Troy, smiled, winked and grunted with pleasure as the bristles of the brush scrubbed her to ecstasy.

'Wotcha cock,' said the man.

Brack had her back to Troy and turned to see whom the big man was addressing. She straightened her spine and looked him up and down.

'What happened to you? You look as though you got hit by a steamroller?'

'Something like that,' said Troy.

'Give me a few minutes,' she said, and disappeared into a Nissen hut at the edge of her plot.

Troy watched the man scrub the pig, wondering if the pig had really winked at him and silently promising himself he would kill Kolankiewicz for giving him a drug that made pigs wink.

'That's a nice shiner you got yourself,' the man said.

Troy rubbed gently at the eye with his hand.

'The other day,' he said, 'when I came through here in the dark. How did you know I was a policeman?'

'Stands to reason, old cock. You was chasing the Major. And I had him tagged for a wrong 'un months back. Besides, I spent a fair bit o' my time 'anging around the likes of you. Gets so I can spot 'em. I did a lot of work before the war for a detective like – amateur, mind, a gentleman – in fact I'd be doin' it now but that he took 'imself orf to the army and one of those 'ush-'ush jobs. Still, he'll be back. And we shall like as not have new trails to follow, new murders to solve and new villains to bring to book.'

The man prodded the pig, who scrambled out of the bath and shook herself like a dog. She brushed past Troy, pausing a moment to rub herself against his trouser leg and ambled off to the other end of the allotment, nose to the ground. The big man drained the water and hung the bath on the side of the Nissen hut.

'Take a look at this,' he said, leading Troy along the narrow path between his allotment and Brack's. 'Know what that is?'

'Cauliflower,' said Troy.

'Broccoli,' said the man with infinite pride in the esoterica of his own knowledge. 'White-heading winter broccoli.'

'A cauliflower by any other name,' said Troy.

'Might smell as sweet, but wouldn't be 'alf as big. I put this in last May. This May, let's say another ten days, and I'll have the fullest, ripest head of broccoli you've ever mistook for a cauli. She'll weigh seventeen pounds I reckon. I gets to eat the head and the pig gets to eat the leaves. What could be fairer?'

Troy looked at the bare, weedy patch that was Brack's.

'Not exactly green-fingered, wouldn't you say?'

'She tries, old cock, she tries. The Major he done the winter diggin' for 'er. All that frost broke up the ground nicely. And when she clears away the weeds she'll find all those leeks she put in in February, nestling under there like little green needles in their 'aystack. There'll be some garlic too. Dunno why she grows that – foreign muck if you ask me – but she did insist.'

'Why do you say the Major's a wrong 'un?' Troy asked.

But before the man could answer Brack emerged from the Nissen hut, dressed in black skirt and jacket once more, her hair combed and brushed, pulling on her gloves.

'Are you are a gardening man, Mr Troy?' she asked in best formal mode.

'I was when younger,' he replied. 'But I have a house in Good-wins Court now – there's no garden attached.'

'I see,' she said, still playing the game for the benefit of the big man. She walked off along the path, slowly, toward the north end of the square, in the direction the pig had taken. The big man was not deceived by distance, physical or metaphorical. He picked up a hoe and returned to weeding his allotment.

'One reason I'd say he's a wrong 'un,' he said to Troy, 'is his paying court to her ladyship. She can't half pick 'em. The odder the better. Don't let her lead you too far, cock. She'll run you ragged.'

Troy caught up with Brack as she left the square at the far side.

'We cannot go to my house,' she said at last. 'You have a man watching it.' She paused. 'Of course, you could order him to leave.'

She stopped and turned to face Troy, awaiting his answer.

'No. I couldn't. I'm not even supposed to be in London.'

'Then I suppose I must come to you.'

'Yes,' he said.

'That is what you want. You do want me to come to you, don't you?'

'I suppose it is,' he said.

'Then I shall.'

They walked on, around the perimeter of the square anti-clockwise, towards the corner of Tite Street.

'What happened? I mean, what happened to your face?'

'I was attacked. Two nights ago. A man.'

'A man?'

'The man.'

'No – you are mistaken. I told you he's gone.'

'How can you be sure?'

'Because if he were here he would have found me. Even with your man at my door, he would have found a way.'

They paused at the corner. Another yard and Troy would be visible to Gutteridge.

'Tonight,' she said.

'Yes,' said Troy.

'As soon as it is dark.'

§ 61

It was close to sunset. He had drifted all day. Aimlessly. He guessed that he had gone out of the house at nine or nine thirty. He had met Brack an hour or so later, and for the time elapsed since then he could hardly account. By four in the afternoon he had drifted into the Russian tea rooms in Davies Street, a little to the north of Berkeley Square. He had not been there in a while, since before Christmas at least. The tea rooms had been opened the previous spring by a couple of Russian women, serving tea straight from the samovar. Troy did not go for the tea – Samovar tea always tasted stewed to him, though the cakes were passable – he went for the sound, the sibilant susurrus of voices speaking Russian. Of voices speaking Russian and making none of the demands on his belonging that his family made. Here he could listen without obligation. Here he could hear Russian without his sisters' moral blackmail – or the contempt with which Kolankiewicz occasionally flung the odd phrase at him. More and more he came to realise the ethnic mix that was North America as Canadians and Americans turned up in uniform ordering their tea and chatting to the women behind the counter in fluent, if accented, Russian. Perhaps his origins did not show after all – two young soldiers sat opposite and chatted in Russian as though not expecting him to understand and discussed how backward they thought the English were. They found the lack of refrigeration a puzzle and the quality of the beer objectionable. Imagine liquid wool, one of them said, and you have English beer. What made Milwaukee famous would do the Brits a power of good.

He listened without looking, learning in the language of childhood that he had grown up to be a member of the most tight-assed race on earth. But he knew that. Tosca told him that with every other remark. Tosca. Her name tumbled through his near-vacant, narcoleptic mind all the way home, to no purpose and no conclusion. While the euphoria lasted he felt strangely free of desire. Cloudy and sexless. He could visualise the ties that bound him to her, floating out in front of him like streamers, but he could not see her, could not conjure up a face to the magic of the word.

Back home, Troy found a note from Ruby on the mantelpiece. 'I can take a hint. Gone home to get some kip. If you need me you know where to find me – at the end of the street from half an hour before closing time onwards. Just don't approach me if it looks as though I've got a fare. I can't afford to lose business just 'cos you have a way of always looking like a copper. Love R. PS. Klankiwitch was mad as hell when I told him you'd gone out.'

It was dark now. He sat in his overcoat in front of the unlit fire, staring at the door. And when he had stared as long as he could he unlocked the door, took off his coat and shoes and crept upstairs to lie on his bed in the darkness. He heard the latch click on the door. He heard a soft shoeless tread upon the stairs. He saw Brack framed in the doorway, slipping her black cloak from her shoulders, flicking back the ever errant forelock from her eyes. Lust batted him in the groin, sharp and hard. The numbness lifted as the desire took him, and with it the pains of all his breaks and bruises returned to rack him.

She walked over to the window framed in the last of the twilight, slowly picking at the buttons on her blouse. Troy got up and stood behind her. She hoisted her skirt to her hips, leant against the window-sill and presented herself to him. He fucked her till he dropped and felt each muscle in his body tear itself free from the next.

He could not be certain, but it seemed that she had picked him up in her arms and lain him back on the bed. She was leaning over him, kissing him on the lips, drowning him in the oh-so-familiar scent.

'What is it?' he asked.

'What's what?'

'Your scent.'

She sat on the edge of the bed pulling off the last of her clothes.

'Je Reviens,' she said in a near-whisper. 'Very costly. Very Parisian. And since the fall of France bloody nigh impossible to get hold of. It's a bit old-fashioned now I suppose. I've worn it since I was a girl.'

Troy knew that. It went with the bicycle and the cut knee and that first embarrassing kiss.

She leaned over him, a hand behind his neck lifting him, the other peeling off his shirt to leave him naked as she was. She stretched herself full length, kissing him below the left ear. He felt her nipples brush his chest and the same old flame go roaring south to his cock. He had no idea where desire would ever find the energy.

§ 62

When he awoke it was light and he was alone. He slipped on his trousers and went downstairs. The front door was locked. A note stood perched on the mantelpiece. It said simply 'Soon' and was signed 'D'.

§ 63

Shortly after lunch Wildeve telephoned.

'Some American woman's been calling for you. Won't leave a name. It's nothing I can handle?'

'No. No it's not. Is there anything else?'

'Bugger all. I'm getting nowhere. For once I think I can honestly say your presence would not make a deal of difference. The Savoy was empty – at least empty of Waynes and Bracks. The doorman recognised him from that mugshot you got hold of. Said he stayed there a lot but he's seen nothing of him since last Tuesday – which was the day we hauled in Diana.'

'Onions?'

'Around and about. He hasn't asked about you yet, so I haven't had to lie.'

Troy did not doubt that Onions would ask. Or that Jack would lie.

That evening he waited quietly for Brack, listening to a concert on the wireless – sunk into a pit of twilight, feeling the ache in his muscles slowly pass, and pushing occasionally at the red cloud that floated into vision. She did not come that night.

Nor did she the next.

The following morning he felt fitter and began to chafe at the bit. By mid-afternoon he had sat all he could and finding he had no further tolerance of the wireless and no concentration for reading, he put on his coat and wandered off past Seven Dials in the direction of Bloomsbury, with no particular destination in mind. He crossed High Holborn, opposite Staple Inn, where Chancery Lane with a poor sense of geometry fails to meet Gray's Inn Road, and ambled on to the junction of Theobald's Road and Clerkenwell Road. A street galleon hove into view, and he caught the number 65 tram, eastbound, rattling and sparking out towards Limehouse. Only when it passed Aldgate East Underground station and clattered out along the Commercial Road did the sense of where he was heading come to him. Alighting at the bottom of Jamaica Street he walked to Union Place, climbed the stairs and knocked on Bonham's door. He could scrounge a cup of tea and catch a tram back the way he had come. There was an evens chance of Bonham being in. He wasn't. Troy leant back against the door, suddenly tired. It had come on to rain the sudden drenching storms of spring. He shoved his hands into his pockets and prepared to wait it out. It might easily die down as suddenly as it had arisen. He felt his key-ring, nestling in the grit and dust, the debris of the bomb blast, that lurked unshakeable in the seam of his pocket – his house key was on it, so was Wolinski's.

The flat smelt dry and dusty. The stale air of emptiness. Troy stood in the outer room, dark and heavy with the weight of books. He almost tiptoed past the rows of collected editions into the inner room. He sat on a chair in the middle, just where he had left it the last time when he had come to search Wolinski's desk. His legs ached. He began to wonder if Kolankiewicz might be right in his fussy concern, and he pushed the red cloud over the horizon once again. The rain coursed down the window-pane, the afternoon greyed into premature evening, the light dropped away. He sat a long time staring through the dimness at the photographs covering the wall, that welter of *Mittel*-Europeana, so reminiscent of family albums his mother kept – the Troys' Viennese phase, the girls as babes in arms, Rod as a toddler, a phase that preceded him and any thought of him. Troy was, as his mother teased throughout childhood, her little Englander. He stared at those decent, well-meaning faces with their decent, well-meaning expressions, lost now in the chaos which their pitifully decent, well-meaning society struggled to keep at bay. Pâtisserie democracy. A chocolate cream finger in the dyke of Europe. There was just one space in the wall of faces, where the shot of Nikolai with Brand and von Ranke had hung. Troy's eyes travelled down the wall from the blank patch to the floor. Something bright and white lay on the carpet, close by the skirting-board. He picked it up and sat down at once, his head spinning from bending so far. It was a single pearl ear-ring on a silver screw fastening, the sort worn by women without pierced ears. He laid it on the flat of his hand and stared at it. It had not been there the last time. Surely not? He was searching as thoroughly as he knew, he would not have missed it, small as it was. He closed his hand around it and looked up at the running streams of dirty water as they made their way across the window – and red came again, and red turned to purple, and purple turned to black and all he could see were those endless, repetitive ranks of *Mittel*-European faces etched on to his retina.

He sat an age in silence with no knowledge of how time passed. The front door opened and he heard feet in the other room. The feet came towards him and he heard a voice speak his name.

'Who is it?' he called back.

'Don't you know me? It's me – Sydney Edelmann.'

'What time is it?'

' 'Bout eight o'clock I should think. How long you been sitting there in the dark?'

Troy knew now it had been an age. Time had passed in monotonous stillness. A curious calm in a terrifying darkness.

'About five hours. I daren't move.'

'Daren't move!'

He felt Edelmann's hand upon his shoulder.

'Daren't move? Why, man, what's the matter with you?'

Edelmann led Troy down the stairs to Bonham's flat. He clung to the banister rail, finding it all but impossible to guess the spaces between steps, the number of steps and where the corner turned.

He heard Edelmann bang on the door. Heard Bonham bellow ' 'Old yer 'orses', and felt himself ushered into Bonham's parlour with a flurry of hands and questions.

'He can't see,' Edelmann said. 'I found 'im upstairs, just sittin' there. Blind as a bat!'

§ 64

Edelmann thrust a cup of universal panacea into Troy's hands – the near-rancid reek of hot milky tea almost made Troy retch.

'You're a bloody fool, aren't you?' Bonham was saying pointlessly. 'You just won't be told.'

Only a knock at the door stopped him from delivering a monologue *in loco parentis*. Bonham had dashed to the telephone box with a handful of pennies to call a doctor. He had arrived with surprising speed.

Troy heard the man bustle in, firing questions at Edelmann and Bonham as though Troy were deaf as well as blind. Troy sipped at the mess of tea, until he felt the man's hands cup his cheekbones to tilt his face upwards, smelt a whiff of pipe tobacco off his clothes. The pencil beam of a surgical torch made a pinprick in his darkness.

'Can you see any light?'

'Yes. There's a dot.'

'You've been in the wars, Sergeant Troy. Bomb blast, I hear?'

'Yes. I took quite a knock on the head.'

'Any concussion?'

'I was unconscious for a couple of days.'

'What? And they let you out?'

Bonham had to have his say, 'Discharged himself, didn't he. Clever dick.'

The beam of light switched to his other eye, a microscopic train at the end of a long tunnel. Then the hands probed his skull, feeling the bumps and scars, the stitches Kolankiewicz had put in.

'These are fresh. Only a matter of days. You've not had these in since the bomb.'

'No. I was attacked last Friday. I got a bit of a kicking,' Troy said almost apologetically.

Troy heard the man draw breath. More than a mite incredulous.

'Have you ever considered selling insurance as a vocation, Sergeant? Your present line will kill you, particularly if you carry on as you are. You should be in hospital but I don't suppose you'll go. You're lucky it's only blindness. Luckier still that it's only temporary. Lots of rest and you will probably make a full recovery. I shall bandage your eyes. For the next few days you will see nothing and your eyes will be forced to rest. Ignore my advice and you may never see again. Do you understand me? First those stitches must come out.'

He felt a twinge of pain as the doctor pulled the stiches, then efficient, gentle hands wrapped his head. Vinegar and brown paper, thought Troy.

'Now,' the doctor said, 'the name of your chief, if you would be so kind.'

'Eh?' said Troy.

'Your commander, your superintendent.'

Troy suspected the worst. Best-laid plans about to go awry.

'Who are you?' he asked.

'Who am I? I'm the Divisional Police Surgeon, Mr Troy.'

Bonham rode with Troy in the taxi-cab back to St Martin's Lane.

'I didn't think. He was just there. I didn't think it mattered.'

'It's OK, George. You weren't to know.'

'I mean it got you looked at quick. He was only across the way. In Leman Street. It seemed natural to send for one of ours.' Bonham paused for thought. 'Maybe,' he began, 'maybe he won't put in a report to the Yard.'

'George, please!' Troy said.

It took some effort convincing Bonham not to stay. Troy pressed home his assertion that he would be fine just left at home. What harm could he possibly come to in his own house? He knew it like the back of his hand. So Bonham left, and Troy fell over every object between the sitting room and the kitchen, and all but scalded himself making tea.

At his fifth attempt he got the gas fire lit and groped his way to the sofa. Later he must make an effort to find the wireless. Now he was almost exhausted and, wondering how he would ever endure it, he settled back into his darkness.

§ 65

Into his darkness came.

The policeman.

'Freddie. It's me. Jack. Are you all right? It took for ever for you to answer the phone.'

'I've been groping around for it in the dark. I banged my shins on the piano and damn near fell flat on my face.'

'Of course. Sorry I wasn't thinking. Freddie – '

He paused. Troy heard him drawing a deep breath. Preparatory to a gabble.

'Onions was in your office when I got in this morning. You know the sort of thing. Perched next to the fire, puffing on a Woodbine. He asked for a full rundown. Everything from the day after Miller was shot. I'm afraid I didn't have a lot of choice. Once that doctor had sent his report in . . . '

'You did the right thing, Jack. Don't worry.'

'He wasn't angry or anything. It might have been preferable. I find his silences between questions a bit of a strain. I rather get the impression he'll be over to see you as soon as he gets a moment. Oh, and your sister phoned. One or the other of them – they hardly ever say – I told her you were in Norfolk. Norfolk's getting to be your Bunbury, isn't it?'

Troy had need of a Bunbury. If there was one thing his life lacked it was a good, irrefutable Bunbury.

Troy waited. Heard the iron tread of Onions's boots on the yard. The prolonged squeak of the door on its hinges.

'Not very clever leaving the door unlocked.'

Troy sat facing in the direction of Onions's voice. 'It does save a lot of arsing about. It's surprising how poorly one can know one's own home.'

'What did you expect?'

Troy heard the swish of Onions taking off his coat.

'I could do with a cuppa. Stay where you are. I'll do it.'

Onions banged around in the kitchen. Troy heard the soft pop of a gas ring going on and the plod of Onions returning to the sitting room, the creak as the sofa took his weight, the rasp of a match as he lit up another Woodbine, the first sweeping exhalation and the waft of smoke touched his nostrils.

'I had a chat with that boy of yours. He's a bright spark. Bright enough to know when the lying has to stop.'

'If I'd told you you'd have suspended me. I'd have been off the case.'

'Aye. For four or five days perhaps. Now you're off it indefinitely.'

'Until my eyes heal,' Troy put in quickly.

'And that's indefinitely, isn't it?'

Troy made no answer.

'That surgeon from Stepney wouldn't put a date to it when I asked him how long I had to do without you. The pity of it is, I could do with you right now.'

Troy was tempted to say sorry, but instinct told him that Onions was already off in a new direction. He had not come to offer sympathy or to accept an apology.

'You're valuable to me,' Onions went on. 'In fact you're the best intuitive detective I've ever met.'

'My intuition didn't serve me too well this time.'

'Oh, you've played the silly bugger — but that's not the point. You took a case with only a scrap of evidence and you pushed it and pushed it and pushed it. You had bugger all to go on, but you identified the victim, you identified the murderer. Don't belittle the achievement.'

'We're close.'

There was a long pause. Onions drew deeply on his gasper.

'No. No. You're not. That's not what I meant. Tell me the truth, Freddie. Are you any further on than you were that day we went over to MI5? Have you anything other than circumstantial evidence? Has anyone seen hide nor hair of Wayne since he killed Miller?'

Troy said nothing.

'You're the best intuitive detective I've ever met,' Onions said again. 'I need you now. But I haven't got you. I've got Gutteridge and Thomson.'

He paused again. Troy felt the soft contempt with which he spoke of Gutteridge and Thomson.

'I've got two murders on my hands. One yesterday, one this morning,' Onions said. 'I could do with you right now.'

Troy resisted the 'Sorry' again.

'Instead I've got Gutteridge and Thomson.'

'You've taken them off my case?'

'I've no choice. Even then they're worse than bloody useless. The only reason they're still on the Force is I can't get anyone else. The only reason they're not in the army is they're too old. That's my hard luck – two dozy buggers even the army didn't want. Too old and too slow. Can't say I didn't see it coming. That's why I kept you out of the forces.'

'What?'

'They wanted you in 1940. I stopped it.'

'You stopped my call-up? You didn't bloody tell me?'

'Did you want to go in?'

'That's not the point.'

'Yes it is! You never made any secret of your dislike of the forces. I kept you 'cos I needed you. Just like you kept the boy. If you'd not put your two penn'orth in he'd have been called up months ago. I need you. I need the pair of you. But I haven't got you, I've got Gutteridge and Thomson.'

'You keep saying that!'

The kettle whistled on the hob. Onions got up. Troy sat in silence until he felt a tap on his arm, heard Onions say 'Don't knock it over', heard the rattle of him stirring his three sugars. Troy let his cup stand. Onions made awful tea. Deepest brown, merely tinted by milk, fit to tan buckskin.

'I keep saying that because it's got my goat. I'm in a pickle. A teenage girl in Golders Green – how respectable can you get? – puts rat poison in the teapot and polishes off the whole family. Least that's the way it looks.'

'What do you mean?'

'Done a runner. Not there to ask is she? And a typical Troy case, two naval ratings quarrel over a prossie and the next thing one of them's found face down in the Serpentine and the other bugger's denying the lot. You get my point? You'd've cracked these nuts in a day or two. But as it happens I don't have you.'

'You've got Gutteridge and Thomson,' Troy said, anticipating the echo.

'More than that,' Onions said. 'Fact is I'll be needing the boy too.' Troy knew he had to appear calm. Onions hardly ever demanded respect for his rank in any other registration but calm. Outrageous questions could be asked, rebellious refusals offered, but not in anger.

'Stan, if you do that we'll lose Wayne.'

'You already have.'

'If you take Wildeve off the case I'll have hell picking up the pieces.'

'I've already got Wildeve. I've put him on to both cases an hour ago. I had to. He'll work as number two to Tom Henrey. Tom's up to his neck as it is.'

Henrey was a Detective Inspector. But for a slight difference in rank and a larger one in the power of imagination he was Troy's peer on Onions's staff. A decent, honest plodder. A man who caused Onions little trouble. There was an obvious question waiting.

'What about me?'

'We'll see. You're no damn use to me blind. And if you could see now I'd put you on new cases too. If you reckon the Stepney murder's still hot when you get back, then we'll see. Happen Tom will crack Golders Green or Hyde Park. On the other hand he might not. Don't get me wrong, Freddie. Laying aside for the moment that you tried to pull the wool over my eyes and you got caught, you did as good a job as could be done – but it pays to know when to stop.'

'It seems like yesterday you were telling me—'

'I know what I told you. Don't throw my words in my face! Like I said, we'll see.'

It was a father's phrasing. The meaningless tactical put-off. No by any other name. We'll see. The opposite of Troy's father's habitual 'If you like'.

'We'll see,' said Troy ironically. 'If I see. Stan, I didn't do this to myself!'

'That just makes it one more unsolved crime then, doesn't it?'

'You know damn well who did this!'

'Don't tell me it was Wayne. It wasn't. He hasn't been seen since Miller was killed. He wasn't at the Savoy. According to Wildeve he hadn't been there since the day you arrested Diana Brack. He's not likely to materialise out of whatever hidey-hole the Yanks have got him in just for the pleasure of kicking shite out of you.'

Troy listened to the awkward pause. Would Onions ask him why no mention of the Savoy had been made in his reports of the interviews with Brack? Onions began to drum the side of his cup with the spoon. The repetitive noise told Troy the meeting was over. Stan had had his say and was not about to let Troy argue. He heard the springs in the sofa scream as Onions's bulk released them. The tweed rustle as he fumbled with his coat.

'I'd best be off. Do you have a doctor looking in on you?'

'Yes. Kolankiewicz will take the bandages off in five or six days.'

'Suit yourself. I'd as soon see a pork butcher as that mad bugger. I'll leave the door off the latch, shall I?'

Onions clunked off the way he had come, leaving the odour of Wills' Woodbines hanging in the air.

Into his darkness came.

The Whore.

Who called each evening between seven and eight. Chattered aimlessly and cooked a meal for two. Troy said all that was required of him – yes and hmm and nodding interjections falling short of the traditional well-I-never. She did not mention or allude to the problem of his sight. Only her presence there in her chosen role made silent reference to the fact of his helplessness. She left an hour before closing time, telling him that duty called, varying the line with the occasional crack about contributing to the war effort.

Into his darkness came.

The Almost-Doctor.

'Troy?'

He awoke from a light snooze. The wireless mumbled softly in the background. A voice he did not recognise had spoken to him.

'Troy. It's me.'

He still had no idea who she was.

'Anna Pakenham.'

'Eh?'

'Kolankiewicz sent me. He said it's time your bandages came off.'

He tried to get up and felt her hand spread flat across his chest to stop him.

'Don't even think about it. Just stay put and let me get on with it.'

'Where's Kolankiewicz?'

'Sawing bone. Literally. He was busy whipping off the top of a chap's head the last time I saw him. He sends fraternal greetings and a thousand I told you sos.'

The slick sound of steel on steel as she cut into the bandages.

'I haven't done this since I was a medical student, so don't move or you may lose an ear.'

'I didn't know you were a doctor.'

'I'm not. I was in my next to last year in 1940. My chap was on Hurricanes. Thought it would be all over for us soon, so why didn't we get married and chuck caution and every other damn thing to the winds. I believed him. As a result I spent the first six months of 1941 thinking I was a widow. The Germans can take for ever to tell you they've got someone in a POW camp. My concentration went completely to pot so I took a sabbatical for the duration. Now – I can't go back till it is over. I work for the Polish beast. And Angus is banged up in Colditz.'

She moved around behind him as she spoke and pulled the mass of bandage free from his head. He had not seen Anna in ages. Curious to think that she would be the first person he saw.

'I can't see,' said Troy. 'I still can't bloody see!'

She took him by the chin, talking straight at him. 'Can you see me at all, Troy? Shapes, light, anything?'

'Not a damn thing!'

'You're going to need patience, Troy. Lots of it.'

Into his darkness came.

The Lover.

He had been a passing-good pianist as a child, neglectful as a young man and nowadays played at best once a fortnight out of

237

duty or boredom. On the afternoon of the seventh day of his blindness he forgot the aching shins, forgave the Victorian upright his mother had given him as a house-warming hint and decided to see how many of the Debussy *Préludes* he could play from memory. He was prompted less by pre-war memories of Debussy recitals – his mother had taken him to see Walter Gieseking in Hannover – than by recent performances of the blind pianist George Shearing in the London clubs. And in a spirit of 'so can I' he fumbled his way to the keyboard and began mangling *Danseuses de Delphes*. He picked up around the fifth prelude and by the tenth was playing a note-perfect *Cathédrale Engloutie*. He broke at seven thirty to let Ruby chatter, ate her meal gratefully, feeling better than he had for days and granted her wish for something she knew, 'You know, something you can hum'. He bashed away at 'The Lambeth Walk', 'Any Old Iron' to her shrieks of laughter, and touched by inspiration switched to Gershwin's 'Someone to Watch Over Me'. He seemed to have hit the spot. He heard distinct sniffles, and when he stopped she pronounced it 'loverly' and said she must dash. Pleased with his efforts Troy took up the tune again. He was still playing it when the door opened several minutes later. He thought it must be Ruby, finding some excuse to return, but as the evening breeze through the doorway brought the scent of Je Reviens to his nostrils he knew it was Brack.

Her fingers began at the top of his ear and ran lightly down his cheekbone. The tip of her little finger parted his lips and her tongue danced over his ear. He stopped, paralysed by the wave of lust that shot through his body, fingers frozen on the keyboard holding down the last chord. He swivelled on the piano stool, to bury his face in her clothes, to swim in the smell of her.

'Hey, baby. Don't stop. I'm kinda fond of Gershwin.'

He screamed out loud, shot upright off the stool and fell back against the wall. He hit his head hard and sank down to the floor. The great gust of Je Reviens came closer.

'Wassamatter, baby? Did I startle you?'

A hand plucked at his. She had not the weight to pull him to his feet.

'Easy now. Come to momma.'

He stood, shaking with fright. Tosca wrapped her arms around him. Kissed him gently on the lips, scenting him into a deeper confusion.

'You've changed your scent,' he said at last.

'And there was I thinking you'd never notice. We just pulled one of our guys out of Paris. Abwehr getting too close. He brought me this as a treat. Reckons you can't get the stuff over here for love or money these days.'

'He's right,' Troy gasped. 'Look. You must go now.'

'Go? I only just got here. I've not seen you for over two weeks. I was beginning to think something had happened to you. You're a very hard man to find. How come you never told me where you live? If I'd known we were this close . . .'

'No. No,' he was almost screaming. 'You must go now! It's not . . . it's not . . . it's not safe!'

'Not safe? Not safe from whom? Oh. I get it. You mean Scotland Yard?'

Troy clutched at the straw.

'Yes. That's it. My Super. He drops in the evenings.'

'You mean he'd give you a hard time for having me around? Couldn't I be your cousin Katie from Kalamazoo?'

'No. No please. You must leave before—'

He felt the flutter of air across his eyelashes. She was waving her hand close to his face.

'Goddammit. You can't see me, can you?'

Troy made no answer. Felt two hands grip his skull and yank his head down. Logically he must be looking into her eyes and she was most certainly looking into his.

'I was right, something has happened to you. Oh my God!'

'It's temporary. Honestly. The bandages came off yesterday. My sight's returning. It'll just take a while that's all.'

If he could be certain in which direction the door lay he would have ushered her towards it.

'Please,' he said, praying she would ask for no more reasons. Praying in particular that she would not ask how blindness had come upon him.

She kissed him again.

'OK. OK . . . but you come see me the minute you can see.'

She kissed him again. He heard her sigh with a sense of finality

239

and knew she believed the lie she had placed on his lips. He heard the door squeak open. She stopped.

'Troy? You still love me, don't you? I mean it's just the eyes. There's nothing else I should know about?'

'Nothing,' he lied. 'Nothing at all.'

It seemed to him at that moment that his life had become bound up in a web of lies – a web entirely of his own weaving. He knew why the smell of Je Reviens on her had struck terror into him. He knew that he had panicked at the thought of her being there when Brack showed up, but there were depths to that yawning back into childhood – besides he had seen nothing of Brack since before the tram ride out to Stepney.

Within the hour the door squeaked its long squeak again. Another wafting stream of Je Reviens. His pulse raced. He held his breath for a seeming age. The latch on the Yale clicked to.

'I had begun to assume the worst,' Brack said at last.

§ 66

After. She sliding off him – him damply detumescent. She kissed him softly on each eyelid, anointing, and lay back to sleep in the crook of his arm. He heard her breathing assume the rhythm of sleep, and in a matter of minutes drifted off to follow her.

It was light when he awoke. She was still there. The first time. He had wrestled a few seconds with double and triple vision before he realised that he could see again.

He found he could focus almost clearly for ten seconds or so by extreme concentration. He held the window, seeing it slide from fours to threes to single vision, then he let his eyes relax and the image dissolved. He tried pulling Brack into focus, close as she was, and slowly a lock of hair, swept over an ear, resolved itself for him. He touched the ear. She made a sleep murmur but did not move. He ran his fingertips down to the lobe and focused harder. What his fingers had felt was a plain gold sleeper ring, pushed through the hole in her ear. The silver-mounted pearl ear-ring was still in the breast pocket of his overcoat where he had placed it days ago. Whoever had dropped it in Wolinski's flat it wasn't Brack. He had almost hoped it was, it would have simplified things enormously – but simplicity wasn't everything.

She cooked breakfast for two. Wrapped in his old silk dressing-gown, fussing at the stove to the baritone burble of the wireless. Chatter would have cut through the awkwardness of it all but she did not chatter – to chatter was unBrack. She placed a boiled egg, perched precariously in its chick-pattern eggcup, in front of him. He watched her fragmenting like silvers of glass in a kaleidoscope. He pulled her into focus and she leaned across to slice the top neatly off his egg. When she sat back he could see her clearly, could see that she was smiling – that wide, beautiful mouth with its even white teeth – and pushing the errant lock of hair back behind one ear. The vulnerability of sleep excepted he had not seen her smile since the night they had met at the Tippett. For the first time he saw familiar features in her face. She bore a striking resemblance to the actress Judy Campbell, so often to be seen in the plays of Noël Coward, and Miss Campbell herself was Greta Garbo sketched by Modigliani.

'What're you staring at?'

'Just staring. Just pleased to be able to do it.'

He watched her eat, left his egg untouched, touched as he was by what he saw as the grace of every movement she made. She was only spooning egg, but to Troy, watching in soft focus, she might have been making all the hand-passes of a Japanese ritual. Precise and positive and incomprehensible.

'Eat your egg,' she said.

And he bent to breakfast, wondering what it was that he could see in her and put no words to. A face to kill or die for – that had been his first reaction to her that day in Tite Street. But that was a world away. He could no longer see quite what he had meant by the notion.

'Have you looked in a mirror today?' she asked as he finished. 'You have a week of stubble.'

Troy put a hand to his face. He had not attempted shaving and had all but forgotten what he must look like.

'Tomorrow,' he said. 'I'm not up to that yet.'

She went up to the bathroom and returned with his strop, his cut-throat and his badger-hair shaving brush. She whipped up a foam at the sink and set a bowl of hot water in front of him. The towel was tucked around his throat before she stated the obvious.

'I shall shave you.'

'Have you done this before?'

'Yes.'

She lathered his face. Troy closed his eyes and searched for the last tinge of burnt cinnamon that still clung to her. Felt the silky rasp of the blade across his throat, gliding up his cheeks, gently shaping itself to his top lip. She said not a word. Troy became acutely conscious of her breathing, a deep slow rhythm softly reassuring him, resolutely seducing him. She wiped him dry. Her fingers rested a moment on his left cheek an inch below the eye, the ball of her thumb playing firmly over the same spot. The steel touched his face again, held still, poised, and then in a quick, hard action bit into his cheek. He opened his eyes, felt the trickle of blood start out across his face, saw her bend down to kiss the wound.

She stood back. Licked her lips, a smear of his blood still clung to the lower. She smiled, but he knew it had been deliberate.

§ 67

Three days later, his eyes functioning normally again, the cut on his face a tiny ribbon of scabs, the red cloud a troublesome memory, Troy returned to work.

It was too early for Wildeve. His desk was neat and piled high in paperwork. Troy's desk was neater still – empty but for his blotter and his calendar. He reached across the desk and picked up the calendar, pages unturned for weeks, the date stuck like a stopped clock at the day of his last interview with Brack. He tore off the thick wadge in a single gesture, and as the pages fluttered down into his waste-paper basket he heard the tap of a hand on the frame of the open door.

' 'Bout time. I was beginning to think I'd imagined you.'

Onions rested his weight against the door jamb. As much as Onions did, he smiled.

'If ever I needed you it was today.'

'Trouble?' Troy asked hopefully, feeling a dark whisper begin to start up in his blood.

'D'ye know the Black Swan, East India Dock Road?'

Troy shook his head.

'Bloke found dead in his room. Blood all over the place. Door locked from the inside. A real Sherlock Holmes-er. Get over there before the locals leave their footprints all over the shop – message timed at seven forty-four. The local bobby reckoned he'd been found about six thirty. Police Surgeon'll meet you there.'

Troy wanted desperately to ask where Wildeve was, when he could get back to Wayne, whether Tom Henrey had solved his cases. Only the last seemed workable, but Onions was ahead of him.

'Take Wildeve – or leave the lad a message. He's nowt else on at the moment.'

Troy looked again at the mountain of paperwork.

'Tom cracked Golders Green and Hyde Park?'

'Not exactly,' Onions said. 'Your lad did. Tom's grateful, but embarrassed, if you know what I mean.'

Troy knew exactly what he meant.

The battery on the Bullnose Morris was flat. Troy waited while it was jump-started. Wildeve came rushing into the garage as the engine spluttered to life and flung himself into the passenger seat.

'Sorry. Overslept.'

'Sleep of the just, eh?' said Troy, easing the car out on to the Embankment.

'You heard? I can't help the feeling that I've somehow blotted my copybook.'

'Solving crimes is your job. Never apologise for it. It's Tom's problem, not yours. Comes the day you run rings around me, then you can worry.'

'I do hope that's a joke, Freddie.'

§ 68

Troy knew the voice at once. It was the same Police Surgeon who had bandaged his eyes and removed his stitches in another lifetime and another place.

'I hope you're rested, Sergeant,' he said.

'I feel fine.'

'You look a damn sight better than you did the last time we met.'

Troy peeled back the grubby white sheet that covered the corpse. A man in his twenties lay in a sticky, crisping pool of blood. Face down, hands buried beneath him, elbows sticking out. He was barefoot, collarless and had rolled up his sleeves. It should have been the old familiar slipper waiting to receive his foot – it chafed like best boot on worst bunion.

Troy looked all around the room, his attention drawn by the sound of gently trickling water to the basin opposite the door, and slowly brought his gaze to rest on the doctor.

'You can carry on,' he said.

Troy sat on a chair by the door, watched the doctor turn the body, stiff with rigor mortis. The room hummed with layers of noise – the sense rather than the sound of the water, the endless creaks of a wooden inn that had swayed with the wind on the same spot for centuries, the stagy whispers from the staircase, and a thunder that to Troy seemed to sound from somewhere deep within him.

'Not dead long, wouldn't you say, Sergeant?'

'Can you put a time to it?'

'Midnight at the outside. Say four o'clock this side.'

Troy glanced at his watch. It was half past eight.

Wildeve hovered in the doorway, behind him a crowd of a dozen or more pressed for the ghoulish glimpse of a corpse. Troy told him to take them downstairs and start questioning – anything to keep them out of the way. Troy looked at the body, upturned like a beetle, stuck on its back, the legs and arms frozen where they'd locked in death. The doctor was cutting away at the shirt-front.

'Stabbed,' he said. 'Right through the heart. I'd've said death was instantaneous.'

'Any other wounds?'

'Hard to tell. You can't get at 'em when they're like this, and I can hardly take a mallet to his knees now can I?'

The doctor stood, wiping his hands. He dropped the towel into his open case.

'I'll have to get him back to the lab, though, to tell the truth, I'd rather leave him till he loosens. He'll not fit on a stretcher the way he is. You can take a look all you want, but you'll see no more than I did.'

Troy knew damn well he could. If death was instantaneous why were his legs twisted together as they were? The man had walked two or three paces and fallen crossing the room when death took him. What was the white stuff in his right ear? Why was the tap still running? He moved to the basin and turned off the tap. Suddenly the room was free of its subliminally dominant noise, and he could hear the doctor grunting softly as he forced the latch on his Gladstone bag together, and beneath that surface sound the slow drumming in his own blood that seemed to him like a syllable beating forth to utterance. He ran his hand around the edge of the basin and looked at a brown ring of fuzz that gathered on the end of his fingers.

Downstairs Wildeve was shouting to make himself heard, but appeared to be getting somewhere.

'This chap – the postman – raised the alarm when he found blood dripping through the ceiling. He and the landlord – that's the little fat chap knocking back the brandies in the corner – forced the door. They both swear the key was turned in the lock on the inside. Trouble is this isn't the sort of place that asks any questions or signs registers – they haven't the faintest idea who he was. Do you suppose it was suicide?'

Troy steered Wildeve away from the saloon and into the snug. With the door closed the hubbub muted. Wildeve was accelerating with the excitement of mystery. Bright-eyed and breathless.

'I tell you, Freddie, this one's a stinker.'

'No – it's not.'

'Door locked. Dead in the middle of the floor. Good God – it's straight out of Sherlock Holmes!'

'That's what Onions said. You're both wrong.'

Wildeve looked perplexed and was about to speak again, when Troy's hand came up to wave him into silence.

'The doctor reckons he died between midnight and four a.m. Let's presume the latest possible hour. He died about five o'clock. And he was murdered. It's pretty damn difficult to stab yourself through the heart. And he was stabbed with a sword.'

'What?' Wildeve was agog with disbelief.

'With a sword. As he shaved. At the basin in his room. Through the panelling that divides his room from the next. He has shaving cream in his ears, the tap was on, and he was about to rinse the basin when someone shoved a sword or something as long as a sword through the gap in the boards. There's blood on the edges of the boards just below the mirror. He took two steps back, clutching his chest, which stopped the blood spraying out, turned to try for the door and fell dead with his legs still crossed. He was a merchant sailor. He was getting ready to sail on the six o'clock tide. Check the charts; if high tide isn't somewhere between six and seven at this time of year I'll eat my hat. If you go through his possessions you'll find papers or a pay-book of some sort. Find out who was in the next room. He'll be long gone, but at least we'll get a description. Pass the description – a name if we're that lucky – to the River Police. Have them stop any ship that sailed on the high tide. Whoever killed him knew him. I'll be at the Yard.'

Troy stood up and reached for the door.

'Freddie – you can't do this. You can't strip the damn thing to the bone and then just bugger off. It can't be that simple.'

'Believe me, Jack; that's what happened. I never said it was simple.'

He walked out.

Wildeve called after him, 'Freddie, I don't know what you're trying to prove, but you don't have to prove it to me!'

But the only word Troy could hear was 'Wayne' as it pounded in his blood and filled his ears with its suffocating beat.

§ 69

Troy sat all day in his office. He stared at the mountain of paperwork on Wildeve's desk and did nothing about any of it. He watched the sun dance the diamond dance of coming summer on the Thames. Coming? He glanced down at the unemptied waste-paper basket, stuffed with discarded pages from his calendar. Coming? It was June the 1st. Summer was already here. God in heaven – how long had he spent in the pit?

At five o'clock he walked along to the Savoy, showed his card and was admitted to the Lady Diana Brack suite, with its view across the river, empty and clean and smelling ever so faintly of Je Reviens. He sat on the edge of the bed and inhaled deeply – not certain of the reality of her presence or the power of his imagination. He sat until dusk – then he ran ragged through the drawers and cupboards. The silks and the satins spilled out pooling a shimmering lake of dresses and stockings, slips and pants on to the carpet. He let a stocking run liquid through his fingers. Buried his face in a slip, felt the rasp of silk on his five o'clock shadow, searched for the familiar and smelt only soap flakes.

There was no man's clothing anywhere to be found. Wayne had left not a trace behind.

Back home, he waited to see if she would come that night. She did not.

Wildeve caught up with him in the office the next morning as they sifted paperwork over eight o'clock tea. Troy thought he was sullenly nursing his grievance. Then he spoke up.

'Of course. You were absolutely bloody right, but that's hardly the point is it?'

'Isn't it?'

'No it bloody well isn't.'

'What have you got?'

'Stoker Alan Bone, bound for Lagos on the SS *Good Hope*. Steamingly angry, denying the lot and guilty as hell. But that still isn't the point!'

'Where are you holding him?'

'Wapping Old Stairs, with the River boys. Freddie, will you stop playing the boss and just for five minutes play the copper?'

'Of course, Jack. If you like.'

'I mean . . .'

'Yes.'

'I mean . . . what would Onions say?'

'He'd congratulate me on the art of delegation, and you on a quick solution.'

'But I didn't solve the damn thing. You did. But . . .'

'But?'

'But . . . not in the right way.'

'Jack, I'm afraid this is a little beyond me. There are no right or wrong ways. Only solutions. Shouldn't you get over to Wapping and give Mr Bone a bit of a roasting?'

Wildeve left. Troy thought the exit fell only marginally short of storming out. He looked at the mountain of paperwork on Jack's desk, and knew it would find itself ignored for another day.

He left the building by the Whitehall exit and caught a bus to Kensington Gore, alighting at the Albert Hall, close to his uncle's office at Imperial.

§ 70

Mid-evening he sat indoors, craving the darkness that June nights denied. He had not even bothered to take off his jacket or turn on the wireless. He mulled over the mass of fact and guesswork that had been his day with Nikolai. Around nine, still cheated of all but the merest touch of twilight, he saw the front door pushed gently open and Brack framed herself in the doorway.

'Where are you? It's black as coal in here,' she said.

'Over here, by the fire.'

He could see her quite clearly. She was dressed to the nines. A black, shoulderless dress, crêpe de Chine or some such, emphasising the length of her neck, the tightness of her waist, the breadth of her shoulders, and topped by a touch of frivolity that scarcely seemed in character – an ostrich-feather boa. She put her cloak down on the chair by the door and spun round for him, smiling, seeking approval.

'You look dressed to kill.'

'No. I dress down to kill. For the Berkeley I dress up!'

'We're going to the Berkeley?'

'Damn right we are.'

'I . . . I haven't got the togs. I don't have evening dress any more. The moths got it.'

'Troy, when did you last go to the Berkeley or anywhere like it? Men haven't worn evening dress since 1940! Mufti is quite acceptable. Just put on a clean shirt and we'll toddle off for a cab.'

'I can't match that. That dress looks as though it cost a packet.'

'Of course it cost a packet! Why do you think we're going out? I've waited six months for this dress. I ordered it from Victor Stiebel before Christmas. I'll be damned if I won't go somewhere and be seen.'

'That's what bothers me,' he said, and sloped off upstairs for a clean shirt.

Slamming the door behind him, he thought that they never had been seen. He found himself simultaneously contemplating the risk and knowing he would do nothing whatsoever about it. She raced to the end of the alley to hail a cab. He followed quietly. At the kink in the alley he thought he heard a sound behind him. He turned, two hands thrust him sharply back against the wall, and a tall man loomed over him.

'Freddie, you fool. You complete and utter bloody fool!'

'Let me go, Jack,' he whispered back.

'What on earth do you think you're playing at?'

Wildeve did not wait for an answer.

'I knew it. I knew it. Damn me, why didn't I see it sooner? Have you taken leave of your senses?'

Troy could see his face now. He looked up into his eyes, expressionless. Wildeve relaxed his grip. Troy heard the familiar squeal of cab brakes from St Martin's Lane.

'Troy,' she called from the street. 'Do get a move on!' He turned his back on Wildeve and walked away.

'Freddie, you can't. You can't.'

Troy did not turn. Wildeve did not follow. He could see Brack now, by the open door of a cab. She could not stand still. She seemed almost to be skipping from one foot to the other. Out of the deepest shadows he heard Ruby's voice say 'Who's a lucky boy then?'

He sat in the back of the cab. She took his hand in hers, and laid her head upon his shoulder. As the cab rounded Piccadilly Circus he could hear his heartbeat. The Circus was almost empty of people. A few people out on the town and apart from the usual gathering outside Rainbow Corner, very few in uniform. One thought intruded, one feeling caused his pulse to race – in his mind's eye he had seen Wayne not Wildeve in that first split second as Jack's hands had grabbed him. He had told himself for weeks now that he would always be ready for Major Wayne. And he had been taken completely by surprise. Worse than this one thought was the doubt about her that had surfaced and sank in that split second, without thought.

'When did you last go there?' she asked.

'To the Berkeley? I've never been to the Berkeley.'

'Were you really such a stuffy old fish, Troy?'

'I suppose I was,' he said to avoid a better answer.

He had found in the police a convenient escape from the social exigencies of class and caste. His brother had accepted what was offered and gone up to Cambridge. His sisters had been presented at court, and had returned giggling at the confusion they had fostered by pretending to be one twin or the other, and agreeing that Queen Mary was 'a bit of an old trout'. One morning in 1931 his father had looked up from the lectern on which he propped his morning paper – 'his', Troy thought, 'his' was always someone else's, the opposition – and asked of the young Troy, 'Well, my little Englander, will you play the English at their game?' It was as though he knew that Troy would not, as though he accepted that his last child was different in some way from his elder children. It was not his habit to force things on any of his children, but in this instance he seemed to be clearly anticipating the response.

'Don't know,' Troy had replied, and left it at that for several years, until the day he announced that he had been accepted into the Metropolitan Police Force.

'Are you sure?' his father had asked. Was all he had asked. And Troy wondered now about the pain he might have given the old man. What had Driberg meant by that remark?

It was not the game – it let him free from the social round. He could do as he wished and to hell with the dreary traipsing around the circuit of sophisticated London. He had not been in a nightclub in years. All in all being a copper was the most marvellous excuse for selfishness he could ever have thought up.

The cab drew up at the corner of Piccadilly and Berkeley Street, opposite the Ritz Hotel. The head waiter at the Berkeley knew Lady Diana Brack by sight and by name. He greeted her as though she were a valued, too rarely seen patron and told her that he would see she got her usual table. They were shown to a green-upholstered banquette.

'Thank you, Ferraro,' she said, 'I don't suppose you could manage a bottle of champagne?'

He disappeared, with her cloak over his arm, saying he would see what he could do. She smiled at Troy across the top of the menu.

'Is this an occasion?' he asked.

'It is and it isn't. I wanted to go out. I was desperate to go out. We seem to have spent a lifetime indoors.'

'A lifetime?' he queried.

She buried herself behind the menu.

'Of course there's no real choice. A five-bob menu is a five-bob menu. I came for the music. Before the war there was such marvellous music. Marvellous music.'

Troy looked across at the empty bandstand. The music stands displayed the name Romero in an italic slant. The name meant nothing to Troy. He'd have known Lew Stone's band or Harry Roy's, but few others. The club was full – as she had said, few men if any wore evening dress, and most were in uniform – an even match of naval officers and RAF types with a smattering from the army.

Five bob translated into soup and fish. A soup so watery it could have passed for Oliver Twist's gruel. The fish was good, fresh river trout, crying out for what they'd never get, fresh Jersey potatoes. The champagne made up for everything. Looking at the golden glow, the racing bubbles in the fluted glass, Troy realised that she too was bubbling in a way he had rarely seen her do.

She told him of her week. It verged on gossip, it approached chatter. She had been to see H. G. Wells at Hanover Gate. Stuck for a response Troy asked simply how he was.

'Old,' she replied.

'Of course,' said Troy. 'He must be eighty.'

'Seventy-seven, actually. But I meant old old. He has been young so long. I had begun to think age would never catch him. Now I think he might not see out the war.'

'It's almost over.'

'Do you really think so? I've been thinking so much lately about after the war.'

'Makes a change I suppose. Most of the time one can get heartily sick of sentences beginning "before the war".'

She grinned and held up her hand as though taking an oath.

'That phrase shall ne'er pass my lips again!'

Then she laughed. And Troy watched as though from another planet. He had not seen her laugh before. It was a moment as awesome as Garbo's first laugh in *Ninotchka*. His feelings glided over one another like oil on water. Her smiles and grins and laughs captivated him utterly, and at the same time the urgency of her speech, the revelation with which she spoke, all put him in mind of the three days he had spent, as Onions put it, beating her senseless at the Yard.

She smiled her perfect smile and flicked back the lock of hair over her eye, holding it there a moment with her hand poised.

'I wanted to ask you about after the war,' she said, and let her hair tumble once more. 'It's something I've never thought about.'

'Nor me,' Troy said.

'What shall we do?'

The question stunned him. Surely he could not have heard her right?

'After the war. What shall we do?' she said again, and he searched in her tone for every possible shred of meaning.

A ripple of applause announced the return of the band. Romero was a stout Latin, well past middle age, with a burnt-cork moustache and thick, Brylcreemed hair pasted tightly across his scalp away from the forehead. He bowed slightly, turned to his band and struck up Cole Porter's 'Night and Day'. The floor began to fill with dancing couples, shuffling along in the slow, public embrace that passed for dancing.

'I love this song. Can we dance?'

'What? I mean . . . I don't even know what kind of dance it is!'

'Slow foxtrot, clot!'

She stood up and stretched out an arm towards him. The pure smile, the black black hair, and the green green green of her eyes drew him from his seat. He took the arm and let himself be pulled on to the dance floor.

'I'm not very good at this,' he murmured.

In her heels she was hardly less than six feet — he found himself level with her chin and constantly looking up. He blundered on, beneath the stars and under the sun, counting himself lucky not to be treading on her feet. Then it dawned on him. Dancing backwards she may be, but she was leading him certainly and securely. She was in his arms and he was surely in her hands.

As the last note trailed off the crowd applauded. She took his head in both hands and kissed him on the mouth. A kiss so passionate he felt bruised. She drew back. Rubbed his cheek where the cut from the razor showed as a small red scar.

'What shall we do?' she said again, and before Troy could say anything blurted out that she must, simply must, just have a word with Romero and dashed off in the direction of the bandstand.

Troy resumed his seat. Sipped at the last of the champagne.

'What shall we do?' He thought — she cannot possibly mean what those words seem to mean. But her tone and the look in those bottle-green eyes told him she did.

Across the dance floor he could see her returning. The grace in every movement was unearthly, a woman without a single gawky gesture. He got up once more. The band went into 'Smoke Gets in Your Eyes'. He extended a hand to her, hoping he could lure her to the seat before she lured him back to the dance, but she stopped a few feet away from him and appeared to be looking past him. He turned to look towards the entrance. Wayne stood on the bottom step holding her cloak. He looked right through Troy to Brack as though he had not even noticed he was there. He spread the cloak like bat's wings, opening out the space into which he invited her to step. Troy looked back. Diana had frozen. The evening's smile had vanished. Then her feet moved, gliding not walking, and as she came level with him he took her hand, holding it gently without force. She glided on past him. Her head turned to look down into his eyes. She floated on until both their arms were outstretched and one of them would have to break the grip. He felt her hand slide across his, her fingernails tantalisingly stroking his palm until only their fingers touched. She stopped, looked at him one last time, her fingertips left his and she fled.

He pushed his way through the crowd of dancing couples and out into the street. People were everywhere. The Ritz was disgorging a host of American soldiers, most the worse for drink. They flowed out across the road, over the pavement up towards Berkeley Square and down towards Piccadilly Circus, singing and chanting. He saw Wayne hail a cab from the Ritz side. He crossed over as a swirl of soldiers came back down Berkeley Street and took him up like a man helpless, drowning in the ebb tide. The last he saw of her was one fleeting, backward glance as Wayne dived into the cab and pulled her in behind him, then the tide surged and deposited him against one of the pillars of the Ritz and he sank down to the pavement and a thousand feet passed over him.

The roar dwindled. The street cleared like mist in a breeze. He sat on the pavement. He did not move. He felt he could not move. His legs were numb and all he felt was the illusive tingle on his hand from the passing stroke of her nails. Feet approached him, pick-pock across the tarmacadam.

'Get up!'

He looked at a pair of high-heeled shoes and followed a pair of silk stockings thighward. There she stood, pigeon-chested again, puffed out with her own anger.

'Get up!' Tosca said, and when Troy failed to move held out a hand. He took it, she pulled him to his feet, let go her hand, bunched it into a fist and hit him hard across the cheek. He tasted blood.

'You bastard!'

She walked off along Piccadilly. A young soldier approached and said, 'Hi, Toots.' And she hit him far harder than she had hit Troy.

He sat down in the road with a bump, pole-axed. Troy walked past him, muttered, 'Terribly sorry', and hastened to catch up with Tosca. All the way to Orange Street she spoke not a word, yet it seemed understood that he should follow. He dared not overtake her.

§ 71

She poured a large bourbon for herself. She did not offer him one. He stood facing her across the table as she went through the familiar routine of kicking off her shoes and discarding her battledress — only now the accompanying silence rendered every action anew and stripped away the veneer of knowledge.

'Y' know,' she said, at last, looking down into her glass, 'I came looking for you to tell you Jimmy was back. I figured you'd want to know. I went to your house, but the hooker who hangs around the alley said I shouldn't bother. She'd seen you get into a cab with what she called "a nice bit of posh" and you'd told the cabbie to take you to the Berkeley. So I walked to the Berkeley and do you know until I saw her with Jimmy I hadn't even bothered to ask myself who this nice bit of posh might be. I mean . . .' her voiced soared, 'I mean . . .' and louder still, 'how dumb can a girl get? You bastard, Troy. You total fucking bastard!'

She sat down at the table, poured herself another drink, knocked it back in one and poured a third.

'I don't have an explanation,' he said.

'Thank God for that. I'd hate to sit and listen to your lies.'

'I have to go,' he said sheepishly.

'How long have you been fucking Diana Brack? That was Diana Brack, wasn't it?'

'Yes,' he sighed.

'And you have been fucking her, haven't you?'

'Yes.'

'So how long has this been going on?'

'I'm not sure.'

'You asshole,' she said, but the ferocity was draining from her voice. A throaty sadness crept in in its place. 'You asshole, you total fucking asshole.'

'I have to go,' he said once more, and turned for the door.

Tosca shot across the room and slammed the door shut with the whole force of her body and squared off to him, shoeless and five foot nothing, shoulders back against the door, eyes level with his chin, staring him and daring him.

'Troy, you leave now and you can never come back. You hear me – never!'

'I can't stay. Wayne is at the Savoy.'

'Yes you can – he ain't going nowhere.'

'What?'

'Six a.m. appointment with Zelly. Sunday morning. And he's tied up all day Monday.'

'All day?'

'D-Day.'

'What?'

'Monday is D-Day. And don't ask me to say it again. I'm not committing treason three times even for you. Jimmy won't run. Jimmy can't run. He'll keep the Sunday meet with Zelly. It's probably the most important of his life. It's what he does with his Saturdays that's got me worried.'

'I don't follow.'

'Take a seat, Troy. We got things to talk about.'

She fought the same old battle with the fridge door and pulled out a pizza pie the size of a cartwheel.

'It's all there is. PX is running kinda low. I guess you ain't tasted it hot yet?'

Troy shook his head. She put a match to the oven and slid the pizza in on its tinfoil tray.

'Don't let me forget.'

She took a second glass from the draining-board, looked dis-approvingly at its greasy smears and shoved it and the bottle across the table at him.

'I'll be glad to get out of this place. It's beginning to feel like a hole.'

Troy looked around.

'You could try cleaning up,' he ventured.

'Don't push your luck, Troy. I forgive nothing. This is purely business.'

'Business? Yours or mine?'

'I don't know. I just know Jimmy is up to something. Something pretty big.'

'D-Day could be rather large I should think.'

'Something ... something that's him. Something very Jimmy. He was on a high today. It was running in his blood. He's on some kind of a mission. He was acting like he always acts when he has something special coming down. He has a kind of rooster swagger to him, and he and Zelly go off into huddles and Zelly gets that dumb-ass worried look as though he thinks Jimmy's gonna drop the both of them right in it. And it's Saturday whatever it is. "I'll take care of it Saturday," he told Zelly. And Zelly says "Sure sure" and just keeps right on sweating.'

She stared into the bottom of her glass again, not looking at him, her voice trailing away almost to nothing. 'Oh God, Troy – I'm scared.'

Troy slipped off his coat and shoes, padded softly round the table, and dropped to his knees. He lifted her chin with one hand. Against expectation her eyes were dry – the look was one of intense concern and, for the time being at least, her emotions seemed to be under control. He had no idea of what she was capable.

'He's gonna kill somebody. I just know it.'

'Do you know who?'

'Jesus Christ, Troy, if I knew I'd've told you five minutes ago! Of course I don't know!'

'Do you know where?'

'Nope – all I know is tomorrow night.'

Troy thought for a moment. He felt the need to reassure her, but had no idea what word or gesture might prove acceptable.

'I'll handle it. Don't worry,' he said, and placed a hand on her stockinged knee.

'Oh for Christ's sake – you've spent the last two months telling me the guy's a killer. You told me he likes it. This is a guy who kills for pleasure!'

'He does,' he said very matter-of-factly.

'Then what the fuck are you going to do???'

'Arrest him. That's my job.'

She sighed in exasperation and he kissed her lightly on her left ear and slid his hand up her skirt and along her thigh.

'Will you stop that!'

She shook her head vigorously, as though he were a small species of insect tangled in her hair.

'Does doing your goddamn job mean going up against a maniac?'

'Won't be the first time.'

He cautiously approached her knickers, thinking all the time that this was no time for caution.

'What in hell are you tryin' ter do?'

'Nothing. Nothing at all.'

And he took her ear-lobe between his teeth. She squirmed and stomped the floor with her stockinged feet.

'Goddamit, Troy! When you first walked in here you didn't know knicker elastic from liquorice! Now you think you can mend any damn thing if only you can get me into bed. Dammit, I don't know you at all, do I?'

Troy said nothing and began a perilous course of trying to tug her knickers kneeward.

'I mean. I never even knew you played the piano.'

'You never asked.'

'What was I supposed to do, go through the instruments of the orchestra – hey honey, how are you on woodwind? – you set for a bash on the snare drum? For fuck's sake, Troy, will you stop that!'

He ignored her. The room began to fill with the smell of melting cheese. A smell so pre-war, so old of old England it was almost seductive in itself, and this turned gently, mingled with the scent of basil and its hint of the exotic, that continental touch, all garlic and black stockings, the forbidden.

'Pizza's almost done,' she said.

Troy said nothing. She lifted her buttocks from the chair and the elastic recoiled on to his hand like a rebounding yo-yo and the silk knickers bunched into his grip as he pulled them towards him.

'You want it before or after?' she said.

§ 72

She read her ten pages of *Huck Finn* as he scrambled eggs and made toast. It was her third time through the book in the time she had known him, she pointed out. They faced each other across morning coffee, sitting on the floor, less than half-dressed.

'Where have you got to?'

'Duke of Bridgewater just got himself tarred and feathered again. There's a lot to be said for knowing when you're in danger.'

She took up the cup in both hands and drank deeply.

'Ah mm ya ya nmmm!'

'Are you working today?' he asked.

'With Armageddon two days away would I not be working? Of course I'm working! Leave got cancelled for almost everybody. Those assholes cluttering up Piccadilly last night were probably under orders to go out and get drunk and make it look like London is still full of Yankees. Haven't you noticed how empty London's been the last week? Everybody's down on the South Coast. I bet you can't get a cream tea in Dorset for love or dollars.'

'So it is Normandy?'

'Did you ever doubt it?'

'Not really.'

'Utah, Omaha, Juno, Gold, Sword.'

'Eh?'

'The beaches. That's what we call 'em. I chose Juno. I figured the war needed a woman's touch. Ike said he wasn't having his boys land on a beach called Fanny, which was to be my first choice, so I went for a goddess instead. My piece of history, not bad, eh?'

She held out her cup for more coffee. He filled it.

'I need you to promise me something,' she said.

'OK.'

'You won't go up against Jimmy alone – like you were going to do last night? You go round to the Savoy with a whole bunch of coppers and you pull him in. Promise?'

Troy thought for a moment. He had half-expected her to ask this. 'I can't do that.'

She slapped the cup down, splashing hot coffee across his naked leg.

'Jesus, Troy!'

'I can't do that because I have no grounds on which to arrest him.'

'Baloney – you spent the last two months trying to arrest the bastard!'

'No,' he said. 'I've spent the last two months trying to get enough evidence to arrest him. Trying to break his alibi. He's still alibied. That statement of Ike's still stands. Why do you think I've received no co-operation from anyone? Because if I succeed I'm calling the Supreme Allied Commander a liar.'

'We all make mistakes. Really, when you get to know him Ike's OK. I mean not grouchy or anything and not too bright. I mean OK for a general – you wouldn't want him to be President or anything like that. I guess someone told him it was all in the national interest, as you guys say – and I guess that someone was Jimmy.'

'Whatever Jimmy has in mind tonight, I need to catch him *in flagrante delicto.*'

'Eh?'

'I need to catch him at it. I need the evidence.'

She was aghast. Her mouth opened and no words came out. She drew breath sharply and made indeterminate noises that led to 'Troy, Troy, Troy, do not go up against Jimmy!'

'I've no choice.'

'Please – Troy, you don't know – you can't imagine – just pull him – a moving violation, anything – just get him off the streets by nightfall. Don't try and take him on.'

Troy looked back at her in silence.

'Then at least get yourself a gun. I know it's not what you bobbies do, but get yourself a gun. You can do that, can't you? I mean that's not asking the earth, is it?'

They dressed. With every other word she called him stupid. Troy gave up trying to explain, and then she looked at her watch and swore.

'Baby, I gotta run. No time. Come see me tonight. Come show me you're still in one piece.'

She stood at her dressing-table, fully dressed, all neat in olive green, fiddling at one ear. She looked down into her jewellery box, slammed something down and said, 'Why does this always happen?'

She turned to Troy. Kissed him on the lips, pulled back, smiled, kissed him again and said, 'Bring 'em back alive!' and dashed out.

Troy looked around for the phone, and after a few minutes' search, found it under the bed with a small mountain of discarded stockings and American magazines and blew the dust off it. He called Wildeve. Wildeve exploded softly in a mixture of anxiety and anger.

'Freddie, where the hell are you?'

'I'm at home. Now listen . . .'

'How long have you been there?'

'What does it matter?'

'I waited outside your house all fucking night!'

Only Ruby, it seemed, had prevented Jack from meeting Tosca.

'I only got in an hour ago.'

'For Christ's sake will you stop lying to me! I was there until twenty minutes ago. Where are you?'

'I can't tell you.'

'Are you at Tite Street?'

'No.'

'You're an ass, Freddie.'

'Quite possibly. But this ass has found Wayne.'

The line was silent for a moment. Troy could almost hear Wildeve think.

'I don't have to ask how, do I?'

'No, you don't.'

'But if you try to tell me this justifies . . .'

'Jack, I'm not trying to justify anything. I've been an ass – you're absolutely right! But right now Major Wayne is sleeping off a heavy night at the Savoy!'

'I'll put Thomson and Gutteridge on to it.'

'Front and back?'

'Of course. When can I expect you?'

'A couple of hours. I need a shave and a change.'

'What if Wayne makes a move?'

'He won't. There's something special coming down.'

'Coming down? What the hell does that...? Oh never mind. How do you know? Has she...?'

'I don't need anyone to tell me, Jack. It's his *modus operandi*. He works by night.'

'Are you saying he's come back just to do another?'

'He's come back to...' Troy searched for the words and could find only Tosca's. 'He's on a mission.'

'Mission? Mission? What kind of bloody jargon is that? Freddie, how do you know?'

'I can't tell you.'

'Will you stop saying that!'

'Jack, just meet me in the shooting range at half past two.'

Troy hung up. A mess of dusty stockings lay at his feet. The only other clear surface was the top of the dressing-table. He yanked on the cable and put the phone down next to her jewellery box. It was open. There in the lid was a single pearl ear-ring on a silver screw mounting.

§ 73

Ex-Regimental Sergeant Major Peacock bore a passing resemblance to the late Lord Kitchener – passing in that a walrus moustache tends to make anyone look like the late Lord Kitchener. He clutched both lapels of his brown, stained warehouse coat and rubbed his thumbs gently up and down whilst looking appraisingly at Wildeve.

'I don't believe I've met yer boy,' he said.

'Detective Constable Wildeve,' said Troy. 'My number two.'

'Bit young aren't yer, lad?'

'I'm—' Wildeve began in a tone of schoolboy resentment, but Troy nudged him sharply into silence.

'Mr Peacock.'

'Mr Troy.'

'A gun if you please.'

Peacock switched his gaze to Troy. Troy had no personal feelings about Peacock one way or the other, but the silent tutting infuriated him as symptomatic of a generation. The assumed air of gravity and the fraudulent pretence of judgement in situations that required only answer or action struck him as the manner in which old men concealed their hollowness. Old men – Peacock could hardly be more than fifty, but a dozen years as an RSM had left him indelibly marked with the importance of his own banality. He was, thought Troy, of the same mould as the old head gardener or the butler in his father's household. Any question, however trivial, put by the boy Troy would be met with concealment, the implication that there were things known to men that were best not known by boys. Adolescence, adulthood even, had not initiated Troy into the mystery. His father, questioned, had ascribed it not to age but to the temperament of the English. Whatever the outcome of this prolonged and unnecessary pause, if, now or at any time in the next ten minutes, Peacock mentioned that he was off to see a man about a dog Troy felt sure he would hit him.

Peacock tugged at one end of the great moustache.

' 'Ow long 'as it bin, Mr Troy?'

'Bin?'

'Since you put in any time on the range?'

'I'm not entering a clay-pigeon shoot. I simply feel the situation requires that I be armed. We have reason to—'

'O' course. O' course. Matter of self-defence. You wouldn't be 'ere if there wasn't a bad 'un out there somewhere with a shooter. Goes without sayin'. What I am sayin' is can you 'andle it?'

Shit, shit, shit, thought Troy.

'Why don't you and I step over to the range. Just see how you're shapin' up. The boy can 'ave a go too. Long as 'e realises 'e don't get a teddy bear if 'e wins.'

Peacock thought his own joke uproarious. He clattered off in his big brown boots in the direction of the range, chortling as he went. Troy and Wildeve followed.

'I'll kill the bastard,' Wildeve whispered to Troy.

'Not if I get him in my sights first,' Troy replied.

Peacock approached the iron and wire contraption that wound the targets back and forth between the bench and the sandbags.

He slipped in two fresh bull's-eye targets and cranked them down to the end.

'I thought we shot at human silhouettes?' Wildeve said.

'You been watchin' too much George Raft. What d'you think we are, the FBI?' Peacock replied.

With a pleasurable flourish he hoiked a huge bunch of keys from under his coat and opened the double doors of a large mahogany cupboard. Twenty to thirty hand-guns sat in a rack of neat wooden pockets, like wine bottles, with their handles facing out. Peacock reached in and pulled out a shiny, black automatic. He filled the clip from the drawer at the base of the cupboard – swift, practised movements, like a music-hall conjuror deceiving the eye – and handed the pistol to Troy. It felt heavy. It felt wrong.

'Doesn't feel right,' he said feebly.

'Different,' Peacock replied. 'Bound to feel different. Lighter. Better power-to-weight ratio.'

Better power-to-weight ratio. That was the most authoritative, genuine-sounding phrase Peacock had yet used.

'Just doesn't feel right,' Troy protested.

'Bang up to date it is. American. First we've 'ad in. Colt company. Point four five automatic. Stop an elephant that will.'

Troy looked at the gun and realised why it had felt wrong. It was the same model as the murder weapon. He laid it down on the bench, surprised at the power of superstition, but unwilling to challenge it.

'What's wrong with the old Webleys?'

'Exackly. *Old* Webleys. You said it I didn't.'

'I'd be happier with what I know.'

'Suit yourself. If you knew the trouble I had gettin' the Colts you'd take it a bit more—'

'I'll try the Colt if I may,' Wildeve put in.

Peacock paused again. Gave Wildeve the ten-second abridged version of his knowing appraisal.

'Right you are, son. Game of you I will say.'

He passed the gun to Wildeve, pulled down a Webley .38 from the rack, held it flat on his left hand and began feeding cartridges into the chamber with his right. A spin of the chamber from the ball of his thumb and he handed the gun to Troy, butt first.

'Mr Wildeve to the right. Mr Troy to the left. No funny business. No showin' off. Fire at will.'

Wildeve's arm bucked at the first recoil and he scored an outer. His second showed more control and took him to an inner, then he placed four bull's-eyes with dazzling speed one after the other.

He grinned at Troy. Troy felt the weight of the Webley. The old bastard was right. He'd forgotten they weighed a ton. It felt like a cobbler's last tied to his wrist. He extended his arm, shaking like a bough in a thunderstorm and tried aiming. That failed, he squeezed off a round in roughly the right direction, felt his arm almost wrench from its socket and heard a tongue-and-teeth-smacking disapproval from Peacock.

'Nice one, Mr Troy. Right on the sandbag. You was out by more'n a yard.'

Troy let fly with the remaining five, and missed with every one.

Peacock reloaded for them. His expression mellowed towards Wildeve. A little skill obviously impressed him. Peacock wound Wildeve's target in and said that there was no point in changing Troy's as it was 'untouched by yuman 'and'. Troy considered the prospect of shooting Peacock instead of the target.

'Mr Wildeve to the right. Mr Troy to the left. No funny business. No showin' off. Fire at will,' Peacock said in his standard way.

The telephone rang by his desk and he disappeared to deal with it. Wildeve and Troy exchanged glances as Troy raised his arm and tried to level the gun. He let it drop again. Wildeve did the same.

'Freddie,' he began in a tone that implied an impending onslaught of questions, 'I don't suppose you could tell me what's going on? Because I think I've been bloody brilliant about not asking. You fobbed me off neatly when you were in hospital after the bomb in Holborn. Perhaps you were right to do that, but you do know what's going on, and I'd feel a damn sight easier about what we're doing if you'd tell me.'

'It isn't exactly simple.'

'I didn't think it would be.'

Troy glanced over his shoulder at Peacock, still busy with his phone call. He squeezed off a round. It thudded aimlessly into the sand.

'I think there's a race on to get to Germany's boffins before the

Russians do. Or before the RAF blasts them all to oblivion. I think that the Americans are using their overseas network and the Resistance in France and Germany to whisk away the brightest and the best. Only something went horribly wrong.'

He nodded at Wildeve, who sent a couple of rounds straight to the bull's-eye. Troy fired a second, as wild as the first.

'They killed the first man – von Ranke – and were clumsy enough to let the body get found. They then covered their tracks as best they could and started all over again. Less than a year later they've got boffin number two – Brand – and the same thing happens. This time they take precautions with the body. But for a mongrel dog in Stepney we'd never have known a thing about it.'

Wildeve fired again.

'In particular I think Wayne is on to the German rocket programme. I know he was in Sweden in March. Coincidence or not, that was when a German prototype went madly off course and came down in Sweden. The Norwegian Resistance crossed over and got most of it. I think Wayne was sent to get bits of it back to England. And I think that's why Miller's diary had so many blanks in it.'

'How on earth do you know this?'

'Can't tell you. But take it as gospel. Nikolai confirmed my source. I spent most of yesterday with him. He has a chunk of this Jerry rocket in the bottom drawer of his desk.'

'It's like something out of *Things to Come*.'

'Nikolai reckons it's something like a flying cigar. Massive warhead, and, worse still, silent.'

'Silent? How the hell can it be silent?'

'It flies faster than the speed of sound. We won't know they're coming till they've hit. Nikolai even named the damn thing – the Jerries call it a *Vergeltungswaffen* – means vengeance.'

'Oh God,' said Wildeve. 'Oh God,' he said again. 'I hate all this spook stuff. Give me plain old-fashioned murder.'

'It's still murder, Jack, for all its new-fangled elaboration.'

'You know there's one thing that doesn't fit. I mean, Wayne's terribly important, isn't he? And we're sticking our noses in and upsetting everybody, aren't we?'

'Like I said. It's still murder.'

'Quite. Coppers all. No argument. But it ... well, dammit, Freddie, it doesn't gel does it?'

'I don't follow.'

'He's so important our top brass are prepared to cover his tracks. That I can understand. What I don't understand is why he had to leave any.'

'They ran. They did a bunk. First von Ranke, then Brand. They were both Communists. Very grateful to be rescued, but not at all willing to be virtual prisoners of Uncle Sam and capitalism. They ran to the one man they knew – Peter Wolinski. But after von Ranke the Americans were ready for Brand, and for Wolinski, and they killed them both.'

'I know. I'd worked that out for myself. That's what doesn't fit. Why kill them? It was excessive. It wasn't necessary. And if Wayne's as important as you say why take the risk of attracting the attention of the Met? It doesn't fit. The risks don't add up. There's something missing. Something we don't yet know about.'

'Excessive.' Troy played with the word somewhere between question and meditation.

'Three men shot to death, one of them chopped into little pieces. Don't *you* think it's excessive?'

Wildeve emptied the remainder of the clip into the target, still looking at Troy. It made no difference to his aim. The echo hung a moment and died. There was a sudden silence as the drone of Peacock's voice in the background ceased with a Bakelite clunk. Slowly Troy fired off his last four shots, trying his pathetic best. Wildeve had hit all six into the centre. So close the six shots scarcely made more than a single hole. Troy had missed with the first four, scored an outer with the fifth and an inner with the sixth. The temptation to smile with small satisfaction was nipped in the bud as the tongue-on-teeth tutting began again and the scrape of the wires on their iron pulleys cut through the air. Peacock clutched both targets, looking pointlessly from one to the other as though any comparison were necessary or other than obvious.

' 'Scuse my French, Mr Troy, but you can't hit the fuckin' side of a barn door now can yer?'

Troy said nothing.

'I don't think God intended people to be keg-handed. You're

all dreadful shots, the lot of you. I'd like it if you'd put some time in, but I do suppose that if I was to ask you'd tell me crime don't wait, so what I will say is . . . this chummy you reckon is out there, well he'd better not be armed, or if 'e is I pray to God 'e's a worse shot than you.'

'Thanks,' said Troy without inflection. 'I'll take the Webley if I may. Jack?'

'I'm happy with the Colt.'

'Rightie-ho. Just the matter of yer chitty.'

Troy pulled out the chit from his pocket, folded double. Peacock bustled back to his desk and unfolded it under the lamp.

'Bit scrawled,' he said after some scrutiny of the signature. 'In a tearing 'urry was 'e?'

Troy said nothing.

'I'll keep the guns out ready like, but if you wouldn't mind askin' Mr Onions to sign again.'

He handed the chit back to Troy. Troy said nothing. Wildeve snatched the chit from his hand.

'No problem,' he said, 'I'll do it in a jiffy. It's only three o'clock. I bet he's still in his office.'

Wildeve took a step towards the stairs. Troy snatched the chit back.

'No,' he said. 'It's all right, I'll do it.'

Troy and Peacock looked at each other. Peacock gave in first and looked at the top of his desk. Troy started up the staircase. Wildeve followed.

'Honestly, Freddie,' he was saying, 'it's no trouble. Why don't you stay here and get in some more—?'

He reached for the chit. Troy screwed it up and shoved it in his coat pocket. They reached the ground floor.

'Oh Lord,' said Wildeve, 'I am an ass sometimes.'

'Indeed you are, Jack. I know it's a forgery. Peacock knows it's a forgery. Peacock knows I know he knows. And let that be all.'

'Are you in the habit of forging the Superintendent's signature?' Wildeve asked.

'Yes. When I think he won't sign. It's simply that on this occasion I made a hash of it.'

§ 74

Four hours later Troy met an acned youth he referred to as Herbert, which concealed his customary *nom de guerre* of Danny the Deserter, in a café in Old Compton Street, and on the promise of twenty pounds at some future date and his silent assent to 'you owe me one', purchased a small Italian-made .22-calibre revolver, from which all identifying numbers had been removed with a steel rasp.

Troy shoved the gun in the left-hand pocket of his overcoat, stepped into the street and turned up his collar against the slow drizzle that was beginning to fill the evening sky – the summer promise of warm rain.

It was still not quite dusk – an endless evening of June – when he and Wildeve relieved Thomson on the Embankment. The look of joy on Thomson's face turned sour when Troy told him to join Gutteridge outside the Strand entrance. They watched him out of sight before Wildeve spoke.

'They call us the tearaway toffs, you know.'

'I'll tear him to pieces if he lets Wayne slip out without telling us.'

'You know, I've been thinking.'

Troy was staring up at the window of Brack's apartment. The rose-coloured light, the flicker of someone passing between the light and the window. The surge in his blood – the rift between wanting to see her appear at the window and the need to see Wayne, to know he was there, within reach.

'A mission you called it . . .'

'Not my choice of words,' said Troy, and almost bit off his tongue – but Wildeve didn't seem to notice the meaning.

'Freddie, are you seriously going to let Wayne run?'

Nothing moved on the third floor back. Troy looked at Wildeve.

'I don't see what other choice I have.'

'It's one hell of a risk.'

Troy said nothing.

'He'll be armed. We won't.'

Troy wrapped his hand around the butt of the little silver revolver and thought better of mentioning it to Wildeve.

§ 75

An hour later it was almost dark. From beneath the trees of Victoria Embankment Gardens that put them in shadow, Troy looked at the sky, asking himself whether the fragment of moon would be enough to follow Wayne by. It peeped intermittently from between the mass of grey cloud that spotted them gently with rain. He drew his gaze round from the cloud to the building and down the façade, past the third-floor window to the glass porch. Wayne emerged from the entrance of the hotel, and hesitated on the threshold. He was clutching a mackintosh and a trilby hat, and he too was looking at the sky. He stuck the trilby on his head, yanked at the brim and made a great show of unfurling his mac, chatting amiably to the doorman as he did so. He flung on the mac, fashionably twisting the belt around his waist and not bothering with any of the buttons. His hands dived into his pockets, brought out a packet of cigarettes and a book of matches, cupped around his lips and lit up. In the brief flare of the flame Troy could see his face quite clearly. It was, he realised, only the third time he had had such a clear view of his quarry, yet the features had etched themselves into memory weeks ago – the softness of the overripe upper lip, the watery blue of his eyes, which even now seemed to be smiling as they had smiled at him long ago in Tosca's office. It was a smile of satisfaction. Troy felt provoked by it. It could mean so many things. Wayne shook out the match with a vigorous wave of his hand and looked once more at the sky.

'Which way do you think he'll go?' Wildeve whispered.

'To the Underground. It's part of his MO.'

'He's not moving.'

'Yes he is!'

Wayne left the porch and turned to his left, heading quickly eastward to the Embankment.

'He's going towards the Temple. Get to the front, Jack!'

'Surely we should stick together?'

'Jack, there's not a moment to lose – for God's sake just do as you're told – make sure those dozy buggers follow on.'

'Freddie, how can we follow if . . .

But Troy was gone. Once more down the rabbit hole.

Wayne paid via one of the automatic machines and went down to the eastbound platform of the District and Circle. Troy stood on the staircase until the train pulled in – a District line bound for Plaistow. When he was certain Wayne was seated he ran for the door at the last second and squeezed into the car behind. Through the connecting doors he could see Wayne, sitting next to an old lady in black and reading the *Daily Mail*. He didn't look up and Troy had not at any point seen him turn to make sure he wasn't being followed. It bespoke a certain cockiness, but it also proved something else. Brack had not revealed to Wayne that she had told Troy about their hideaway. Troy took an emotional pleasure in this – this one vestige of loyalty she had shown him, for the truth was that he had not been at all certain that she would keep the secret or that she was capable of keeping any secret.

Wayne ignored the stops, and did not even look up from his paper until the train pulled into Mark Lane, where the District and the Circle parted. It was a likely place to change. If he did Troy would have a very hard job concealing himself. Wayne peered at the platform, as though making certain of the station name, and went back to his paper. As the train pulled out Troy began to suspect that Wayne was heading for Stepney. It seemed absurd. Absurd that the murderer should return to the scene of the crime. A cliché of tacky novelettes. At Whitechapel Wayne got out. Perhaps it wasn't to be Stepney after all? But then he turned left along the Mile End Road, crossed over in front of the Blind Beggar pub, and turned sharply right at the top of Jubilee Street.

Troy kept as far back as he could, and when Wayne turned left into Adelina Grove he raced to the corner. Wayne was fifty or so feet away and walking resolutely in the direction of Stepney Green. Still he did not turn. Keeping to the doorways, fearful that his footsteps would sound like horses' hooves in the quiet of the empty street, Troy moved at a crawl and as he reached the corner of Hannibal Road and Jamaica Street – or what was left of Jamaica Street – he realised that Wayne had vanished from sight. He was only a few feet from Cressy Houses, a few flights of stairs from

Wolinski's flat, but Miller had never recorded any visit by Wayne to the flat – what he had recorded was Wayne's meetings in the Bricklayers Arms, outside which Troy now found himself. He pushed cautiously at the door marked Jug and Bottle and found himself in the off-licence, a mere cupboard of a room with scarcely the space to swing a jug or bottle. The landlord had his hands full with a Saturday-night crowd, and less than an hour's urgent drinking time left till closing. He was alternately berating a young serving woman for her slowness and yelling 'Now, now, gentlemen, 'old yer 'orses,' at the customers. Troy stepped back from the counter, out of the light, and began to search the crowd. Wayne must stand head and shoulders over the average Londoner, he thought, and he could not be hard to find. Yet he could not see him above the mob. The young woman moved away from the bar and turned to the row of optics on the back wall at the same moment the landlord did and for the first time Troy had a clear view across the bar to the far end where it curved round to meet the wall and ended in a hinged flap. Wayne was hunched over a pint of stout, burying his height by propping himself on his elbows. He was deep in conversation with a small man on a bar stool who sat on the corner and so had his back to Troy. There was something familiar in the curve of that back, it was almost hunched, or was it the way the man leaned to hear whatever it was that Wayne was saying? Then the man turned and he knew it was Edelmann. Edelmann spoke to the barman, pushed a half-crown across the counter to him and as his order was taken gazed idly round the room, so idly as to let his gaze meet Troy's, so idly as to let their eyes lock – and neither he nor Troy could look away, and Major Wayne could not but notice. He had the glass to his lips, and as his eyes flicked across at Troy to see what Edelmann was looking at his lips froze and he put the glass down untouched and fled.

'Shit!' said Troy out loud. He turned to bump into an old man carrying a jug for his beer and found himself stuck, wedged against the counter, with no room to pass. He pushed the old man back into the street. The man fell with a moan and a 'bugger' as the jug smashed upon the paving, and Troy ran. Wayne had stolen a march and was halfway down Union Place – a quick glance over his shoulder at Troy and he disappeared down Stepney Green, running towards a patch of rubble where a lone chimney-stack stood out like a lighthouse.

Troy cursed his luck. Why did Edelmann have to be there? Why did he have to spot Troy? Why, given what he knew about Wayne, was he talking to him over a pint like an old mate? Why was Wayne running? Why was Troy chasing? Wayne could not now do anything – not a damn thing except run the both of them ragged. The rendezvous was blown. Whoever Wayne had come to meet – whoever Wayne had come to kill – whoever, whoever, whoever – the word rang in Troy's mind. Would he ever know?

He jumped over the remains of a house wall and found himself once more on the exposed kitchen floors of the ruined houses of Cardigan Street, among the nettles and the brambles of 'the farm', where the boys had chalked up their game of hopscotch. Wayne was nowhere to be seen. Troy ran on towards the chimney-stack. Suddenly Wayne appeared from behind a length of wall just high enough to have concealed him – but he wasn't running away, he was walking towards him. Troy had to stop or they would meet nose to nose. It was a foolish position – he felt foolish – he slipped his hands into his pockets, and found little reassurance in the silver revolver nestling there. He found himself in the shadow of that great chimney, with the moon peeking out and the gentle rain upon his face beginning to mingle with the rivulets of his own sweat. Thirty feet away Wayne stopped – hands deep in his mackintosh pockets, the rain running off the brim of his trilby. Somewhere in the distance a siren sent up its plaintive wail – the usual false alarm, there had been no raids for weeks now. It seemed to Troy that he could hear the rain louder than he could hear the siren, seemed that he could hear Wayne breathe louder than he could hear his own heartbeat. Then sound subsided into silence, and the distant purr of an engine wafted across the night sky with all the power of an illusion.

'I figured it was time we met,' Wayne said.

Troy said nothing. Troy could think of nothing. He watched Wayne's hands, wondering which pocket held the Colt, and trying to remember whether the man was right- or left-handed.

'I hear you had a high old time while I was away.'

He paused to let Troy speak, but Troy didn't.

'Was she good?'

Troy gripped the butt of his revolver, and searched out the trigger with his index finger.

'Was she good?' Wayne repeated. 'I mean, she can be so very good, so very, very good, but when she's bad – Oh man, she is better.'

And he took both hands out of his pockets and touched thumbs to fingers to form two emphatic winged zeros in obscene appraisal – then he let his hands relax and locked the fingers across his midriff.

Looking back, with endless time in which to recuperate, in endless pain with which to exercise hindsight, Troy examined the move a thousand times. What was it that had made him slip his fingers from the gun and take his hands from his pockets and lock them together as Wayne had done? What was it? What had it been? Some gentlemanly gesture of fair play? Some dreadful, latent Englishness that told him it wasn't cricket to be holding a gun on a man who wasn't holding one on you?

The last thing – he could have sworn he heard the drone of an aeroplane engine as the shot rang out and blew him to the ground. There was awful, searing pain in his left side, and a sensation of warm tea pouring out across his shirt. His face was in the mud, the mud was in his eyes as he looked up at Wayne, still standing there with his fingers locked, staring down at him from under the sodden brim of his hat.

Wayne unlocked his hands, and looked off to his left.

'Finish him,' he said softly.

Troy could not see. He lay on the side where the bullet had pierced him. He strained his eyes and twisted his neck and fumbled in his left-hand pocket for the gun. A tall man in black, black shoes, black pin-stripe trousers, a glistening black raincoat and a wide-brimmed black hat was bearing down on him – a large automatic pistol hanging loosely from his right hand. Troy could not make out the face, nor any feature of it. He tugged at the revolver as the man walked slowly out of the shadows towards him. He pulled as hard as he could and slithered around in the mud and the blood, but the weight of his body was on the gun and the hammer had caught on the lining of his coat. He looked round again, twisting to see over his own shoulder. The man had stopped and was slowly raising the pistol to aim at Troy's head. Troy tugged on the gun. It tore free with such force that his whole body twisted round towards his assassin and in a single sweeping movement he had levelled the gun and fired. He had missed. Oh God, he had missed!

The man stood with the gun still aimed at Troy. Why didn't he fire? Troy asked himself. Then the arm dropped – the man swayed gently as though pushed by an invisible hand, fell over backwards and hit the ground full length, scattering mud, and still clutching the pistol.

Troy staggered to his feet. It seemed to him it took an age as he pulled each limb free of the clinging mud and the downward pull of pain. But Wayne had frozen. Troy tried to raise the gun again, but the pain was more than he could bear. Still Wayne would not take the risk, he did not move. Overhead the drone of the plane came closer. Troy fought his own muscles and managed to level the gun, Wayne extended his arms, put up his hands either in silent pleading or an unconscious gesture to ward off bullets. The drone was right above them now, smothering, enveloping, blurring, deceiving, deceiving – the power of suggestion. Behind Wayne shapes seemed to form out of the darkness, the stones uncurled, the bricks spoke, a murmur rose up to meet the drone from above. Shapes became figures, murmurs became voices, the drone became a boom, a deep bass rumble, roaring in his blood, bending the world in front of him as he tried to keep Wayne in focus, tried to keep his grip on the trigger. He aimed his gun, his finger would not move. He could not pull the trigger. Then thunder exploded all around him and it seemed to Troy that the earth had opened up and swallowed him.

§ 76

'You're a very lucky boy,' the nurse told him when he first awoke, but his first waking lasted only minutes and he drifted into painless sleep and into dreams in which Brack kissed him better, as she would put it, and kissed him, and smiled as she never smiled.

When next he awoke a different nurse told him he was in the London Hospital, and that he was going to be all right, and then she too said that he was a very lucky boy. Troy asked what day it was and was told it was Wednesday, but that meant nothing to him, as he could not remember what day it had been the last time he had been aware of days. He was in the London Hospital, in a room to himself, and it was a Wednesday. It was 1944 – or at least it had been when he last thought about it. He couldn't be at all sure of the month though. He slept and dreamt of the cellar where he and Bonham had found the pieces of Brand – only the pieces were him and he lay like a rag doll on that stinking, mouldering pile of lath and plaster, with the smell of death mingling with the smell of carbide, only the power of his dream had changed the smell of carbide to the scent of Je Reviens, and he could not see her, yet she must be there. He craned around, his neck aching – there was a tall dark figure over by the furnace door, and when he turned it was Bonham, and Bonham smelt of Je Reviens.

The next day the pain returned and with it memory. He had killed a man. Almost certainly he had killed a man. The gun had been aimed at his head and he hadn't missed – by some fluke he hadn't missed. He lay for an hour after his breakfast. The traffic hummed in the road outside, a nurse came and opened the windows, telling him it was a bright, sunny morning and the fresh air would do him good, and there was Wildeve. Standing in the doorway.

'Jack – who was he? Who did I . . . ?'

Onions strode in past Wildeve, clutching his Homburg hat to his loins. Onions hated hats. The occasion could not augur well if he had seen fit to wear a hat. The nurse bustled out past him and told them not to tire Troy. He had had a nasty wound and he was a very lucky boy.

Onions laid his hat on the trolley and stared out of the window for a moment, made the smoothing gesture, running his hands along the side of his head as he stood gathering his thoughts.

'I really don't know where to begin.'

He turned to face Troy. Fixed him with his eye.

'You disobey orders, walk off a case, forge my name on a chit for weapons issue, buy an illegal gun, stage a shoot-out at the OK Corral – the list is endless!'

Onions leaned over the foot of the bed, both hands in a fierce grip on the bed rail.

'But for the boy here you'd be dead. Do you realise that? If he hadn't had the gumption to try and head you off you'd be on a slab down the mortuary. Why, Freddie, why did you do it? Couldn't you see the danger you were in?'

He held up a hand. He didn't want Troy to answer. Not that Troy would have done.

'The boy tells me you said Wayne was on some kind of mission. Is that right? A mission. He'd come back just to do one more job. There was someone he had to kill. Couldn't you see who that was?'

For once he seemed to require an answer, but Troy stared back at him in silence.

'The only mission Wayne was on was to kill you – a private vendetta. He laid a trap for you – him and that woman of his – and you walked right into it. Wildeve saw it for what it was. Were you blind to it?'

Troy looked at Wildeve. His entire expression, even the posture of his body said 'Sorry' – but Jack had nothing to be sorry about. Troy knew he had saved his life. Among the shapes and murmurs as the bricks had come to life he had recognised a shape and a sound that were Jack. Wildeve shook his head. He had not told Onions about Brack and Troy. Troy looked back at Onions – if Onions knew about his affair with 'that woman' it would surely have been top of his endless list?

'Not only that – Wayne was not your man. You spent twelve weeks on the case – you told me he had a killer's nature, enjoyed killing, and now it turns out some other bugger did it. He was too proud to get his hands dirty. Wayne didn't kill Brand, didn't kill von Ranke, didn't kill Wolinski. He had some hatchet man do it for him. Some bugger you'd never even suspected existed.'

Troy had shot said bugger dead. The most prominent thought in a welter of conflicting thoughts and feelings was who was this man, had they identified him yet?

'Who was he?' he asked, scarcely audibly.

'Tell 'im!' Onions barked at Wildeve.

'Er ... we don't know – we don't have the body. Wayne got away with it. He had a car parked by the Green, ready for his getaway. He bundled the corpse in and got clean away. All I got was the gun.'

'Satisfied?' Onions turned on Troy in fury. 'Pleased with your result? 'Cos that's all there is!'

'No,' Troy whispered.

'No?' Onions roared.

'We have Wayne as accessory after the fact to attempted murder – mine.'

'You're out of date, Freddie. It's murder, the whole thing, all the bloody way. Edelmann's dead.'

Troy was stunned. What had Edelmann to do with this? He had left him in the Bricklayers Arms.

'Edelmann?'

'Dead. Shot with the same gun that cost you half a kidney.'

Troy paused. He was not at all sure how Onions would react.

'Then we've got him,' he whispered.

'Got 'im! Got 'im! You're out of date, laddie. Do you know what day it is?'

'Thursday,' said Troy. 'It's Thursday the ... '

'Thursday the second day after D-Day to be precise. D-Day was Tuesday. Normandy's so full of scrap-iron looks like a totter's yard. They sent Wayne over to France on the first day. We can't touch him!'

'What?'

'The only chance we had was to get him within our jurisdiction. In France we have to convince the military – and they've got alibis like a bookful of meat coupons! He's gone, Freddie, gone for good!'

Troy lay back and closed his eyes.

Onions lowered his voice – a little of the pain went out of it. 'I'd suspend you – as a rule. But the quacks tell me you'll be out of commission for three months – mebbe more – so we'll let things be, let sleeping dogs lie, and sleep is what I suggest you get.'

He picked up his hated Homburg.

'I'll be in to see you at the weekend,' he said in something approaching a neutral tone, and then he too was gone.

Wildeve came over and sat on the side of the bed. Minutes passed with only the buzz of traffic in the street outside to break the silence.

'It's all right,' he said. 'They say you're going to be OK.'

'OK?' Troy said.

'You've lost part of a kidney, but really you can lose a whole kidney and still have all your gubbins work OK.'

'Gubbins,' said Troy without meaning.

Wildeve geared up for the inevitable.

'I don't quite know how to tell you this. I rather guessed Wayne would head for Stepney. It all seemed like unfinished business to me. Truth to tell I've been preparing for it for weeks. I kept in touch with Edelmann, ever since you first took me to that railway arch. I think he liked you really – it just didn't do for an old Bolshevik to let it be known.'

This was bewildering – the speed of it all. What was he talking about? How had Jack known to go to Stepney? Troy had not known himself until . . .

'How did you figure it out? Copper's intuition?'

'If you like.'

It was like hearing himself speak – his phrasing, his tonality, Wildeve's utterance.

'Although it would be nearer the mark to say that Wayne had asked too many questions of all those misguided heroes – I felt there was something else. I was wrong. Killing you could hardly be that something else – so something else still is – if you see what I mean.'

That, to Troy, sounded even more like Troy.

'On Saturday I didn't do what you told me to. I went into the Savoy and phoned Edelmann. Then I caught a cab straight to Stepney. If the traffic had been lighter I might even have got there before you. Edelmann had his rent-a-mob waiting. We'd agreed on that. He tried to keep Wayne as long as he could, but he couldn't hold him at all. As it was Wayne knocked me flying as he came out of the pub. I was out for a minute or so – Edelmann picked me up – that was a mistake, really we couldn't afford to lose that time. It cost us dearly. When you took off after him, we followed, but we were too far behind. I heard the other bloke take a pot-shot at you, but he came out of nowhere – took me completely by surprise. I saw you shoot him and I was running towards you when the bomb hit and . . . '

'Bomb? I got hit by a bomb?'

'No. Not hit. It landed a hundred yards off, but you were standing on the roof of that damn cellar – the shock wave shattered it. It looked for all the world as though the earth had opened up and swallowed you.'

The earth had swallowed him. He remembered the feeling – and the dream, that explained the dream. He had been in that damn cellar – it wasn't just a dream.

'Wayne picked up the gun and threw the dead bloke over his shoulder like a sack of potatoes. I couldn't believe it. I know Wayne's a big bugger but it was as though the other chap weighed nothing at all. Then he saw us and he started shooting.'

Wildeve plucked at the sleeve of his jacket – shoved a finger through the bullet-hole.

'You were lucky,' Troy said softly.

'Edelmann wasn't. The bullet that missed me killed him – poor sod. I caught Wayne with a half-brick and made him drop the gun, but he ran – even with the body on his shoulder he ran. I still can't believe it. Why didn't he just drop the body and have done?'

Troy thought about this. He thought he knew the answer.

'But you got the gun, you said?'

'Oh yes – and prints aplenty. If we could ever match them up to Wayne he'd hang.' He paused. 'Tell me, Freddie, did you really not know it was you he'd come to kill?'

'No. Did you?'

'No – I hadn't a clue. Instead . . . ' He shrugged.

'Instead he killed Edelmann,' said Troy.

Wildeve nodded, tears in the corners of his eyes.

'Where are my clothes, Jack?'

'What?'

Troy swung himself off the bed, felt a surge of pain to his gut, and flung open the bedside cupboard.

'Freddie, what are you playing at?'

His clothes lay in a neat pile in the cupboard – he reached for his trousers.

'We have work to do.'

'Freddie!'

'You heard him – I'm not suspended. I hold the King's Warrant. Do you have a car?'

'Yes – your old Morris is out front – but we can't . . .'

'Oh yes we can. Help me with the shirt.'

Wildeve stood dumbfounded.

'Jack! For God's sake!'

§ 77

They roared along the Embankment. Down to Chelsea. All the way to Tite Street.

'I tell you I've searched Tite Street. She's not there. The girl's not seen hide nor hair of Diana since Friday night. Accept it, Freddie, she's done a bunk. Poor bloody Gutteridge has been out there day and night!'

Troy was having difficulty breathing. He had moved too quickly, and the shock of finding a six-inch cut in his side and a row of more than a dozen stitches had dented his first rush of energy. He had somehow imagined himself intact – at the very least showing a minute hole where the bullet had entered.

'Not the house,' he whispered. 'The square.'

'Come again?'

'The square. Where the old boy had his pig.'

They shot past Constable Gutteridge, who had perfected the art of sleeping upright with his eyes open, and pulled up by the patchwork fences of the square. Getting out of the car winded Troy – Wildeve had to pull him from the seat. Troy led the way between the potatoes and the cauliflowers to the Nissen hut where Brack kept her tools. The pig was in her sty, poking her nose over the corrugated iron pen and snuffling pleasurably in the morning sunshine.

The door to the hut was padlocked. Wildeve kicked it in, flicked on his torch and stepped inside.

'Oh God,' he said. 'Oh God!'

Troy caught the torch as he dropped it. Wildeve began to buckle at the knees and staggered back into the daylight, retching violently into a neat, emerald-green row of new potatoes, bobbing gently in the breeze in defiance of pathetic fallacy.

Troy shone the torch again. He knew what he had seen, but unlike Wildeve he must look for ever and so must look again.

She was naked and weighted down in the tin bath by a broken piece of fireplace marble dumped across her midriff. Her eyes were open and a tiny black spot, just like the one he had imagined in his own side, marked the centre of her forehead. The tub was full, but still shallow enough for her nose and fingertips to break the surface and float like tendrils of weed on a stream. So curiously is the human mind constructed that Troy thought of Millais's Ophelia, floating with her bunch of posies, more beautiful in death than life.

Even with the water to suppress it the smell of death had come to fill the air. He had noticed it as soon as they entered the hut. He stepped outside and leaned against the steel wall of the hut. Wildeve had stopped puking, and seemed to be hunched over in silent tears.

'Why would he do such a thing?' he asked. 'Why . . . I mean . . . did he shoot her or did he drown her or did he what?'

'He didn't drown her. That's just an attempt to keep down the smell. And he didn't shoot her. I did.'

Wildeve looked up, wiped a strand of saliva from his lips on to his jacket sleeve. The big man was hurrying towards them down the path, the light glinting on his bald head, and the pig was grunting in anticipation.

''Ere! Just the chap I want. Would you adam'n'eve it some blighter's pinched me tin bath – y'know, the one I uses ter scrub the pig.'

'I've found it,' said Troy simply.

'Thank Gawd for that. In the 'ut, is it?'

Troy slumped forward, felt the blood drain from his head. The big man caught him, sweeping him up in his arms as a father would a small child.

' 'Ere, old cock, are you all right? You don't 'arf look pale.'

The big man carried him back to the old Bullnose Morris and laid him gently in the passenger seat.

'Guard the hut,' said Troy. 'And if I were you I wouldn't go inside.'

'Right you are, old cock. Just like old times. You will be back, won't you?'

'Yes,' Troy said feebly, 'I'll be back.'

Wildeve leaned his forehead on the steering-wheel – still breathing thick and fast.

'I don't understand it, Freddie. I just don't understand it.'

'Take me to Orange Street,' Troy said softly.

'I ought to take you back to hospital.'

'Orange Street,' said Troy.

Wildeve pressed the self-starter and slipped the car into first.

'Where is all this going to end?' he asked.

'Orange Street,' said Troy. 'It ends with Orange Street.'

§ 78

Troy made Wildeve wait in the car. At the first landing he thought his body would tear itself apart. He had never known such pain. He pressed on, knowing that if he took too long Jack would come looking for him, his palm firmly planted on his stitches, feeling the familiar sensation of warm tea spreading out across his shirt. On the top floor Tosca's door was locked. He fumbled in his jacket pocket for his key-ring and found the key she had given him. He opened the door slowly, letting it swing back on its hinges. He took one step inside and let the wall take his weight, leaning back breathless to look at the mess. The coffee-pot stood half full upon the table as though she had made for two, her unconscious not acknowledging that he had not returned. A half-eaten pizza graced the dining-table. *Huck Finn* lay face down upon the ironing board. Her stockings dried on a line above the sink, oddments of discarded clothing clung to chairbacks and scattered themselves higgledy-piggledy in her sluttish way – and there was blood everywhere. Blood on the sheets, blood on the walls, blood on the floor. Crisp and dry and brown. A slaughterhouse in the attic. Blood, so much blood he could taste it – it was on his tongue and on his lips – but it was his blood he could taste, his blood not hers, his blood and the blood which trickled between his fingers, coursed down his leg and puddled at his feet merely added to the gore.

§ 79

Troy slept. An age rolled over.

Into his sleep, into his waking came ... a stream of visitors.

His mother – arthritic, between two walking sticks and two daughters, making her first visit to town since the death of her husband. She would speak no English to him – but Russian has a thousand different words for fool.

Brother Rod – chest beribboned – the returning hero – head of the family – came to tell him everything was OK, and that the room was paid for and he need want for nothing. Troy should care? Of course he cared. There was nothing in the world he wanted more than to be alone.

Bonham – clutching his helmet between his knees as he peeled an orange of immense rarity into it. The vapour filled the air. They both inhaled in silence, a blast of the past. Bonham stuck his head in his helmet, nose to the peel, refusing to eat one single segment of what he had brought for Troy, and breathed deeply and pronounced it 'Christmas'.

One day he awoke from a midday nap to find Kolankiewicz, and Anna and a child. Anna stood with her back to him, looking out of the window, watching the play of June's searing light upon the buildings opposite. Kolankiewicz was playing cards. Troy realised the boy was Shrimp Robertson. He was teach ing Kolankiewicz three-card monty. Kolankiewicz professed never to have heard of it. Troy watched as Kolankiewicz was allowed to win twice, and enjoyed the child's surprise as Kolankiewicz said it was his turn now and watched him fleece the boy for more than half a crown. Anna turned, saw that he was awake.

'Hello, stranger,' she said.

Kolankiewicz and the boy looked up from their game.

'Mr Robertson has something he'd like to say to you, Troy. Haven't you, Mr Robertson?'

She looked directly at the boy as she finished her sentence. He looked awkward but did not blush. He approached the side of the bed and addressed Troy.

'We thought you was a tosser,' he said very matter-of-factly.

'Yeeees,' said Troy, not knowing where the conversation was leading.

'Only then my dad read in the paper as 'ow you were on to some bloke as killed that feller we found in bits. Only it wasn't some feller at all, it was some posh bird you found in an 'ut down Chelsea way. It was the posh bird wasn't it who killed that feller?'

'Yes,' said Troy. 'It was the posh bird.'

'And probably killed the shadowman as well.'

'Who?'

'Shadowman. That's what we called Wolinski. Well – it's what my dad calls him. 'E's the local barber see, down the Mile End Road. No matter what time o' day 'e come in, Dad says, 'e's got five-o'clock shadow.'

'I see,' said Troy.

'And then we realised you wasn't a tosser, you was an 'ero.'

'When did you decide this?'

'Well – you got shot, didn't you?'

'Does that make me a hero?'

'Not 'arf! Anyway we 'ad a whip-round for yer and we got 'arf a dollar. 'Cept I just lost it to this gent 'ere.'

How, Troy wondered, would the child feel about his heroism if he knew that he had taken the beating of a lifetime on his own doorstep – from a woman he so euphemistically called 'the posh bird'?

'Would it,' Troy began, 'appease your injured vanity to know that you'd been taken by a master? I know of no one in the Met or the forces of the entire Home Counties who would sit down for so much as a game of snap with this gent 'ere.'

The boy looked bewildered by this.

'Allow me,' said Kolankiewicz, and handed Troy half a crown in pennies and ha'pennies, sending them cascading across the bedspread.

The nurse came in and told them Troy must rest. Anna kissed him and ran her fingers through his hair, and told him she had always known he was a fool. And Troy could only guess at how much she knew.

By the door, with the nurse holding it open as a hint, the boy paused. Something on his mind.

' 'Ere. It was the posh bird shot you too, wasn't it?'

'Yes,' said Troy.

Troy slept. An age rolled over.

The nurse brought in a card. Someone asking to see him. Troy picked it up. The front read 'Frederick, Marquess of Fermanagh' and gave his Irish address. On the back it read, 'I must see you, please.'

'Tell him "No",' said Troy.

After all that they had the same name. But he could not remember that she had ever used his.

§ 80

A week or so after his return to the hospital a spluttering car, pinking badly, seemed to cruise across the skies. So vivid was the noise he could see it in his mind's eye – a clapped-out old banger, worse, far worse than his old Morris, out in the street pouring forth a plume of black exhaust. But it wasn't out there in the street – it was up there in the sky. Then it cut out and he heard a swishing like a falling bough tossed down in a storm, then a bang like the gates of hell slamming shut and every window in his room turned to crystal fragments, showering his bed with their sparkling shards. He was not cut, merely dusted. The nurse bustled in. Said 'Deary, deary me', kicked the brake free on the base of the bed and steered him out into the corridor.

He had heard it, he had heard it! The whole point, Nikolai had said, was that one would never hear it coming!

'If you can hear it you're dead!'

December 1948

§ 81

It had not been a good war. He had hated it. Once it was over, he missed it badly.

He returned to work in the October. Onions's wrath had turned to silence. It was understood that his promotion could go to hell. Wildeve made Sergeant. It was his due. He had coped marvellously in Troy's absence and had emerged from the mess of the 'Tart in the Tub Affair', as the Yard so cruelly dubbed it, with not a stain on his record. To the best of Troy's knowledge Jack never told anyone about Troy's relationship with Diana Brack, and when Troy had reported the murder of M/Sgt Larissa Tosca, US Army, and had described her as an 'informant', Jack had asked no questions and made no guesses. For a while he and Troy shared a rank as well as an office – then in the summer of 1945, two days after VJ day, three days before his thirtieth birthday Troy's promotion came through. He had made Inspector. Onions had relented.

All the same – the thought of resignation passed through Troy's mind every working week. Even a boom in post-war crime had not reconciled him to his profession. He hated the peace even more than he hated the war.

Brother Rod did not share this view – he had ended the war a hero, festooned with medals, and had got out of it at the earliest opportunity. He had announced his intention to stand for Parliament as soon as Churchill had dissolved the coalition. That summer he stood for South Herts and when the long, slow count had been completed found, to everyone's surprise but his own, that he had won the seat for Labour. By 1948 he sat on the front bench as Wing Commander Sir Rodyon Troy, Bt., RAF (Reserve), MP, DSO and bar, DFC, number two at the Air Ministry. Rod loved the peace. Peace, like war, had been very good to him. Few things, if any, upset him.

'Why is Tom Driberg asking me for your home number?' he asked, clearly upset.

'I don't know,' said Troy. 'If you give it to him we'll find out.'

Troy heard a muffled few words as Rod spoke to his secretary with one hand across the mouthpiece.

'Freddie – I don't know what you're up to, but one doesn't want to get too close to Driberg – he has a certain reputation. It's bad enough him buttonholing me at tea-time!'

'I'm not mixed up in anything that need worry you. If Whitehall 1212 is somehow not good enough for him, then by all means give him my home number.'

'I didn't even know you knew him.'

'He used to come to the old man's natter and nosh – as you used to put it – don't you remember?'

'No – I don't. I could hardly forget him though, could I? Wonder where I was?'

He rang off. Troy wondered. He had not seen hide nor hair of Driberg since that day in '44 when he had been out to the coast to see Inspector Malnick. To judge from his journalism Driberg spent a lot of his time abroad. He knew from listening to Rod how well this went down with the Whips' Office.

At home in Goodwins Court – Troy sat at the piano. He had just discovered Thelonious Monk and was pootling through music that struck him as curiously attractive whilst totally alien. What, he asked, had Debussy bitten off when he first used ragtime in *Children's Corner*? Then the phone rang. It was Driberg.

'I need a word. Could you come over to my flat?'

'You can't come here?'

'Not really. It's private. It wouldn't do to be seen visiting the home of a policeman.'

'But it will do for a policeman to be seen visiting your home?'

Driberg declined the bait and gave Troy an address in Knightsbridge. Troy said he'd be there in an hour. He hoped Driberg hadn't had a run in with the police again. If he had, there was bugger all he could do about it.

It was a cold December. Days and nights of unrelenting, bitter frost – made worse by a paucity of rations. Even bread, that grey mush, was rationed now. He drove to Knightsbridge wishing he had a car with a heater, wrapped in two overcoats and a balaclava helmet. A welcoming blast of heat greeted him as Driberg prised open the door and ushered him in. He had lost more hair at the temple, but what there was still rose up in ridges like corrugated cardboard, still gave him the look of a startled dog.

'Very good of you, Troy,' he said. 'Very good indeed.'

Driberg peeled back the layers of coats and Troy felt two stones lighter.

'If this is private, I can take it it's got nothing to do with my being a policeman?' Troy ventured.

Driberg opened the door from the lobby to the sitting room.

'Did I say private? I meant delicate.'

Troy knew that.

A man sat with his back to him in a high armchair. All Troy could see was the top of his head. At the sound of their entry he did not get up, but hunched lower and leant forward. Driberg led off, striking out for the drinks and offering Troy a large Scotch. Troy walked slowly round to the fireplace to face the other guest. Curious how one can tell so much from the top of a thinning pate.

'Neville?' he said cautiously, a little incredulously.

Pym glanced up from his glass, still clutching it two-handed. He was pale and looked as though he hadn't slept in days. Time had not been kind to him since their last meeting at MI5 more than four years ago.

'Hullo, Troy. Good of you to come so soon.'

Driberg appeared next to him, warming his backside at the roaring fire, shoving a large Scotch into Troy's hand.

'You couldn't call me yourself?' Troy asked.

'I wasn't sure you'd take the call,' said Pym. 'We didn't exactly meet under auspicious circumstances the last time, did we?'

'I have the distinct impression this meeting will be no different.'

'It's a delicate matter,' Driberg chipped in.

'Isn't it always?'

'Won't you sit down, Troy? I think it best for Pym to tell you in his own words.'

Troy perched on the leather-topped club fender and sipped at the whisky, and decided to let Pym get on with it. Whatever it was it would not be private and he was almost certainly there in his professional capacity.

Pym sat back. It took him a while to gather himself. Driberg stared off into infinity. Troy sampled a first-rate single malt.

'I spent last night in jail,' Pym blurted out suddenly.

Troy nodded sagely and looked into his glass, trying to break eye contact.

'I was arrested in the Holloway Road and taken to the police station ... also in the Holloway Road and I ... er ... I ...'

'Neville,' Troy cut in sharply. 'Please, just spit it out.'

'Oh God,' Pym groaned. He gulped at his whisky and began again, and the pained formality gave way at once to something more desperate.

'I was in a lavatory in the Holloway Road. I suppose it was about half an hour after closing time. That's usually the best time. The drunks have had their piss and rolled off home – you know damn well that anyone still hanging around a gents' lavatory is after the same thing you are. There's some very tasty rough trade in that particular bog – a fair bit of young stuff too – I go there quite often. Catch the Piccadilly up from the West End – cab back if I meet anyone I feel I could trust to take home. Last night was a good night – there were half a dozen of us – no one I really knew – we wanked each other off – a group job – you had your work cut out knowing what belonged to whom. Then it happened. This uniformed copper, big as a house, bursts in – "Right you are, you filthy bastards" – and they all ran for it.'

Pym stopped. He was trembling and his voice was going fast.

'Why didn't you run?' Troy asked.

'I couldn't. Nor could the boy I was with.'

He stopped again, drained off the last of his Scotch. Driberg took the glass from him at once and returned with it almost full.

'I was ... I was on my knees giving the boy a gobble.'

'Boy?'

'I say boy – he looked sixteen. At least.'

'So you got nicked?'

'Yes,' Pym croaked.

'A constable?'

'Sergeant – does it matter?'

'A constable would make life easier. How old was he?'

'About forty I suppose.'

Troy didn't fancy his chances of trying to talk sense to a career copper who was still in uniform at forty, had enough rank to know what was what, and would, beyond a shadow of a doubt, not take kindly to the intercession of a Detective Inspector ten years younger than he was.

'He took us both to the local nick. I've no idea what became of the boy. They pulled me out at six o'clock this morning and charged me with gross indecency. I lied about my name – so they turned out my pockets and found my driving licence and a couple of letters. I told them I was a journalist. They didn't question that.'

'What do you do these days, Neville?' Troy asked.

'Good God, Troy, haven't you grasped the point of all this? I'm still with MI5!'

There was a sudden silence in which Troy could hear the clock tick and the hoarse rasp of Pym's breathing.

'You begin to see why I sent for you?' said Driberg. 'Neville came to me. I called you. I felt you might be ... *simpatico.*'

'Oh I see only too clearly – but what the hell do you think I can do about it?'

'I'd be grateful for anything,' Driberg said in a friendly tone.

'I can't have this come out,' said Pym. 'I'm finished if it gets out. I'd lose my clearance – they'd say I was wide open to blackmail – even if I beat the charge and walk out of court with an apology from the police I'd lose clearance and they'd have me out in a jiffy.'

'Five could get this dropped just like that, far more easily than I could,' said Troy. 'Is there no one you can trust?'

'That's not the point, Troy. Who I might trust is irrelevant – there's no one would trust a queer!'

'What I was thinking,' Driberg said gently, 'is that if you could take the matter up – get Pym off with a caution perhaps – it might never emerge that he wasn't a journalist – it need never reach the papers.'

Troy looked from one to the other. For the life of him he couldn't think why they had picked him – apart from the fact that they both knew him — why they should think he would be in any way, as Driberg put it, *simpatico*. It remained, nevertheless, that he was.

He took out his little black notebook and turned to a blank page.

'What was this Sergeant's name?'

§ 82

'I'm telling you,' he said with grotesque emphasis, 'he had the lad's cock in his mouth and he was sucking it!'

'I don't doubt it,' said Troy.

'I saw him with my own eyes! I pulled the bugger off with my own hands!'

'Is the boy known to you?'

'No — we've nothing on him.'

'Did you keep him overnight?'

'No, I took him out the back, and I thrashed the shit out of him.'

Troy wondered what deal they had been able to reach with the boy. Let off in return for a statement against Pym?

'How old was he?'

'Sixteen. If he'd been any younger I'd've taken your mate out and thrashed the shit out of him too.'

Pym had been lucky — lucky not to get a beating — although if he had it would have given Troy a better position from which to negotiate — lucky to have picked on a boy the right age, though he doubted that had mattered to Pym at the time.

'He's not my mate.'

'Isn't he? You're a poof's runner for queer bastards you don't even know?'

If Troy had had any illusions that rank would matter to this man, they vanished. He could not be reasoned with, cajoled, and Troy doubted very much whether he could be bullied.

'I know why you're 'ere,' he went on. 'I can hear it in your voice. You've got the same accent. He's one of your own, isn't he? What is he, an old mate from schooldays? Eton was it?'

'Harrow,' said Troy pointlessly.

'And that puts you above the law, does it? A poncey education and you think there's one law for the rich and one law for the rest of us? Is that it? Well sod it, Mr Troy, that's not the way it's going to be. I know you, Mr Troy – I shouldn't think there's a copper in the Met that doesn't know you – you're known as one of the best – time was everyone was talking about you – towards the end of the war you were the stuff of legend – there were more stories in circulation about you and the Tart in the Tub case than there were about Dr Crippen and the Edinburgh body-snatchers put together. You're known, Mr Troy – you're a character – but this is beneath you, and I'll tell you to your face, you should have better things to do with your time than running errands for queers. He's going down, Mr Troy, and that's all there is to it.'

§ 83

'Neville, it's Troy. Not good news I'm afraid. The man won't budge. If he were a constable I could consider going over his head, but no local Inspector is going to risk overruling one of his sergeants – the rift it would create in the nick would be ruinous.'

'I see,' Pym said in a breathy, exhausted way. 'So it's I who shall be ruined?'

'We could try for the best brief.'

'The best briefs are not likely to want to touch a case of this nature, are they? I thank you, Troy,' an arch huffiness crept into his voice, 'but I don't think there's much else *we* can do.'

Pym rang off and Troy was left holding a dead line. The 'we' had been emphatic, cutting even. Troy did not think that he had deserved it.

Days passed. Troy thought about the matter, but found it made him angry – and he pushed it to the back of his mind. Less than a week before Christmas Pym called him on his home number.

'I don't suppose you could come over to Albany?' he said.

'No, Neville, I don't think I could.'

'Please, Troy. It's important.' He paused. 'Shall we say nine o'clock? It's the last thing I shall ever ask of you.'

Troy should have heard the warning.

The door was off the latch. Pym was in the fireplace with his brains all over the wall. He had put the barrel of his service revolver to the roof of his mouth and pulled the trigger. A blood-spattered envelope with Troy's name on it stood propped against the clock on the mantelpiece. Troy flicked a piece of grey matter off one of the circus-red chairs with the edge of the envelope and sat down to read the letter. It was dated 19 December 1948 and Pym had inserted the time, for good measure, as 8.35 p.m.

Dear Troy,

I take the easy way out – I trust you will not think it the coward's way. I have posted letters to Driberg and to my father. If you could see that news of my death does not reach them before my letters do, I would be grateful.

There is a little I can do for you in return – Wayne's real name is John Baumgarner. He's a Colonel in the Central Intelligence Agency – which is what they call the OSS now. They were jolly pissed off with him for letting that mad bitch walk around with a licence to kill, but really he was too important for them to let you have him. He's under strict orders never to set foot in Britain again. At the moment he's running the airlift in Berlin.

Yours,
Pym.

§ 84

'I need you to get me on a flight to Berlin.'

'What?'

'Rod – I have to go to Berlin.'

'Are you mad? Stalin's got the city sewn up like a camel's arse!'

'Why do you think I'm phoning you?'

'Freddie – we're airlifting every damn thing except tap water or they'd starve. Dammit, man, we're even flying in coal!'

'That's why you have to do this for me. I can't get a civil flight. You have to get me on an RAF flight.'

'Official, is it?' Rod asked.

'Would I be asking if it weren't?' said Troy.

'OK. OK. Leave it with me. I make no promises but I'll see what I can do.'

Troy put the telephone back in its cradle. Wildeve was staring at him. Tapping his teeth with a pencil and staring.

'I've been thinking.'

'I can see that.'

'What jurisdiction do you think we have in Germany?'

'I've a warrant. Signed by a British JP. Part of Germany's British. Part of Berlin's still British.'

'Yes – but that's subject to military law. Not civil. Besides, what are your chances of catching Wayne in the British sector?'

'Bugger all I should think,' snapped Troy.

'Quite,' said Wildeve. 'In fact, while you've been busy with the coroner and chasing flights I had the whole thing legalled. Freddie, you can't lay a finger on Wayne—'

'Baumgarner!'

'Baumgarner,' Wildeve went on. 'At least not while he's in Germany.'

'I have to try, Jack. Can't you see that?'

'Indeed I can. I think you've been very lucky in ever picking up the scent again. Luckier still that Onions has decided to spend Christmas in Warrington, sampling the delights of black pudding and hot-pot.'

'If I fail, he need never know. If I pull it off, then nothing succeeds like success.'

'Quite,' Wildeve said again. 'I just think we need a little help as well as a lot of luck.'

'Such as?'

'I've a chum who's just been assigned to liaise with Interpol. Let me see if I can come up with a name. What we need is someone on the Berlin Force. Someone with just that spark of imagination on which you and I have come to pride ourselves but which we know all too well is sadly lacking in your average man about the beat.'

Wildeve grinned hugely. 'Leave it with me.'

§ 85

Rod came through for Troy. Found him a place on an RAF Douglas Dakota out of Brize Norton, bound for Gatow Airfield in Berlin, via Hannover, late in the afternoon of 22 December.

Rod walked Troy out to the aeroplane, across the black tarmac. Lit only by the lights buried in the runways and swept by a bitterly cold wind, night on an airfield gave Troy the sense of Christmas as though the hundreds of lights were candles that miraculously refused to flicker with the wind. He felt fat and heavy wrapped in an RAF sheepskin flying jacket, on top of his own overcoat and jacket – a bizarre black Santa Claus waddling out to the waiting sleigh. The Dakota's twin propeller engines were already turning over as Rod helped him into the vast cargo bay and sat him on one of the hard wooden benches that lined the fuselage. It was barely possible to hear him speak, but he seemed hell bent on trying.

'It'll be bloody cold once you get airborne.'

'It *is* bloody cold! And we're still on the ground!'

'Don't be an ass, Freddie, I mean cold like you've never imagined. I found the important thing was to keep the hands and the ears well covered. The pilot will ask you to put the helmet on just before take-off. It lets him talk to you, and it adds another layer.'

'Why would he want to talk to me?'

'It's not a passenger flight, Freddie. He talks to his crew. Technically that includes you. All I'm saying is do as you're told. By the way,' Rod shouted, 'this came for you. Phoned through to the CO's office about ten minutes ago!' He stuffed a small brown envelope into Troy's hand. Troy tore it open. It read, 'Dieter Franck. Inspector at the Uhlandstrasse Police Station. Brit. Sector.

Speaks good English. Honest as the day is wotnot. Expecting you this p.m. Best. Jack.'

A flight sergeant stuck his head in the door and saluted.

'There'll be a slight delay, sir. Another six or seven minutes.'

'Thank you,' Rod said. 'You know, Freddie, it's still second nature to expect to be saluted. I don't suppose the habits of wartime will let go easily.'

'I know. You told me. You had a good war. History was good to you,' said Troy flatly.

'And you didn't.'

'Doesn't much matter one way or the other in my business, does it?'

Rod weighed this up. The engines lowered their revs. Troy could hear himself think for the first time.

'I used to think,' Rod resumed, 'that you'd had a lousy one.'

Troy said nothing. To shrug was pointless, it would be a gesture lost beneath the multiple layers that swathed him. He tried very hard to assume an expression of utter unresponsive blankness.

'Just after the action – around 1945, suppose, I thought you were going completely potty. But I started to think about it and for the first time I looked at the way things had gone for me, and yes you're right, I do think I had a good war . . .'

'Imprisoned by the British, shot down by the Krauts and bunged a couple of gongs as a consolation prize!'

'Not at all. I felt no bitterness about being interned. As for being shot down. I spent a couple of hours in the drink off Sheerness and got picked up. Not a mark on me. On the whole I got off lightly. The war was, as you put it, good to me. I rather think I enjoyed it. But you didn't did you? You got shot –'

'Twice.'

'Stabbed.'

'Four times.'

'Bombed.'

'Twice again.'

'Beaten up.'

'More times than I can count. Look, Rod, what's the point you're trying to make? You're not telling me all this tosh just to let me know I missed a trick by not volunteering.'

'I really thought you'd had an awful time . . . '

'Of course war's an utter fucking picnic! Millions get slaughtered for the benefit of the nostalgia of the survivors . . . '

'Not what I meant at all. I thought you'd been battered every which way for a while. Then, looking back, I remembered my first command. My first squadron in forty-one. The chaps I had under me then used to astound me. The way they ran to those crates, the sheer eagerness to get in there, into the thick of it. I wondered if I'd ever been like that. I knew I hadn't. I realised what they had that I hadn't. What they were that I wasn't. They had the killer instinct. And I knew that because I'd seen it in you. I'd seen it in you even when we were kids. You hated me for years after I pushed you off your bike, and for a dozen other things that should have been inconsequential. Nothing petty or spiteful or momentary, but unremitting hatred. That unforgiving, relentless pursuit.'

'That's the business I'm in. Some call it justice.'

'Just as well. I'd hate to think you were on your way to Berlin just to settle an old score.'

'Rod, I'm a policeman. The sweetest, the most beautiful words in the English language are "I arrest you in the name of the law", I don't have to kill him. I don't have to kill anybody. The law is the law and that should be enough.'

Rod patted him on the side. On the coat pocket. Right where Troy had his revolver.

'No harm in asking though, was there?'

The Dakota picked up revs again. The sound of the propellers swamped them. There was no space in which to say any more. Rod smiled and climbed down the steel ladder to the runway. Troy wrapped his hand around the gun and asked himself why God had so ordered the world as to make elder brothers into know-alls.

§ 86

A stout, miserable corporal, buried beneath an army greatcoat, met Troy at Gatow field.

'I've gorra a jeep and the CO sez I'm to take you anywhere you want to go,' he said in best Birmingham misery.

'Thank you, er...' Troy looked at the stripes on his arm. 'Corporal ... er.'

'It's Clark, sir. Lance-Bombardier Clark actually, sir. Artillery.'

'Known as Nobby?' Troy ventured.

'Swifty,' the man replied. 'On account of me being five foot six an' fifteen stone. I'm a translator. Anything you need to say – just put it through me. I'm fluent in German.'

Troy found this hard to believe. The man scarcely seemed fluent in English.

'Do you know the Uhlandstrasse Police Station?' Troy asked.

'Indeed I do, sir.'

'I'm meeting an Inspector Franck.'

'I know. He phoned to say he's gone home.'

Troy sighed.

'You are two hours overdue, sir. He said he'd see you around noon tomorrow.'

Troy sighed again. Half a day lost already.

'I'd better find somewhere to stay,' he said.

'All taken care of, sir. You'll be at the Officers' Club on the Kurfürstendamm.'

§ 87

By noon Troy and Clark were waiting for Inspector Franck in his office. It was hardly warmer inside than out. Troy put a hand to the radiator – it was stone-cold. Clark flipped the lid on an old iron stove.

'There's a spark of life here, sir. I imagine the main boiler's out of fuel. This looks a bit like a make-do-and-mend job to me.'

'Are we going to hear that phrase the rest of our lives?'

'Now if we had a bit of wood...'

Troy looked out of the window. A ragged army of navvies was clearing up what was left of the building across the street. A large man in a fawn mackintosh was gathering an armful of wood – he scurried back across the rubble and out of sight. A uniformed constable brought in two cups of coffee. He said something to Troy. Troy looked at Clark.

'He says this will warm you up, sir.'

Troy sipped at the coffee – hot it was, but it tasted as though it had been used and reused for days, squeezing the last drop of life from the bean. He pulled a face.

'I know,' said Clark. 'Welcome to Berlin.'

The door burst open and the large man Troy had seen in the ruins across the street came in clutching his booty. He rushed to the stove, flipped open the lid with his elbow and shoved in as much as the belly of the stove would take.

'It's a slow process,' he said, 'but bit by bit we are feeding most of Old Berlin into our pot-bellied stoves. That's the third building in this street we have stripped back to nothing since the blockade began.'

He dusted down his coat with the palms of his hands.

'Franck,' he said extending a hand and smiling broadly. 'Dieter Franck. Please call me Dieter.'

Troy introduced himself, side-stepping his Christian name, and introduced Clark as his driver.

Inspector Franck stretched out his hands and warmed himself as the stove began to roar. He was, Troy guessed, about the same age as himself, though wearing less well. He was thickening at the waist, and thinning at the hairline, but his smile lit up his wide, chubby face with a disarming impression of honesty. Rare in a copper, he thought.

'To business. Your colleague, Sergeant—'

'Wildeve,' Troy prompted.

'Yes, yes. Sergeant Wildeve called me yesterday morning. I believe you are in pursuit of Colonel Baumgarner?'

'I have a warrant for his arrest.'

'Ah . . . how I envy you!'

Inspector Franck surrendered the stove to Clark, opened a filing cabinet next to his desk and took out a fat file bound with string. He slipped off the string and let the file fall to the desk-top with a demonstrative thud. A couple of black and white photographs spilled out. Baumgarner was fatter than Wayne, and was drifting into double chins and a puffiness around the eyes. Troy supposed he must be about forty now – but there was no doubt that it was the same man.

'Baumgarner arrived here just under two years ago – in January last year. I started to hear rumours concerning him by about June – gossip on the underworld grapevine – and then I began to see evidence that went some way towards confirming what I was hearing. The Colonel is a man who has to have a sideline, whatever he does – in Berlin it's weapons and it's drugs.'

'Drugs!?!'

'Morphine. Stolen or – since Baumgarner is in the position he is – diverted from legitimate shipments into the underworld, sold on the black market at extortionate prices. I found that alarming – but that was nothing to what I heard next. Germany, as you would expect, was awash with weapons at the end of the war. Every thug who wants a gun can own one, but most prized of all are American weapons – souvenirs of victory, much more precious than a German gun. The teenage thug who can wave a Colt or Smith and Wesson in the face of an enemy cuts more ice than he would with an old Luger. Wayne caters to this market. He supplies an already well-tooled illegal little army with even better weapons. He is in effect funding an underground war.'

'What evidence did you find?'

'Young toughs picked up with the weapons. More talk of a mysterious supplier. And since last autumn half a dozen gang killings all of which point back to the trade in guns and drugs. Nothing that actually fingers Baumgarner, but plenty that adds weight to rumour. Informers say the source is a foreigner. Some speak of an American specifically. One or two even name him, but no one who's seen him first hand commit any crime. Most think he's German, but then his German is as good as mine. It's Baumgarner, I know it. I've spent a lot of time on the Colonel. I have built up a profile. I think I understand him very well – not, of course, that I've ever met him.'

Troy sat back to listen – the notion that Baumgarner could be 'profiled' was fascinating – it was the new vocabulary of police work – he half expected it to be gobbledegook.

'Imagine a type of man, a man driven by God knows what – his hormones, his chemistry, whatever – driven to satisfy certain needs only in action. A man who needs must live on the cutting edge of life – life without danger is nothing. In wartime all countries need men like this – they search them out and they use them. The British, after all, turned them out in their hundreds, men and women alike, parachuted them into occupied France to take their chances against an utterly ruthless enemy. But the mask of legitimacy is distorting. The edge is less the edge if it is in some way sanctioned. If you are Colonel Baumgarner then the OSS and the CIA are your natural fields – nevertheless their sanction channels these drives to its own ends, so they find another way out. Men like Baumgarner need their sidelines – and it's quite essential they should be illegal. For a while I think penetrating the Berlin underworld, turning it into his private market-place satisfied his drives – but it's tame stuff after a war like he had. It demands the ultimate transgression – sooner or later only murder will do. So, comes the time some teenage thug double-crosses the good Colonel or tries to threaten him and he becomes the first victim, and the victims tumble like a row of dominoes, and bodies start to turn up all over the city.'

Dieter paused. 'You're saying nothing, Inspector Troy. Does this not sound like the man you knew? I admit I've had less than two years to study him, compared to your—'

'I had just under fourteen weeks. I had no notion of a profile of Baumgarner until you began to speak. I met him face to face only three times. The first time he asked me for a light, the second he said nothing, and on the third he tried to kill me.'

Dieter laughed ironically. For a few seconds Troy was left to wonder what the joke might be.

'Well, bang goes that theory. That'll teach me to get philosophical. I was about to hypothesise that the key to Baumgarner is that he doesn't kill in person. That it would be too easy for him. The gossip has it that he has a henchman, a tame thug, some young psychopath who pulls the trigger for him. I had deduced that the pleasure in killing for Baumgarner is in the control, the manipulation of another human being. A human gun he can point and say "Kill". I've been relying too much on gossip, perhaps it's meaningless.'

Troy was hesitant. He had accounted to the Yard the exact details of the attempt on his life, but thereafter had thought of it in a mental shorthand. In saying Baumgarner had tried to kill him, he was eliding the truth, and eliding memory, but it accorded with the way he thought of it. Baumgarner had tried to kill him. The mechanical, toneless way he had said simply 'Finish him' was audible still.

'No, no. You're absolutely right. In London in '44 he had four men killed in just the way you describe. I was to have been the fifth, but he didn't pull the trigger in person.'

'A henchman? A psychopath?'

'A . . . a . . . woman,' Troy said, and knew he could explore this subject no further without lying.

'Odd,' Dieter said. 'But the pattern stands, does it not?'

'It does indeed,' said Troy. 'I suppose you'd like him off your patch?'

'Of course – but first I need watertight evidence.'

'I've got that.'

Dieter raised an eyebrow.

'I've a gun with his fingerprints on it. A forensics report that matches the gun to bullets recovered from the murders he had committed and half a dozen witnesses to him shooting a man in London.'

'Personally?'

'Back against the wall. He was cornered. It doesn't blow your theory that a cornered man, however manipulative, will kill without proxy?'

'No. Not at all. It . . . delights me in a curious way to know that he can slip up and to know that we stand a chance of getting him.'

'I have to get him back to England.'

'I know. That's what I told your Sergeant. If your warrant ran here I'd gladly drag the bastard off the streets and hand him over to you in handcuffs but . . . ' Dieter did not finish. He got up and stretched.

'Tell me, would you like to see our quarry?'

'Of course. Do you know where he is?'

Dieter shook the fat file and spread out dozens of pages on the desk.

'You don't speak German, do you?'

Troy shook his head. 'Schoolboy, and getting worse every year.'

'This one is in English.'

He pushed a dozen photographed documents across the desk to Troy.

'It's his diary. How on earth did you get this?'

'There are no secrets in Berlin. At least not any you can keep for very long. I had his office ... mmm ... "burgled". Quite discreetly. I have his diary for the whole of December. Alas, if he records meetings with the thugs they're in some sort of code, but his work is there in plain English, and today at noon he is distributing Christmas presents to children at the Fredericksplein in the French sector. All part of the limitless goodwill of our new-found Uncle Sam.'

'Beware this Uncle,' Troy said. 'He's like The Man Who Came to Dinner. He never leaves.'

Dieter leaned over and stabbed at 23 December with his index finger.

'We can be there in twenty minutes in your jeep.'

§ 88

One bombsite looked much the same as another to Troy. The RAF had left scarce one brick standing upon another, and if they had, Troy fantasised, then it required only a single Russian soldier to come along and boot the last brick off the next to last to have done with Berlin. To Dieter they were familiar landmarks. Troy sat in the back of the jeep with the canvas flapping wildly about him, while Dieter leaned in close to Clark and shouted instructions in German. All the same, when they jerked to a halt it was in the middle of what seemed to be yet another nowhere.

Dieter turned to Troy. 'We'll attract less attention if we walk the last few blocks. If Herr Clark would not mind waiting here?'

Clark flipped back his greatcoat and pulled a dog-eared volume of *Penguin New Writing* from the map pocket on the left thigh of his army trousers.

'Don't worry about me,' he said, 'I'll be fine.'

A few minutes later they approached the back of a sizeable crowd, gathered in what had once been a square, if not of some elegance – that seemed unPrussian – then of some grandeur.

The focal point of the hubbub, the adult murmur pierced by the shrieks of delighted children, appeared to be an army truck.

From the back of the truck a hatless figure in a grey gabardine mackintosh was holding court on the fringe of vision. Troy elbowed his way a little closer, Dieter followed behind muttering apologies in German. He caught Troy by the sleeve.

'Be careful, Troy. You don't want to annoy these people. If there's trouble, waving a warrant card will get neither of us out of it. It's their occasion – they'll let nothing get between them and the contents of that truck. They're people who've had nothing for their children since the thirties. Do not tread on toes, figuratively or literally.'

'Sorry, I have to see him,' Troy said. 'That is Baumgarner, isn't it?'

'Indeed it is. And if I tried to arrest him now they'd tear us apart.'

Troy looked towards the truck again. It was Baumgarner – doling out chocolate and fruit and gaudily wrapped presents to a host of squealing children and adoring adults. He played the audience like the ringmaster in a circus, or a pantomime dame, working their sense of anticipation and teasing out the rewards in rapid German that meant nothing to Troy, but if it amounted to no more than huckster's patter he would not have been surprised. Baumgarner was fatter – the photographs now supplemented by his appearance in the flesh. He was thickening rapidly about the middle. The lean, vulpine shape was distorting, maturing into something else, something coarser, more bestial still. But the look was the same. His eyes rolled across the audience, at one point looking directly at Troy with not a hint of recognition, limpid blue and careless, as though the world at large meant little to him, as though his words and his thoughts made no connection – and as the fat huckster played his mob, the wolf's mind lurked behind those smiling eyes, lean and hungry, and regarded them as just so many sheep. Troy glanced to either side of him. These Germans were thin and threadbare – the grubby, frayed overcoats had seen too many winters – the grey, hollow cheeks, the prominent, staring eyes had lived too long in the iron fist. Troy found an unbidden comparison fighting to the surface of consciousness – they put him in mind of those photographs from the final weeks of the war, when Belsen was taken, its gates opened and the first British soldiers across the line encountered the living dead. Once acknowledged it seemed absurd – these Germans were alive and reasonably well, their deprivations were slight, their bellies grumbling rather than permanently empty, and if they were wasn't this what they deserved?

Their eyes lit up, laughter and cheers rose in their throats at what Troy took to be jokes on Baumgarner's part – bellowed out so they could be heard to the limits of the crowd. Each time he threw an item from the back of the truck, there was a surge in the crowd as they jostled for possession. A Hershey bar spun out towards Troy and landed two rows ahead of him – a dozen or more children descended on it like piranhas. Troy had seen nothing like it in England in the entire course of the war.

'I've seen enough,' said Troy.

Dieter led the way back to the edge of the crowd.

'He's got these idiots eating out of the palm of his hand,' said Troy.

'What you must understand, Troy, is that this man is a hero.'

'What?'

'He is a hero to those people because they are so desperately in need of heroes.'

They stopped in front of a five-foot-high pile of blitzed red brick.

'In 1945 we were a defeated nation – a people indoctrinated with the belief that we could not lose, but we had lost. It was essential – psychologically essential – to identify in some way with victory. I had not long been back in the city myself when Churchill chose to pay a visit. I heard this story from half a dozen people who saw it. He was being driven through the ruins, a landscape just like this one, when the car and his escort found themselves virtually surrounded by Germans – the Berliners came as close to the car as they could get, one or two even managed to press their faces up against the window. Then it dawned on Churchill's guard that they were not hostile. The old man insisted on getting out. They had stopped by a heap of rubble just like this one.'

Dieter climbed the few steps to the top of the heap.

'Churchill got out, and with the aid of his stick he scrambled up the little pile of Berlin's remains. He lit up one of his Havanas, he made the V sign and waved at the crowd, he put his hat on the end of his stick and he held it aloft and blew a smoke ring at the sky, and they cheered and cheered and cheered.'

Dieter did the Churchillian V and threw in a few gratuitous grumbles about 'Narzis', and took a bow before his non-existent crowd.

'In the end his bodyguard had to beg him to come down. And when he did the crowd fell over each other to be able to clap the old man on the back, just to be able to touch him. I tell you, Troy, the Pope doesn't get such a reception as Churchill had. He was like a saint to them.'

'A saint without honour in his own country. We threw him out of office,' said Troy.

Dieter leapt to the ground.

'An irrelevance if I may say so. Churchill is a citizen of the world. On that day he was a German. More precious to them as their conqueror than the memory of Charlemagne, Bismarck and Hitler put together. Today Baumgarner is German. Baumgarner is the symbol of victory. And this crowd is merely a fragment – Baumgarner is untouchable.'

'You said not an hour ago that you'd drag him off the street in handcuffs if you could.'

'I would if I could, but I can't. If you and I can get him out of Berlin, then it is, as they say in the USA, a whole new ball game. Let us have no ideas that we can lay hands on him in this city. It's his. He's bought it lock, stock and *Bierstein*. The good guys – the harmless burghers you just saw – as well as the villains. I don't know what we can do, but I do know it must be done outside this city.'

Clark drove them back to the police station. Troy's mind turned over a tumult of ideas. Berlin flashed by unnoticed.

'What do you mean by "code"?' Troy asked.

Dieter leaned across the desk and ran his finger down one column of the dark, grainy photograph of Baumgarner's diary.

'See for yourself. Last Wednesday – JBP at 2200 the KG.'

'I wouldn't call that code,' Troy said. 'It's simple abbreviation.'

'But just as obscure. We do not know who JBP is and the KG could be any one of twenty locations. Look,' Dieter flipped forward a page to the last week of December. 'Home Run. 55K. Now who is Home Run and is 55K a weight or a sum of money or what?'

Troy's attention was seized by 27 December. The first day after today, the 23rd, for which there was any entry. He let his finger stop under the date, and Dieter picked it up as his cue.

'See. Again. Who is LH133? Where will he be at 10.00 hours? What is Id 2200? Freud's phone number? And there, the following day what is DC at 0145? And at last we have a full name, but George Town is a made-up name if ever I heard one!'

'Dieter. You said you learnt your English in England?'

'I was there from 1938 to 1941.'

'Before the Americans arrived. And you've never been to America?'

'Make your point, Troy. If I've been stupid I'd rather know at once.'

'LH133 looks very like the way airlines have taken to abbreviating flight numbers. Id is quite possibly Idlewild – the New York international airport. DC is surely Washington. And you're reading far too much into George Town. Even to seeing a space where there isn't one. Georgetown isn't a person it's a suburb of Washington. The bugger's going home!'

'Why would he fly on a civil airline? With his resources?'

'I'd hate to cross the Atlantic with the US Air Force if I didn't have to. I flew with the RAF to get here. Not the height of comfort. He's flying home by the easiest means.'

Dieter snatched the diary from Troy's hands and cursed aloud. He picked up the phone and spoke to the operator. Troy looked over his shoulder at Clark, wondering how much attention the man paid, but he had his nose in his book, his greatcoat open and his legs splayed around the stove. If he'd heard what was said his utter indifference added to his translator's discretion to create a solidly impervious front.

A couple of minutes later Dieter put down the phone, looked straight at Troy and blew a silent whistle of appraisal.

'I have an old friend in the airline's office. There is a flight from Berlin to New York at 10 a.m. on the 27th. And Baumgarner is booked on it.'

'Stopping where?' asked Troy.

'Hannover and Shannon.'

'Shit,' said Troy.

'Shannon is in Ireland, is it not? Your writ does not run in Ireland?'

Troy paused momentarily, sighed deeply, and stated the inevitable. 'We can't let that plane land at Shannon,' he said softly.

'Troy – this is fantasy! How do you expect to divert a plane?'

Dieter pushed back his chair and stood up. He stood by the stove and warmed his hands at it. Clark looked up as the shadow passed across his gaze, but went back to his book without a second glance.

'Troy – perhaps I have misled you about the way things can be done here. I obtained the copy of Baumgarner's diary by subterfuge. My own action – my own responsibility. It's deniable. If you have any thought that we can ask them to put down in London without the proper permissions, forget it. Right now Berlin is a city where you can buy a gun on a street corner but you cannot ask a bureaucrat to cut a corner. Do you see what I mean?'

'Can your friend find out the name of the pilot?'

'Troy, please!'

'Can he?'

'Yes.'

'Good. I don't propose to ask favours. I don't propose to say a damn thing to any jobsworth bureaucrat. Just get me someone who can be bribed.'

§ 90

Clark and Troy went back to the jeep.

'Time to kill, eh, sir?' said Clark. 'Would you like to see a bit of the city?'

'I've seen enough builder's rubble to last a lifetime.'

'Oh, there's more to it than that. There's the Brandenburg Gate, there's the Reichstag – if this were the LCC there'd be a blue plaque saying "Marinus van der Lubbe" was here – as it is it's only in chalk.'

They sat side by side in the jeep. Clark not even turning the key in the ignition without some indication from Troy.

'I don't want the tourist guide. Take me to a café – anywhere you like,' said Troy.

'There's bound to be a mobile at the Tiergarten, I should think.'

'Bit nippy for standing around outdoors, wouldn't you say?'

'Yes, but the Tiergarten might interest you as a policeman – the tram-conductors don't call out Tiergarten any more, they just yell "Black market".'

The coffee at the mobile canteen contrasted pleasantly with that at the Uhlandstrasse – it was fresh and it was real. And it was probably stolen. Troy looked over the top of his cup at a mêlée of human scarecrows – stickmen with brown-paper parcels, stick-women pushing prams without babies. It all looked too familiar – the pre-war newsreel footage of a nation in retreat. The universal refugee. Except that these people were going nowhere. They circled, they collided and they spun off each other like billiard balls.

Clark unwrapped into a surprising volubility.

'The Inspector's a bit of a philosopher wouldn't you say, sir?'

'I've despaired of ever getting the short answer – but I suppose he knows what he's talking about.'

'Oh yes. The re-respectablisation of Germany. Not a bad Ph.D. thesis or perhaps a paper for the Fabian Society.'

Troy looked sideways at Clark – wondering what he kept hidden beneath the wall of unwavering misery.

' 'Cept he's wrong,' Clark added.

'How so?'

'Well, sir – it comes down to one question. A dozen ways to frame it, but just the one question. Whose soul do you want to buy? Whose grandmother would you like to own? Whose babies would you want to see baked in an infant pie and washed down with virgin's blood? In this city if it isn't nailed down it's for sale. I don't blame the Inspector for putting it in the best possible light – it's his country after all – but I think he's wrong. If you don't mind me askin', sir, how much money did you bring?'

'Two hundred and fifty – sterling.'

'Well, sir – I reckon that could buy an archbishop and still leave a bob or two over for the odd gross of virgins. One airline pilot should be no trouble. In the Berlin Stalin has fashioned everyone is on the fiddle – and I mean everyone.'

'Everyone?' asked Troy.

Clark lowered his voice, added a hint of mock confidentiality, 'Tell me, sir, are you a married man?'

'Why do you ask?'

Clark whipped open his greatcoat – nylon stockings, silk knickers and frilly garters hung from a cat's cradle of string and safety-pins.

' 'Cos if you are – I'm bound to have something in her size.'

Point made, he closed his greatcoat.

'I sold this bloke the coffee as it happens. Best NAAFI dark roast. Not bad at all.'

§ 91

Troy did a deal with Clark. He swapped his day-old *Manchester Guardian* for Clark's *Penguin New Writing* and retreated to the meagre warmth of his room on the Kurfürstendamm. It was hard to concentrate. Jack's 'honest as the day is wotnot' had been meant as a recommendation – but Troy found himself wondering if it might not become a liability. He did not wholly believe Clark's theory of Berlin – it was a bit like the Berlinisation of everything. On the other hand Clark had pointed out that most police stations in the city were serving decent coffee.

It was dark when Dieter called him.

'Troy, I have the name of the pilot of LH133. Marius von Asche, and he's right here in Berlin. He has two days off before the New York flight.'

'Can we see him?'

'I have talked to him. He will see me, but he won't see you. Not yet.'

'What?'

'It was fine till he realised you were English. There are some of us who are unforgiving – I take it as a sign for the worst.'

'What do you mean?'

'I mean only that I have certain misgivings.'

'For Christ's sake, Dieter, spit it out!'

'I can't, really I can't.'

'Then let me come with you.'

'Troy, that really isn't possible.'

'Then you'll have to do the deal.'

There was a silence – exactly as Troy had expected.

'I . . . er can't do that.'

'Dieter, I have the money. I'm not about to let this slip through my fingers!'

'Troy, please. You must leave this with me. Perhaps if he sees me and sees that I am above board he will agree to meet with you.'

He rang off. Dieter, Troy thought, was so far above board he was in the crow's nest.

§ 92

Troy was waiting when Dieter arrived at his office the next morning. He stared out of the window. The constant hum of planes overhead set the glass in the windows vibrating. In Berlin there scarcely seemed to be a moment when there wasn't a plane overhead. London's sound for so many years had been the mournful wail of the siren. With peace it struck Troy as being a constant human babble, louder than the traffic. The Berlin sound was the narcotic throb of piston engines and propellers. You went to sleep to it, you woke up to it, you lived to it. Clark was oblivious to it, and assumed his position draped around the stove, nose deep in Graham Greene's *Stamboul Train*, having taken the precaution of bringing his own wood and his own coffee. By the time Dieter walked in the stove was throwing out enough heat to set the lid on the coffee-pot wobbling.

'My that smells good!'

Clark glanced up from his book.

'Help yourself, sir. A present from the NAAFI.'

Dieter did not question Clark's use of the word 'present' – he poured himself a cup and sat behind his desk, savouring the aroma of the coffee like a man long deprived. As he tilted the cup to his lips, his eyes met Troy's. Troy was not in the mood for the small pleasantries of the morning.

'Well?' he said.

Dieter set down the cup.

'Tell me. What did you do in the war?'

'Has this got anything at all to do with von Asche?'

Dieter took another sip of coffee.

'Yes. Indulge me a moment.'

'I was a policeman.'

'Why?'

'Why? Because it's what I did, it's what I do, it's what I believe in.'

Dieter was nodding in an understanding, utterly infuriating way.

'Quite, quite. I spent the war in England and in Norway as a member of Special Operations. I arrived back in Berlin with the Americans in 1945.'

Troy had guessed as much.

'It was, as you put it, what I did. What I believed in. Von Asche was in the Luftwaffe.'

'So?'

'He flew some of the last ever sorties over London. He boasts that he was bombing London right up until D-Day. It was what he did. It was what he ...'

'What he believed in? What the hell has that got to do with anything? Nobody can believe in that now!'

'Exactly,' said Dieter with a note of finality that caused even Clark to look up and betray his eavesdropping.

'So the man's a Nazi! And since that's impossible as an ideology he believes in what? Money?'

'I would guess that he believes in money, money and more money. He means to give us a very hard time. His exact words were – "I hope your friend has enough". How much do you have by the way?'

Troy told him. He whistled softly.

'That's three months or more's income, Dieter.'

'I know. I hope it's enough to satisfy the hopeless. He has agreed to meet. Two o'clock in the lobby of the Wilhelm I Hotel.'

Clark looked up from his book again.

'Do you know it?' Troy asked.

'Posh it is, sir. In so far as Berlin has any posh left. A little bit of gilt and velvet among the ruins, you might say. From a copper's point of view I'd say the important thing is that it's got more exits than a rabbit warren, and it seats upwards of a hundred and fifty. Whatever happens happens in public. I'd say your bloke's watching his back. Coffee's good too, if you catch my drift.'

He held the book up and winked hammily at Troy. It seemed to give him a curious pleasure to be able to hint at his alternative income in the presence of two policemen. Troy wondered if he'd ever get a cup of coffee in Berlin that hadn't first been part of a shady Clark deal.

§ 93

Young waiters in moth-eaten maroon bum-starver jackets darted hither and thither distributing one-inch portions of strudel and fruit cake sliced as thin as bacon. Every so often one of them appeared with a long-handled dust-pan and a broom and endeavoured to keep up a losing battle with the flaking plaster that fell like a lazy snowstorm all around the customers for afternoon tea. Posh and gilt was not a bad description. The gold leaf was peeling, the ceilings and walls were cracked and the carpet threadbare – but the Imperial crest manifested itself at cornice height wherever a yard or more of plasterwork remained intact, and the Prussian eagles peeped out of an interlocking pattern around the holes in the carpet. A shabby elegance also characterised most of the clientèle. Too cold to give up topcoats, most of them sat fully wrapped, a forest of stale wet wool and astrakhan, taking a lush, loud pleasure in the pretence of a world into which the twenties and thirties had never intruded. They gossiped and clattered crockery fit to drive the frost from their bones and relished a convivial Christmas Eve, rendered all the more convivial by common hardship. Morality restored, Troy thought, the Germans reminded him of those English for whom the siege of London by the Luftwaffe assumed the tinge of a golden era of *bonhomie* and comradeship in the face of deadly adversity. For a moment he felt quite at home.

Von Asche was not what might have been expected. He was pale, ascetic, a little camp and delicately scented. A pinch-thin face, an aquiline nose and delicate, long-fingered hands, with finely manicured nails. The backs of his hands, his cheekbones and his forehead shone tightly – the polished tones of plastic surgery for burns. He seemed oblivious to the lack of heat in the hotel. An old black coat with a worn fur collar hung over the chairback as he defied goose-pimples in his black double-breasted suit. It was, Troy decided, showing off. His narrow, boy's waist would have been lost in the overcoat, and burdened with the weight of thick sleeves he would not have gestured so freely with his long fingers and their overlong almond-shaped nails.

He had stood and offered his hand to Troy. Troy shook it. Dieter ignored the hand and sat. A boy in a bum-starver appeared from nowhere, tray held high, and dotted a *cafetière* and three tiny cups in front of them and was gone. Von Asche took a silver cigarette case from his inside pocket. The catch was a white stud, a semi-precious stone in an oval silver hoop, inset with a small black swastika. When Troy and Dieter declined the offer he lit up and drew deeply. He reached for an ashtray in the centre of the table and flicked ash – index finger crooked to tap at the king-sized American cigarette. They sat with their obligatory black-market coffee untouched, waiting on the obligatory pause.

'Two policemen,' he said. 'I don't know whether to be flattered or intimidated.'

The evident relish he took in the situation was relish only when demonstrated. He meant to rub their faces in it.

'Still. I suppose all this must be terribly important to you. Who is this man, this passenger you want to see diverted to England?'

'I can't tell you that,' Troy said.

'Oh, come, come, Herr Troy. Play up and play the game.'

Troy said nothing. As far as he was concerned the bastard could quote the whole of 'Drake's Drum' to prove that he was *au fait* enough with the English to send them up – all Troy wanted was that he should name his price.

'This man – surely not a German, or your colleague here would arrest him in the street? Are we talking about a British citizen or an American? You can hardly expect me to lack curiosity.'

'It's an American,' Troy conceded.

'Ah, ah, ah!'

Von Asche blew a smoke ring and took pleasure in the moment. Troy could feel Dieter bristling, hoped he would stick to his promise not to interfere.

'So dog eats dog. I can't tell you what pleasure it gives me to know that the victors have fallen out amongst themselves. Not that it will get you what you want any cheaper.'

At last money.

'So you'll do it?'

Von Asche strung out the pause. Troy dreaded Dieter's intervention, preferring to let silences run their course. Speaking to fill another man's silence usually led to indiscretion.

'To land in England?'

'Yes.'

'A fault of some kind – an emergency on the aircraft?'

'Whatever you like.'

'And where would I land?'

'West London. There's a new airfield under construction on the far side of Hounslow. They call it Heath Row.'

'Aha.' He paused to inhale and exhale at length and then added, 'I always wanted to see England.'

'So you'll do it?'

'I had hopes that I might see it sooner – say about 1940, but that was not to be. All the same it would be nice to see England.'

He smiled – the man was taunting Troy. Defying him to blow it by a crude statement of patriotism.

'You'll do it?' Troy repeated.

'How much money do you have?'

'I'll pay a hundred pounds. Cash,' said Troy.

Von Asche threw back his head and laughed.

'No, no, no, Herr Troy. You have much more than that. What did you bring? Two hundred and fifty?'

'Two hundred.'

'Try again.'

'Two hundred and fifty. And that's my last word.'

Von Asche stubbed out the end of his cigarette and immediately lit up another. He blew the smoke at Troy and smiled.

'Your last word. I see. I think the last word should be mine, don't you?'

He leaned across the table and dropped his voice to a stagey whisper. *'Und das Wort Ist "Tausend"!'*

Troy felt Dieter rise in his chair and gently extended an arm to prevent him.

'I can't pay that!' he said softly, almost without inflexion.

'Then perhaps this American is not quite as important as you think.'

Dieter could be contained no longer.

'Troy, this is madness. The man is a crook!'

'Quite,' said von Asche, utterly unperturbed by Dieter. 'What you ask is crooked. That is why you came to me, is it not? If you want this crooked act performed by this crook, then the price is one thousand pounds. Cash!'

'Two hundred and fifty in cash. I'll write you a cheque for the balance.'

Von Asche shook his head gently from side to side.

'No, no, no, Herr Troy. Cash. I'd hate to find that your cheque bounced or that your colleague here appeared with handcuffs when I tried to cash it.'

He turned his gaze on Dieter, smiling, silently mocking him, delighting in his discomfort. The shiny skin around his eyes crinkling like Cellophane.

'Troy,' Dieter said, brimming with anger, 'you cannot do this!'

Troy ignored him. 'Cash it is,' he said.

Dieter got to his feet, ostentatiously took a banknote from his pocket and threw it down next to his cup.

'Enough is enough. I'll be in the jeep.'

Von Asche looked up at him. There was a silence in which the roar of the room became audible while they waited for Dieter to get clear.

'He doesn't seem to share your passion,' von Asche said at last. 'What did this man do that you want him so badly?'

Troy got up and put a banknote down on top of Dieter's.

'The price is a thousand. Money's all you're getting,' he said.

'As you wish. I'll be taking Christmas lunch here tomorrow. Twelve until two. I suggest you join me then. If, of course, the Berlin Police find such a transaction indigestible, you might come alone.'

He let out a colossal cloud of smoke and smiled at Troy.

'I'll be here,' Troy said.

§ 94

Out in the street Dieter was stamping his feet. Troy found it hard to tell whether this was anger or a measure against the biting cold. Clark sat in his jeep, still reading, buttoned up almost to the eyebrows. Dieter turned at Troy's approach.

'Good God, Troy, what have you done? What have you done? A thousand pounds? This is madness, utter madness! You haven't got a thousand pounds!'

'Get me to a phone and I will have.'

Dieter seemed to weigh this up for a second or two and then sighed deeply.

'OK. OK. We must go back to the station and book the call.'

It was gone six and the electricity was off again by the time the operator called back with the international connection to Troy's family home in Hertfordshire. Apart from the occasional crackle the line was clear enough, and Rod heard Troy out in silence.

'Right, Freddie. Let me get this straight,' were his first words and Troy knew at once that he meant to argue. 'You want me to get on to the bank, at half-past six of a pitch-black Christmas Eve, dig old McCrimmon out of his club or whatever bolt-hole widowers have on Christmas Eve. Get him to draw out an order for seven hundred and fifty quid, wire this to a bank in Berlin which will then have to open up especially to enable you to pick up the cash, with which you will then bribe a German pilot to fake an emergency landing in England, at which point you will step in with your Bow Street warrant and arrest this bugger you've been obsessed with since the war. Now tell me, Freddie, have I got it right – this is in essence what you're asking me this Christmas Eve?'

'Yes,' seemed almost inadequate as an answer.

'Have you taken complete leave of your senses?' Rod exploded. 'For Christ's sake, Freddie, it's Christmas Eve. My children are shaking their presents under the Christmas tree to see if they rattle, your sisters are upstairs swapping frocks and dirty stories, my wife is pouring sherry for everyone, your mother is asking awkward questions about what time you'll be arriving this year and why is it only you that has no sense of punctuality. What am I to tell her – that you've gone barking bloody mad?'

'I know what I'm doing.'

'Jesus Christ, man. You're a policeman. You can't cook up schemes like this!'

'Rod – please do this. It's important. You can do this. It's not a lot to ask.'

'Of course I can do it. The point is I won't. I won't dig out McCrimmon at this time of night—'

'Rod – we have millions with that damn bank!'

'That's not the point. He's an old man. He has a right to be left in peace. I won't do this to him and I won't let you do this to yourself. It's an obsession – can't you see that? For Christ's sake, Freddie, just walk away from it. It's over. It was over years ago. You can't go on living your life on some ancient pain.'

There was a loud clank as Clark flipped open the lid of the stove and threw in another strip of Old Berlin. In the red light of the flames Troy could see Dieter watching him through the darkness, hands supporting his chin, elbows on his desk, meeting his gaze eye to eye. It was obvious that Rod's harangue had been audible in the room. There was a whispered exchange at the other end and a rattle of Bakelite, and another, deeper, accented, world-weary voice came on the line.

'Freddie – is Nikolai. Come home, my boy, it is over. It is a wise man who knows when to quit.'

'I can't do that.'

'Yes you can – or this thing will kill you.'

Troy put the receiver back in its cradle. Dieter was still watching. He sat back and took his chin off his hands.

'It's Chrismas Eve,' he said.

'I know. People keep telling me.'

'My wife will be cooking supper soon. I should be home to put my girls to bed. Why don't you join us? The meat is thin, but the wine is plentiful. Who knows I may turn into a real Prussian and break out the Schnapps.'

Troy looked at Clark. He was invisible from the waist up, but Troy could hear the turn of pages as he ploughed on through his book.

'Can you get me on a flight out?' he asked.

'Not tonight I can't.'

'That's OK. Tomorrow will be fine.'

Clark leant down to look at his notebook by the glow of the fire.

'The morning could be tricky. Lots of RAF types going west. Late afternoon's OK. There's a charter going right through to England round about six. You wouldn't have the stopover at Hannover.'

'That's fine,' Troy said softly, feeling the first wash of resignation flow over him. 'Six will be fine. Who knows, I may take the tourist trip.'

'Is there somewhere I can drop you gents?' Clark asked.

Troy turned to Dieter. 'Can we walk to your house?'

'Yes. Only a couple of miles.'

'In that case no, Mr Clark. Take the night off. It's Christmas Eve.'

Clark rose and stuffed the book in his thigh pocket.

'People keep sayin' that,' he said.

He reached into the depths of his greatcoat and plonked down a small package on the desk in front of Dieter.

'A little something for the missis, sir. What would Christmas dinner be without a glass of brandy and a nice cup of coffee to follow? Mind you, I can't fix you up with the brandy. Well, gents, I'll bid you goodnight, and I'll see you at Gatow tomorrow, Mr Troy.'

He left. The lights flickered on for a second or two, then the power surged, the bulbs popped and they were in darkness once more. It seemed to Troy to be an apt symbol of his life for the last week or more.

§ 95

Gently, Dieter warned Troy that he would prefer not to talk shop when they got home. He liked a life apart from his work. Troy could not imagine what such a life might be like. He had lived so long in one world alone.

Dieter swept two small girls into his arms as they stormed him at the threshold. He told them to say hello and goodnight to Mr Troy, and bundled them upstairs to bed.

Frau Franck – Cosima – was small and blonde and talkative, – as quick in English as her husband. She took his coat, offered him a glass of Hock and sat him down in the narrow, high living room, festooned with home-made decorations, down to a home-made tree sitting by the window. Dieter had cobbled it together from more bits of Old Berlin, slapped on the branches at right angles to the main stem, and given it a lick of green paint. It looked like Christmas with Marcel Duchamp. Under its branches, gathered around the zinc bucket in which it stood, were dozens of brightly wrapped presents. Troy remembered how neatly Rod had used the idea of Christmas to get him to come home.

When the children had been read to and persuaded against nature that they should sleep, Dieter came down and he and Troy and Cosima shared ten ounces of pork that otherwise might have better fed two. The wine was plentiful. Rather than Schnapps, Dieter found two inches of pre-war Armagnac that had somehow escaped British bombs and Russian infantry.

Dieter was different in his different world. He chatted in a low-key manner. The tendency to make a thesis of everything seemed to have been brushed off on the doorstep. He had a talent for small talk. He was constantly affectionate towards his wife. He covered her hand with his frequently. Pressing it rather than holding it. An habitual gesture – a reassuring conjugality. Cosima had passed the entire war in Berlin. She had seen the world turned upside down, dissolved into dust and all but blown away. Troy watched the nuances in their gestures as he listened to this tale of hell. He had seen nothing like it, he thought, since the death of Ethel Bonham. Even though the constant touching, and the way Cosima would gently biff his shoulder with her head like a young cat, was remote from the spare intimacy of the Bonhams, the image – the metaphor – stood. They fitted each other like gloves. It was startlingly natural. It had beauty, containment, safety, peace and pleasure. It occurred to him that this was a way of life he had rejected, or that had somehow passed him by, and at thirty-three was unlikely in the extreme to be offered him. And he didn't miss it one jot.

Midnight struck. What church bells remained in church belfries rang out. Troy felt he should be going. Felt he should leave them to an intimacy that was fascinating to watch, but in which he had no place.

'Let me call you a cab,' said Dieter.

'I'd rather walk,' said Troy.

'It's two miles!'

'All the better,' said Troy. 'I need the air.'

He thanked Dieter for all he had done and set off along the empty streets back to the Kurfürstendamm. He wondered if the not unpleasant feeling that spread softly within him was relief and freedom from the impossible pursuit – or just Hock and Armagnac. It's over, he told himself. It's over.

It was, Troy thought, remarkable how far he had strayed. His frustration with Dieter had given place to something approaching gratitude that he had stood firm and honest at a point when Troy was ready to break any rule, bend any law. It was snowing gently, flakes the size of half-crowns billowing down around him, a white night magic in the small hours of Christmas Day. All the world was white. Somewhere in the gathering snow behind him he heard a squelch – a wet footstep – and turned to look, then all the world was green. Green of a rather pleasing shade, the old Victorian green of a good billiard table. His father had had one in just this shade.

§ 96

Troy lay in a fitful half sleep on the long, peeling white verandah of his father's Hertfordshire house. He had no idea why he was there. It seemed years since he had lain like this, yet he was unmistakably conscious that he was in some stage of the slow convalescence from one of the many childhood illnesses that had dogged him throughout those years. He was warmly wrapped, almost to the neck, cushioned and propped against the head of an old oak and iron porter's trolley, like a piece of baggage awaiting collection. The sun shone in the west. Down the garden, off towards the end of a lawn that covered more than an acre he could see the large stooping figure of his paternal grandfather, Rodyon Rodyonovich. Well into his seventies, still the Slavophile, a simple-life disciple and friend of the late Count Tolstoy, he was dressed in the manner of a Russian peasant and swung the heavy scythe against the long grass of the unkempt lawn in the fond pretence that it was good Russian wheat.

Troy's father had bought this house in the late summer of 1910, for no other reason than that the long, south-facing verandah struck him as being faintly like home. Laughingly, he called the crumbling

Georgian pile his dacha. When one of the natives shrewdly observed that there was no higher ground between this small village in the English Home Counties and the mountains of the Urals, his father's attachment to the place became complete. 'There is nothing,' he would say, biting back near hysterics, 'there is nothing between me and Moscow!'

In the November of the same year Tolstoy had died a peasant's death in a railway hut at Astapovo, attended only by his family, his followers, the Bishop of Tula and the world's press. Rodyon Rodyonovich knew it was time to leave. Only the old man's world status had kept the secret police at bay. Without him there was no future in Russia for a Tolstoyan. Before Christmas he was in Hertfordshire, where he lived out the rest of his life, dressing in the coarse linen costume of the peasant, refusing to learn a word of English, writing long letters to *The Times* (which his daughter-in-law had to translate on his behalf), preoccupying his grandchildren with tales of the old country and the peaceful revolution, and quaffing vast quantities of claret.

The old man had dropped his scythe and lumbered closer. His huge hands rested on the verandah railing – Troy could count the hairs on the backs of his fingers – and he leaned his bear-like face down towards his grandson.

'Are you awake?' he asked in Russian. He looked off somewhere over Troy's right shoulder. 'I don't think he's awake yet.'

Troy struggled to open his eyes and realised he was blindfolded. There was the distant sound of dripping water and the smell of mould and decay.

'Take it off,' said a woman's voice in Russian.

Troy blinked into the light of an unshaded overhead bulb. There was a small woman, two men flanked her like colossal bookends. They were in a cellar.

'Wassamatterbaby? Light too bright for you? My boys hit you too hard?'

Troy looked at the two men. Large, dark and anonymous in their heavy black overcoats. Broad, brutal Slav faces. The one very much like the other.

'Do we need them?' he asked.

She waved the two men towards the door. It thudded behind

them, and in a swift upward movement Troy seized Tosca by the throat.

'I thought you were dead!'

'Take it easy, baby,' she gasped.

His grip tightened.

'I thought you were dead!'

He had her back against the brick wall. Anger gave him a strength he did not feel.

'I thought you were dead! There was blood all over the place!'

'Let me go and I'll tell you!'

Troy eased his grip. He felt his legs would buckle under him, but he stood looking down into the clear brown eyes.

'I thought you'd spot it.'

'Spot what?'

'You know. It's an old trick. I felt sure you'd get the message. Oh, Come on, baby. We talked about the goddam book the first time we met. Remember? *Huck Finn?*'

'The blood group matched yours. I had it checked against your army medical record. I really thought you were dead. Huck Finn used pig's blood!'

'Oh come on. Where in hell d'you think I'd get a live pig three blocks from Trafalgar Square? Besides it took less than a pint. You splash it around enough and it can look like a real mess.'

'A set-up?'

'Sure. What else?'

'An NKVD set-up?'

'We got a new name for it now. New initials too.'

'And I suppose we're in the East now?'

'Well – I don't think we're in Kansas any more, Toto.'

§ 97

Spent seed did not send Troy tumbling into a vulnerable, satiated sleep. Tosca slept. Troy felt he would never sleep again. Understanding so little, nettled into a stinging alertness. The back of his head throbbed. He wrapped his shirt around him and stumbled into the sliver of light that came from the crack between the shutters. The light hit the cracked linoleum floor, a rough shard beneath his feet. How often had he shuffled around her bedroom, in and out of the light, working out the pieces she had put in front of him, so seemingly casual, teasing him like a child with the jumbled mess of a jigsaw puzzle.

As ever her eyes flicked open. Not even a flutter of the eyelids to drag herself from sleep. She woke instantly, totally, hard-eyed and staring.

'Oh God, Troy. Do you never sleep?'

'I was waiting.'

'Waiting for what for Chrissake?'

'For you to tell me what a fool I've been.'

'OK. You've been a fool. The complete horse's ass. Now come back to bed.'

'How long did you string me out? Feeding me titbits. From the start?'

'You don't want to go into that. Really you don't.'

'You played me for a fool. I think I deserve an explanation.'

'Oh my. Have you turned into a pompous asshole or what?'

He had drifted too close to the bed. A powerful hand snatched him back. Her left foot shot out, biffed him lightly in the belly and pinned him to a sitting position. Her grip on his arm was fierce. She squirmed upright, looking straight into his eyes.

'You want it? You'll get it. Could be a long story. I have to go back a few years.'

'I've got the patience of Job,' Troy said quietly.

'No, Troy, I don't think you have. You have the fucked-up self-martyrdom of one of those boring Christian saints.'

It was the most complex notion Troy had heard pass her lips.

'OK. OK. Picture this, you complete pain in the ass. 1905 – my dad, like your dad, gives up on the revolution. He gets out of Russia. He thinks it's never going to happen. So he sails for New York. Settles on the Lower East Side, where the wops and the Jews live, a dozen or so to a room. There he meets my sweet little Italian momma, only seventeen years old when he marries her in 1910 – in 1911 I come along. Born an American, raised an American.

Then *it* happens. The revolution does come, and the old man can't wait to get back – he's itching for it, but he can't get there. Everybody in Europe's fighting everybody else. It's 1919 before he can get a passage to St Petersburg. All three of us make the crossing. I puked every day for two weeks. But the old man is happy – he dumps us in a crummy apartment in Moscow, flourishes his party card and suddenly he's gone – we don't see the bastard for nearly two years. He fights for Mother Russia, the reddest soldier in the Red Army – by the end of the war they're pinning medals on him so fast they have to use a fuckin' stapler. So, he comes home, one eye gone, three fingers missing and a chestful of ribbons. He looks like Halloween. I guess I'm eleven or twelve. My Russian's fluent – which is just as well, on account of all my mom can do is struggle with her mishmash of English and Italian and scream that she wants to go home. We don't. We're here for good he tells her. And just to show her he uses privilege and gets her a classy apartment and enrolls me in the youth wing of the party. And every night she cries herself to sleep.'

Troy's mouth opened to speak and Tosca's hand flashed out at the intake of breath, her fingertips resting on his lips.

'Whatever it is, keep it. Just shuttup. You wanted it all. So shuttup or I stop.

'Now. It's 1924. Lenin's been dead about three months. Trotsky's losing out. May Day parade's over. The goons are climbing down off their podium and some lunatic cries "Long Live Holy Mother Russia" and points a gun at Trotsky. So what does my father do? The stupid bastard bursts out of the crowd and throws himself in front of Trotsky and takes a full magazine right in the chest. Well, of course, he gets a hero's funeral. We already knew he was a hero, but to tell the truth this really doesn't count for much with my mother. All she can think of is that they're burying him in three different places – 'cos one eye's in Siberia somewhere, and the three fingers are in the Ukraine. The day after his funeral she asks to leave – like a kid in a school she hates she says "Can I go home now?" 'Cos she's had the Union of Soviet Socialist Republics. Well, you'd expect they'd say no. And they go on saying no – until '31 when I'm told to present myself at Party Headquarters. They've cooked up a lulu of a scheme. Am I a loyal party member? Of

course I am, I say. After all to say no is to ask for a one-way
ticket to the salt mines. Even at twenty I know that. How did
I see the future of Europe? I stumble through that one. It's kind
of a biggie. I seem to recall something about the inevitable
collapse of the evil British Imperialists as the irresistible workers'
movement wells up in the rainy little islands. Cut the crap, says
the head brasshat, in so many words. The Brits are out of it.
Let 'em drink tea. What about the Germans? Like I said I was
a shrewd twenty-year-old. It's Hitler I said. He's your problem.
A year or two, maybe five and the little corporal could be
chancellor of the paper republic. That was the right answer.
Jackpot. Hole-in-one. How would I like to go back to the
States? they ask. For a second or two this throws me – one
minute we're discussing Germany. Now it's America. But I get
the message. Momma can go home, but I have to go with her
and I have to go as an agent of the Soviet Union.

'I said it was a lulu, didn't I? They fix us up a phoney past to
explain the twelve years in Russia – we've been picking lemons in
the hills above Naples or some place like that. And as we're both
American citizens we've no trouble getting back in. I enlist. Do
my basic training in Virginia, and go to serve Uncle Sam, but really
I'm serving Uncle Joe, 'cos what worries the Russians is that when
the war comes – and they'd no doubts that it would – America
will stay neutral, that they'll let Europe go under and Russia with
it. So – they need people on the inside. I guess I was one of a
dozen, maybe more, working my way up, working my way closer.
I didn't have a clue what was going to happen, I didn't have a clue
what I believed.

'Then, a few months after basic training I was posted to a desk
job in Washington. It was April or May of '32. That spring thousands and thousands of poor people, First-War vets most of 'em,
marched on Washington, camped around the edge in a colossal
shanty town. All they asked was a bonus payment – something they
were owed anyway for doing their bit in the war. Do you know
what the home of the brave and the land of the free did to its poor?
They bulldozed their shacks and shanties, and MacArthur, Ike and
that lunatic George Patton turned the cavalry loose on those
walking bags of bones. I was there. I saw that. Troy, if I didn't

believe in what I was doing before, I sure as hell did after. Life, liberty and the pursuit of hogwash.'

'And what do you believe now?'

'What? What? What in hell gives you the right to ask me what I believe?'

Tosca leapt from the bed, banging heavily on the floor. Her fists pounded each shutter in turn, sending them crashing into the window. She turned to face him, red with rage, her arms in the air, her breasts shaking with the weight of anger.

'Troy, Troy, Troy. What do *you* believe? Don't answer that! I can tell you. Troy, you believe nothing.'

She knelt at his feet, took his hands in hers and pulled him down to her. She held him by the head, face to face, their noses almost touching, one hand spanning the lump on the back of his head and the cut on his temple, the other palm spread across his cheekbone.

'Troy,' she whispered hoarsely, 'if you believed in anything it would be in justice or whatever you want to call it, or maybe the rule of law. I prefer justice. At first I used to think that's what drove you. Justice. That's not the way it is. The guys you catch could swing or walk free for all you cared – you love one thing only, the pursuit. You have a sense of means without a sense of ends. You can't see beyond the pursuit. You're like some fifth horseman of the Apocalypse. After War and Famine comes the Avenging Demon. Never asks where it's all leading but never gives up. It's as though you're no part of the system that follows, the system it all fits into. I am. I know what I do. I know what connects with what. You don't. You never did. So you can't ask me what I believe.'

From saint and martyr to demon possessed in a thousand easy moves, thought Troy. Her mouth closed on his. As she pulled back from the kiss to look at him, four years of rage and pain welled momentarily in his eyes. Tosca licked the tears, kissed Troy on each eyelid, on the forehead, all over his face. Pressed into the flesh of her cheek, smothered in the smell of Tosca, he said as clearly as he could, 'I honestly thought you were dead.'

'Well. It's time to fuck the ghost.' And she tore the shirt from his back.

§ 98

The radiator creaked and strained in the corner, occasionally kicking out with a knock that echoed around the building in a slow diminuendo. Troy stood in the window looking down into the street. The greyest of days. The streets empty of people. A joyless Christmas morning silence, broken only by the near-sub-liminal hum of aeroplanes. Tosca had been an age in the bathroom. He was fully dressed. Hands in his overcoat pockets, waiting again. There was a gentle rap on the door. Troy opened it. A small, dark man, buried in a huge grey overcoat, his face half-hidden by a scarf wrapped up over his chin and a trilby pulled well down on to his forehead.

'Excuse me,' he said in near-perfect English and swung his attaché case forward to indicate his wish to come in. Troy stepped aside. The man set down the case on the bed and turned back to Troy. Troy wondered whether Tosca had a gun, and what he should do if the man produced a weapon. The man unwrapped a layer of scarf revealing the kind of face that has five-o'clock shadow all day, and pushed his hat further back on his head. He looked to Troy to be about forty-five.

'At last,' he said.

'At last?' said Troy. 'At last what?'

'At last we meet. A little late, but not too late I believe to express my gratitude.'

Troy stared. He could not place the face, he could not place the accent. A Czech, a Pole, one of those airmen that used to be so abundant in England only a few years ago?

'You weren't to know what you were doing for me. But believe me, it helped my faith in humanity to know that my death was not ignored. Strange as it may seem it gave me a grudging respect for the Metropolitan Police that I had scarcely felt in all my years in London.'

A sepia photograph, a paler patch on patterned wallpaper where it had once stood came flashing back through Troy's mind, even to the mundanity of the flowered pattern itself.

'You're Peter Wolinski,' he said.

The man glanced impatiently at the bathroom door.

'Yes,' he said, 'and if you will forgive me this will be but a short reunion. If you would be so good as to tell Major Toskevich I called.'

'Toskevich?'

'If you ever have to adopt an alias, Inspector Troy, you will find it easier to adjust the closer it is to your own name. But, then I suppose that was exactly the logic your late father employed. He never ceased to be one of us you know, but I doubt there was any way he could have told you. Well, I'll bid you goodbye.'

He opened the door, and Troy grabbed him by the sleeve.

'My uncle too?' he asked.

'Good Lord no. A complete maverick. What nation in its right mind wants a secret agent who tells the truth from a soapbox at Speaker's Corner? Only the most far-fetched paranoiacs in the Secret Service could ever think he was one of us.'

With that he was gone. Troy turned to the case. He listened to the sound of running water in the bathroom. He flicked the catches on the case and opened the lid. It was empty but for a fat bundle of crisp, white five-pound notes. He looked once more at the bathroom door. It had opened noiselessly and she was standing in it. Fully clothed and made-up. She bent to pull on her shoes, saying as she did, 'Go ahead. It's yours.'

Troy picked up the bundle and riffled a few sheets.

'Are they real?' he asked.

'Of course they're not real. You think I'd waste a thousand smackeroos on a fuckin' Nazi? We ran 'em off by the wagonload during the war. Never got used. I just helped myself to a handful.'

'Dieter said there were few secrets in Berlin,' Troy sighed.

'Von Asche'll never spot the difference. They're the best. Pay the guy and take your chance. It's a good scheme. I could have thought it up myself.'

'Was the messenger your idea too?'

'No – I think Peter was just curious. I think he felt he had to prove something to you. I guess after four years he wanted to let you know he was still alive. Something like that. You know these Poles, they're not like you and me. They're half-crazy to begin with.'

'You and I are alike?'

Troy split the bundle into two and stuffed a wad in each pocket of his overcoat. Tosca slipped on her fur coat and told him it was time to go. Out in the street Troy asked how he would get back.

'No problem. We're only on the Schadowstrasse. The end of the block and you're back on Unter den Linden. You could practically spit through the Brandenburg Gate.'

'What do I do?' he asked, clueless. 'Just walk across?'

Tosca slipped an arm though his and tapped his shoulder lightly with the side of her head – walking along in the bitter biting cold like young lovers.

'Of course,' she replied. 'With me along, you think anybody's going to ask you a damn thing? Just walk right into the British sector. I am known in these parts. Believe me, baby, I am known.'

She eased her grip on him slightly and kicked out a few paces in mock goose step.

'I don't think anyone's going to find that funny,' Troy said.

At the Brandenburg Gate four soldiers stood bored and cold. Troy wondered if they would salute Tosca or block his way. They looked, but there seemed to be not a flicker of recognition or concern on their faces, and as Tosca stepped under the arch two of them shouldered their rifles in a semblance of duty and moved off. The arch was chipped and scarred from bullets, parts of it flaked and crumbled almost before the eyes, the dust of a thousand-year Reich.

'I'll see you at Gatow tonight,' she said, and pecked him on the cheek, the perfect wife seeing off her commuter husband on the 8.10 from Weybridge.

'What?'

'I thought the RAF wangled you on to a night flight out?'

'They have. But how the hell do you expect to get into a British base?'

'Oh baby, this is so elementary. Two and two are four – you get my drift. Now, Gatow is an airfield. That means planes land there, right? Now how do planes land – yes I know they have pilots – but, my stupid angel, they also need air traffic control or they'd be flying up each other's asshole like New England turkeys in a blizzard! Who do you think runs air traffic control? We do. Not a single damn plane could make it down the air corridor to land if we told the Krauts on this side to pull air traffic control.'

'Your world,' he said, 'is composed of so many shades of grey ... it isn't even worth guessing any more.'

'Suit yourself – but Uncle Joe and the Missouri haberdasher have a few little deals going here and there. I wouldn't be surprised if Stalin hasn't got a tasteless tie for Christmas. Trust me. I'll be there. Pay the Kraut and get out to Gatow. And don't mess around. I don't have all day. Bob Hope's playing Tempelhof tonight. I wouldn't want to miss him!'

'Curiouser...' said Troy.

'It's all part of the game.'

'...And curiouser,' he said. 'I don't suppose you knew my father?' She shook her head, grinning.

'Or Tom Driberg?'

'Now you're being silly.'

She pecked him on the cheek again, turned, and with what Troy would have said was a skip in her step, set off quickly back down Unter den Linden. Troy looked to the guards. One of them made a beckoning motion, pointed to the West and then turned his back on him. Troy walked through the arch, hearing the sound of his own shoes clatter on the flagstones in the vast silence as though he were the only person in all Berlin. Everywhere the piles of rubble had been turned into shining white mountains by the overnight snow, but nothing on earth could make the man-made ruins seem natural. A landscape in white, slashed by jagged lines. It reminded Troy of the day nearly five years ago when he and Bonham had followed the ragtag army of Stepney schoolboys out to the ruined streets on the Green. Another white, dazzling landscape of war's detritus. The silence shattered. Planes overhead. No more Heinkel, no more Dornier. Douglas Dakotas droned and purred. Rising out of Tempelhof.

Clark showed Troy to a booth in the mess at Gatow. The mess was three-quarters empty, but the dozen or more men at the bar seemed hell bent on making up for it by celebrating Christmas as loudly and as drunkenly as they could. It seemed a bleak variety of joy.

'Just the single men who weren't allowed full passes, sir. The married men are off the base and anyone who got a pass has somewhere better to go. You'll be fine here.'

He looked out of the first-floor window at the snowstorm swirling past the window and down to the ground, where snow-ploughs battled to keep the runways clear.

'I wouldn't bet on anything running to order, if I were you.'

'That's OK,' said Troy. 'You get off. I'll be fine.'

'I'm sorry it's all been a waste of time, sir.'

Troy looked at Clark. It wasn't mere pleasantry. The man meant what he said.

'It hasn't. I paid von Asche at lunchtime.'

Clark looked surprised, then a smile broke the front of deceptive misery.

'Have you told Inspector Franck, if you don't mind my asking?'

'No. I think he'd rather not know, don't you?'

Clark shook Troy's hand, a little awkwardly.

'Been a pleasure, sir.'

'No, Mr Clark, it's been an education.'

Clark set off down the room. He'd just reached the door when Tosca backed in, wearing her Master Sergeant's uniform, shaking the snow from her coat. She almost collided with Clark, threw him a friendly grin, said a quick 'Hi, Swifty', and rushed up to Troy breathless and beaming.

'Gee, get a load of this weather.'

She flung herself down in the booth, opposite Troy. It was the same uniform, the same face, only the haircut was different. He could hardly believe it.

'I thought I'd never make it.'

'"Hi, Swifty"?' Troy said. 'Hi, Swifty! You know Clark?'

'Sure. And he knows me. Where the heck d'you think I got the coffee you had at breakfast? I told you, I'm known in these parts. I come here quite often. Though every time I have to put on this damn uniform it gets tighter. I'm surprised it fits at all after all these years.'

She breathed in and patted her stomach.

'Is there anyone you don't know?'

'What's that supposed to mean? As if I can't guess.'

'How long have you known Wolinski?'

'Nowhere near as long as you think I have.'

'But he was a Russian agent in London, wasn't he?'

'He wasn't there to sell chopped liver.'

'But you didn't know him?'

'Will you drop this. Jesus. I told him it was a dumb idea to show up now. It would only set you thinking. No. I didn't know him. Now can we talk about something else!'

'When you left London. When you faked your death. What was I supposed to believe?'

'That I was dead. I had to do that. I really had to.'

'You left everything behind?'

'Of course – I had to throw you off the scent. I knew you'd come looking – if you lived that is – and I knew that if you thought I was alive you'd never give up. There was a real danger that you'd blow my cover. My job was over – I wasn't there to watch Jimmy, I'd no idea what he was up to till you came along – and I wasn't there to control Wolinski – I mean, I never even met the guy till 1946 – I was there to see that nothing about the opening of the second front was held back. With D-Day the job was done. I guess they wouldn't have pulled me so quickly, but once you had your shoot-out with Jimmy I could see all hell breaking loose. Zelly turned purple – maybe permanently – and Jimmy found himself shipped out to France on day two.'

'They told the Yard it was day one.'

'Well – they would, wouldn't they? Day two was bad enough. They sure as hell weren't going to let Jimmy risk his neck on day one. I mean, even Churchill wasn't allowed over on day one!'

'So you gave up everything?'

'Sure – it would have been a convincing murder if I'd packed first! I lost some good stuff. I had this cute little silk dress . . . and I could have used my jewellery.'

Troy needed no reminding of her jewellery.

'I have something of yours,' he said gently.

'You kept a souvenir?'

'Yes. I have your copy of *Huckleberry Finn*.'

'That's OK you can keep it.'

'And I have a pair of silver-mounted pearl ear-rings.'

She looked at him quizzically, smiling sweetly, as though foxed by the choice he had made from all she had left behind, but in seconds the realisation hit her. She buried her face in her hands, bent her head – spoke through the fingers.

'Oh God. Where did you find it?'

'In Wolinski's flat. Not the first time I went there, not the second. The third. You dropped it in that middle room of his. I suppose it was some time in May. You went there after you and I met, after you and I had discussed the case – of which you now tell me you knew nothing.'

'I did know nothing. Do you really think I'd've let you get mixed up with Jimmy without telling you everything?'

'I don't know what to think. I'm inclined to think you fed it to me bit by bit – you strung me out – you used me.'

'No I didn't! I never knew Wolinski. I was never part of anything he did in the East End. His path crossing Jimmy's was a bad coincidence. Every one of us had an emergency number to call – after Brand was killed – and believe me I didn't know that was the trigger – Wolinski called me. He needed to get out straight away. I plugged him into the network, got him the money he needed to disappear. I never met him. I dropped the money in a dead-letter box. Then you come along. There's no reason to think I need have anything more to do with it all. Then he calls me from Scotland. He's left his code-book in the flat – some goddam mathematics textbook. I tell him to forget it. No one will spot it, and we'll never use those codes again. He won't hear of it. Dumb bastard says he'll come back and get it. So I do it. It took for ever to search it out. I must have been there more than ten minutes. I guess I lost the ear-ring scrambling up his goddamn bookcases. The only thing I kept from you was the fact that Wolinski was still alive. But there was no way I could tell you that. Dammit, Troy, if you think I used you try asking yourself about the other women in your life. Did I use you like my private warrior 'cos I couldn't fight a man's battle myself – 'cos that's what Muriel Edge used you for. Did I string you out by the dick until it was time to blow you away – 'cos that's what that mad—'

'Don't say it!!!'

'Sorry,' she said for the first time in all the time he had known her.

'Why does everyone call her "that mad bitch"?'

'Maybe because she was?' Tosca ventured carefully.

There was a brittle silence, offset by the roar of the drunks and the roar of propellers.

'Should I post the ear-rings to you?'

'Nah. I'll pick 'em up the next time I'm in England.'

'The next time you're in England?'

'Sure.'

'If you come to England I shall be duty bound to arrest you as an enemy of the crown.'

'Boy – you should hear yourself. "Enemy of the crown"!'

'I'm serious.'

'Awww. You won't arrest meee!!!'

'Why wouldn't I arrest you?'

'Because, silly, if you arrest me you don't get to sleep with me.'

'If little else,' Troy said, 'at least your vocabulary is improving.'

§ 100

Heathrow was referred to as an air port. Troy presumed that this fiction was in some way meant to distinguish it from such places as Croydon which had always been called an aerodrome or Brize Norton which remained an air field. It was a linguistic elevation, a sleight of tongue. What it amounted to on the physical plane was a shanty town of shacks and bulldozers, mountains of frozen mud, on the very fringe of London – so far out as to seem like another country. In this weather, Troy thought, it might as well be the North Pole.

The wind caught at the powder-fine snow, whipping it into small white eddies around the legs of the first passengers as they came down the steps on to the freshly brushed tarmac, thanking God loudly that they had touched down safely and asking each other what the problem could possibly have been. Troy stood between the crowd and the warm reassurance of the building, and they parted around him like a river to a rock, foaming busily to either side, seeming oblivious to him. Baumgarner was nowhere to be seen. Over their heads Troy thought he caught sight of an exceptionally tall man at the back. He drew his revolver and stood with it in his left hand, hanging at his side. Suddenly he was visible. Someone screamed and pointed and the crowd spread out to either side of him in a rush of fear. No one stood between him and the man now standing at the foot of the aircraft steps.

Baumgarner had an unlit cigarette between his lips and was patting down his pockets looking for matches. His right hand went into his overcoat pocket. Troy levelled the gun at his head. As though he had heard the silent gesture Baumgarner looked up and noticed Troy for the first time. He drew out his hand, tore a light off a book of matches and put it to his cigarette, cupping both hands against the wind. He inhaled deeply, blew a single smoke ring to the sky and returned Troy's gaze. The moist, laconic blue eyes, the provocative pout of the upper lip – he smiled faintly. The right hand returned the matches to his coat pocket and stayed there, wrapped into a fist. He took the cigarette from his lips and spoke in the long, careless, Western drawl that had rung in Troy's ears for so long.

'Curious isn't it, Troy? You only have to kill just once to get a taste for it.'

Just for the pleasure of the sound Troy thumbed back the hammer on the revolver.